The Lions and the Wolf

Blood Harvest at Cannae

Garrett Pearson

Published by Morepork Publishing

Cover Design: More Visual Ltd

ISBN: 13-978-0-473-63698-2
ISBN: 13-978-0-473-63701-9

For Stephen S. and Paul L. and memories of a wild childhood.

Glossary

Ancient Country & Place names:

Aecae – Troia in the province of Apulia, Italy

Arretium – Arezzo, Italy

Ariminum – Rimini, Italy

Beneventum – Benevento Italy

Carthage - Now within modern day Tunisia

Capua – In Campania, Italy

Cartagena Nova – Cartagena, southern Spain

Casilinum – Ancient town in southwest Italy

Drepanum – Trapani, western Sicily

Gades – Cadiz, Spain

Gaul - France, Belgium, Switzerland, Holland and Northern Italy

Geronium – Ancient town in southeast Italy

Icosium – Algiers

Iberia - Northern Spain

Igilgili – Jijel, Algeria

Lilybaeum – Marsala, western Sicily

Massilia – Marseilles, France

Nubia - Northern Sudan

Numidia – Algeria

Perusia – Perugia, Italy

Picenum – In the Marche district, Italy

Placentia – Piacenza, Italy

Rusucurru - Delles or Dellys, Algeria

Saguntum – Sagunto, Spain

Salmantica – Salamanca, Spain

Saldae – Bejaia, Algeria

Spoletium – Spoleto, Italy

Tarraco – Tarragona, Spain

Tarascon – In Provencal, France

Trasimene – Lake Trasimeno, Italy

Victumulae - Outpost or township somewhere in the Po valley

Prologue

Italy, Autumn of 217 BC

Rome has suffered another catastrophic defeat from Hannibal and his Carthaginians by the forest and shores of Lake Trasimene. The Roman Consul, Gaius Flaminius has been killed in the fighting and his legions destroyed. The Roman senate attributes Flaminius's defeat to his lack of attendance to religious protocols expected of a Consul before taking office, rather than he being outmanoeuvred and outgeneralled by Hannibal.

Rome however is in shock, the citizens once more at the gates seeking news of loved ones from the few legionaries that have survived the battle and begun returning home. The senate is in turmoil and recalls the remaining Consul, Gnaeus Servilius Geminus and his legions to defend Rome.

The senate decides upon an unusual, almost desperate measure, whereby the office of Dictator is resurrected and given to one, Quintus Fabius Maximus along with full dictatorial powers. Fabius, in complete contrast to Flaminius calls for all religious protocols to be observed before committing to the task of battling Hannibal. Fabius is to prove very different in his methods of waging war compared to the men holding office before him.

Meanwhile, Hannibal has moved eastwards to Picenum and the Adriatic coast seeking supplies to recondition his men and horses as his troops are suffering from scurvy and the horses from mange. The coastal area proves fruitful and men and animals are well victualled, even some sour wine (acetum) is secured and used to treat the horse's coats and skin. However, with his army living off the land, Hannibal must keep moving and marches south into Apulia before turning back westwards. He encounters Fabius and his legions at Aecae and offers battle; Fabius declines to fight giving Hannibal yet further credence as an unbeatable General.

Hannibal marches on through Samnium, burning and pillaging around the city of Beneventum before entering Campania and the fertile Falernian district seeking further supplies, allies and support from tribes disaffected from Rome. Fabius follows and attacks Hannibal's foraging parties and water details but still declines formal battle.

Baldor, now a Captain of his own cavalry troop has fought bravely at Trasimene. Within a few days of the battle and under the command of Hannibal's cavalry commander General Maharbal, he successfully leads a blocking force to cut off a belated Roman relief column of four thousand cavalry (equites) sent from the second Consular army of Gnaeus Servilius Geminus. This entire cavalry arm under the command of Propraetor, Gaius Marcus Centenius is slaughtered or captured. However, Baldor has once more incurred Hannibal's displeasure when he speaks up on behalf of his Roman prisoners.

His enemies within the Carthaginian army, both old and new also remain a threat whereby he must watch his back. Adding to his woes, he suffers domestic troubles when his tent is robbed and burnt, his servant murdered and his lover killed or kidnapped. With his woman, tent, money and belongings gone he is living in the tent of Andulas, a Gallic warlord and comrade in arms.

Centurion Cornelius Scipio has fared little better than his nemesis, Baldor. Having fought at the battles of Ticinus, Trebbia and Trasimene, he has now suffered three defeats by the Carthaginians, the last two being catastrophic. Having narrowly escaped the slaughter at Trasimene and a murderous attack by bandits in which he was injured, he returns briefly to Rome. Frustrated at what he sees as arrogance and incompetence by his Consuls as well as a refusal to learn how Hannibal wages war, he's further angered by domestic troubles when he and his betrothed argue over his giving away of her gift to him and his decision to return to the war once again.

So, as the Romans once more gather their legions under the Dictator Quintus Fabius Maximus, they trail Hannibal. Thus, both Baldor and Cornelius must once more take the path of the warrior.

Part 1

Make your enemy see what you wish them to see and not what is.

Anon

Chapter One

Near Mount Callicula in the Ager Falernus district, Campania, Italy. Early autumn of 217 BC.

Baldor closed his eyes and lifted his face to the sun enjoying the morning's mellow heat. The days were changing, becoming shorter and losing the fierce heat of the summer the air cooler and fresher. He breathed deeply enjoying the sweet smell of the grass and trees while listening to the gentle rush of the stream over the stones. A bee flew past; its buzz almost lethargic as if it, like the land was tired and ready for rest.

"This looks like trouble." Armaco grunted as he nudged Baldor and pointed to a fast-approaching horseman.

The rider lashed the reins either side of the horse's withers as he sought speed from his tired mount. Raising clouds of water spray he forced it across the shallow stream to where Baldor, Armaco and his officers waited by the carts being loaded with the fresh water supplies.

"Captain! … Captain!" The rider called as he reined in hard next to Baldor. "Roman equites coming up the valley inlet on our right flank."

"How many?"

"Two turmaes at least sir, plus some twenty or so auxiliaries."

"Around eighty then?"

"Aye sir and by their speed I'd say they know we are here."

"The bastards are becoming persistent." Armaco growled as he hefted his spear and pulled his shield around from his back just as Baldor placed a halting hand on his shoulder.

"Take the laden carts and ten men as an escort and head for camp."

"What! They already outnumber us by almost two to one, how in

11

Baal's name are you …"

"Just do it!" Baldor snapped as he turned towards a large canvas covered wagon and whistled.

The cloth flaps opened and a score of archers spilled out onto the sward.

Armaco chuckled and shook his head. "You crafty young bastard! … Sir." He added quickly when Baldor glowered at him. "All right! I'm gone, I'm gone!" He shouted as he forced his mount around. "Drusus, move those bloody carts out! Andaal! You and your men, on me!"

Drivers clambered into seats and whips cracked. Horses leapt forward in their traces the cart axles creaking as they sped away from the stream towards the trees while Armaco and his escort cantered alongside escorting the convoy away.

Baldor was already by the archers' cart pointing back to the valley mouth and issuing brisk orders to the officer.

"Clitus! Spread your men either side of the valley entrance but under cover. Start taking the Romans down after the first score or so have passed you; I need you to split them up for me. I'll move my lads further back into the valley to the flat ground; we'll charge whatever survives your arrows."

"Aye sir, aye."

The old archer divided his men into two groups, sending each running for the cover of the scrub growing on opposing sides of the small, doglegged valley inlet. Baldor watched as the archers scrambled up the small inclines and quietly disappeared into the brush and scrub then signalled for his cavalry to fall back and reform further up the valley. Halting and turning them where he judged he had enough distance to make speed back to the entrance, he settled himself at the head of the small group then turned to issue his orders.

"We need to buy time for the carts to get away. The archers will break the Romans up as they come and hopefully kill most, we'll take the rest. They may know we're here but they won't expect us to be ready for them but wait for my command."

With the horsemen in position and shields and spears ready, the men quickly settled into an edgy silence. Only the gentle rush of the water and a horse tossing its head and snorting disturbed. With battle and the risk of death or injury only moments away tension filled the air. Some men dropped their heads in prayer, while others looked blankly on and quietly mouthed their reverences. Some produced good luck charms or tiny effigies of their God and reverently rubbed them, staring at it as they prayed. Others eased a necklace from beneath their shirt to hold or kiss the suspended talisman as they spoke their venerations into the breeze and sky. Baldor stared ahead. With his own piety long gone, he had no devotions to offer and instead listened and watched intently for his enemy, preserving as many of his men's lives as possible his only concern. Running over the plan in his head he deemed it simple enough, simple was good, less likelihood of something going awry. He swallowed nervously as he waited, he needed the archers to reduce the odds quickly and for the timing of his advance to be right or he and his remaining warriors were in for a hard fight. His mouth was desert dry. Swallowing hard again, he loosened his spear butt from its socket on his mount's tack, too late now to change anything. As time seemed to stretch, self-doubt in his abilities to command well surfaced, along with the familiar oily, gut churning pre-battle nerves, would they ever stop he wondered?

The rumble of approaching hooves grew louder causing some of the Carthaginian horses to whicker and stomp. Talismans and effigies quickly disappeared as men's hands tightened around spear shafts and shield straps. As the noise grew in volume faces twisted into grimaces and men fidgeted, a horse reared. Baldor listened intently trying to gauge how far the Romans were away before they would come into view. A moment later and deciding the time was right; he motioned his horsemen forward at the walk before quickly taking them to a canter. The troop now rode back towards the valley entrance, the hidden archers and where the Romans would soon appear. Their enemy for the moment still unseen.

The thunder of both sides' hooves now made it impossible to gauge the Roman position. With the relative short distance between the Carthaginians and the valley mouth where the Romans would enter, Baldor had to ensure he and his men would be at the gallop. Knowing he'd had to guess at the timing he could only hope to have it right. Just as he raised his spear and called his men to the charge, the lead horses of the Roman cavalry rounded the corner at the gallop. The first two dozen equites spilled into the valley proper and seeing the charging Carthaginians coming at them quickly raised their spears. A trumpet blared, the brassy tones rising above the rumble of hooves and the Romans spread from column to line in a brave display of red-faced shields, gleaming mail shirts and crimson crested helmets.

To the Roman rear and along the valley sides, the archers sprang up from the scrub and loosed a volley into the passing mass of men and horses. Their second arrow was already on the string then following in the wake of the previous just as the first struck home. Men seemed to sprout feathers then tumbled from their mounts, horses too went down to the feathered death. Whinnying in pain, they stumbled and fell, their speed catapulting their riders along the sward, the bodies tripping others coming close behind them, others collapsed dead, crushing their rider as they went down. Carnage followed as the archers continued to loose into the chaotic maelstrom of men and horseflesh.

Meanwhile, Baldor and his warriors clashed with the leading Romans, the air rent with a terrible din of battle cries, colliding horseflesh and the clatter of iron on wood. Mounts emptied of riders as spears pierced flesh, warriors grabbing for swords as the fight quickly turned into a melee of swirling horses and men. Baldor roared his hate as he and his first adversary clashed. The Roman was fast and struck first, Baldor ducking behind his shield to avoid his opponent's spear, it glancing noisily off the brass boss. Dropping low and thrusting underarm, he drove his spear hard under the Roman's shield hitting the man just above the groin. The Roman groaned horribly and rolled back off his mount taking Baldor's spear with him. Baldor immediately reached behind his shoulder for one of the two falcatas he wore crossed over his back and kicked his mount on seeking a new opponent. The next Roman, seeing Baldor bearing down on him, hurled his fighting spear at him in a desperate bid to kill or drive him away while snatching for his spatha. The heavy spear lodged in the shield face weighing it down and forcing Baldor to drop it. The Roman, sensing advantage pressed forward to the attack. Baldor however, grabbed for his second falcata and kicked his mount hard towards him. Surprised, the Roman raised his shield as Baldor forced his mount alongside then delivered a rain of fast, accurate blows to both shield and spatha blade. Shocked at the speed of the coordinated attack the Roman tried to counter and lost his sword arm at the elbow as Baldor chopped it off with one swipe. The man screamed as the limb fell and blood misted the air; he was still in shock when Baldor's next stroke cut deeply into his neck. Before the man fell dead off his mount, Baldor had moved on. Glancing quickly around at the fight, he saw his men were having the better of it, if Clitus and his archers could kill or stall the others they had a good chance of winning while giving Armaco time to escape with the water. His horse suddenly whickered and shuddered beneath him, its pace changed to an unsteady stagger. Recognising a dying animal, he swung his right leg over its neck and dropped lightly onto his feet. A moment later the horse collapsed, the Roman javelin lodged deep in its chest having burst its heart. The javelin thrower and another unhorsed Roman sensing an easier kill rushed towards him. One man retained a fighting spear while the other snatched one from the ground as they manoeuvred to either side of him. Without a shield and taking on two spearmen, Baldor knew he was in trouble. Holding both falcatas out defensively his eyes darted from one man to the other, his mouth twisting into a snarl as the men came at him together. A horse dashed past behind the two Romans, there was a flash of metal, a spray of crimson mist then the horse was gone and one man fell forward. The other glanced about then ran at Baldor, spear lowered. Baldor swerved to one side and the spear scraped over the side of his mail shirt. The Roman retracted the spear quickly and thrust again, Baldor stepping back and swinging his falcata to chop the shaft. The wood didn't shear but the spear was forced down. Baldor spun his body in a circle along the spear shaft closing on and just passing the man, then slashed a falcata down across the back of his thighs. The heavy blade cut to the bones and the man collapsed, a moment later the other falcata cleaved his neck just under his helmet.

"Are you all right sir?" A trooper shouted as he reined alongside while throwing Baldor the reins of another horse. Baldor nodded his gratitude and raised a bloodied sword in salute. "We have them sir, they're surrendering!"

"Watch in case anymore ride past Clitus." He pointed the bloodied blade back to the valley entrance.

"Aye sir."

Meanwhile to the Roman rear, those attacked by the archers were already turning about and trying to extricate themselves from the chaos and the relentless feathered death that poured down on them. The archers continued to take the Romans down until they rode out of range, only a dozen or so making it away and back out of the long, narrow entrance to the valley.

In the main valley the few Romans that remained alive began throwing down their swords and calling for quarter. As always, with battle nerves replaced by adrenalin and then the euphoria of survival it took time for the killing to stop and despite surrendering the men died. When it was found that only four wounded Romans survived and thus hardly worth the trouble of taking back to camp, they too died quickly from well-aimed sword thrusts. The men were dead before Baldor could stop it, chewing his lip hard he turned away seeking Clitus.

The old archer and his men were already making their way into the valley proper toward Baldor's men. Clitus jogged up to Baldor's horse.

"They're gone sir, though most are down and dead, aye. Barely a handful got away."

"Good man, Clitus. Any casualties?"

"None sir, none. A few nettle stings and thorns in the legs from the scrub there and a sore arse from where I slipped in some fresh cowshit and went down hard."

Clitus turned to show the back of his tunic covered in green shit, Baldor suppressed a chuckle while his nose wrinkled from the pungent grassy stink.

"You'll not be popular in the wagon Clitus but let's begone, back to camp."

"Aye sir, aye. Hurry on lads!" He shouted, as he waved his men away from looting the dead equites and into the wagon.

Baldor rode back to his warriors and called for the casualty list.

His men were busy helping their injured while finishing off and looting the fallen Romans. His Hypolokhagos stepped up.

"Three dead sir, five wounded but not critical."

Baldor nodded, quietly relived at the light casualties. "Mount the men up, tie the dead across their horses and let's begone, that was a reasonable size group we just encountered, I'll not wait for another to come along."

"Yes sir. Mount up! ... Mount up!"

Baldor paused to look around the small valley while his men reluctantly left their robbery and mounted quickly then formed column. He felt the heat on his face again from the morning sun as it slipped from behind grey-banked clouds shedding light onto the valley floor and reflecting brightly from the stream. The yellow of the gorse and broom shone brighter as the sunlight fell on them, the dew-wet grass lush and bright green. The beauty however blighted by the dead men and horses, severed limbs and the blood-red stains in the grass. Turning away, he trotted to the front of the column and waved the men on.

Arriving back in camp he placed his report with one of Hannibal's adjutants then made his way through the canvas city to his quarters at Andulas's tent. He was met by the big Gaul himself along with Armaco, both making to hold his mount's bridle as he dismounted.

"All good?" Armaco asked.

"Reasonable, you got the water safely back and we won the fight but we have three dead and my horse was killed under me."

"Well, that's good isn't it? … Not the horse, I mean the odds are good for what we've achieved."

"Not if you are one of the three dead." Baldor replied flatly. "It just seems a high price to pay for one day's supply of water for our men."

"Needs must Baldor, needs must." Andulas said quietly then clicked his fingers to a slave who stepped forward bearing a bowl of rosewater so Baldor could wash the blood from his hands and face. "Come … come." Andulas urged. "There's wine and food, you must be hungry."

The three men sat for their midday meal in the shade of the tent awning, as always, Armaco seemed to have the most to say.

"What is it with these Romans of late?" He mumbled as he stuffed hunks of bread and cheese into his mouth. "Since this Dictator, Fabius took command we've had determined attacks on the water and forage details, yet the old goat refused our offer of battle at Aecae." He swilled the food with a huge gulp of wine. "And he had the high ground and forty thousand men with him, what more did the old bastard want?"

"More than forty thousand men I guess." Andulas chuckled.

"Hah! He's just a chicken-hearted bastard."

"I'm not so sure." Andulas replied sagely. "See, those troops he has will be mostly new and green …"

"He'll have Geminus's legions though?"

"Aye but that'll only account for a third or a half of his force at most, not great odds to be taking us on." He smiled. "What think you, Baldor?"

The younger man dipped some bread in his wine and nibbled it before he replied.

"Well, from what I've heard this Fabius is a markedly different character to those before him …"

"That's true, he's a bloody coward."

"I don't think he's a coward, Armaco. He fought a successful

17

campaign against the Ligurians some years ago and the Romans have elected him Consul twice, he must have something of worth."

"Well, it's not a pair of balls!"

Andulas chuckled though Baldor remained serious.

"If the Romans elected him Armaco, he'll be no milksop, believe me."

"Why won't he fight then?"

"Well, their previous tactics aren't working so it seems he's taking a different approach."

"Hah! He and they are just afraid of us now is all?" Armaco growled.

"Cautious and wary I think, not so much afraid." Baldor reaffirmed.

"How so?"

"Well, look at their tactics for a start. They remain unchanging and unimaginative and still rely on wanting clear ground and a heavy infantry encounter …"

"They had that at the Trebbia and still lost!"

"Yes but we surprised them in their camp before dawn then forced them across a freezing, swollen river, ambushed their rear and flanked them. If you remember, we still couldn't hold their push forward."

"He still wouldn't take us on at Aecae though and they had the advantage!" Armaco argued.

"All right then, look at their previous leadership quality. The first Consul underestimated us and the following two have been drawn into our traps because they wouldn't practice caution, perhaps this Fabius is going to play it differently?"

"What, winning by attacking foraging and water details?"

"Well, it's certainly made our lives difficult; we need lots more men now to protect them whereas in the past we could send the women for water."

"Is that what Hannibal thinks?" Armaco asked with a smirk.

Baldor shrugged disinterestedly.

"Still out of favour with the General then?" He quipped and laughed as Baldor's expression soured. "I told you your high ideals would bring trouble for …"

"Armaco! For Epona's sake put your tongue between your teeth and keep it there." Andulas chided.

Armaco raised his hands as if to say all right. Baldor however retorted sharply.

"It's what I think Armaco! What I can see and if you looked past your bloody nose and prejudiced opinion for a moment you might see it too!" Baldor snarled and pushed his plate away, stood quickly then stormed out of the tent.

"Baldor! … Baldor! For Baal's sake, man! I'm teasing! Oh, for the love …" Armaco called after him and went to rise.

Andulas placed a hand on Armaco's arm and spoke quietly. "Let him go Armaco. He's not in a great frame of mind right now; you just hit a raw nerve is all. Let him have a little peace and some time on his own."

Andulas poured more wine for them both while Armaco shook his head, adjusted his eyepatch and grumbled under his breath. The men drank and resumed their meal, neither spoke for a while. Eventually Armaco looked up from his plate and cast his eye around the tent then spoke quietly.

"Have you learned anything of his woman?"

Andulas nodded slowly. "Maybe, my informer picked up word of a tall redhead being sold to a slave trader from Casilinum or Capua."

"Capua! That's a bloody long way from where she was stolen!" He shook his head then smiled grimly. "But not so far from here."

"No, not too far, though still a risk for a small party, for that's all we can risk if we go looking."

"I take it Baldor doesn't know yet?"

"No and we say nothing until we can be surer." Andulas held his finger over his lips.

"He took her loss badly eh? I thought she was just another woman to him, albeit a beautiful one."

Andulas shook his head slightly. "He's no womaniser and you should know him better than that by now Armaco! You're his oldest friend. From the little I know she was the first woman he'd lain with since he lost his wife back in Carthage three years since. Anyway, what about your enquiries for his stolen gear. Any word of his ivory hilted falcata and silver dagger? They should be readily identifiable if they are still within the camp and that ornate Roman Tribune's helmet he had should stand out like dog's balls."

"No, nothing yet. Unless we strike lucky it could take time, the camp's a huge place and it's like looking for needles in a haystack."

Andulas looked thoughtful. "Maybe the thieves would have had more sense than to sell the items here anyway?"

"No, I've thought about this Andulas, and I don't think so. Most thieves are lazy bastards believe me; I've dealt with such scum before. They wouldn't have gone to great pains to sell the gear subtly. Like you, I have a good man making discreet enquiries and casting his eyes about in the camp, he'll find them it'll just take time."

Andulas was quiet for a moment, his brow furrowed in thought. "If this Bomilcar Bodeshmun is behind the robbery and kidnap surely he would have insisted upon careful disposal of anything that was taken?"

"Regardless of what he stipulated, unless it was his own men that did the robbery and I doubt that it was, the stuff will not be that well-hidden, I know."

"But Baldor's woman, if my source is correct, it would seem she was taken afar."

"It's not so easy to hide a woman as tall and striking as Lasairiona."

Andulas nodded sagely. "Aye true, true … and she was a beauty."

"Is! … She is a beauty Andulas, and we will get her back!"

Andulas raised his eyebrows and smiled. "Gods above! It's not like you to be so optimistic, positive even."

"Huh! I'll show Baldor that I'm not just the irritating loudmouth that he thinks I am."

"I'm sure he doesn't think that."

"I'm not so sure of late; I just seem to make him angry. His sense of humour seems to have left him."

"He's just having a hard time of it at present; think on it, first the trouble with this Bodeshmun and his sidekick, Sakarbaal, then the argument with Hannibal. After which he's robbed, his servant murdered and his woman taken."

Armaco nodded slowly. "Aye, when you sum it up you're right I suppose, I'd better find him and make amends."

"Finish your meal first; give him time to cool off."

The men returned to their meal but were disturbed a short while later when Baldor reappeared. He walked up to the table and bowed his head to both.

"Brothers, I crave your pardon for my temper and manners."

Armaco beamed and stood offering his hand. Baldor instead threw his arm over Armaco and pulled him close. "I'm sorry for my harsh words, you didn't deserve that."

"Well, I should watch my tongue." Armaco mumbled grudgingly.

"No Armaco! No, you shouldn't. You're my friend; you're both my friends, my family even and warriors deserving respect." He reached out and placed a hand on Andulas's shoulder. "Speak as you will, Baal knows you both have the right."

"Come Baldor, finish your meal." Andulas smiled and leaned over to pull out a stool then topped up Baldor's cup with wine.

The three sat for a while enjoying the food, just when Andulas called for more wine a servant appeared along with a messenger.

"My Lord, sorry to disturb but this man has a message for Captain Targa."

Andulas gestured with an open hand for the man to speak. The man turned to Baldor.

"Captain Sir, General Hannibal seeks your presence at a meeting in his tent immediately."

"Thank you. My compliments to the General." The man bowed and left. Baldor stood and picked up his helmet. "Brothers, excuse me."

Baldor was one of the first officers to arrive at Hannibal's tent; served with a cup of wine he was ushered through to the meeting table where Hannibal waited.

"Good day, Captain." The salutation formal and stiff.

"Greetings sir." Baldor dipped his head.

There was an awkwardness between the pair. Not so dissimilar in age and until recently friends, they eyed each other. Baldor lowered his gaze first.

"I've seen your report, Captain. The Roman attacks on our water details are growing bolder and more aggressive it seems?"

"Yes sir."

"About eighty men you say?"

"At least sir."

Hannibal nodded slowly. "Your losses were minimal and you brought the water safely back. Well done."

"Thank you sir."

Hannibal looked away as other officers entered the tent.

"Welcome gentlemen! Please be seated." He gestured to the table.

Baldor noticed the warmth in the greeting towards the new arrivals compared to his cooler reception. Quietly cursing himself for his past transgression to Hannibal, he sought a seat for himself. He was heartened however, when General Maharbal slapped him on the back and offered his hand.

"How's life lad, all well?" He smiled.

"Yes sir." He lied. "Thank you, and yourself?"

"The bones ache a little Baldor but at my age it's to be expected, along with the need to piss in the night." He laughed and pulled up a chair next to Baldor. Their chatter was interrupted by a thickset man stepping through the gathering crowd towards them, a wine jug in hand.

"A top up, gentlemen?" He said as he made to fill both cups.

"Sir!" Baldor smiled warmly and started to rise but the man eased him back into his seat.

"Mago, to you Baldor." The man amended genially.

"Mago!" Maharbal said as he laughed then turned offering his hand.

"My Lord to you if you please, General!" He corrected and laughed heartily as he put an arm over each man's shoulder.

"Reprobate, more like!" Maharbal laughed and punched Mago playfully. "It's bloody good to see you."

"It's good to be seen for I swear the alternative has little appeal."

The men's laughter and camaraderie was interrupted by Hannibal calling the meeting to order. Adjusting his eyepatch, he took the floor. Baldor noticed a change in the young General's usual relaxed demeanour. There was a guarded stiffness in his body language followed by a quiet seriousness in his tone.

"Gentlemen, welcome." He said then paused to swallow hard. "I fear … I fear I have led you astray."

A chorus of denials came back at him, which he raised his hands to quieten.

"We won't accept that, brother!" Mago shouted and backed again by hearty denials from the men at the table.

Hannibal bowed his head graciously. "Thank you." He said quietly. "But hear me out." Silence fell as the men settled and readied to listen. Hannibal breathed deeply and gathered himself before speaking. "I was reliably told that Capua would open its gates to us and thus I expected to be safely ensconced within now. As you know this has not transpired and I fear that the time we've tarried here has seen this Fabius back us into a corner. He's brought up his legions far quicker than I anticipated and holds all the bridges over the Volturnus River, at least one of which we need to cross if we leave this valley by any other pass than which we entered from."

"Hah! The bastard won't fight though." Mago shouted.

"He doesn't have to brother. The bridges are fortified, while he and the rest of his army are on the hill yonder and he has four thousand legionaries blocking the pass exit. Just like the Spartans at Thermopylae."

"Aye but they lost in the end!" Mago growled as he frowned and shrugged.

"Only through treachery brother. Not from the might of the Persian force coming forward."

"Can we come up behind or outflank them then, just like the Persians did?"

"Aye! Use our Spanish mountain troops they can climb, they'll sort Fabius's legionaries." Maharbal added.

"As good as the Spaniards are I don't believe they would gain a foothold against heavy legionaries without support."

"Can we use the pike phalanx to smash our way out through the pass at the same time the Spaniards attack?" General Gisgo asked.

"That was my thoughts too, General but reports say the ground is rocky and broken at the pass mouth, so no place for the phalanx, if the legionaries get in amongst the pikemen …" Hannibal just raised his hands in a hapless gesture.

Baldor was shocked. For the first time it seemed they had been outmanoeuvred by the Romans and trapped but worst of all, Hannibal the master tactician, seemed at a loss as to how to extract them.

"Needless to say, gentlemen we cannot stay here with winter coming on. We have a few more days of grazing for the cattle and horses and then we'll need to move, our own supplies will also be running low by then too. Therefore, I'm open to ideas … think on it and we'll reconvene tomorrow. If we cannot see a way clear then brute force is our only option though I foresee our casualties being high."

As the meeting broke up, Baldor went to the horse lines and taking his mount rode out towards the pass mouth.

Chapter Two

"Hurry up, damn you! ... Move it if you want to be in here tonight!" A grizzled sentry bellowed to the cart driver while his comrades began pushing on Casilinum's huge bronze-sheeted wooden gates, drawing them closed.

The cart creaked and rocked over the cobbles as the driver goaded the horse quickly on. Once through the gates, an overweight and lethargic guard halted him.

"Hold there now! What are you carrying anyway?"

"Slaves for the market sir."

"Show me."

The driver stood and pulled the canvas cover off the cart to reveal an iron cage that held half a dozen folk; all were male except for one. The guard stepped closer and looked the human cargo over. Most of the men had their heads down staring at their feet; others dropped their gaze as the guard's eyes fell on them. Only one man glared back, his eyes bright like fanned coals, his face a mask of hate. The guard banged a stick on the cage bars in front of the man's face, the man never flinched and just continued to stare.

"I'd make that bastard into a eunuch." He growled. "Cut some of that hate out of him." He laughed as he looked to the corner of the cage. "Where's the pretty redheaded Gallic bitch from then?"

"I don't know sir; I just transport them on behalf of my master, Thaddeus Rufus Antonius."

The guard peered closer, a salacious leer spreading over his face. "I could enjoy some time with her ... why is she bound and the others aren't?"

The driver shrugged. "All I know sir is, she took a knife to the last man that tried to take her against her will."

"Feisty bitch eh!"

"Aye sir, she killed him."

"Gauls eh! The bastards don't know when they're beaten; a sound whipping will sort the bitch's manners."

"I agree sir but the instructions I have are she's not to be marked, it affects the price see and then there's talk or a suspicion that she's Gallic royalty. It's all about the coin she can fetch."

"Gallic royalty!" He snorted. "Hey bitch! Was your father in charge of a pigsty and a few peasants?" Lasairiona didn't answer; she just returned an impassive stare while the two men chuckled at the jest. "Hey Princess! I'm talking to you!" He laughed as he hit the cage bars again with his stick

Lasairiona moved her eyes slightly to look at the guard's face and gave a contemptuous sneer.

"Oh, there's hate in them eyes! Are you a hater girl?" He chortled as he pushed closer to the cage bars. "Need a good man to hump some respect into you, eh? … Hey, bitch! Has the cat got your tongue?" His banter was drawing the other guards across to the cart. With an audience, he slipped the stick through the bars and prodded Lasairiona in the stomach. "Need a man to fill your belly girl and put a smile on your face? Look here lads, a Gallic Princess and that's a right royal pair of tits she has." He laughed as he lifted the stick and went to prod Lasairiona's breasts.

Lasairiona pushed the stick away. When the guard went to prod again, she moved with tiger-like speed and raising her bound hands grasped the stick and pulled hard. The guard was pulled forward, his face slamming hard up against the bars. Lasairiona spat in his eyes. Instinctively he released the stick his hands moving to clear his vision; she then rammed it back at him fast and hard through the bars, the blunt end hitting him in the mouth. He howled in pain as the stick burst his lips and smashed his front teeth, the blood running down and off his ample chin.

"Bitch!" He screamed while spraying blood and pieces of broken teeth. "I'll kill you … I'll kill you."

He forced a hand through the bars and grabbed for Lasairiona's leg, his fingers sinking talon-like into her calf and making her yelp as he tried to drag her towards him. She lashed out with her foot trying to kick him away. When he pushed his other arm through the bars to help secure his hold she kicked it hard to the side against the bars making him shriek again as the bone snapped like a dry twig.

"Bitch! You damned Harpie! I'll kill you!" He shouted as he pulled his arms back, the broken one hanging at an angle. "Give me that bloody spear." He tried to snatch a spear from one of his comrades.

"Stop sir! Stop! The driver shouted from his seat. "If you kill her you'll have Master Antonius to answer to, she's his property."

The other guards wrestled with their large comrade as he tried to secure a spear. The commotion grew louder as the cart driver jumped down from his seat and joined in to help control the guard, everybody shouting at once.

"What's going on here? … Stop! Stop!" An officer bellowed as he appeared from the Watch room and ran towards the chaos.

Some of the guards heard him and backed away immediately, others were struck by his stick as he set about them in a bid to restore order. The pandemonium stopped quickly and men settled.

"Stand-down! I won't tell you again!" The officer growled at the guards. "Now! What in Jupiter's name is going on?"

"Sir … sir I just need to be on my way with the cart. These wretches here are Master Antonius's property and …"

The officer held up his hand to stop the driver's outpouring. "Master Antonius? … You're his man you say?"

"Aye sir."

The officer seemed to stiffen. "My apologies for the inconvenience you've suffered. There's no harm done I hope?"

"No sir, no. Not to the goods anyway, I'm not so sure about your guard though."

"I'll deal with him. You don't have to mention this inconvenience do you?"

"No sir."

"Good man! Please, be on your way. You two." He snapped at two guards. "See this fool to the Orderly and then lock him up."

The Officer looked up to the cart as it moved off and to where Lasairiona was on her feet. She threw the stick at the officer's feet then spat.

"You'll learn pretty girl, aye you'll learn." He said quietly.

****

"My Lord … My Lord!" Armistarr hissed as he shook Sakarbaal awake. "We need to be up and away, General Maharbal is marshalling a troop for patrol and we're included."

Sakarbaal threw the blankets off and rolled out of the low camp bed. Finding his feet, he staggered a pace or two as the sleepy muscles refused to work then made his way to the night bucket to empty his bladder. Still weary, he quickly washed his face then dipped his head in the washbowl and dragged his fingers through his hair. Gasping at the cold water and waking up, he quickly pulled his tunic on just as his servant appeared to help him with his armour and weapons. Slipping the leather undershirt over his tunic, he staggered as his servant dropped the appropriated Roman mail shirt over his head, once in place across his shoulders and the weight distributed it felt more comfortable. As the servant knelt to lace the cavalry boots, Sakarbaal fastened his dagger belt and dropped his sword baldric over his shoulder. Slinging a shield over his back and snatching up his magnificently crested bronze helmet, he exited the tent to where Armistarr waited holding both horses.

"Come My Lord, we need to catch up."

Mounting quickly the pair collected war spears from a wooden rack then set off in the wake of the departing patrol. Cantering along the side of the column, Sakarbaal made his way to the front and General Maharbal. The older man looked up, scowled and grunted as the younger reined in.

"Good of you to join us, My Lord."

"My apologies General, I overslept."

"Leave the whores and the wine alone of an evening young man and you'll not be taxed to rise of a morning."

"Yes General." Sakarbaal replied quietly.

"Now, as you know our lads in the water details and smaller patrols have been taking a thumping of late. Thus, General Hannibal wants us to take a look and set things aright if we can, hence the larger than usual patrol."

"Yes sir."

Maharbal beckoned him closer so they could talk without shouting above the rumble of hooves. "You're new to my command, My Lord."

"Yes sir."

"You don't come on recommendation." He growled. "But rather from under a cloud owing to all this trouble between yourself, Lord Bodeshmun and Captain Targa." He held up a hand to stifle Sakarbaal's reply. "Captain Targa is my friend and has proved himself a brave and capable warrior." Sakarbaal, expecting a put down or at least a veiled threat against him dropped his head. "That aside, I don't hold grudges so this could be your chance to begin anew and show me your mettle, Baal knows we have plenty men to fight with the Romans without making war on ourselves."

Sakarbaal brightened. "Yes General. I'll endeavour to give my best."

"Good! After all we are on the same side, My Lord."

"Yes sir … and I believe I have been wrong in my anger towards Captain Targa. I'm seeking to put things aright."

Maharbal gave a curt smile. "Good to hear, I dislike officers fighting among themselves, let's leave that to the Romans shall we?"

"Yes sir."

"Scout coming in sir, at the gallop." Maharbal's standard-bearer interrupted as he called and pointed into the distance where a horseman appeared in front of a rising dust cloud, his head down beside his horse's neck as he sought speed.

Maharbal scanned the foreground then turned to Sakarbaal. "Have the column form line."

"Sir!" Sakarbaal relayed the order and a trumpet blasted, the men peeling away from the column and spreading into line.

Moments later the scout reined up in front of Maharbal.

"Sir! There's a Numidian patrol behind me, they've been cut up badly by a large Roman patrol who are in pursuit."

Maharbal nodded and looked to the distance where the scout pointed. "How far behind you?"

"Ten, maybe twelve stades, sir."

Maharbal glanced around and then side to side and seeing small copses to either side of his flanks, he turned to Sakarbaal his commands coming fast. "Take half the troop into that wood yonder." He pointed. "I'll take my half into the other. The Numidians will come this way back to camp, let them through then we'll hit the Romans in their flanks as they pass between us. Wait until you see me break cover then we hit them together. Do you have it?"

"Aye sir!" Sakarbaal signalled to his men and pulled hard on his reins twisting his horse about and digging heels into its flanks as the troop divided.

Settling his men back from the edge of the trees, he dismounted. With his heart pounding as if it would burst from his chest, he edged forward to watch while keeping in cover of the dark trunks. With the sun still low the forest remained cool with the floor still damp from the night, the earthy scents of vegetation and leaf mould filling his nose.

Thirty or forty sand-coloured ponies came into view, the brown-skinned warriors low across their backs as they raced across the sward. A stade or so behind them, in the lee of the Numidian dust came the Roman equites. In contrast to the lightly armed and simply attired Numidians, the Romans were a blaze of colour. Sun glinted from bronze helmets and mail shirts, scarlet cloaks billowing behind them, their large circular shields hiding most of the rider.

Sakarbaal slipped back to his mount. "Get ready!" He managed to call to his men.

His muscles felt slack and his legs weak forcing him to pause before trying to mount his horse. Gritting his teeth and fighting down the need to vomit and piss, he managed to mount. Struggling to breathe and with hands wet with sweat, his heart thumped as if he'd run a huge distance. Sticking his spear in the earth, he pulled gloves over shaking hands and turned to his men. He went to speak but his tongue stuck to his mouth forcing him to swallow hard and try again. When he vomited instead, Armistarr, seeing the difficulty took up the call while raising his spear.

"On My Lord's command!"

Spears raised in silent reply. Horses jostled and bridled as they sensed the nervous tension from the men. Seeing Maharbal's men burst from the trees opposite and not trusting himself able to speak, Sakarbaal nodded to Armistarr. Mumbling a quick but earnest prayer, he pulled his shield around from his back then hefting his spear overarm, dug his heels in his mount's flanks sending it springing forward.

"Attack! ... Attack!" Armistarr bellowed and the horsemen broke from the tree line following their leader. Battle cries started up, the horses whinnying in protest as they were forced quickly up to speed. Out front, Sakarbaal's fear was replaced by adrenalin and he felt as if he and his mount floated over the ground. Strangely, the shouts and cries of his men and the rumble of hooves faded to silence as he galloped towards the Romans. He thought he shouted his war cry but couldn't be sure. The equites were falling into disarray as they tried to slow their headlong gallop after the Numidians and turn to face Maharbal's men coming at their flank. Now, hearing and seeing Sakarbaal's men charging their other flank completed their confusion as men tried again to turn their mounts to face the new threat bearing down on them.

A moment later, Sakarbaal was on top of the first Romans. His world snapping back to normal speed as his mount careered into a Roman pony bowling it over. The noise also returned suddenly, coming like a thunderclap with horses whickering and screaming, men shouting and roaring in anger, else howling in pain amidst the clatter and rattle of weapons on wood. Sakarbaal, adrenalin fuelled fought like a madman and forced himself through the equites, Armistaar riding close and protecting his Lord's side as the Carthaginians burst the Roman patrol apart.

The fight was short and brutal. The Romans, surprised and attacked on both flanks were scattered and slaughtered. As a handful turned their mounts and tried to escape, the Numidians, having regrouped howled like demons and gave chase. Unencumbered with armour and on fast, agile ponies they quickly closed the gap to hurl their javelins into the backs of the fleeing equites. As the fighting stopped and the Carthaginians dismounted to see to their wounded and loot the fallen Romans, Maharbal came alongside Sakarbaal.

"Well done My Lord, they didn't know which way to turn." He cast his eyes over the gore splattered Sakarbaal. "No injuries I trust?"

"No … no, thank you General."

"Good, see to your men then let's begone."

Sakarbaal saluted and turned to Armistaar. "Can you …"

"Yes, My Lord. You are all right? No …"

"Yes, yes, thank you." He managed a smile before waving the man away then dismounted quickly and vomited again, having had no breakfast the remains of the previous night's wine splashed his boots red. As the hot flush left him, he began to shake. Leaning his head against his horse for support while gripping the reins and riding blanket, he tried to hide his shaking hands while mumbling into the horse's flank. "Baal Almighty … father above, my thanks for bringing me through this today. Tannith, mother of us all thank you for sparing your son." Pulling a heavy gold chain from his neck bearing a glyph of Tannith, he reverently kissed it. Reaching for his water skin and taking a gulp, he rinsed his mouth then took a long draught. Removing his helmet, he tipped the remainder over his head. Taking a deep breath, he felt his heart rate slowing and the shaking easing then stopping and he began to feel a little better. He was about to mount when Maharbal appeared again along with a richly attired warrior.

"My Lord, a moment."

"Yes General."

"May I present, Prince Massinissa of the Massylii tribe of Numidia."

Sakarbaal bowed his head and held a fist over his heart. Looking up he saw the young man was magnificently armoured and quite different to the simply dressed warriors that trotted their mounts up behind him. A fringed, white wool tunic overlaid by a gold coloured, fish scale mail shirt covered a broad chest; a bronze Roman helmet framed his dark-skinned face and trailed a long white horse tail from the crest down over his shoulder, his weapons and shield however remained Carthaginian. The man offered his hand.

"My thanks for your intervention, Lord Sakarbaal we were being hard pressed."

Sakarbaal dipped his head again. "You're welcome your majesty."

"I shall see you are rewarded when we return to camp."

"Thank you, majesty but there's no …"

Massinissa had already turned away and signalled to his warriors to follow him.

When Sakarbaal looked to Maharbal and shrugged the other just chuckled.

"He'll be a King someday and Kings find it hard to say thank you. Anyway, we've done well, there's nigh on four hundred equites dead and our losses are light. Here, take this." He passed a bloodied sack over. "Give my compliments to General Hannibal along with our report." Sakarbaal stared at the red-blotched sack. "It's the head of one, Lucius Hostilius Mancinus, a Prefect or so he said. I'll give you the details as we ride."

****

"Well, we're here again Cornelius." Gaius said as he shaded his eyes and looked down from the hillcrest at the smoke rising from hundreds of Carthaginian campfires in the vale below. With little wind, the grey-blue columns gradually coalesced into a huge cloud that sat high above the valley.

"Yes and I think this time we have Hannibal bottled up, we just need Fabius to make a bloody move and attack."

Gaius chuckled. "Gods above lad! Are you ever happy? You whined and moaned about Tiberius and Flaminius being rash and now you complain about old Fabius being overly cautious."

Cornelius ignored the jibe his young face serious. "Aye I did, because those two were impetuous and wouldn't listen or scout properly. Fabius has played the long game and worn Hannibal down but now needs to take the bull by the horns and attack."

Gaius slipped his magnificent trans-crested helmet off, mopped his sweat-wet head and studied the view before him for a while before replying. "So, you don't see any possibility of another ambush or trickery then?"

"No, not this time. Hannibal is penned in and needs to break out for supplies or starve."

"I'm not so sure about him starving, that's a lot of cattle he has down there and at least one of them smells good." He chuckled and sniffed appreciatively at the salt-sweet tang of roasting beef drifting on the air. "However, I agree his mounts, pack animals and moveable larder there will all need fodder and winter is not so far off, so no new grass growth."

"Exactly, so he has to move and as you know all the exits from the valley and the bridges are blocked and can be easily defended. We have him this time Gaius! There's no space for him to manoeuvre, play tricks or use that damned cavalry of his to any great affect."

Gaius chewed his lip then pointed with his vine stick to the valley. "Aye but at the same time we are also limited for movement. The only bit of open ground is broken and not ideal for our heavy lads so the best we can give him is a good mauling."

"That would be a start though wouldn't it? We've won nothing of note against him since he entered Italy. Yes, we've harassed and slaughtered his foragers and water details of late but we need a battle, a win. It doesn't have to be huge but a victory is what we need to put some pride back into the troops while letting the Carthaginians know they're not invincible and that Hannibal makes mistakes just like other men."

"And you would advise what?" Gaius chuckled again.

"Don't mock me, Gaius!" Cornelius snapped without looking up from watching the Carthaginian camp.

"I'm not! I'm asking you a question." Gaius frowned as he retorted sharply.

Cornelius turned back at the sharp response and dipped his head. "I'm sorry, that was uncalled for."

"Apology accepted." Gaius growled before moderating his tone slightly. "I'm merely asking, as one Centurion to another what you would do if the decision was yours?" Cornelius began manoeuvring himself from lying on his belly into a better position to talk. "Well?" Gaius pushed, still a little rankled from the earlier rebuke.

Cornelius, somewhat chastened cleared his throat. "I would send the velites up either side of the valley heights to secure them and prevent any possibility of Hannibal's Spanish Mountain troops trying to outflank or come behind us while advancing the heavy infantry up the valley floor to engage the Carthaginians head on." He paused to ease his back up against a boulder.

Gaius nodded slightly. "Go on."

"The velites and the main army advance as one to sweep the valley top and bottom, with the cavalry out on the wings preventing anyone trying to slip past us. We could drive the Carthaginians before us if we rout them. Then, with the other exits from the valley barring this one all being narrower and easily defendable, we could pin them between us and destroy them."

"Men trapped like rats tend to fight like them; it would be a hard fight."

"Maybe but we have the manpower and the men are keen for battle, Fabius's dallying is wearing thin, that's another reason he's back in Rome, he needs to defend his delaying tactics to the senate. We need to strike now while we have the advantage, as I said we have them this time."

"H'mm, it seems a reasonable, perhaps possible solution." Gaius said quietly. "Quite a few 'ifs' in there though. If we take and hold the heights, if we advance together, if we rout them?"

"Gods above! Can you not see it?" Cornelius growled. "And you're the one who's always game for a fight."

Gaius heard the frustration in Cornelius's words along with a rising temper and took a moment, trying to control his own ire at the sharp tone before replying. However, when Cornelius stared at him as if demanding an answer, the senior Centurion in him, unaccustomed to being growled at or questioned by subordinates won out over friendship and he snarled.

"Yes I can see it Cornelius, I'm not bloody stupid! All I'm doing is playing Hannibal's advocate and testing your theories. I would have thought such an approach prudent before committing to battle? Jupiter knows that was always your way!"

The angry retort quickly sobered Cornelius and he dropped his head in shame. "I'm sorry again Gaius, truly I am. I don't mean to take my frustrations out on you. You're my best friend as much as my senior officer, you look out for me, teach me soldiering and treat me as a son, you of all people deserve better from me."

The ready apology quickly soothed Gaius and the loyal and trusted friend in him resurfaced. He sighed as he uncorked his canteen.

"Here, you bad tempered little bastard! Have a drink, its wine not water. It's some of that good Falernian I've been saving." He smirked as he prompted Cornelius to drink then chuckled and quipped the moment Cornelius's lips touched the canteen. "Not too much!"

Both men started to laugh then Cornelius took a long draught.

"That's good." He said as he wiped his hand over his mouth.

Gaius smiled. "Makes you happy eh? You should drink more."

"Thank you." He quickly tipped the canteen again and gulped.

"Whoa! Buy your bloody own. One sup is friendship the second a bloody liberty!"

Cornelius gulped again and filled his cheeks then smiled and offered the canteen back.

Gaius took it while shaking his head and laughing. "That's more like the Cornelius I know. Now, what in Jupiter's name is eating you? …" He waited as Cornelius shuffled then fidgeted, just when he was going to prompt again Cornelius started to speak.

"Nothing … everything." He bit at his lip and his head fell forward.

"Take your time lad but let's have it all out." He glanced about. "There's no one near or in sight so we have some peace."

Cornelius looked away, his eyes vacant and trance like, his lips moved but no sound came out. Gaius offered the canteen again and after another gulp, the younger man found voice.

"I just want this over Gaius or a win at least; we've fought Hannibal thrice in major battle and three times he's beaten us, this last twice brutally. Fabius just needs to stop following Hannibal like a sheep and attack him and this time … this time I think we can beat him, don't you?"

Gaius looked at Cornelius and smiled before replying. "Yes, I think we might just have caught him this time and remember just because he's won some battles it doesn't mean he's going to win the war. So what else is eating you?"

There was another long silence as Cornelius just stared into space. Gaius waited patiently while sipping from the canteen then passing it over. Cornelius drank absently before he turned to Gaius, his eyes glistened wetly, full, and ready to spill tears. He fumbled with his helmet strap; loosening it he pulled it off and dropped it beside him in the grass then dragged the liner from his head and gripped it tightly in his hand. His fingers flexed and closed around it, his body shaking slightly as he looked from his hands to Gaius and back again.

"All … all I have seen is slaughter. Good soldiers wasted because of the foolishness and pride of supposedly greater men. Such a waste Gaius, such a bloody waste!" The first tears spilled down his cheek, which he didn't bother to wipe away. "Then that last time, at Trasimene there, a day after the battle, the Carthaginians chased … they hunted us down like animals." He shuddered at the memory he conjured. "We survive that only to be ambushed by bandits, Romans, our own people! The very folk we're spilling our blood for, for Jupiter's sake! … Bastards!" He subconsciously rubbed his arm and ribs as if remembering the injuries suffered from fighting the bandits. "Then … then, when we finally reach home no one seems to understand." His voice dropped to a harsh whisper the tone as bitter as bile. "Least of all Aemilia." He was quiet for a while and cuffed at his cheeks wiping the tears. "I'm tired Gaius, tired of fools, weary of waste and slaughter and of people that should understand but can't or more likely don't want to.

I'll fight, I'll do my duty but with Jupiter as my witness I need to see a bloody victory." He paused again and just when Gaius thought he was finished, he began again. "How do you do it Gaius? How do you keep your composure, a brave face?"

Gaius didn't answer, he just offered the canteen again and the pair continued to drink. When he was sure Cornelius was finished, he spoke quietly.

"Well lad, I've some years of experience over you for a start. By my reckoning this is my eighteenth year with the legions." He smiled. "That's almost as long as you have been alive. I've seen defeats before too but I know we'll bounce back. I've seen my share of fools as well but as you've noticed, they tend to eradicate that problem by getting themselves killed. Sadly, they take good men with them but I've learned to accept that is the way of it, wars are not won without casualties. I've also learned that the enemy, as good as they may be, or think they are or we think they are, will eventually make a mistake. Until then I'll do my duty as best I can while trying to keep myself and as many of my men alive as possible." He paused to wipe his mouth. "As for people … well people, I've learned to take as I find and they in turn must take me as they find and thus sometimes as hard as it can be I'll end the friendship. You just have to ask yourself, is Aemilia worth fighting for? However, …" He held up a hand to stop Cornelius speaking. "However, bear in mind she's a young woman from a sheltered background and probably scared half to death with what's going on and what might happen to you, so you may need to make some allowances."

"She was so angry though, she wouldn't listen."

"Give her some time, Cornelius and yourself but in between now and our next visit home, I need you to be the best you can be, not just for yourself and me but for the men." Cornelius nodded slightly. "As for Fabius, we have no say in his tactics; all we can do is our jobs as best we can. Yes, I think we should fight and fight soon but that said I have to hand it to the old goat, he hasn't lost us too many men of late."

"But he's gained us nothing!"

"Has he not? We've had breathing space to raise new legions and he's took some of the ease from the Carthaginians by attacking their foragers, water details and their raiding parties."

"But it's all small scale."

"There's more than one way to fight a war Cornelius and from small acorns mighty oaks do grow. Furthermore, building on small successful actions will grow the men's confidence and build experience ready for the big test, the big battle when it comes. For me it makes sense to nibble away and win a morsel at a time until we are ready, strong enough and in the right place to win that final test. So come on lad, bear with me a little longer eh? Be patient and keep your head up. You look after me and I'll look after you, I swear it."

Cornelius finally smiled as Gaius offered his hand and the pair grasped forearms in warrior fashion.

Chapter Three

Just after first light the morning following the meeting, Baldor was back at Hannibal's tent seeking an audience.

"Captain?"

"Greetings General."

Hannibal saw the urgency on Baldor's face and gestured him through to the meeting table. "What brings you to me this early ... trouble?"

"No sir, no. I think ... I think I have a plan that will help us out of this valley."

Pouring wine for them both Hannibal settled himself comfortably and looked to Baldor.

"The floor is yours Captain." Baldor hesitated and Hannibal raised his eyebrows. "Go on."

"General ... General." He paused to clear his throat. "Before we go further can I offer my apologies for my obstinacy when we spoke of the Roman prisoners after Trasimene?"

Hannibal's brow furrowed. Adjusting his eyepatch, he breathed deeply then rested his chin on his hand looking sternly at Baldor from a dark eye, taking time to reply. When he spoke, it was quietly, the tone civil but firm.

"Captain, advice and opinions are welcome as are disagreements but not when I give you an order. An order means you will obey; be it right or wrong and whether you like it or not, an order is an order. Am I understood?"

Baldor bowed his head. "Yes sir, absolutely. I am sorry for my disobedience."

"No more, Captain."

"No more, sir."

"Apology accepted." A trace of a smile played on Hannibal's lips his dark eye now strangely warm as he offered his hand. "Now, this plan?"

Baldor took the offered hand and managed a smile along with an involuntary audible sigh of relief.

"I was thinking of a diversion sir, or rather diversions which may allow us to exit the valley without too much of a fight."

"I'm all ears Captain, as you know we are disadvantaged at present with Fabius and his legions on the high ground … so, these diversions?"

"We have some thousands of cattle in our herd. What if we were to split the herd into sections then divide them amongst the army and drive them ahead of us as we march out, they would provide a buffer for us and if we stampede them just before we close on the Romans, I venture they'll not stand in the way of that. We'd lose our cattle but hopefully deter, even prevent the Romans from fighting us until we wish it."

Hannibal sipped his wine, deep in thought.

"It's a good idea Baldor, I like it and it has promise. I would willingly lose the cattle before I'd lose men." He sipped his wine again. "Let's think more on this, have you eaten?"

"No sir."

"Then let's discuss further, over breakfast."

Escorting Baldor to a side table laden with food, he gestured he should help himself. The bread was fresh and still warm from the camp ovens, the smell making Baldor's stomach rumble. Hungry, he collected up bread, fresh butter and fried eggs that still sizzled gently atop a heated plate before adding a helping of fresh fruit for after. With laden plates, the pair returned to the table and Hannibal pushed a map across to Baldor.

"As you know, Fabius has placed four thousand legionaries in the pass mouth at the base of this saddle. He, the rest of his army and his cavalry under his Master of Horse, Minucius, is camped on this nearby hill." Baldor watched as Hannibal traced his finger over the parchment. "I think your idea has merit and if we make our move after dark we can better hide what we are at."

"After dark sir? Would that not be too great a risk?"

Hannibal grinned. "It's a greater risk yes, but with careful planning it should work, I've done such before successfully back in Spain. When I say after dark, I was thinking the third quarter of the night when sentries are bored and dozy. Moving then could further lessen the chances of casualties. And …" His grin eased into a smile and finally a chuckle, while Baldor looked on clearly puzzled. "And considering Fabius seems very reluctant to fight anyway methinks we can trick him to ensure he stays that way."

"I'm sorry sir, I don't quite understand?"

"Well, as we know Fabius has made no move to fight us in full battle. He's certainly learned from his predecessor's mistakes; I'll give him that." He chuckled again. "Instead of battle he's relied on skirmishes to harass or hinder our patrols and forage details and so challenge our sense of ease, just like you witnessed yesterday morning. I have to admit he's done that admirably well and in truth caused us more trouble than Scipio, Sempronius and Flaminius put together.

However, I digress. He now has his best chance so far to attack and inflict serious casualties on us when we exit the valley. However, here's the rub, he's a cautious man and if we can make him believe it's a trap and not just a withdrawal, I surmise he'll still procrastinate and once again do nothing."

Baldor's mouth creased into a wide grin. "So, we use his caution and delaying tactics against him, even when he has the best chance of beating us or at least giving us a mauling."

"Yes!" Hannibal's face displayed a boyish mischief. "Remember Baldor, if you can make your enemy see what you want them to see, not what is or in this case seeing as it will be dark, do what you want them to do." He laughed at his own jest. "Fabius will think he could be walking into a trap but which will instead be a ruse to cover our movements; I'll wager you what you wish, he won't move against us."

Baldor's face lightened as he saw Hannibal's enthusiasm. "I think I've another idea that helps us further and even allows for him attacking us should he suddenly grow bold."

Hannibal could not hide an excited grin and gestured Baldor should continue. "Go on Baldor, don't lose the thread now."

"When you speak of him seeing what we want him to see, what if we were to tie torches onto the horns of the cattle. Then before we move the army out in the darkness, we light them. That will panic and frighten them and help us drive them towards the Romans. From a distance it could look like an army on the run and thus if Fabius does decide to attack he'll go for the cattle instead of us."

"I like it Baldor, I like it! So instead of splitting the cattle and the army into sections you now think we should drive all the cattle at the Romans at the pass mouth while the army moves out under cover of darkness."

"Yes sir, I think that would work. If we use a token force to keep the cattle moving the bulk of the army could perhaps extricate themselves unscathed."

Hannibal chewed his lip and his eye closed for a moment as he thought the manoeuvre and numbers required through. "We'll use two thousand cattle; that should be sufficient. The remainder we'll take with us as we still need to eat." He smiled at Baldor. "I'll send two thousand camp followers and drovers to drive them and keep them moving, along with an escort of two thousand light infantry." He paused and cupped his chin deep in thought, then pointed back to the map. "See here, there's a saddle above the pass mouth just opposite the hill on which Fabius and his main army are camped. If we aim the cattle at that it could draw the legionaries away from their post below as they may think they're being outflanked, leaving the pass mouth open for the army?"

Baldor watched where Hannibal indicated on the map. "And Fabius sir, if he were to grow bold and attack?"

Hannibal smiled. "Let me ask you that question. Pretend you're Fabius. It's the middle of the night and you're roused from your slumber by panicking guards. You ask what's happening only to be told they're not sure but you may be suffering an attack or the Carthaginian army is trying to escape the valley in the darkness. Half asleep, you look for yourself and all you can see are hundreds of torches moving over the saddle above the pass mouth and all you can hear is the rumble of hooves and the cries of men. Now, do you attack in the darkness when you are unsure of what's happening and can't see? Have you a plan to control and co-ordinate your men for such an event? Or is that bastard Hannibal laying another trap as he did at the Trebbia and Trasimene?" Baldor just stared at Hannibal. "What will you do, Fabius? ... Come on! What will you do?" He badgered, while giving a wide grin.

"I ... I need to know what's happening, I ..."

"Come on Fabius, make a decision. Now!"

"Stand-to ..."

"Do you attack?"

"No, 'Stand-to' until the situation becomes clear."

"Which it won't because it's dark and you are cautious." Hannibal grinned. "I'll wager my last silver shekel Fabius will not move, Baldor."

Baldor shook his head gently a smile teasing the corners of his mouth.

"You're tricking him because he expects to be tricked!" Baldor started to laugh. "Baal almighty sir! I think you have the measure of it, the measure of this Fabius."

"Maybe Baldor but this was your idea." Hannibal gripped Baldor's shoulder and smiled warmly. "Between us we have merely thrashed it out and embellished it but the credit for it is yours."

Baldor flushed under the praise. "Thank you, sir."

"Thank you, Baldor! And I much prefer it when we are friends."

Baldor smiled warmly and placed his hand over his heart. "Me too sir."

"We'll meet with the command group later today and go through the plan with them; I expect it will only take a day or so to prepare for the manoeuvre so we could be on our way as early as tomorrow night. We'll ensure the men are fed and ready to go and then play our trick on our Roman friends. The timing is ours to control, all the Romans need do is do nothing." He laughed loudly. "Come … come, finish your breakfast."

The pair returned to their food. Hannibal, clearly delighted with the plan and jovial struck up general conversation and reverted to his usual teasing of Baldor.

"And how is your sultry redhead, Baldor not taxing your body too much?"

Baldor's cheerful expression disappeared and he swallowed hard.

"You won't have heard sir. My tent was robbed and burned, my servant Sulis murdered and Lasairiona taken."

"What! When was this?"

"On or about the day General Maharbal and I gave you our report on the action against Centenius's cavalry."

"That was some time ago now, why … why was I not informed?"

Baldor dropped his head and spoke quietly. "I had just angered you sir over the Roman prisoners, I thought it best not to bother you with my domestic troubles."

"Damn it, Baldor! I may be your General but I'm also your friend, the first is business but the second personal you should have come to me."

"My pride wouldn't let me sir."

"Damn your pride, Baldor Targa!" Hannibal exclaimed. "And stop calling me sir! I told you, when we have privacy it's Hannibal."

"I'm sorry Hannibal."

"No, no I'm sorry. Do you have lodging?"

"Yes, I'm staying with Lord Andulas."

Hannibal left his food and disappeared into his private quarter of the tent returning a moment later with a wooden chest. Opening it up, he fished out a sizeable leather bag, which gave a dull but heavy thump as he dropped it on the table in front of Baldor.

"It's Roman silver Baldor. Take it and see that you purchase a tent, victuals and a slave. I know prices are high for some commodities but that will see you comfortable."

"Thank you, sir I mean thank you Hannibal but I cannot."

"Why can you not? It's a gift."

"Andulas already offered me silver and then a loan when I refused, if I take it from you now, he may feel insulted. He's taken me in and fed me at his table and will not speak of me owing him anything."

"Well pay him with some of that."

Baldor half smiled. "Gallic sensitivities Hannibal. My head might end up on a spear."

Hannibal nodded and chuckled. "Aye! True, true! My Lord Andulas is a good and proud man ... however though, this is no gift, no loan but a reward for your plan."

Baldor looked stunned and shook his head slowly. "But to devise, propose plans is ... is part of my job as a Captain."

"H'mm, it is and as your General, choosing to reward good advice is my prerogative." He pushed the bag towards Baldor. "Your reward for a good plan that will undoubtedly save men's lives." Before Baldor could say anything Hannibal had closed the chest and returned it to his quarter before resuming his seat at the table.

"Thank you ..."

"No thanks necessary Baldor, that silver was earned. Now, what do you want to do about your redhead? Do you want to try and find her?"

"Yes." He replied quietly.

"Have you any idea where she may have been taken and by whom?"

"None. Malo looked at the tracks to and from the tent and all he could determine was three men entered but only two left. We found the remains of two bodies in the tent one of which was female and one male. We surmise the female's body to be Sulis."

"Aye, they would take the younger woman; she would fetch the higher price." Baldor nodded. "And the dead man?"

"A thief? I can only surmise Lasairiona killed him, as you know she can be formidable."

"You are sure they took her? She hasn't ran? I mean no insult by that." He added quickly.

"I'm sure. We'd grown ... close over these last months." Baldor looked uncomfortable at the admission.

Hannibal just nodded sadly. "I'm sorry Baldor, very sorry to hear this. I did notice a cheerfulness in you for some months and despite my teasing, I recognise when a woman is good for a man, she seemed to bring you happiness."

Baldor chewed his lip and nodded while bringing the subject back to the robbery. "Malo could see by the depth of the boot prints that one of the two men that left was carrying a load, most likely Lasairiona."

"Do you think it was a random attack or has someone a grudge against you?"

Baldor shrugged. "The only enemies I have here in camp that I know of are the Lords Bodeshmun and Sakarbaal."

Hannibal raised his eyebrows. "Aye, they certainly bear you no love."

"But I cannot accuse as I have no proof and in all honesty I would not envisage either to stoop so low."

"H'mm, no you cannot just accuse but as far as stooping low I am not so sure. Men without honour are plentiful and I didn't like what I saw in either of those two."

"I've known Sakarbaal most of my life and don't think he would agree to or condone such a ..."

"Come on Baldor, think on! Remember his sister? She planned and would have paid for your murder! Why should her brother be any better a person? As for Bodeshmun, he's a powerful Lord and used to getting what he wants, he'd not be unpleased at your misfortune though he wouldn't dirty his own hands to do it."

"But murder and theft? Sakarbaal? No, I cannot see it. Bodeshmun however ... I don't know him."

Hannibal shrugged. "For an intelligent and battle-hardened warrior Baldor, you still hold high ideals of men and honour. I'm not saying that's a bad thing." He said quickly. "But be wary of men my friend, not all are like yourself."

Baldor sighed resignedly. "Aye, Armaco has told me so, many times."

"Baal bless Armaco, your friend and watchdog." Hannibal smiled trying to lighten the conversation. "Listen, here's what we'll do, should you wish. Once we are clear of this valley and settled for the winter, take your troop and find your woman if you can."

"My entire troop sir?"

"Aye, methinks Fabius will be less inclined to attack a force larger than water detail size, especially after tomorrow night." He chuckled.

Baldor bowed his head. "Thank you, sir."

"Just don't get yourself killed doing it Baldor or I will be angry with you!"

Hannibal smirked and Baldor managed to laugh. The pair were picking through more of the fresh fruit when the door guard interrupted.

"General, sorry to disturb but Lord Sakarbaal from General Maharbal's staff requests an audience."

Baldor stiffened and made to rise. "I'll excuse myself, sir."

"Stay Baldor, finish your breakfast." Hannibal said as he put a restraining hand on his shoulder and eased him back into the chair then stood to receive the visitor. "Send him in."

Sakarbaal removed his helmet as he was ushered in. He bowed his sweat-wet head to Hannibal and though his face and mail shirt were splashed in blood, he smiled warmly, until he saw Baldor.

"Er … Greetings of the day General and compliments on behalf of General Maharbal."

"Greetings My Lord, you are bloodied but unhurt I trust?"

"Yes sir, thank you, and your pardon I should have washed before requesting your time."

"Tis no matter My Lord." He smiled. "You and the General are both hale?"

"Yes sir, thank you."

Hannibal looked at Sakarbaal then glanced towards Baldor.

Sakarbaal cleared his throat. "Good day to you, Captain Targa." The greeting respectful and sincere.

Baldor dipped his head. "Lord Sakarbaal."

There was a brief silence as the three men eyed each other. Hannibal noticed both Sakarbaal and Baldor looked uncomfortable.

"You bring news My Lord?"

"Yes … yes General." Sakarbaal, still surprised by Baldor's presence struggled to find his words.

"And …" Hannibal prompted and pointed at the bloodied sack in Sakarbaal's hand.

Sakarbaal pushed his hand into the sack and grimaced slightly as he pulled out a head by the hair. The dark, short-cropped curls declared the head Roman. The eyes were mercifully closed, the mouth hanging slightly open above a neatly severed neck.

Sakarbaal cleared his throat. "A one, Hostilius Mancinus, sir. The leader of a very large Roman cavalry patrol that we clashed with this morning, some four hundred equites or so."

"Fabius is growing bolder then?"

Baldor looked on, watching as Sakarbaal wiped sweat from his brow as he replied.

"Er, no sir. Not according to this Mancinus anyway. Fabius is in Rome at present and does not return here for another three days."

"That was very obliging of this Mancinus to tell us?"

"A strange man sir. He seemed very bitter towards Fabius while bemoaning the loss of all his men."

"You killed them all?"

"Everyone sir." He swallowed hard. "They thought a Numidian patrol to be easy meat, so the General taught them otherwise and cut them to pieces."

"Our losses?"

"Twenty-seven dead and thirty-three wounded sir."

Hannibal nodded appreciatively at the numbers. "Very light casualties My Lord, well done to you and General Maharbal!"

Sakarbaal seemed to relax slightly. "We ambushed and cut them up before they knew what hit them, sir." He smiled briefly and shrugged. "They're poor horsemen and still have no light units only heavy and those large shields just get in the way and they've still no bridles on their horses."

"And this Mancinus?" Hannibal asked impatiently.

"Sorry sir, General Maharbal offered to let him go so to carry the tale back to the Roman camp but he asked permission to take his own life owing to the disgrace of his defeat. To save time the General helped him on his way, then we tied his body across a mount and sent it back towards the Roman camp anyway."

Hannibal chuckled. "Excellent My Lord, excellent! Thank you for news of the victory but more importantly for the information regarding Fabius. Do you think it correct?"

Sakarbaal swallowed hard again and glanced at Baldor then back to Hannibal. "I think so sir … yes, yes." He reaffirmed. "This Mancinus had nothing to gain by lying about it. The General did ask him if Fabius had finally grown some balls and were the Romans finally going to fight." Hannibal laughed but bade Sakarbaal carry on. "He just said someone had to do something about us and that Fabius could go to Hades for all he cared."

Hannibal nodded sagely. "Thank you, My Lord and my thanks to General Maharbal. Go and take breakfast then rest you've earned it."

"Sir." Sakarbaal bowed his head and placed his fist over his heart. He turned quickly to Baldor and dipped his head. "Good day Captain." Still carrying the head, he turned to go.

Hannibal returned to his seat. "What think you of that, Baldor?"

"Well, if that Mancinus is to be believed it seems the Romans are less than happy."

"Not that!" He chuckled. "The respect for you and your rank from no less than Lord Sakarbaal? Finally!"

Baldor shrugged. "I surmise it was because of your presence sir, nothing more."

"No Baldor, no." He smirked. "I see a change in our Lordling there. Yes, I warned him of respect towards you but what he offered today was freely given."

"Maybe he's finally seeking peace between us or at least civility?"

"Would you accept peace if he offered it?"

Baldor sighed then nodded slowly. "Yes, yes I would."

"Despite all that has happened between your family and his?"

"I've known his family and Sakarbaal all my life and his elder brother Adharbal, he and I were good friends as children." His head dropped. "I didn't want to fight or kill him. Their elder brother Carthalo however, I do not regret killing."

Hannibal shrugged. "Men should think before they quarrel and from what you told me, you had to defend yourself. However, what about their sister, Serfina? She's quite a Harpie is she not? She's tried twice to have you convicted through the law courts then when that failed, was prepared to pay for your murder. Do you think she's behind your robbery?"

"I thought about that but reasoned it's me she wants to kill, robbing and burning my tent then killing and kidnapping my people is hardly a satisfying revenge."

Hannibal nodded and settled back in his chair. "I dislike fighting and bickering among my staff, so if you and Sakarbaal can find an accord that would please me."

"Yes sir, though please don't ask the same of me with Bodeshmun for I cannot." Baldor's face was grim.

Hannibal smiled. "You do have trouble dropping the sir." He chuckled and waved Baldor's response away. "I'll take half a win Baldor and between you and me if this Bodeshmun should fall to a Roman sword I won't be unhappy. Now, what do you think of this information we've gained from this Mancinus?"

"I'm inclined to believe it sir it seems the man had nothing to gain by lying."

"Agreed and when the information is given freely without torture I am more disposed to believe it, what's more, we can maybe test the truth of it and watch and wait for Fabius returning."

"So we'll wait three days before we move?"

Hannibal was deep in thought and didn't answer straight away. Baldor prompted again.

"We wait, sir?"

"Yes … yes." He said quietly, his gaze fixed on the tent wall. A moment later, he seemed to return from his thoughts. "We can afford to wait a little longer, four maybe five days to be sure that Fabius is back in camp and exercising restraint, we don't want some hot-headed Prefect taking charge and attacking us do we?" He chuckled again and reached for the wine jug then gestured to the cups. "I know it's early for a drink, Baldor but I have a good feeling about this, let's just watch and wait for a few days."

"Yes Hannibal." He said as he smiled and nodded towards the cups.

"And then as I promised before Lord Sakarbaal arrived, once we are out of this valley and safely into a winter camp, you can go and find your woman."

Baldor left shortly after to see to his duties and stepped out briskly through the tents, his heart lightened from the renewed friendship with Hannibal.

"Captain … Captain Targa!"

Baldor turned quickly towards the voice and saw Sakarbaal. Still holding his helmet, his other hand immediately reached for a falcata hilt. Sakarbaal slowly raised both arms from his sides, hands open and well away from his weapons. Baldor frowned and dropped his hand down from his blades, hooking a thumb in his belt but not too far from his dagger.

"Lord Sakarbaal!" He said levelly then sighed.

"Can we talk?"

Baldor nodded. "If you wish, what do you want?" He asked flatly while stepping closer towards a guard post before motioning Sakarbaal to join him.

"Peace … peace between us."

"I offered peace Sakarbaal and received blows for my trouble."

Sakarbaal dropped his head. "I'm sorry." He mumbled quietly.

"What did you say?"

Sakarbaal raised his head and stepped closer while extending his hand. "I'm sorry for what has passed between us and for my behaviour." Baldor stared into Sakarbaal's eyes seeking falseness and found him staring back at him. "I'm sorry Baldor, I believe I was wrong."

Baldor slowly placed his hand in Sakarbaal's, his senses however, sharp, his nerves on edge and poised to move if he saw trickery. There was a long silence as the two men just looked at each other.

"Why now, Sakarbaal? I don't surmise you have a sudden liking for me."

"Respect, Baldor. I respect you, surely it's a start?"

Baldor shrugged. "I accept your apology. At least now we can be civil and it will please the General." He nodded slightly, withdrew his hand and turned to go.

"Wait! Wait you if you please."

Baldor turned back. "I'm listening."

"That day we fought … you tried to dissuade me from a fight but I would have none of it … you could have killed me and you didn't."

"I didn't want to fight you Sakarbaal and certainly didn't seek your death or that of your brother Adharbal. However, I will make no apology for the death of Carthalo; for my wife's death was his doing." Sakarbaal tried to interrupt but Baldor stopped him with a raised hand. "Furthermore, your sister Serfina sought and paid for my murder, which I also will not forgive so if you cannot accept that, then know now, there can be no peace between us."

Baldor noticed a brief but surprised look on Sakarbaal's face at the mention of his sister before he continued quietly.

"I've thought much on what has transpired Baldor and I believe Carthalo to be in the wrong and I swear by Tannith, mother of us all that I know nothing of Serfina's doings … however and more importantly I am sorry for the death of Aiticia, truly."

Baldor saw sincerity on Sakarbaal's face and replied quietly. "Thank you." He turned to go again.

"Baldor … Captain, I mean it I am sorry." He looked Baldor in the eye and extended his hand once more. "Can we start again?"

Baldor rubbed a hand over his jaw as if contemplating and then took the offered hand. "Very well."

Each mumbled, 'peace be with you' as they shook hands.

Chapter Four

In preparation for the coming march, Baldor laid his meagre possessions out on the camp bed to check and inspect. Apart from the spare tunic, which he'd purchased since the robbery, they were all that remained of his previous belongings, a bronze helmet, an acquired Roman mail shirt, a pteruges belt and a pair of greaves, two falcatas, a dagger, waist belt and a round shield.

Settling himself cross-legged with his back against the bed, he sighted the first falcata blade for nicks and imperfections then after testing the edge against his thumb began rubbing a whetstone methodically over the blade. With Andulas and Armaco out on patrol and the servants and slaves about their work, he had peace and time to himself to ponder his situation. As he worked he thought of the offer from Hannibal to take his men and find Lasairiona, having the men at his disposal was one thing but where to begin looking for her quite another. He knew she would have been taken far from the camp and with the locality mostly in ruin, likely to be some distance away, perhaps even sold overseas by now?

Finishing the first blade, he rubbed it all over with unwashed sheep's wool, the lanolin a good defence against rust. Picking up the second blade, he began the process anew while pondering his strange relationship with Lasairiona. She was strikingly beautiful. However, when first given to him as a slave after he'd slain her father, a brutal and tyrannical Gallic warlord, at the siege of Victumulae he'd abhorred her presence. Owing to Gallic attitudes to blood feud and vengeance, he thought she would attempt to kill him at the first opportunity. However, despite being Gallic nobility, life with her father had not been idyllic and she had to his surprise, accepted her servitude with a quiet sufferance.

Fairness and civility from him had led to respect from her and which eventually brought both together in mutual, sensual comfort. Though he now cared deeply for her, he couldn't say it was love, the pair really growing together from adversity. She, by caring unstintingly for him and his injuries and perhaps making the best of her lot as a slave, he, seeking a woman's comfort after the death of his wife, Aiticia some three summers since.

That painful jog to his memory had him putting the sword and stone to one side and pulling a silver cameo from around his neck. He ran his thumb carefully over the warm metal that bore Aiticia's image. He stared at it for a while, the finely chased lines showing the head and shoulders of a beautiful young woman with cascading, lustrous tresses and a fine-featured face set upon a long, elegant neck and his mind conjured memories of better, happier days. A lump rose in his throat as he remembered when his thoughts were just that of his beautiful wife and hopes of a family, his only concerns the family business of building ships and turning a profit. He swallowed hard and whispered.

"You'll always be in my heart my love; you're gone now but not forgotten."

He kissed the image as his eyes filled. Slipping the cameo back into his tunic he bit his lip and returned to his sharpening. Enough now he thought, the pain of Aiticia's death was not as sharp as it once was though he reasoned it would never leave him. Nor would the guilt he felt for it as he still blamed himself and his temper for causing her demise. Two brothers of the Samilcar family had died at his hand as he'd sought vengeance for Aiticia's death, and though he felt vindicated for those killings they had brought him no comfort, only a blood feud with the men's family. Shaking his head and putting the old, grim thoughts firmly to one side, he returned to his work.

Attempting to leave the past in the past, he brought his thoughts back to the present and the disappearance of Lasairiona and the murder of his servant, Sulis. His face took on a sudden bitter look as he thought of Lord Bodeshmun, was Hannibal's supposition right? Was he behind the crimes? The man had previously insulted and almost killed him, so one day no matter what, he'd seek redress and kill him. Then, remembering being told revenge is a dish best served cold, he forced the thought from his head and took up the blade and stone again while seeking more positive thoughts. Despite his woman trouble, his stolen wealth and loss of his other armaments, his mood turned light owing to the constructive meeting with Hannibal and the curious, peace-making turnabout by Sakarbaal. That was one enemy less to worry him, though he would still watch the man carefully. He smiled to himself as in his mind he could hear Armaco's words, 'Lordlings! Don't trust the bastards!'

Thankfully, his dire monetary situation had disappeared owing to his recently acquired silver, enabling him to pay his way again and not having to rely on the charity of others, which pleased him. Riches or at least silver, not that they bothered him greatly and which he knew he could acquire again remained a necessity to live. Only the ivory hilted falcata willed to him by his former commander, Captain Balaam and the silver chased dagger given him by Hannibal in recognition of saving Mago's life bothered him, those items had been precious to him.

It was early in the evening before Andulas and Armaco returned from patrol. Hearing their relaxed chatter and laughter as they approached the tent he reasoned all had gone well and made his way out to meet them. Servants were already holding their horses while the men dismounted and passed over spears and shields. Baldor dipped his head.

"Hail brothers, I trust all is well. No mishaps on patrol."

The pair dipped their heads in turn.

"All good Baldor." Andulas said as he smiled. "Methinks that thumping General Maharbal gave those equites the other day has quietened the Romans down again. We only saw two small patrols but they kept their distance, they watched but didn't interfere with us getting water. I guess Fabius is back and keeping a tight rein on his men again … come!" Throwing his arm over Baldor he guided him toward the tent again then turned his head to Armaco who was still by the horses and ferreting in a large tack bag. "Bring our find in with you to meet Baldor." Shooing servants bearing bowls of rosewater to wash and a tray of wine and cups and telling them to wait a moment he turned to Baldor again. "We thought this might make it feel a bit more like home for us." He gestured to Armaco who shuffled in, his cloak gathered in front of him covering a sizeable odd-shaped lump.

"Ugh! The little bastard has pissed on me." Armaco scowled as he pulled a grey puppy from the wrappings of his cloak and held it by the scruff making it yelp. "Here!" He thrust the pup at Baldor while using the cloak to wipe his corselet.

Andulas couldn't resist a chuckle as Armaco continued to grumble then throw his cloak to a watching slave. The puppy, safely cradled in

Baldor's arms was busy sniffing him and trying to climb up his chest to lick his face. Baldor laughed as the pup continued trying to find purchase as it climbed, stroking and trying to settle it he smiled widely while talking softly to the pup

"It likes you." Andulas said, looking pleased with himself.

"He? … She?" Baldor lifted the pup to look. "She's wonderful."

"Hah! Wait till it pisses all over you." Armaco growled.

Baldor took a seat and lifted the pup to see it better; it was probably only two or three months old. The ears had been cropped to points; the broad, stubby head wrapped in spare folds of shorthaired, wrinkled grey skin leading to a black snub nose and long flews. A white mark shaped as a lightning flash centred on its chest and stood out against the grey coat. The short, thick legs that ended in huge paws a sure sign the dog would grow large, the folds of additional loose skin across the body more evidence of growth to come, the tail thick and whip-like.

"Where did you find her?"

"She was just wandering near a copse and yapped at us; there was no sign of any others or any people. I surmise she'd been left behind or become lost as folk fled the farms and such. I think she's old enough to be away from the mother, so she'll manage solids if we break them up a bit."

The pup gave a little sigh, looked about then seemed to settle in Baldor's arms while staring at the men from sleepy brown eyes, its head resting between its front paws. As Baldor continued to stroke and talk softly the pup's eyes flickered and closed.

"What are we going to call her?"

"Trouble!" Armaco snapped.

"How can you say that you miserable wretch, she's beautiful."

"Wait till it pisses and shits all over the place then see how you feel about it." Armaco grumbled, then removed his helmet and slumped into a chair.

Andulas roared with laughter and called for wine. "I've seen these dogs before Baldor, the Romans call them Molossian. They're strong and very faithful and she'll grow to quite a size, folk would have had such to hunt with or raise as watchdogs for the farm and to keep wolves at bay in the fields near the hills."

Baldor, still cradling the dog called for a servant demanding food and water fit for a puppy. When the servant looked lost, Andulas intervened.

"Soak some of that hard bread in milk and chop up some meat and fat into mush for later."

When the servant reappeared, the pup's nose seemed to twitch and her eyes opened watching intently as the bowls were laid on the floor. Baldor set her down and she walked straight towards the food. He laughed as she strutted on the unfamiliar carpeted ground.

"She'll be hungry and thirsty I imagine." Andulas said as he watched.

"Huh! I know how it feels and now the bloody dog is to be fed before us it seems!" Armaco grumbled.

"Don't you want to wash first?"

"No Andulas, I just want to eat and swill this dust out of my throat with some wine."

"Very well, we'll eat now." He clapped his hands and a servant appeared. "We'll take dinner now."

"Yes, My Lord." The servant scuttled quickly away alerting the others to begin serving the food.

Baldor was now laid on the floor watching as the dog finished the milk and bread then sat upright, head up, licking her lips and watching the men.

"She looks very regal don't you think?" He asked.

"Yes quite a lady." Andulas added.

"That's it, Issa … Issa, that's what we'll call her. Issa means her little Ladyship."

"Issa it is then. We better find Her Ladyship a fitting bed methinks no carpet or bare floor for her." Andulas chuckled as he wandered the tent picking up and discarding cushions before settling on a sheepskin. "This will do and it'll keep her warm."

The moment he laid the skin in the tent corner the pup, unbidden, walked towards it and curled up on it while keeping the men in view. As the men took their places at the table and settled to eat, Issa, seemingly content closed her eyes and slept.

****

In the Roman camp, a droning cornu signalled a meeting for the commanding officers at the tent of the Dictator, Quintus Fabius Maximus. The atmosphere in the camp was tense, expectant, both officers and legionaries keen to exploit their superior tactical position over the Carthaginians and go to battle. After weeks of trailing and skirmishing with the enemy and with comrades to avenge for the slaughter at Trasimene, the men's desire for war was like that of the hungry wolf that stares longingly at the sheepfold.

The officers, dressed in full armour filed in and took their seats around the table, helmets placed close at hand in readiness for the hoped-for call to action. Fabius however appeared in just his tunic and without armour; men looked askance at one another at his casual state as they waited for him to speak. When he took his time pouring wine and taking reports from two scouts, his Master of Horse, Marcus Minucius Rufus spoke up.

"Sir … sir what are your orders, do we march?"

"Patience, Marcus. Let me deal with the scouts first."

"But time is pressing sir; we've fervently awaited your return from Rome and are ready for battle, the men are eager and …"

"I said wait until I finish with the scouts!" He snapped.

Marcus's face flushed the colour of his hair at the put down and he snatched for his wine cup and quaffed it to hide his embarrassment, clicking his fingers to a servant, he signalled for a refill. Eventually Fabius finished with the scouts and picking up a cane turned to the table while summoning servants to place a map board on a stand at the table head.

"Now gentlemen, as you know we have Hannibal trapped here in the valley." He traced the cane across the map illustrating his words. "The only logical exit he can take is the one below us here, which we've blocked with four thousand legionaries."

"Do we advance into the valley sir?" Came from the table.

"No! No, we do not …" Anxious, fretful mutterings started up from the table drowning Fabius's words and he slapped the cane hard on the tabletop stopping the talk. "There will be no advance yet! We wait! Hannibal is running out of fodder for his animals and supplies for his men and will soon be forced to march, when he does, then we'll attack him." The men just stared, their disappointment and frustration clear on their faces. "As you all well know, catching an army on the move before it can deploy is the time to strike." The veiled criticism at Flaminius's calamitous march past Lake Trasimene did nothing to endear Fabius to his men. "The Carthaginians will not only be hungry and strung out on the march they will be disadvantaged as we have the benefit of both time and ground. Also, we'll ensure that there's little space so Hannibal cannot use his cavalry arm to any affect and the narrow, broken ground as they leave the valley will only hamper their pikemen."

Marcus tried again. "Sir, we have them bottled up as you say and thus I urge you to strike now! The men are ready for battle, eager for it, strike while …"

"And I say no!" Fabius snapped while staring hard at Marcus. "I care not what the men are eager for, our tactics of shadow and small, sharp strikes are effectively hampering Hannibal's efforts to forage and to secure a winter camp. Furthermore, our delaying has allowed time to rebuild and train our depleted legions rather than throwing good men after bad."

Fabius's further hinted disdain of the Trasimene catastrophe and the men cut deep and the mood at the table darkened further for many there had lost brothers, fathers and uncles at Trasimene. Marcus, angry beyond belief jumped to his feet.

"Enough sir! By Jupiter, I say enough! This is not the Roman way, following an enemy around like sheep then behaving like slaves and cowards and shrinking from the fight."

Fabius, incensed at the insolence and the insinuation at what he knew was said about his character behind his back, of he being Hannibal's 'pedagogue' or slave and merely following him about, rounded on Minucius.

"How dare you, sir! How dare you!" He spat, though it seemed Marcus was not to be cowed as he responded just as furiously.

"I dare because I'm Master of your Horse and I'll speak up for what I judge is not right. We are Romans! We engage and fight our enemy in the field, face to …"

"Open your damn eyes man and you'll see Hannibal is not doing that, he fights like a brigand, with no honour. Thus, we must change our tactics to suit. Jupiter knows our previous efforts have borne no fruit. I will fight him as it suits us and not as he wishes and denying him battle on ground of his choosing is a must …"

"There'll be no ground left if we don't stop him soon! He's destroying everything and what he hasn't fired, slaughtered or trampled you have had us do it! Gods above Fabius! We've burned our own land, destroyed our crops and driven our folk off! As Romans in our own country we are shamed, this is beyond sufferance, how can you just stand by and watch it happen?"

Fabius's brow furrowed deeply his features twisting in anger.

"I suffer it because I must, we must! I'll stop him when I am sure I can beat him and beat him without the loss of most of my men and command."

"We could beat him now, down there in that valley."

"Yes, we could but a Pyrrhic victory is not what the Republic needs right now."

"How would it come to that?"

Fabius shook his head in disdain. "Because many of our men are new, raw. Not that I doubt their bravery or resolve to win." He got in quickly. "But they're up against a seasoned force and a seasoned force that is trapped!"

"Trapped! Exactly my point! Now's the time to strike."

"Is it? Good military acumen dictates that men with no way out will fight to the death for they have nothing to lose." Minucius tried to interject but Fabius raised his voice to dominate the diatribe. "Use your wits man and think above your singular cavalry actions for once and see the bigger picture! His army is slowly starving, his cattle beast and his horses, if not so much his men as yet but either way, he needs to move out of that valley and soon. The longer he procrastinates and does nothing the better it is for us, as he only grows steadily weaker. We will attack the moment his army begins to move clear of the valley and the ground suits us. When he's arrayed in column, he is far easier to attack than solid formations with their backs to the wall. Is it not?"

"Yes sir." Minucius said quietly. Realising the good logic to Fabius's argument he looked crestfallen, raising his hands as if acknowledging defeat, he took his seat again. Fabius, comfortably dominant once more and somewhat soothed by the ready deference attempted to smooth Minucius's ruffled feathers.

"Once we have them on the move, then you and your equites can get in amongst them and show these Carthaginians our Roman fortitude and destroy them."

Chapter Five

As arranged, the Carthaginians took their evening meal, watered their wine and drank sparingly then settled to rest. To any Romans watching the camp there was no change in the usual behaviour, just an army settling down for another night. However, when dusk gave way to darkness the Carthaginian camp came to life. Without the signal of trumpets, men began gathering up belongings, packing down tents and strapping on armour and weapons. Cavalryman went down to the horse lines and prepared their first mount for riding while stringing their reserve mounts ready to move. The campfires however were kept well fed with wood along with the sentries' braziers so to give an impression of normality while wagons were loaded and horses readied. The camp women encumbered with small children climbed into wagons settling their charge's snugly amongst the cargo, small babies being wrapped tightly and held close. The single women gathered in groups and fell in behind the troops, ensuring that if battle did come they'd be no hindrance to the warriors. This well-planned, quiet bustle belied the efforts to dismantle a camp by firelight and prepare an army for the march.

The cattle required for the operation had been separated from the main herd and now men set about tying torches to their horns ready to be lit on command. The work was difficult, the beasts anything but accommodating as they tossed their heads and pushed and shoved to be away from the men. Baldor watched as the servants loaded the last of Andulas's belongings and tent sections onto the carts, with nothing large of his own to transport, he took leave of Andulas and Armaco.

"I'm called to the General's tent for a final briefing. If I can, I'll be back but if my orders change I'll find you come daylight."

Andulas, heavily armed and decked in mail offered his hand. "Epona bless and keep you Baldor."

Baldor shook the proffered hand then threw his arm over the Gaul. "Epona's blessing on you also Andulas and my thanks for feeding me and giving me a bed."

"No thanks necessary Baldor, it's no loss what a friend gets … tomorrow eh?"

"Tomorrow." Baldor bowed his head then turned to Armaco and embraced him tightly. "Baal keep you and bless you."

"And you." Armaco muttered, unused to showing affection he returned the embrace awkwardly. "I've got your horses should you need them, if not I'll take them and see you on the morrow. Stay out of trouble eh! If I'm not there to look after you, Baal knows what could happen." He punched Baldor in the shoulder in a rough show of affection and smiled.

Baldor smiled and nodded. "Andulas, you're in command until I return." He bowed his head again to both then disappeared into the darkness.

Arriving at Hannibal's tent, he found it just a shell, the contents and furniture already packed and loaded on wagons. The officers gathered inside standing in a group, exchanging pleasantries while waiting for the meeting to convene. The warm night and the number of men crammed into the tent made the air stale, the odour of male sweat adding a sourness. It wasn't long before Hannibal stepped up under the light of one torch to address them. He smiled widely, his manner jovial and seemingly relaxed despite the complex situation.

"Gentlemen, thank you for foregoing your beds and sleep but we must be about our business. Tonight, is perfect for us, Fabius is back in camp and the clouds are hiding the moon but we'll still wait until the third quarter of the night before making our move. By then the Roman sentries will be chilled and weary and should they still rouse the legions, men dragged from their beds at that time of the morning will be groggy and not at their best, as you all saw at the Trebbia." He managed a chuckle that brought low laughter from the men. "Now, we will drive the cattle at the small saddle just to the side of the pass mouth, that should draw the legionaries as they will think we're either escaping or they're being outflanked. With the pass mouth open the army can march out."

"And Fabius, General?"

"I'm gambling that he does nothing General Maharbal, and you know I don't gamble unless I know I can win."

There was more low laughter from the men.

Mago asked. "So, Fabius maintains his usual stance but we may lose those cattle and the men driving them to an attack from the legionaries at the pass?"

Hannibal looked serious and nodded. "It is possible, brother. It all depends on how well those legionaries respond. However, as I said, they'll have been rudely roused from their beds so won't be at their best as they have to don their mail then run uphill to see what's afoot. Thus, they'll arrive breathless and not in battle order, even if they did, the cattle will help break them up. Therefore, I think our light infantry will be able to get in amongst them and give them a beating."

Mago chewed his lips and nodded slowly. "Do you want me to lead the infantry?"

"No brother, I want to use the caetrati, our light Spanish troops, and Captain Tercero has stepped forward for the task."

"It's still heavies against light though; it'll be a hard fight." General Gisgo grumbled. "No disrespect to you or your men Captain Tercero for I've seen you fight." He dipped his head graciously. "I'm just concerned that we can't support you if the fighting becomes heavy."

"I'm reasoning manoeuvrability and speed will overcome heavy armament and tired legionaries." Hannibal countered.

Tercero bowed to Hannibal then turned to face the assembled men. "Gentlemen, I thank you for your concerns but both my men and I are confident we can do this. We need to be out of this valley and I think this is the best chance we will have. We are a mountain people, at home on the hill; the cattle will be our heavy support."

This raised a murmur of laughter and Gisgo nodded and clapped Tercero on the back.

"What happens if Fabius does move against us, brother?" Mago asked.

"He'll have to find us first. Remember, we'll be marching in the dark, only the cattle with Captain Tercero are bearing torches. Would you attack in the dark against something you couldn't see?"

"I wouldn't no but going by past performances these Romans are not so bright."

Again, the room filled with laughter.

"If Fabius were to move and if it looks like he could cut us off, we'll make a stand. However, I tell you, this is Fabius, Fabius the cautious who is expecting to be tricked so we'll oblige and trick him into doing nothing. As you all know, he is happiest doing nothing." He had to hush the men as laughter broke out. "Don't think me overconfident or that I underestimate him, I don't! He is far wiser and has caused us more trouble than his predecessors. However, I'm sure that I've judged him aright and caution will hold him in check."

Baldor listened intently to the diatribe and despite the assurances; he heard and saw some of the tenseness in the men. With the plan being his, he felt responsible for the men about to undertake what many in the room clearly thought to be high-risk night manoeuvres. Light troops outnumbered and pitched against heavies and an enemy that may or may not move, then a battle in the dark. He also knew and liked Tercero having fought alongside him at the cavalry action after Trasimene. Taking a deep breath, he spoke up.

"General!"

"Yes, Captain Targa."

"Sir, as you know I've scouted the mouth of the pass and the saddle, may I accompany Captain Tercero, I could be of use to him."

Hannibal hesitated for a moment then nodded. "Yes, Captain you may, though you understand it's not a cavalry action."

"Yes General." He managed a smile. "I'll do my best to keep up."

Hannibal grinned and the men chuckled. Tercero stepped towards Baldor and offered his hand.

"Thank you, Captain Targa. For me this will be easier than our last fight for we have no river to cross and no horses to ride."

The pair smiled as they remembered Tercero's horror at climbing up behind Baldor, both fully armoured as they swam the horse across a deep, swift river. Being an infantryman with an abject fear of horses and unable to swim it had tested the Spaniard's mettle.

Hannibal called the men to order. "The order of march is our African infantry to the front followed by the cavalry, the baggage train, then the cattle and camp followers, the Gallic and Spanish heavy infantry to bring up the rear. We must be ready to move when we see the torches lit and the cattle moving up the saddle and then march the moment the scouts confirm the pass is no longer defended and open for us. Are there any more questions? … No? Very well then, to your regiments and may Baal bless and keep you all."

With murmured responses and bowing heads, the group broke up.

Tercero led Baldor in the direction of his men while bringing him up to speed on the finer points of the plan.

"We'll travel light Baldor, small or no shields and little in the way of armour, best to leave that mail shirt and heavy helmet off as we will have to move fast."

"It's all I have Tercero, my leather armour, helmet and padded shirts were stolen when my tent was robbed and burned."

"Bastards! What kind of scum rob a man of his armaments? No matter my friend, come with me." He diverted Baldor to the still growing mass of wagons, finding his men's baggage section and his own cart; he jumped up on it and began ferreting through his chests and boxes. "Take the mail and helmet off Baldor and pass them up you can leave them on the cart with my belongings."

Baldor threw his helmet up then unfastening his falcatas and harness from his shoulders and his waist dagger belt, bent over and shrugged out of the mail shirt then hefted it up to Tercero. Standing in just his tunic and boots, he waited as Tercero continued to search through his effects.

"Hah! Here we are, try these." Tercero passed a harness of three interlocking bronze discs down and a simple, un-crested leather helmet. "I'll give you a hand in a moment, just let me stow your gear safely." Baldor slipped the hardened leather helmet on, with his thick hair, it was a little tight but it would suffice. Tercero jumped down from the cart. "How's the fit?"

"Good and so light."

"Let me help you into the harness, you can fit your falcatas over it in a moment, here hold this." Having Baldor hold the simple bronze tri-disc in place over his upper chest and heart, Tercero fastened the leather harness straps over his shoulders. "How's that feel, tight enough?"

Baldor flexed his shoulders then twisted his torso about. "Very comfortable and light."

Tercero nodded. "As you can see it's a long way from total protection but it's not restrictive and you won't tire as you would from your mail shirt. Speed and manoeuvrability is the essence of staying alive when wearing this. Here, I'll help you with your falcata harness."

Baldor added his waist belt then flexed his body trying different positions and stretches, amazed at the flexibility and weightlessness he now had, he grinned. "Now let's see what kind of infantryman I make."

"Better than I as a cavalryman, I'll warrant! Spear?"

"No, it's not my favourite weapon; my blades will keep me safe."

"Take these though." He passed over two javelins. "They're light and very useful … one more thing." He led Baldor across to the fire and raked out some of the charred wood. Rubbing his hands on the blackened timber, he wiped them across his nose, brow and cheekbones. Turning to Baldor, he began smearing the charcoal over his face. "Cover the high spots Baldor, anywhere that torchlight may reflect from." Baldor rubbed his hands on the burnt wood adding more black to his face. "Arms and legs too Baldor, make yourself harder to see."

Smeared in charcoal and soot and with Baldor more suitably attired the pair set off to find Tercero's men, the drovers and the cattle. They talked quietly as they walked.

"Can I ask Tercero, what made you step up for this, I know you like a fight but this is during the night and far from an ideal situation?"

Tercero chuckled. "Purely self-promotion, Baldor. That and Hannibal offering me the command of two thousand men and a chance to prove myself with a night manoeuvre. If I can win this, my prospects for promotion will hopefully gather momentum. What of yourself, what's made you leave your horses?" He chuckled again.

Baldor's reply however was serious. "This diversion was my idea so I feel I should be here to share the risk. And when I heard you were to command it, I reasoned that I should support you as you supported me against Centenius's cavalry after Trasimene."

Tercero halted the pair of them from walking and thrust an open hand out. "You're a good man Baldor Targa, may Dercetius bless and keep you." Baldor smiled and shook his hand while dipping his head in respect. "Dercetius is our mountain God." Tercero explained. "And we are going to a mountain are we not?"

Baldor grinned. "It's steep enough!" The pair laughed and strode into the darkness seeking the men and cattle.

Tercero called up his unit commanders for a briefing. Materialising out of the darkness with their skin also blackened, they formed a tight ring around him and Baldor as he explained his plan.

"We bring all the cattle forward of us and to the base of the saddle, so when they stampede we're well out of their path. When the drovers fire the faggots on their horns they're going to panic and the moment they begin to run we follow. Captain Targa tells me it's a long climb up the saddle. However, we must keep up with the cattle and then be ready for battle as we think the Romans at the pass mouth will also move up the saddle thinking we're trying to outflank them. They're legionaries not velites, so they'll be heavily armed but shocked from the rude awakening and tired from the run up the saddle. The cattle will also surprise them and help break up any semblance of formation, ensuring we can get in amongst them … Questions?"

"We attack as soon as we see them, sir?"

"Yes, don't wait for orders or trumpet blasts, just kill the bastards as you see them."

"Do we hold them or drive them off, sir?"

"Either we just need to buy time for the army to move out of the valley."

"And then sir?"

"Then we'll extract ourselves." There was an awkward silence before Tercero cleared his throat. "In truth it could be a hard fight and the very worst case is the whole of the Roman army could eventually bear down on us. Come daylight we may have to make a run for it."

Chapter Six

The cattle were all massed ready for the night's manoeuvre. Some trying to lie down owing to the time of night while others milled about, lowing loudly, and unsettled with the drovers at pains to keep them from wandering. Eventually they settled down and for the moment were relatively quiet, just the odd one tossing its head and trying to dislodge the torches tied to its horns while lowing as if in complaint. With so many beasts jammed in close proximity, their smell was very strong and the ground already wet from their urine and glutinous droppings. Baldor, having stood in such felt the warm shit squelching between his toes, the pungent stink causing his nose to wrinkle. He and the two thousand Spanish caetrati waited quietly, ready for the chaos they were about to unleash once the torches were lit and for the battle they were sure was to come. As always, that time just before combat was the worst, when men considered their mortality and every sense became finely tuned. The time when men suddenly appreciated things around them, simple things like plants and trees, the scent of the forest or the sweet smell and green hue of the meadow, the blue of the sky, a flight of birds or the drone of a passing honeybee. Now, waiting in the pitch darkness men could see nothing, their comrades just mere shapes in the murk, the air thick with the stink of cattle and the nasal piercing stench of their piss and shit. Was this akin to waiting to enter Hades with the darkness, the lack of colour and fear of what could not be seen and what awaited?

Baldor swallowed hard. Despite the amount of fights he'd been in, he felt a tremor in his leg, forcing it still with his free hand he quietly cursed it and hoped they would move soon. Combat, despite all its horrors seemed a kinder alternative to this waiting. He also felt lost without his horse, a horse to a cavalryman was more than a means of transport or combat, it was a support, a friend. A friend that could be patted and stroked, the smell of their coats pleasant, the animal a simple, comforting distraction while waiting for battle to commence. The weight and security of the mail shirt was also gone, the comfort and robustness of his bronze helm exchanged for light, hardened leather. His new, loaned equipment despite its weightlessness and as comfortable as it was, now left him feeling unprotected, naked. Also, with Tercero up front briefing the drovers, he didn't know any of the men that stood alongside him and he felt very much alone. His mouth was bone dry, his stomach quietly churning and his bladder felt full to bursting. Trying to ease that discomfort he lifted his tunic and tried to piss, only a dribble came. The cold fingers of fear came next, creeping into his body and pulling at his heart, trying to steal his courage. Thoughts slipped into his mind that told him to run, to get away from this coming madness, this chaotic fight in the darkness amidst terrified cattle.

"Light them up! … Light them up!"

The order was hissed around the men and the drovers began applying fire to the torches. The moment fire was held near the cattle, mayhem ensued. Animals bellowed and leapt away from the flames and each other, their terror reaching new heights as the torches on their own horns were set alight. Some were knocked over as beasts close by went berserk, careering and crashing into others from fear of the flames. Men leapt to one side as the pandemonium increased as more and more animals had their horns fired. As the beasts made to run, more drovers armed with two torches apiece lined their route shouting and waving the torches ensuring they moved in the direction of the saddle. As fear spread chaos amongst the herd, trying to light more of the torches was akin to taking your life in your hands. More than a few of the drovers died from horn thrusts as animals tossed their heads wildly from side to side trying to escape the fire, others too slow to move were knocked over and trampled as the living, fiery leviathans began to stampede. As the animals raced away, the spectacle took on the appearance of a river of fire but surging uphill not down.

With the cattle fleeing into the darkness, some of the drovers assigned to the infantry lit torches to give the men some light and they also began to move. Trotting behind and matching their gait to that of the cattle the men gradually increased their speed as the animals spread out and raced away. The noise grew quickly with cattle bellowing and lowing, the thunder of hooves and cries as some animals lost their footing and went down to be trampled by the others coming behind. The occasional scream also rose above the turmoil as a drover too slow or caught in the wrong place also went down, the terrified cries cut mercifully short. Baldor, as frightened as he was at the prospect of a battle in the dark began a loping run relieved that the action had finally begun and the waiting over. His hand holding the javelins was wet and clammy from the nervous wait and swapping the javelins into the other hand; he dried it on his tunic before changing back and drying the other. The going grew hard as the incline steepened quickly; thankfully, the grass remained short with only the occasional depression and broken rocky scar. The speed and poor visibility had some men trip and fall; most regained their feet immediately, others more slowly as they limped on with sprained or twisted ankles. A few suffered broken bones and had to remain where they fell as the warriors raced on in the lee of the cattle, the animals their shock troops should the Romans appear. Baldor's foot slipped from underneath him as he stood in more cowshit sending him stumbling into another man. The man growled a curse but neither fell and they blundered on into the darkness.

With no enemy contact yet he wondered at the effectiveness of the deception, would the legionaries move up from the pass mouth and attack? Would Fabius move in support or would Hannibal be right and he would do nothing? His calves and ankles were already aching from the stumbling run over the uneven ground, his lack of vision contributing to the difficulty. His thigh muscles began to burn as he forced his way uphill, unused to running his heart hammered in his chest from the exertion, while his breathing came in short, fast gasps. These physical difficulties only added to the fear that he may have to fight for his life in the darkness at any moment. The other fear and this time unseen was he had no idea how far he had to run; all he could do was try to keep up with the others and hope his body would not let him down. Despite his earlier reservations about giving up his usual equipment, he was now glad he'd taken Tercero's advice and equipment and left the mail shirt and heavy helmet behind otherwise he wouldn't have gotten this far.

Above the noise of the cattle, the shouts of the drovers and his heavy breathing he thought he heard the first sounds of combat up ahead. Moving a javelin into each hand, he glanced about at the men around him with torches and peering into the small pools of light he looked for the enemy.

Suddenly, to his right a man holding a torch stopped abruptly as if he'd hit an invisible wall. The man collapsed to his knees and then fell back over his legs with a pilum protruding from his chest. The torch fell to the floor but illuminated an advancing, long oval shield and a half-dressed legionary that was snatching for his sword. Baldor didn't slow down but swerved to his right and at less than ten paces hurled his javelin at the partly lit silhouette of the Roman. At the close range and with the man unarmoured the javelin thumped into his chest the slim head bursting out of his back. Baldor, still at the run jumped over the dying legionary then had to sidestep quickly to avoid a cow that suddenly appeared out of the darkness. One torch was gone from its horns the other had loosened and swung down burning the animal's skin. It tossed its head wildly and jumped erratically as it ran trying to shake the burning brand off.

Still running and watching the darkness ahead for comrades or more Romans, Baldor couldn't see anyone. Sensing he was alone he was about to stop but was instead pitched suddenly forward, headfirst as his foot hooked under a body in the grass. He hit the ground hard, the breath driven from his lungs, his forehead smashing into the earth. Breathless and only semiconscious but still gripping his javelin he tried to get up. His senses swam and his legs wouldn't respond. Falling back down, he was hit again, this time in the thighs as another man fell over him but managed to gain his feet and run on. Curling up as best he could to protect himself from further hurt, he waited as more warriors ran past. It went quiet once more and not hearing anyone else coming close, he tried again to rise but only managed to get to his knees.

A voice behind him startled him and he rolled away while pulling his dagger from its sheath.

"Stop! … Steady, I'm on your side." The man shouted as he pushed his stick into his belt and raised the torch. Baldor stared up at a big man, a drover. Recognising the garb and the language, he nodded and lowered the dagger. "Are you wounded?" The man asked.

"No … no, I fell … I'm just …"

The drover, seeing him trying to get up, reached down and began hauling him to his feet by his harness. Baldor was slow to move.

"Can you stand?"

"Yes, yes I think so." He managed as he gripped the man's arm his other hand using the javelin as a staff to help him rise. "I just … just need to catch my breath." His head pounded from the impact with the ground and he tasted blood, his teeth having bit his tongue when he fell. He spat and dragged a hand over his mouth.

"We need to keep moving, can you …" The drover's words were cut off as he gasped and crumpled leaving go of Baldor who staggered for balance. The man groaned horribly and fell to his knees dropping the torch and grasping at a pilum lodged low in his belly. Baldor, still unsteady reached up for a falcata hilt and missed but managed to bring his javelin up just as a legionary, bellowing his war cry attacked him at the run. In the darkness, the Roman ran onto the javelin point, it sliding and scraping over his mail shirt but forcing him hard off balance and off his feet while knocking the javelin from Baldor's grip. Baldor was still grasping frantically for a falcata his coordination awry, when the Roman recovering quickly from the fall leg-swept his ankles taking his legs from beneath him and he hit the ground hard again. The Roman rolled towards him his feet lashing out to kick, trying to land a debilitating blow and keep Baldor on the ground while his hand grabbed for his dagger hilt. Baldor groaned as the man's boot hit his legs repeatedly, the hobnailed soles tearing his skin. Still concussed and finding it difficult to synchronize his movements he recognised the need to fight for his life. Fear delivered a huge dose of adrenalin and he rolled quickly away and forced himself to his feet.

The Roman was also on his feet and the small light from the fallen torch showed him coming at Baldor with a dagger and a gladius. Reaching to his shoulders with both hands, Baldor finally managed to pull the falcata's from their scabbards and he crouched slightly ready to move. With the fight now suddenly more than even, the Roman hesitated and as Baldor took a step toward him, he turned and ran into the darkness. Unsure of where the man had gone, Baldor twisted this way and that in case he came back at him from the side. His ears strained listening for the sound of the man's boots while his battered senses processed the background noises, his muscles readying for immediate action. Time seemed to standstill, he could hear noises of combat and men shouting and the occasional lowing of beasts and thudding hooves. He saw torches hurtling past but other than that, he seemed to be on his own again. Taking a moment, he settled his breathing and flexed his fingers around his sword hilts testing his grip. Battered, bleeding and horrified of the darkness that stole his vison and brought enemies out of nowhere he was about to pick up the fallen torch then realised it made him a ready target. Deciding he was safer taking his chances in the dark, he sheathed one falcata and kicked around in the grass until he found his javelin.

Seeing a handful of men following well behind a moving torch and heading the right way up the saddle he moved closer while keeping back from the light, there was still safety to be had in numbers. The men glanced at him briefly and he raised a hand, recognising familiar garb they paid him no more heed. The advance was slowing now as men wearied from the constant uphill push, while the sporadic combat continued in the small irregular size groups. The drovers had lost what little control they'd had over the cattle the beasts now running every which way, some remained in groups others careering singly still trying to escape the fire.

The advance was now more difficult owing to the ground being dotted with bodies of both Romans and Spaniards, along with cattle that had succumbed to the flames else fallen to break limbs and now groaned and thrashed pitifully. Some of the dead animals were now fully on fire, the carcasses hissing and spitting as the body fats caught alight and fed the flames that roared and grew in height devouring the animals. The burning lards and greases trickled from the beasts like miniature rivers of flame, which in turn set fire to the parched sward. The stink of burning hair, skin and meat mixing with the reek of cow shit and acrid smoke from the grass.

The firelight illuminated some of the scene and the Spaniards stepped wide of it. Suddenly torchlight appeared in front of Baldor's small group which identified legionaries. The Romans, like the Spaniards were in open order but rudely roused and completely surprised, many were without helmets and mail shirts though most had brought a shield. Baldor's group reacted first and javelins flew across the few paces into the advancing men just as they prepared to rush the Spaniards. In the darkness most javelins missed or lodged in the shields. However, the ones that found their mark punched into the men with such force that they fell immediately. Baldor, having thrown his javelin was already reaching for a second falcata ready for the close quarter fight that was coming. A legionary ran at him trying to batter him with his scutum, a gladius held close to the shield edge ready to stab and disembowel. Baldor raised his leg and stamped hard at the large shield while knocking the gladius aside with his falcata. The Roman was stalled by the blow and Baldor followed on quickly with both blades, one battering the shield the other engaging the gladius. The Roman was surprised and overpowered by the force of the counterattack and gave ground. Baldor pushed the man back while moving to his side trying to get behind the big shield to stab. The Roman held his nerve and counter moved while watching Baldor over the shield rim and thrusting with the gladius to hold him off. Baldor went to kick the shield again but the Roman moved fast pushing it forward knocking him back off balance. Stepping quickly after him he roared as he thrust the gladius at Baldor's belly. Baldor twisted sideways, the blade screeching as it glanced off the small breastplate into his tunic and slicing skin where his belly had been only moments before. The Roman, missing the killing stroke was over-extended, his sword arm out from the side of the shield and his shoulder partly exposed. Baldor swept a falcata down and the Roman groaned as the heavy blade chopped into his shoulder muscle and smashed the bone beneath. Screaming, he backed away his arm drooping. Baldor went after him determined to finish the fight; the legionary unable to lift his gladius anymore raised the shield to fend him off. Unsure of the wound on his side Baldor attacked in a fury, keen to kill the man so he could look to his injury. With the Roman unable to use his blade, Baldor kicked and battered the shield hard forcing the man backwards, a final kick sent him sprawling. The Roman was still screaming his hate and trying to rise when Baldor kicked the shield to one side and killed him with a stab to the chest.

Breathless, he peered into the darkness and listened as best he could. Satisfied there was no one close he stuck one falcata in the ground while holding the other ready, then pushed a hand into the rent in his tunic, flinching as his fingers tentatively probed the wound. The skin was slippery and warm with blood but to his relief, the cut had not penetrated his vitals though it would require stitching. With no sounds of fighting nearby and taking a chance, he squatted by the dead Roman and hacked a piece of his tunic away. Undoing the man's dagger belt and discarding the dagger and sheath, he threaded the belt around his midriff and under his harness straps before stuffing the wad of material inside his tunic. He winced as he pushed it against and over the wound then keeping it in place fastened the belt over it.

After taking a moment to settle his nerves and catch his breath he set off into the darkness again, a falcata in each hand at the ready. The ground had levelled out now and the going easier on his legs and lungs, realising he was on the saddle top itself he wondered if the Spaniards had halted or kept moving.

****

On the opposing hill, Fabius's camp was seething with legionaries roused from their beds by the sound of trumpets blaring the 'Stand-to'. Still dozy, they snatched up their weapons and equipment and hurried to their assembly points marked out now by torchlight. Optios and Centurions, still strapping on their own weapons and mail as they ran bellowing and harassing their men into order. As the men formed ranks, Cornelius, still half asleep and fumbling to fasten his helmet strap seized a torch and prowled amongst his century. Remembering the hard lesson learned from the surprise attack at the Trebbia, he checked the men had all their weapons, water bottles and kit. Trying to maintain calm in front of his men he wondered what was afoot, more Carthaginian trickery or was this going to be a battle fought in the dark? As much as he desired combat, the thought of a battle in darkness frightened him as neither him nor his men had training or experience of such. The recollection of his father's awe at Hannibal being able to conduct and win at such doing nothing for his nerves. After barking at a few men for missing items of kit and sending them sprinting back to their tents for it, he was back at the front of his century; his concerns interrupted when Gaius appeared. Straightening his back, he saluted.

"Good morning, sir what's our orders?"

"We stand-to until the situation's clear Cornelius. At present it looks as though the Carthaginians are moving out over the saddle."

"All of them, sir?"

"It looks that way; going by the number of torches and noise there's certainly a huge amount of movement up the hill and over the saddle."

"They've avoided the pass mouth altogether then?"

"Aye, I guess Hannibal's doing what he's always done and took the hard road."

"And our lads at the pass mouth?"

"It seems they've took the initiative and moved up to the saddle to attack them."

"Do you think we'll move in support?"

Gaius shrugged. "I don't know lad; the orders haven't come down yet."

Cornelius grimaced as he remembered the chaotic fight when the Numidians had attacked the Roman camp in the darkness near the river Trebbia, triggering the events that led to the catastrophic Roman defeat later that morning. He looked to the east hoping to see the first chinks of grey light but the sky remained star-speckled and black. The camp however, was now bathed in an orange glow with hundreds of torches aflame, helping drive back the darkness. To his comfort the men at least seemed well arrayed and prepared this time. As the shouted orders ceased and a strange quiet fell back over the camp the army waited to hear what Fabius would do.

"We need to move now, sir!"

"Do we Minucius? Do we? I think not." Fabius growled as he raised his hands to silence the furore and clamour building from the men in the tent.

"For the love of Venus, sir they're escaping over the saddle! This is our chance to stop and destroy them whilst they're on the march and to support our legionaries."

"And I say no! What's more, who gave those men leave to abandon their position at the pass mouth and attack?"

"They're doing what any full-blooded Roman should do and marched to battle." Minucius retorted.

Fabius, incensed at the implied insult, rounded on Minucius and stepped quickly towards him looking as if he would strike him. His face red with anger and barely able to control his anger he lowered his arms though his fists remained tightly balled. "Damn you Marcus Minucius Rufus! Damn you to Hades! You misspeak yourself!"

"Sir, the men at the pass would be forced to move else they'd be outflanked." Came from one of the officers, intervening in quiet tones and trying to restore calm. Fabius ignored him, his attention and ire still focused on Minucius though he lowered his voice.

"Use your wits man and as I told you before, see the bigger picture. We don't know where all the Carthaginians are, is that the whole army moving over the saddle or are there more waiting in ambush for us?" When Minucius tried to speak Fabius pressed on. "Moreover, do you wish to fight a battle in the dark when you have no idea where the enemy are and in what strength and when you're carrying a torch that makes you an easy target?" He glared at Minucius who returned the look with an icy stare though a twitch in his face betrayed his fading confidence for verbally attacking his senior officer. Having demonstrated his dominance to all, Fabius scanned the men's faces. "Do you understand? We don't move until the situation is clear?"

A disjointed low chorus of 'Yes, sir.' came back from the room.

Nodding, he issued his orders. "The men will stand-to until dawn. We will reassess the situation once it's light. Should daylight bring advantage for us we will attack, until then we'll release scouts and wait. Am I clear?"

The officers left the tent to relay the orders down through the chain of command and on to the waiting men. Before long, Gaius summoned Cornelius to him.

"Yes sir."

"We stand-to Cornelius, at least until dawn. Let the men eat what they can but keep them ready just in case anything changes."

Cornelius was unsure whether he was relieved or disappointed at the order but saluted and turned to address his men.

****

The saddle had quietened with the coming of dawn, the fighting having stopped with men on both sides exhausted from combat and the undulating terrain. Men took the chance for a drink and those that had a morsel of food or that could stomach it ate, others strapped wounds and looked to help comrades. Of the cattle that remained alive, the torches on their horns had long since expired or in many cases simply fallen off. Some wandered aimlessly looking to crop at what long grass there was, others laid down between the opposing warriors, injured or simply drained from the night's exertions and fear of the fire. As the light came full, Baldor and the Spaniards could see the growing strength of the legionaries as more arrived from the pass mouth making a blocking force to prevent the Spaniards advancing further.

Tercero found Baldor. "It's good to see you my friend." He grinned as he offered his hand.

"It's good to be seen." He managed a smile as the pair shook hands. Tercero saw the bloodied tunic and improvised bandage.

"I trust that's not serious Baldor?"

"No, it's bloody sore but it's just a flesh wound."

"The God's are good then, you're all right and from what I've seen our casualties are not too bad. Though that could change." He gestured towards the thickening ranks of legionaries.

"What now then, Captain? Do we try to extract ourselves? Have you any idea of the situation with the army."

"From what I'm told our camp is empty and it looks like Fabius hasn't moved so I hazard a guess the plan has worked. Now I need to see about getting us off this saddle."

"How can I help?"

"Would you tally up our men for me? The hale, wounded, and dead then we can see what our strength is."

"Yes Captain."

The pair separated, Tercero dispatching men to find answers for his next questions; how many legionaries were arrayed in front of them and was there another way around them. Baldor, moving amongst the men questioning unit commanders on casualties and the men's condition while adding the figures in his head. Now that the fighting had stopped and his body cooled, he noticed the aches and stiffness in his legs and body more and the need for a drink and some food. Swigging from his water bottle he nibbled at the dried meat and piece of bread he'd brought; it squashed almost flat from his falls during the night.

Armed with the figures of the living, wounded and dead he was looking for Tercero when he heard a shout to 'Stand-to'. The call quickly repeated, and men rose swiftly to their feet and readied themselves, refitting helmets and taking up their weapons as in front of them the legionaries were marshalling. Baldor cursed quietly. With the element of surprise gone along with the cloak of darkness and the Roman ranks thickening and forming maniples, it was going to be a hard fight. He surmised he was going to have to run for his life, as the light Spanish troops would be no match for the legionaries' toe to toe. Suddenly, the Roman ranks seemed to belly and push forward, their previous order falling to chaos as men turned to look behind them, the sound of battle suddenly loud in their rear. Baldor smiled then laughed in relief as he saw more Spaniards appearing behind the Romans, Hannibal had sent a rescue force for his men on the saddle. The arriving Spaniards were still only caetrati and thus light infantry but the element of surprise along with fresh troops was decisive. The realisation of being caught between two forces was not lost on the Romans and they scattered. The men with Baldor didn't wait for the order to attack and just hurled themselves at the Romans. The cattle panicked once again, desperate to be away from the fast-approaching, yelling men they ran amok, back towards the stunned Romans causing more chaos and scattering them further. The battle quickly dissolved into small group or individual fights and with the legionaries separated and easier targets, the agile Spaniards swarmed around them like hounds pulling down deer.

Tercero found Baldor and bellowed above the din.

"We need to finish this else be past them and gone Baldor, Fabius is mobilising and coming this way." He pointed to the Roman camp on the opposite hill where a blaze of colour from standards, shield faces and helmet crests told of the Roman legions finally on the move.

The fight was going out of the Romans on the saddle. Surprised during the night, exhausted from the climb, battered by cattle and a mobile enemy and now caught between two forces they fled. Tercero turned to Baldor.

"I'll take a unit and give chase to make sure they don't rally. Can you push on and lead the men off the saddle and follow the army?"

"Yes, yes but …"

Tercero didn't wait for Baldor to finish. "We'll catch you up." He called as he and a sizeable force of men began running after the fleeing Romans.

Chapter Seven

It was much later in the day when Baldor, Tercero and the Spaniards caught up with Hannibal and the army heading northeast. Footsore, aching and weary he and Tercero made their way to the front of the column seeking their General. They found him riding on the last remaining elephant.

"Captain Targa, Captain Tercero, well met!" Hannibal called down as he dipped his head and held his hand to his heart while guiding the elephant to the side of the column and stopping it. He waved the column on then placed his hands on both animal's ears and pushed downwards. "Down Sirus! Down." The elephant lowered its head and eased gracefully to its front knees; Hannibal swung his leg over the beast's neck and dismounted. He patted the animal's trunk as it turned its head towards him. He looked the men up and down quickly; both were heavy eyed, battered looking and covered in filth. Dust stuck to their sweat-damp clothes and caked their skin, their tunics and hands spotted and stained brown with dried blood. Both bore smears of green from grass and cowshit, the stink still upon them. Hannibal immediately offered his water bottle. "You are both hale I trust?" His face showed concern when he saw the improvised bandage on Baldor's side and his bloodied legs and Tercero with a forearm swathed in a bloodstained bandage. The pair returned the compliment while saluting amidst nods and grins before swapping the bottle quickly between them and drinking heartily. "Your smiles tell me of success?"

"Aye sir! A great success, and the army, are all safely away?"

It was Hannibal's turn to smile. "Oh yes! The army, the baggage, the women, servants and the remainder of our cattle and not a Roman to trouble us."

"There's a few less to trouble us now, sir." Tercero quipped.

Hannibal laughed and threw his arms over the men's shoulders. "Come, come let's find us a wagon and you both some food and we can sit and talk."

Commandeering a wagon and having the driver make room amongst the goods; Hannibal climbed up then reached down to each man in turn giving them a hand up. He smiled as both men emitted sighs as they relaxed amongst the baggage, both glad to take the weight off their feet.

"I won't keep you overlong as you'll be weary but I surmise you will want to eat? So while we wait for the food tell me of the night."

The men took turns relaying details of the night's action and the casualty list. Hannibal nodded appreciatively at the light losses and then burst into laughter when told that the men had even brought some of the cattle back.

"Baal be praised!" He chuckled. "When I sent the relief force to get you, I didn't expect to extract both you and some cattle! How much damage did you do to those legionaries? Poor Fabius, he'll be red-faced this morning and no doubt having to explain himself. How I love it when a plan comes together. Now, after you've eaten find my physician, a one, Synbolus and have him treat your wounds and charge the costs to me."

****

The lightly armed Roman velites that raced upwards to the saddle ahead of Fabius and his legions were met by the surviving legionaries and wounded colleagues on their way back down. Most were half-dressed, weary from the previous night's climb and bloodied from the fight. Helping or carrying comrades with crippling injuries, their faces spoke of defeat but also of anger having been left unsupported. The velites pushed through the legionaries and onwards to the saddle itself and saw the carnage. The sward was littered with carcasses of burned and slaughtered cattle interspersed with discarded weapons and men's bodies most of which were Roman. The grass around the cattle was soaked and stained scarlet with the animal's blood else blackened and scorched when the animal had burned. Some still smoked and smouldered along with the men who had fallen dead alongside else been trampled beneath them. The morning breeze carried the stink of burning animals and the sickly-sweet stench of roasting human flesh, the macabre harvest already drawing the ravens and crows, the birds alighting amongst the bodies to peck and tear. Apart from a few crippled beasts that remained on the ground and lowed pitifully nothing else moved, the Spaniards having slaughtered most wounded legionaries before departing with the relief force. With reports of the dead and the now disappeared Carthaginians relayed back to Fabius; the Romans turned back to their camp to plan their next move.

The mood in Fabius's tent as he addressed his command group bordered on mutinous. The leader of the outrage was once more Minucius who was out of his seat, leaning on bunched fists and shouting belligerently up the table at Fabius.

"You cannot be serious sir! Over a thousand of our men are dead, trampled by beasts and slaughtered in the night by nothing more than murdering brigands, the enemy gone to the Gods know where and you plan to do nothing?"

"You will hold your tongue sir and do as I command!"

This time however, Minucius was backed by others around the table and the clamour for action grew. Fabius hammered his wine cup repeatedly into the tabletop until the men quietened. However, before he could address the men the Legate broke the tense silence.

"Sir, we beseech you! We cannot suffer more of …"

"You will all do as I command! Is that clear?" Fabius thumped his fist hard on the table. "This is a military camp not a Greek democracy … I said silence!" He bawled when another tried to speak up. "We will break camp now and march, we'll follow the Carthaginians whom the scouts tell us are heading northeast again. We'll maintain our shadowing and harassing tactics until I can see a way to bring our forces to bear at our advantage."

"Gods above man, you've just missed your opportunity! We had them, right there in the valley, trapped!"

Fabius turned on Minucius, his eyes narrowing and face flushed with anger "This is my final warning to you Minucius; I will suffer no more of your unwanted advice on how to wage war. I've been at such business while you were still sucking on your mother's tit!"

Minucius glared hatefully at his superior officer, his lip curling into a snarl. "I will not be silenced sir! I, like these men here are freeborn Roman citizens, freeborn! And we have a voice."

"Which I need not heed! I am duly elected Dictator and that means my word and commands are law." Minucius tried to interrupt but Fabius pressed on quickly. "If you don't like the commands I give, you have my leave to go. Return to Rome and explain to the senate why my Master of Horse has abandoned his post. Else resume your seat sir, hold your tongue and listen." Minucius hesitated, a heavy scowl twisting his face into a mask of thinly disguised rage bordering on contemptuous hatred. The men around the table were now silent and watching intently to see what he would do. "Well?" Fabius pushed as the silence lengthened.

Minucius slowly eased back into his seat.

"Your orders sir?" The Legate ventured quickly, his question dissolving some of the tension.

Fabius dropped or hid his previous anger. "As I said, we break camp now and march. Minucius, I want riders out following this Hannibal, once we know exactly where he and his army are headed I want flying columns to ride around and get in front of them. From there, your men will burn and destroy ... silence! ..." He bellowed, as unrest and protesting murmurings started up once more from the table though less in volume than before. "Will burn and destroy anything of use to the Carthaginians." He reaffirmed. "They have to live off the land so we must make it difficult for them to do so. As distasteful as this is, either we destroy our crops and goods and starve them or they feed themselves then destroy what's left anyway." He looked around the table seeking discontent or objection again but found only quiet if reluctant acceptance. "Gentlemen, we are done here, to your commands and break camp."

"How many?" Cornelius asked while stuffing gear into his kit bag, his tone incredulous.

"Around one thousand." Gaius growled.

"A thousand legionaries slaughtered by Spanish caetrati! How in Jupiter's name did that happen?" He grunted, as he hefted the bag up to a cart driver.

"I'm not surprised at all."

"But heavies against light?"

"Think about it. Our lads would have been surprised at that time of night for a start and most likely still half asleep. Then they leg it up the saddle in the dark, most likely under equipped with no chance to form up and have to fight agile, wide awake warriors while dodging stampeding cattle."

"Cattle?"

"Aye, the crafty Carthaginian bastards fastened torches to the beast's horns and our lads at the pass mouth mistook them for the Carthaginian army trying to escape over the saddle."

Cornelius shook his head. "Hannibal again, what a devious, clever bastard!"

"Aye, a bastard all right!" Gaius spat into the dust.

"What's Fabius planning apart from breaking camp?"

"We're to follow …"

"And?"

"We'll fight if and when the ground and time suits us. For the moment he's dispatching cavalry units again, to push ahead of the Carthaginians to implement a scorched earth policy to prevent them re-provisioning."

"Gods above! How much more of our country are we going to burn?"

"Needs must lad, we have to deny them sustenance and ease of movement to forage."

"Try telling that to the folk whose farms and livelihoods you are destroying."

"Well, it is what it is Cornelius and that's the orders."

"I understand the military logic but what of the people? If we cannot defend them and it seems clear to all that we can't, what's to stop them throwing in their lot with Hannibal?"

Gaius shrugged. "Well so far we seem to have been lucky with that. Apart from a few Gallic tribes there's been no great move to side with him and I've heard no rumours of sedition or desertion from other Latins." Cornelius fell silent, deep in thought. "Look on the brighter side Cornelius, at least Fabius hasn't lost us a huge number of troops."

"True but we need a battle; the men are ready for it."

"Agreed but as you said it's a battle we must win so I must somewhat agree with Fabius as to picking our time and ground. The old goat may be cautious but he's no one's fool."

"Sir, the men are ready and we can move out." An Optio said as he approached and saluted Gaius.

Gaius raised his stick in acknowledgement. "Come on Cornelius, we'd better move, let's be up and doing at least." He clapped the younger man on the shoulder and stepped out proudly one hand on his sword hilt and the other swinging his stick.

****

The Carthaginians pushed on north-eastwards seeking a site for a winter camp their pace slow owing to the baggage train and the portable larder of cattle, goats and sheep. Pillaging and burning as they went they slaughtered or enslaved any of the populace who resisted while turning the land into a desolate, scorched graveyard once more in a bid to bring Fabius and his legions to battle. The size and strength of their forces involved in the destruction deterred Minucius's small flying columns from action, they being restricted to merely shadowing and watching as the land went up in flames. Despite this brutal provocation from the Carthaginians and almost mutiny from his command group, Fabius still refused battle.

Hannibal, having learned from collaborators and his spies of Fabius's own property being directly in the path of the destruction, tried a different tack to force him to battle. Having his army purposely march around the property, they left it alone, Fabius's people, his fields and orchards remaining untouched and intact. This giving rise to the rumour that Fabius was in Hannibal's pocket and which saw him recalled to Rome again to explain his military dalliances to the senate and the reprieve shown to his property when all around him had burned.

Approaching the settlement of Geronium and judging it suitable for a winter camp, Hannibal offered generous terms to the citizens. The populace however, refused the entreaties and instead set fire to some of the buildings before fleeing and leaving the Carthaginians to invest the town. The Carthaginians settled in quickly making the town into a grain store and stabling for their still vast herds of cattle, sheep and goats. A camp was set up outside of the dilapidated town walls for the army with commands for a palisade and deep ditch to be constructed around it. Moving their wounded and sick troops into the camp and feeling secure at last, Hannibal released two thirds of the army, some to forage and harvest crops others to pillage and burn as far afield as they dare while leaving the remaining third to guard the camp.

Baldor, noting the permanence of the camp and the shortening autumn days announcing the coming of winter and thus an end to the campaigning season, approached Hannibal for permission to begin seeking Lasairiona.

"Come Baldor, let's walk and talk." Hannibal ushered Baldor out of the tent while passing him a heavy cloak. "Here, the evening is chill but pleasant with the last of the sun; we should enjoy it while we have it as winter will soon be upon us."

"Yes sir." Hannibal frowned at him and raised a fist in mock threat. "Yes Hannibal." He corrected himself and smiled.

"Let's inspect the ditch and palisade while we talk and enjoy this." Hannibal waved a wine pitcher. "It's Falernian, the good stuff, it seems the Romans can do somethings right." The pair chuckled as they walked and drank. "What is it I can help with Baldor?"

Baldor cleared his throat. "Well, seeing as how we are settling for the winter I wondered if I could begin searching for Lasairiona."

"Ah yes, I promised you didn't I?"

Baldor looked uncomfortable. "I don't like to ask but …"

"No, no you are right to ask for you have done me and the army great service and I did promise. However, I need you to wait a while longer, let me explain why." He offered the wine again while giving a small shiver and drawing his cloak tighter around his shoulders against the stiffening breeze. "I have word that Fabius is again called to Rome, to answer I imagine for his delays and why his property is still intact." Both men laughed. "He's left his Master of Horse in charge, a one Minucius whom I'm told, is a very different man to Fabius."

"You expect trouble?"

"Yes, while the master is away I think the servant will want to play. I'm reliably informed that the Romans are desperate to fight so I would have the use of your quick wits and your men."

"Always, Hannibal." He dipped his head and placed his hand on this heart.

"Good man!" Hannibal accepted the wine back and took a long drink before smacking his lips appreciatively. "I'm told this Minucius is battle hungry and like all Romans he seeks glory. He wants to shine above Fabius and humble us."

"Another Tiberius then?"

"Not quite, he's not that reckless but he is seeking a battle and before Fabius returns I surmise."

"And we must be ready."

"Yes we must. However, we also need to be careful, for with winter coming I want to use the time to rest and recondition the horses as they have had an exhausting summer. They need some meat on their bones and their coats conditioning again, which means our most effective fighting arm is at a reduced capacity.”

“I understand Hannibal.”

“Once we've bettered this Minucius I promise you, you can go with all your men and my blessing and find your woman. Have you any news of her? I surmise she may be difficult to find being one captive among thousands for as you know we've flooded the slave market this last while.”

Baldor nodded. “I do have a lead or at least a rumour.”

“Excellent! Tell me.”

Andulas has been making discreet enquiries apparently, well, he about Lasairiona and Armaco about my stolen gear. They didn't say anything to me until I told you were granting me time and men to search.”

Hannibal beamed. “They're good men Baldor, good friends and such are hard to find in this world.”

“I know; I owe them both much.”

“And they you! Friendship is a two-way thing, and you are only reaping what you've sown.” Baldor smiled. “So tell me, what have they learned?”

“Andulas's informant learned of a tall redhead being sold in the slave market in either Casilinum or Capua; he's remained in the area to make more enquiries and is expected to report back again shortly.”

Hannibal nodded sagely. “It's a pity you didn't know that earlier for we have left both places behind. However, if you have a specific area to search that will make it much easier and not so much a needle in a haystack. And when I think on it your woman will stand out as she is strikingly beautiful and quite different to most.”

Baldor's head fell forward and he looked sad. “Yes, yes she was, she is.” He corrected.

“I'm sure you'll find her and in good health my friend, a woman like that would not be treated badly or whored for she would have been expensive.” He saw Baldor wince. “I mean no disrespect by that Baldor.”

“I know and you're right.” He said, as his eyes took on a faraway look, his mind lost in a memory for a moment. “I just didn't realise how much she meant to me until she's gone. She cared for me unstintingly after Bodeshmun and Sakarbaal wounded me, more than cared; it wasn't just a servant doing her work.”

Hannibal saw the hurt and anger playing on Baldor's face and passed the wine pitcher. Baldor took a long drink and it seemed to help him as he managed a small but sad smile as he passed it back, Hannibal clapped him on the back warmly.

"And Armaco, what's he found out about your belongings? If he finds the men that stole from you or committed the murder I'll see them hung or crucified." Baldor didn't reply immediately. "Baldor … Baldor?"

Baldor just stared ahead, his eyes in a trance like gaze, when he finally spoke his words came out slow and deliberate, the tone a low growl. "You won't have to Hannibal, for I'll kill them! Not so much for the theft but for the murder of Sulis and the abduction of Lasairiona." Hannibal heard the grit and anger in his voice but before he could reply, Baldor carried on though he turned to look at his General. "I mean no disrespect to you or the military law in the camp Hannibal, but this is personal."

Hannibal looked at him intently before taking a deep breath and sighing. "The law is the law, Baldor and I cannot, will not, change it for you nor any man." He held up his hand to stifle Baldor's retort. "What I will do is make a deal with you. If the men are found in the confines of the camp, they will suffer military justice. However, should they be found outside the camp and away from anyone who will carry the tale back, then you kill them." He held up his hand again to stop Baldor interrupting, his tone formal and serious. "Just make sure you have the right men and that I don't come to hear of it … am I clear Baldor? Don't force my hand for I've no wish to nail my friend to a cross … furthermore, we didn't have this conversation."

"Yes and thank you."

"Like you, I abhor soldiers preying on one another. Whether it's brawling, stealing or murder. However, I have a duty to maintain the law and ensure things are done correctly and openly in front of all."

"Yes Hannibal, I understand."

"Good … on the other hand, you're my friend and I'm angry for what you've suffered so I also understand the need for vengeance as much as justice. Just be careful how you obtain it."

"So, we must wait a little longer before going after the girl, you say?" Armaco growled as he bit and tore at a lump of beef before chewing noisily then gulping it down and picking at his teeth seeking a piece of trapped meat.

"Yes, Hannibal expects trouble from this Minucius and soon."

"Well, surely there's enough men without our lads?" He swilled the meat with a huge guzzle of wine.

Baldor shrugged. "We're short of cavalry with so many of the horses being rested, so we're needed."

"If the Romans are going to be active it's best we wait anyway, it's going to be difficult enough getting into Casilinum without tangling with any large Roman patrols along the way." Andulas added as he poured more wine for them all.

"Lasairiona is definitely in Casilinum then, not Capua?" Baldor asked.

"Yes, my informer was told on good authority from one of the town guards, that he remembered a woman fitting Lasairiona's description causing trouble at the gate. He said she's likely a slave in the house of a one, Thaddeus Rufus Antonius."

"How in Baal's name does your man learn all this?" Armaco asked before quaffing his cup of wine and belching loudly.

"Did I say my informant was a man?" Andulas asked as he chuckled then tapped his nose with his finger when Armaco made to ask more.

"Maybe I could buy her back? I have the silver."

"Possibly Baldor, we could try that first. It would be easier than trying to take her by force."

"Hah! You two hardly look like slavers!" Armaco grumbled before taking another drink.

"Maybe not but I can look like a Gallic Lord and a Lord needs slaves does he not?"

"True! And I can pass as your bodyguard but what about Baldor? He doesn't look like a Lord to me and he's too young to be a killer." He smirked.

Baldor picked a grape off the plate and threw it Armaco, bouncing it off his head.

"Peasant!" Armaco tut-tutted and shook his head. "See what I mean? A Carthaginian peasant would not a Gallic Lord make!"

Andulas chuckled and Baldor hurled another grape at Armaco who snatched it out of the air. Baldor smiled and nodded approvingly at Armaco's hand speed.

"Children! Manners at the table, remember I'm the barbarian!" The three men broke into laughter. "Think on though Armaco, his hair is long enough to tie back and if he grows a moustache he could look like part of my retinue."

"Aye, a servant! That'll be about right!" Armaco quipped.

"Servant maybe but I'm fluent in Gallic, it's what we do with you that may be difficult." Baldor made a show of looking thoughtful. "I know! You could be a slave to a servant, me!"

"Hah! Just get me in there and I'll sort things out while you two play at Lords and servants."

Andulas tapped the table, his face turning serious. "Gentlemen, all jesting aside we need a plan and a good one. Getting in to Casilinum may be easier than getting out so I suggest we put our heads together. Anyway, I have a couple of ideas …"

****

Thaddeus didn't take his eyes from the activity in front of him, raising his arm and holding a wine cup absently in the air while a slave stepped quickly forward refilling it from a golden pitcher.

He sipped the wine then suddenly scowled and shook his head in distaste. "Too ugly to keep." He said quietly to a nearby servant while nodding towards a woman, which two men paraded in front of him. "Sell her on. Next!"

The servant clapped his hands twice and pointed to the left, the two heavily built men standing on a raised platform a few paces away hustled the woman slave away to a pen before returning with another held between them. Thaddeus turned to pick fruit from a platter on the small table beside him before looking back to see what the men had brought out. He paused in midbite. This next woman was taller than both men that held her and she didn't struggle with her captors, her composure remaining proud and regal. She looked at Thaddeus then the men beside her with an air of contempt. The servant bent to whisper in Thaddeus's ear.

"This is the woman, sir."

"The one who beat the idiot guard at the gate?"

"Yes sir. The seller told our man that they think she's barbarian royalty."

"Aye, they would say that to raise the price no doubt."

"Er, yes sir undoubtedly."

Thaddeus gazed at the thick, fox-coloured hair that fell below the woman's shoulders and her beautiful eyes that glinted like shards of blue sea ice and which emanated a look just as cold. Only the dirt and dust from travel and the faint trace of a bruise that marked one cheek and the temple above it marred her beauty. Ignoring these small trivialities Thaddeus swallowed quickly, a lecherous smile lifting the corners of his mouth.

"Mind you, she doesn't look like the usual Gallic trull; I think she's worth a better look."

"Yes sir." The servant nodded and signalled to the men that they should turn her around slowly so their master could view.

Clad in a buckskin dress, Thaddeus couldn't determine much of her shape except the other outer hints of her beauty, her long neck and shapely breasts. After she'd been turned about full circle, he took another drink.

"Strip her; let me see what I've paid for."

The servant clicked his fingers and the two men quickly removed the woman's dress and undershirt, leaving her naked except for her calf-length sandals, again she didn't struggle but maintained her proud composure. Thaddeus shuffled his overweight frame forward in his chair staring, his interest caught, the wine and fruit forgotten. She was truly beautiful he decided, a little over tall perhaps but beautiful, nevertheless. Her skin unblemished and pale like the mountain snows, her breasts rounded and full, her limbs long and shapely, her mound coloured like her hair. The men turned her about to show firm, curvaceous buttocks and long firm thighs.

"She'll do! Burn those barbarian rags and have her washed and dressed in keeping with civilised society. Give her over to Tacita and put her to work in the kitchens until I decide what to do with her. I don't want her marked! If she needs a beating make sure there's no damage."

"Yes sir." The servant signalled to the men and they led Lasairiona off to a different pen.

Thaddeus beckoned the servant close. "Keep her out of my wife's sight; she doesn't need to know about her. Am I clear?"

"Yes sir, perfectly."

Chapter Eight

Baldor laid back on the heaped floor cushions enjoying the sunlight shining through the open tent door and warming the interior. Yawning, he clicked his tongue while beckoning to the pup.

"Issa, Issa come!"

The pup wagged her tail and looked up from where she laid on the sheepskin. Getting up, she picked up her leather chew and padded across to Baldor then climbed onto him settling herself across his chest, dropping the chew she licked at his face.

"She's taken to you, Baldor." Andulas said. "And I knew you would like her."

Baldor smiled widely as he stroked Issa then picked up the chew, Issa immediately biting on it and tugging. "She's beautiful. I've never owned a dog nor lived with one but she's great company. You had dogs at home did you not?"

"Aye, too many probably, hunting dogs and house dogs. I find they sometimes make better companions than people, present company excepted." He grinned. "They're always happy to see you, they forgive quickly and they're faithful, all they ask is some food, a bed and to be with you."

"You say she'll grow large?"

"Yes, she'll be a big, powerful dog when fully grown."

"Let's hope she's house trained before then or we'll need a bigger shovel for the shit." Armaco added.

"And you clean it up, when?" Baldor asked flippantly.

"Huh! You know what I'm saying. Animals belong outside." He grumbled.

"Well, we let you live in here." Baldor quipped and sniggered,

Andulas burst into laughter at the jest and sprayed wine as he coughed and almost choked on it.

"Sharp this morning aren't we? Watch you don't cut your tongue, boy." Armaco grumbled.

"Boy is it now?" Baldor smiled. "That makes you how old?"

"Old enough to give you a slapping."

"I'll set my dog on you!" Baldor laughed and turned Issa to look at Armaco. The pup just wagged its tail. "Go get him Issa!"

"If it pisses on my gear again I'll make it into a spit roast."

Baldor got up along with the dog and walked across to where Armaco relaxed on a couch. He placed Issa on Armco's lap.

"Say you're sorry Issa and the bad-tempered old man won't hurt you."

"Get the mangy animal off me!" Armaco went to brush Issa off but she was heavier than he thought and instead the pup dropped her chew and managed to lick his hand. "Ugh!" He went to move her again and she caught his hand in her mouth, her tail wagging and body swaying ungainly in excitement as she tugged at his fingers. As Armaco tried again to move her, she mouthed his hands playfully. Pulling her by the scruff of the neck, he brought her close to his face. "Go! You little Cerberus … go lose yourself, you harbourer of fleas!"

Issa just looked at him from dark eyes then licked his nose.

Baldor and Andulas chuckled as Armaco dropped Issa onto the cushions on the floor. Picking herself up, she jumped back onto the low couch and climbed up on Armaco again full of play. Trying to push her off only excited her more and she chewed at his fingers then threw herself at his face licking him again. Grabbing hold of her, he tried to push her off but she gave an excited growl and locked her teeth on his leather arm bracer pulling and tugging at it. He lifted his arm expecting her to drop off but she hung on to the bracer while emitting little growls. Before long Armaco was laughing and play fighting with her.

Baldor got up and went to take Issa back.

"Get off, Baldor! She's not just yours!" Armco chuckled as he wrestled with the puppy.

"You won't be pissing and shitting on our gear as well will you Armaco?" Baldor said as he laughed and sat back down, leaving man and puppy to play.

As Armaco finally wearied of Issa and pushed her firmly away, she moved to Andulas then back to Baldor seeking more play until she too, worn out from the exertions and diminishing responses from the men curled up next to Baldor, gave a small sigh and closed her eyes. The men, enjoying their wine and good food, the downtime from patrol and the pleasant autumn warmth also gave in to tiredness and the talk stopped. Baldor looked at Issa, smiled and gave her an extra pat as she rolled onto her side.

Laying back on the cushions again, he stared absently at the tent wall and smiled when he heard the steady breathing and soft snores from Armaco and Andulas. Left alone with his thoughts he gazed at the pup sleeping so peacefully. Peace? … Peace was just a distant memory now having been at war and constantly on the move for almost three years. His previous life had been so different, an ordinary everyday life with a beautiful wife, a home, servants and a thriving business far removed from war. He lifted the silver cameo from his neck and gazed at the finely chased image, his Aiticia. A lump rose in his throat and he quickly tucked the silver back into his shirt. She was long gone but not forgotten, and his heart still ached at the thought of her demise and though he'd extracted a terrible vengeance for her death, it had brought him no peace.

He wondered then at the robbery and murder done at his tent, such things happened in the camp but was it just bad coincidence that it had been his tent or was this Bodeshmun behind it? Now, he had another woman that needed his help and before she was lost or killed in the chaos of the war. Perhaps this time he could do something before it was too late. His hands tightened into fists and his lips twisted into a snarl. A growl of frustration rose in his throat. Someone was going to pay and pay with their life and there would be no mercy. Lord or common soldier it mattered not, if he found them they would pay.

He sneered at himself for his bitter thoughts; Gestix had been right when he told him vengeance brought no peace, all it would do was even the score, a life for a life. Thinking of Gestix, his friend and brother in all but name brought another lump in his throat then tears. Biting his lip to stem his emotions failed and a dry sob accompanied the tears spilling down his cheeks. The big man who'd helped raise and care for him had been killed in the first clash with the Romans at the Ticinus, another loss and a void that couldn't be filled. Regardless of finding peace or not, Gestix's death, at least in Baldor's thinking had set him on a vengeance trail against the House of Scipio and the former Consul Publius Scipio, the man responsible for Gestix's death. But what of the son, Cornelius?

And this strange life bond they shared from childhood. Now, during this war, fate had brought them together on the battlefield more than once and each had given the other life rather than taking it, the Gods alone knew how that was going to play out. He smiled bitterly and reasoned that enemy or not, he couldn't kill Cornelius for their strange bond ran deep and thus he'd save the hate for the father. Cuffing away the tears, he tried to place his grief in perspective for many had suffered more than he. Many friends were dead and gone, Andulas had left his family and home to fight and Armaco's injuries to his legs meant he would never walk easily again. He at least remained alive and whole, his injuries and his broken heart were all recoverable.

The sudden blast of a trumpet sounded the 'Stand-to'. Repeating quickly across the camp it snapped Baldor from his thoughts and brought a rude awakening to the men and they quickly roused themselves. Shaking sleepy muscles and rubbing their eyes, they called for weapons and news of what was afoot. Baldor, seeing Armaco struggling with his damaged legs went to help him up but had his proffered hand shrugged off.

"I'm all right, I can manage!"

Issa, sensing the men's agitation as they hurriedly shrugged into their mail shirts ran around their feet, barking and wagging her tail. She yelped when Baldor, his head still lost in his shirt, stood on her paws and he fell over her. Picking himself up, he scooped her up, ruffled her ears gently and deposited her into the arms of the nearest servant.

"Look after her!"

With trumpets still sounding throughout the encampment the three men hurriedly strapped on weapons and helmets as they dashed outside to find the camp in chaos. The duty guard units were already marching past the tent towards the gate while those who were stood-down to rest snatched up weapons and ran to their assembly points. Baldor grabbed the arm of one of the officers leading a small infantry detachment in the direction of the gate.

"What's happening, friend?"

"Romans, Captain and seeking battle in front of the camp, it seems they've finally found their balls!"

Baldor nodded his thanks and turning saw his signallers arriving at his tent at the run. Before the men could speak, he was shouting orders while following in the wake of Andulas and helping Armaco in the direction of their mounts, he, dragging his legs in an ungainly hobble and cursing his impediment.

"Sound our stand-to now!" Baldor yelled at the first signaller and then cupped a hand over his mouth to help direct his words above the hubbub. "I want our men at the horse lines and mounted ready to go now! … In full battle array!"

"Yes sir!"

"Stay here and send any messenger from the General to me, I'll marshal our men ready."

"Yes sir!" The signaller blew the exclusive notes that would see Baldor's men assemble for battle then stood by the tent waiting for any messenger that may come from Hannibal.

"You! With me, now!" He bellowed, while pointing and beckoning to the second signalman to follow him.

At the horse lines, men were arriving at the run and hurriedly throwing riding blankets and sheepskins over their mount's back, strapping them in place before mounting quickly. Horses whickered and reared at the excitement while men shouted and cursed, the clatter of weapons adding to the noise and chaos. As the troop began forming into an ordered unit, a mounted messenger appeared.

"Captain Targa! … Captain!" He called while forcing his mount through the chaos, his head twisting this way and that anxiously seeking Baldor.

"Here!" Baldor called and raised his arm.

The man reined his horse up hard in front of Baldor, it rearing at the abrupt stop, its spiralling dust cloud catching it and momentarily shrouding both man and horse.

"Sir! … Captain! … Compliments and a message from the General."

"Yes soldier?" Baldor dipped his head in salute. He swallowed hard, his heart thumping in his chest; this was trouble.

The messenger pointed back towards the front of the camp. "The Romans have attacked some of our foragers in force sir, they cut them up badly then chased them back here." His horse reared again as a small group of riders forced past shouting for people to clear the road, the messenger having to shorten the reins while patting the horse's withers and talking quietly trying to settle it.

"And?" Baldor snapped. "Out with-it man, quickly!"

"Sorry sir! The General is rallying our men and leading a sortie to screen the camp; he hopes to hold the Romans until more of our men return from foraging and give support."

"What can we do to help meantime?"

"The General asks that you bring your entire troop immediately and support his right flank, the fight's looking to escalate as the Romans are in strength and deploying more infantry and cavalry."

Baldor looked towards his men and bellowed. "Mount up! … Mount up!" His horse skittered as he shouted and waved at his men then looked back at the messenger. "How many are they?"

"Thousands sir!"

"Baal Almighty! … I only have three hundred and fifty-three men here. The rest are on patrol or sick but we'll do what we can."

"The General has sent for General Hasdrubal and his men as well."

"Where's General Hasdrubal? … Hurry up!" He growled over the messenger's shoulder as another handful of his men appeared.

"South of here sir foraging, so it may take some time for him to arrive. It seems the Romans have caught us out this time."

"Fabius comes at last then?"

"No Captain, it's his Master of Horse, Minucius that commands."

"Minucius eh? Tell the General we're on our way, soldier." Baldor nodded and saluted while forcing his mount around to the front of his assembling troops and waved them forward. "Come on! We're needed!" The urgency clear in his voice.

The men that were already mounted followed in small groups and ones and twos, while calling for their comrades still arriving to hurry on. Strung out, they had to ride around and through the chaos of other warriors forming up or running to their positions. Scattering the camp followers and slaves before them they pushed through the panicking throng towards the camp entrance. Warriors shouted and cursed at folk to get out of the way, the slower to move being shoved else battered and knocked aside by the horses as they forced a passage down the road. Once clear of the gate, men and horses quickly fell into column and the troop banner along with the standard of Carthage was raised. Baldor glanced back and seeing that most of his men had caught up, shouted to his signaller.

"Sound the advance, that'll let the General know we're coming."

The trumpeter blew the notes and Baldor took his troop to the canter then quickly onto the gallop, racing across the plain towards the huge skirmish developing on the open ground. Surprised by the number of Romans arraying, he took some comfort when he saw warriors hurrying from the camp to reinforce their comrades and the Carthaginian ranks slowly thickening. On the left flank, fighting was already heavy as the Romans sought to push past and attack the Carthaginian camp. The hasty but stiff resistance however, managing to halt the Roman rush and who instead now tried to turn the Carthaginian flank inward. An undulating blast of trumpets had the wide Roman centre give a huge roar and attack at double pace. It hit the Carthaginian centre in a loud clash of metal on wood and forced grunts from men as they took the heavy impact. The hastily formed and still thin Carthaginian lines wavered and bellied but held intact, though they were pushed slowly back under the pressure. The wide Roman frontage forced Hannibal to thin his lines further to extend his ranks and prevent the Romans overlapping his centre.

Leading his men towards the right flank, Baldor saw more legionary maniples arriving and noticed their huge numbers. The officer he'd spoken to by the tent was right, the Romans had finally found their balls, were here in force and it seemed had caught the Carthaginians unprepared. Hannibal and his personal guards were at the front and centre of his men, fighting while closing them into one defensive block and trying to support the heavily pressed left flank with arriving troops. Out on the Carthaginian right flank there were only light troops, and the Romans were moving quickly to attack and turn it in on itself, seeking to squeeze the Carthaginian centre.

Lifting and turning his spear Baldor raised it above his shoulder. Pulling the shield around from his back and looking again to his signaller riding alongside, he yelled and signalled for the charge. The trumpet notes blew loud and vibrant and his men roared battle cries and raised spears. The clamour rose to new heights as the horses raced forward, heads tossing and whickering, hooves drumming and kicking up dust and stones as the riders spread into line. The men made a gallant display with gaudily painted shield faces and streaming, colourful horsehair crests, the sunlight flashing from their bronze helmets as the line surged.

"Hold the line! … Hold the line!" Bellowed above the noise.

The Romans in front of Baldor's men were velites not legionaries and though there was a large number of them, they fought as skirmishers do, in open order. Seeing the heavy Carthaginian cavalry bearing down on them at speed they began to panic. With no legionaries close enough to support and form a shield wall to protect them and repel the horsemen, they began to peel away.

A loud groan turned to cries and screams as Baldor's men hit them at the gallop, the Carthaginians riding into and through their open ranks like a surging river flowing around small islands else swamping them. Men went down like ninepins, some dying on the cavalrymen's spears some battered to one side by the charging horses. Many were trampled and crushed in the chaos by their comrades as men scrambled to be away from the cohesive, heavy attack. As the Carthaginians penetrated the velite ranks deeply, the sheer mass of men forced their pace to slow, the riders finding the enemy panicking but still grouped thickly about them.

With spears broken or gone, the cavalrymen snatched for their swords, the combat turning into a heaving, swirling maelstrom of horses and men. Baldor lost his spear as it lodged deep in a man's chest. Dropping his shield, he drew both falcatas and laid about him, the heavy blades chopping into the lightly armed velites, splitting un-helmeted heads and cleaving un-armoured shoulders. Digging a knee into his mount's flank, he forced it round about in tight circles else kicked it forward to scatter the Romans and prevent attempts to hamstring the animal. The battle noise grew in volume again as men shouted in fear or hate. Screams rose above the clang of weapons as blades pierced and cut flesh. The horses, wild-eyed with fear whickered, stomped, or died as they were forced amongst the velites, blood spraying all as the fighting became intense. The velites were almost corralled now and being driven before the cavalry, the wounded, if they fell being trampled underfoot. Hannibal, seeing Baldor's cavalry driving the enemy back and securing his right flank, could now concentrate on the Romans attacking his centre. However, seeing more legionaries marshalling quickly behind them he looked desperately to his rear for more men.

As Baldor's cavalry onslaught turned the velite's attack he saw a mass of Roman cavalry forming at their rear, wary of being outflanked himself, he had the signaller sound the recall. With enough men, he could have engaged their cavalry and likely driven them off, allowing him to then attack the edge of the unprotected Roman centre but for now, he had to content himself with the success he'd had. As the velites continued to retreat the discipline of his men saw them halt and regroup. Repositioning his unit to watch the Roman cavalry and menace the edge of the Roman centre, he hoped their presence would at least ease the pressure on Hannibal.

Meanwhile the fighting on the Carthaginian left flank was intensifying as Roman reinforcements continued to arrive and were fed towards it determined to break or turn it. Hannibal, still desperately short of men attempted to counter it with heavy troops as they arrived in handfuls from the camp.

Cornelius and his men moved up, taking position to the rear of the Roman centre they made ready to advance in support.

"Shields!" He shouted. A clatter of wood answered his command as men disappeared behind the wooden wall with only protruding spear shafts and helmet crests showing. His heart was already thumping hard, was this it? The fight he'd been waiting and praying for? The chance to hit back and hit hard? A victory at last?

He could see the Carthaginians were hard pressed and appeared drastically short of troops and apart from the few cavalry on their right flank, there was no sign of any others, yet.

Roman trumpets blared over the din sounding a regroup and Centurions began extricating their men from battle to reform alongside the newly arrived troops ready for one big push. As the front ranks of both sides separated, some small individual fights continued as battle-rage ran hot, while the officers on both sides bellowed at their men to withdraw and rest. Men slowly fell back and into the line, mopping at sweating brows and gasping for breath some leaning on their shields for support, all glad of a moment's respite.

Cornelius glanced behind him and saw more equites and legionaries arriving in his rear and he smiled. At last, it seemed the Gods of Rome listened and favoured their faithful sons. The ranks thickened quickly and Cornelius waited anxiously for the command to attack. He rested a hand on his gladius hilt, his other holding his vine cane, which he tapped against his greave, the motion helping hide his nervousness. Facing forward, he eyed the enemy while mumbling his prayers through a very dry mouth.

"Juno, mother of us all I ask your protection, please keep me safe through this fight." Expecting to hear the command to advance at any moment he began easing his gladius from its scabbard. "Fortuna, Goddess, give us luck this day and should you call my fate I beg you, let me see ..." Suddenly more trumpets sounded, followed quickly by a huge roar from the Carthaginian ranks and pulling him from his reverences. Looking past the Carthaginians arrayed in front of him, he saw thousands of cavalry and infantry spilling over the hill in their rear. "No, no! ... Jupiter Almighty, no!" He growled. "We had them, we had them!" He glanced at the other Centurions off to his right and left, they like him now looking to Minucius's command group for signals.

The shouts from the Carthaginian ranks had men looking back to where others pointed and cheered. Hannibal shaded his eye then beamed a smile.

"Baal be praised! It's General Hasdrubal and his men." He laughed. "If these Romans want a battle I'll give them one now." The small hill to the south of the camp was now full of spear points and helmets that flashed and gleamed in the autumn sun. Hasdrubal's men came on like a wide silver stream, a mixture of cavalry numbering in their thousands with lightly armed Spanish infantry running alongside. Hannibal summoned his signallers. "You! Send a runner back to the camp and have any remaining troops and the guard units march out immediately."

"Yes sir."

"You! My compliments and thanks to Captain Targa, he's to hold his position on the right flank. I'll send a messenger to General Hasdrubal to support on the left as he arrives. Let's see how the Romans like the odds now?"

With the fighting paused both sides stood off glaring at each other across the bloodied sward like dogs ready to fight over a bone. The air, already thick with the stench of spilled guts, blood and shit became charged as the tension mounted. All the while men edged and fidgeted, the ground in between the armies littered with the dead and dying most of which were Carthaginian. A few men still moved, some trying to crawl away others sitting up and holding their injury, a few forcing themselves to their feet and staggering back towards their own men. Centurions still looked to Minucius to see if he'd attack again before the Carthaginian reinforcements arrived, just then the Roman trumpets blared across the field sounding retiral. Cornelius cursed and pushed his gladius back in the scabbard then shouted his orders.

"Facing front, back up twenty paces."

Behind him, all along the Roman lines other maniples followed suit.

As the legions continued to back away the Carthaginian lines erupted into jeers and taunts then began hammering their weapons on shields. At their rear, General Hasdrubal's men began to arrive, his Spaniards thickening the infantry lines and his cavalry moving to the left flank. As the noise from the shields became a solid deafening rhythm, Baldor watched as his comrade's ranks swelled and wondered if Hannibal would order the attack. However, as the Romans continued stepping away, he realised the chance of further combat was diminishing, Hannibal it seemed happy was to let them go this time, reinforcements arrived or not. His study was interrupted by the arrival of a second messenger, the man having to shout above the din.

"Captain, compliments from the General. Once the Romans are off the field, please stand your men down and convene at his tent without delay for a briefing."

"Yes, soldier. Thank you."

The officers arrived at Hannibal's tent still in full battle array and looking exhausted. Their sweat-wet faces and damp tunics caked with dust, their armour blood spattered and some with flesh wounds, Hannibal himself in no better shape. Some chairs remained empty as many men were still on patrol or foraging. As usual, Hannibal welcomed his men personally and served their first cup of wine, his face however was grim. When all were seated, he began.

"Gentlemen, thank you for your fast responses and bravery today. Methinks this battle was unexpected perhaps by both sides, going by the Roman withdrawal when the odds evened. General Hasdrubal, Captain Targa, my thanks for your timely arrivals and actions." He dipped his head to both men. "General Gisgo please furnish me with our casualty list as soon as you have it."

"Yes, sir."

"General Hasdrubal, dispatch some large cavalry patrols to make sure the Romans keep heading back to their camp."

"Already done sir."

"Prince Massinissa, would you aid General Hasdrubal's heavy patrols with some of your light cavalry."

"Already done General."

"General Mago, check the camp perimeters and reinforce the guard units."

"Done brother. Sorry, done General." He corrected quickly.

Hannibal beamed. "Thank you! Thank you all. That should see us well secure again." He paused to sip his wine and clear his throat. "Now! It seems I have misjudged this Minucius and his ambitions. According to my spies, he was left in command while Fabius returned to Rome but with explicit orders to continue shadowing us but not engage us for battle. I did expect some trouble but not on this scale, it's also unusual for a Roman officer to disobey his commander so flagrantly!" Baldor gave an involuntary twitch and shifted in his chair as he remembered his own transgression. "However, it seems the servant has more balls than his master! And if the master can't control him then we must cut off his balls and teach him a lesson for his temerity." His lips twisted and he snarled preventing any laughter from the men. "I swear, if this Minucius want's battle we'll give it to him but on our terms and as Baal is my witness, this time we'll be ready."

****

"He's calling it a victory!" Cornelius blurted, his voice heavy with scorn.

"Keep your damn voice down man!" Gaius hissed and pulled Cornelius in the direction of the camp's edge and out of earshot.

"How can we claim a bloody victory?" Cornelius persisted. "We left them in command of the field."

"Because our Master of Horse says so and we estimate their casualties at around six thousand while ours are less at five thousand."

"A Pyrrhic victory then! Jupiter knows we can't afford many more of those."

"We've bloodied their nose, that's what you wanted wasn't it?"

"Yes!"

"Well then?"

"Just one more push and they'd have buckled, Gods above! We had them, we bloody had them!"

"Their reinforcements were coming up fast though."

"But their right flank was weak with just a few hundred horse and nothing in the way of infantry to support it, their left flank almost broken. Just one more push …"

"Time and chance lad." Gaius shrugged.

Cornelius sneered. "Maybe, but I still think fast attacks on both flanks would have seen them broken. We had the men to widen our frontage which would have forced them to widen theirs, reinforcements or not."

"I think the idea was to catch them unawares before any reinforcements returned."

"Well, we were just too bloody slow!"

Gaius shrugged again. "Give them their due they rallied quickly and that was Hannibal himself in their centre, he's got balls."

"Aye, it just seems to be us that are lacking in that department!"

"I'd keep that opinion to yourself."

The pair were silent for a while; Gaius uncorked his flask and offered it.

Cornelius took a gulp. "Do you think Minucius will try again before Fabius returns?"

Gaius smiled. "I'd wager my eye teeth on it; he's had a taste of success … of a sort and come away wanting. Today proved we can catch the Carthaginians out, so he won't leave it there I'll warrant. There'll be a battle and before Fabius gets back."

Chapter Nine

"Sir, the redhead as you requested." The guard said as he pushed Lasairiona into the room and closed the door quietly behind him.

Thaddeus turned from the window and stared at Lasairiona from over the rim of his wine cup. Nodding appreciatively at what he saw, he gestured to the wine jug and another cup.

"Ah! My barbarian Princess. Would you like some wine?" Lasairiona didn't reply. "No? Not rich enough for your royal Gallic taste? …" He shrugged and chuckled to himself as he refilled his cup. "I must say you look more civilised now that you're washed and out of those filthy rags." Perching his corpulent frame on a settle he patted the cushions next to him. "Here! … Come here, sit." Lasairiona looked at him briefly and then quickly around the room Thaddeus laughed as he saw her look at the window. "Go ahead Princess, have a look, there's no way to escape from here."

Lasairiona edged to the window and peered out across the large garden then straight down into the well-lit, paved courtyard a floor below. A guard padded across it, a heavy club in one hand and a huge Molossian hound pulling on a leash in the other.

"Jump if you wish?" He chuckled and gestured to the window; the chuckle suddenly replaced by a snarl. "However, know that when your legs break or you've suffered some other injury and are no longer of use, I'll leave you for the dogs to tear apart. No one robs me of what I've paid good silver for and you girl, you cost me dear!" Lasairiona turned back from the window. "No, I didn't think you'd jump, it seems there's some sense in that pretty redhead of yours … hah! Brains as well as beauty. A rare commodity!" He laughed and sipped at his wine. "So girl, are you going to stand there all night or come and sit? … But bear in mind I'm not a patient man."

Lasairiona stepped cautiously across to the settle and sat at the opposite end. Thaddeus sighed and got to his feet, placed his cup down and casually walked behind the settle, Lasairiona watching his every move. He stopped behind her and tut-tutted softly.

"You really are trying my patience girl." The speed of his hand belied his size and he snatched at her hair. Taking a firm hold, he dragged her across the settle to where he'd been sat. "I said I'm not a patient man and yet you insist on testing me!" He twisted his wrist tightening his hold in her hair and making Lasairiona yelp, holding her until she stopped struggling, he leant close to her face, his wine scented breath strong in her nose. "Now Princess! You'll sit here, take a drink, speak when spoken to and behave like the royalty they tell me you are." He twisted her hair savagely again, gave her face a light slap then let her go. Resuming his seat, he poured her a cup of wine and watched as she straightened herself on the settle and glared at him. "Drop the insolent look girl or I will have you whipped."

"You won't whip me, I'm worth more unmarked." She spat.

"Aha! So, you do have a tongue. However, I suggest you curb its manner. If I choose to whip you girl, I'll happily take the loss in your price for the pleasure it will give me … so don't test me!" He passed her the cup. "Drink!" Lasairiona took the cup and sipped while watching Thaddeus over the rim. "Now that you are being civilised, tell me, can you dance, sing, recite poetry or tell stories?"

"No."

"Nothing! … What can you do to entertain me then?" He tut-tutted again. "It seems I've paid for your body and nothing else." Lasairiona gave a nervous look though Thaddeus just chuckled and seemed to settle back on the couch. "So, tell me, where do you come from? What's your story, are you really Gallic royalty? … Well?"

Lasairiona chewed her lip, her mind fathoming whether talking would help her. Was he looking to rape her, whip her or was he just enjoying baiting her? What to do? She would rather die before she'd let him violate her but there was nothing visible she could seize and use to defend herself with if it came to that, no heavy bowls or jugs, not even a fruit knife. The thought of a slow death if leaping from the window didn't kill her or being savaged by dogs, was no solution.

"I'm …" She paused, cleared her throat and raised her head proudly. "I'm the daughter of Lugobelinos, son of Maponos, son of Teutorigos Chief of the Cenomani tribe, we were allies of Rome."

"So, allies of Rome eh and a Princess in all but name?"

"I'm not a Princess; I'm a Chief's daughter." She answered quietly.

"Oh!" He chuckled. "Perhaps I should let you go … but there again who will pay me for what I've paid for you." He raised his hands in a hapless gesture. "You were damned expensive!"

Lasairiona felt a faint surge of hope. "My man … my man may raise the price."

"Your man?"

"Yes."

"Your husband?" Thaddeus suddenly looked unsure.

"No … no, we are not wed."

Thaddeus rolled his eyes. "So where would we find your man and how did he come to lose you in the first place, or did he sell you himself?" He burst into laughter enjoying his own wit.

Lasairiona's head dropped. "I was kidnapped from his tent whilst he was at battle."

"At battle? But we Romans don't take our women to war, what were you doing in a military camp?" He asked quickly. For the second time Thaddeus looked unsure, was this woman a Mistress of some high-ranking Roman? He looked again at her and saw not just an attractive woman but a beauty, a Goddess, someone a man would risk his all for, including his life. Clearing his throat and recovering his composure, he asked as casually as possible. "So who is your man? If … and I say if, I were to seek to recover my money who would I ask for?"

"My …" It was Lasairiona's turn to look unsure.

"Well?"

"My man … my man's name is Captain Targa."

"A Captain? Don't you mean a Chief Centurion or Camp Prefect?"

"No, he's a Captain … a Captain with General Hannibal's army."

Thaddeus burst into laughter and some relief. "Ah, a Carthaginian! Well, that changes everything. Tell me, what was an ally of Rome doing in a Carthaginian camp and in the bed of a Carthaginian Captain?"

"I was taken as a slave when my township of Victumulae was sacked."

"And now the slave has risen in status to a lover but not yet a wife? … How wonderfully sweet."

"Will you offer him a price for me?"

"My, my, you're confident that he will want to pay!"

Lasairiona's face fell but gathering her composure she raised her head proudly again, her beauty evident despite her angst. "Yes, he will pay, he's a good man."

Thaddeus's expression hardened. "Willing to pay or not, he's also an enemy of Rome and thus I can have no truck with him. Would you have me crucified for collaborating, girl?"

He chuckled and made another mock show of raising his hands in a hapless gesture. He got slowly to his feet, stretched and yawned then suddenly leapt at Lasairiona, seizing her savagely by the hair again while snatching hold of her dress and dragging her across the settle. "Furthermore, I think I'll keep you for myself." He snarled. Using his ample body weight, he pinned her on the couch then moving the hand from her hair, he used both to rip her dress. As the pain went from her head, Lasairiona twisted and flung her body trying to get him off, her elbows digging backwards, hard into his ribs. As heavy as he was she was strong and she flung him off, landing him on the floor with a heavy thump.

"Bitch! You damned bitch! … Guard! Guard, in here now!"

The door burst open and the guard entered at the run. Seizing Lasairiona by the hair and her arm, he tried to force her back down on the settle. She stamped her foot hard repeatedly on his toes and he let go of her.

"Get hold of her, man!" Thaddeus yelled. The guard stumbled after her; seizing her by the dress, he cuffed her hard on the back of the head sending her staggering. "Don't damage her you bloody fool! Restrain her!"

The guard snatched Lasairiona's arm again and twisted it up her back, she flung her other arm backwards trying to hit him in the groin and missed. He forced her arm higher and she groaned in pain and ceased her struggling. Kicking her in the back of the knee, she went down, he using his body weight to force her flat to the floor.

"I have her sir!"

"She'd better not be damaged! Tie her hands then fetch Arya, tell her I have need of her talents, I have a troublesome girl that requires disciplining but without damage." Pulling a leather cord from his pouch, the guard went to tie Lasairiona's hands. "No, you fool! That'll cut into her skin, use this." Ripping a strip from her dress, he passed it to the guard. With Lasairiona bound, Thaddeus held her down with his foot pressed on her back while the guard disappeared seeking Arya. "You'll regret this behaviour, Princess." He growled. "Arya will teach you some manners; she deals with all my troublesome girls. Let's see how brave you are then." He leant hard on her back making her gasp. "You think that hurts? Wait till Arya has finished with you."

Shortly, a raven haired, elegant woman with an Amazonian physique appeared with a cane in her hand followed by the guard carrying a short, heavy bench. The warm beauty and greeting on her face towards her master changing to a cruel mask as she eyed Lasairiona.

"You sent for me sir."

"Ah, my beautiful Arya! This vixen here requires disciplining and teaching some manners."

"As you wish sir, I …"

"It's no good caning her girl; I don't want her skin marked. She was much too expensive for that!"

"Yes sir, the guard told me. Allow me please; I have a technique that will suffice both requirements." Thaddeus smiled and gestured she should continue while stepping back as Arya placed her foot on Lasairiona's back and spoke to the guard. "Put the bench down here then tie her ankles to it so the soles of her feet are uppermost." Thaddeus gave a wicked giggle and poured himself another cup of wine then eased back on the settle to watch. The guard lifted Lasairiona's lower legs resting her shins against the edge of the bench, tying them in place with cloth strips given him by Arya. "Gag her well!" She said while tying her hair back and removing Lasairiona's sandals. "All is ready, sir."

Thaddeus looked at Lasairiona, she gagged and bound and face down on the floor, her legs tied to the bench. Satisfied she was secured he dismissed the guard.

"You may begin Arya but make it nice and slow, teach her that she needs to obey."

"Yes sir." Arya purred wickedly as she sat on the bench. Rubbing the cane slowly over Lasairiona's soles she tapped them gently as if letting her know what was to come. Lasairiona was already struggling against the heavy bench when Arya brought the end of the cane down across the sole of one of her feet, she screamed into the gag. Arya worked the cane from one foot to the other while looking to Thaddeus each time for the signal to strike. He, delighting in seeing the pain inflicted gave the command slowly, watching excitedly until Lasairiona appeared to pass out.

"Wonderful Arya! Wonderful and no visible damage."

"She'll be unable to walk or work for a few days, sir."

"No matter … no matter, the bitch can reflect on her behaviour later in the box … a little more perhaps?" He gestured to the cane again.

Arya reached for the small water flask and tipped it over Lasairiona's head, the cold water bringing her back to consciousness.

"I best use this now, sir. This way the skin won't split." Arya produced a short but flexible piece of wood the same length as the cane and about two fingers in breadth.

"Please lay on, Arya but slowly again my dear." He said, the perverse delight lighting his face.

Lasairiona thrashed and twisted as the wood slapped her soles, her cries strangled by the gag. As the beating continued, she went suddenly still and Arya knelt close, checking her.

"She's swooned again; shall I fetch more water and revive her sir? I can then take the wood to the back of her calves and thighs and bring fresh pain." She flicked Lasairiona's dress up exposing her thighs and buttocks.

Thaddeus, clearly enjoying the spectacle looked as if he was about to agree then looking lustily at Arya beckoned her to him.

"No Arya, as much as I'm enjoying watching you work I think we must call a halt."

"She's strong sir and I will be careful; I won't mark her."

"No Arya, no." He smiled as his voice thickened with lust. "I have need of your other talent." He began pulling his robe open. "Come; show me the delights of your other skill."

"But what of your wife sir? I have no wish to be whipped again, she has a heavy hand."

"Gone … gone to Rome. I promised her jewels of her choice." Arya looked at him quizzically, he explained. "It seems I must atone for our last dalliance Arya. She only gave you a thrashing, but she is punishing me by bleeding my purse dry! Come; show me what the old Harpie did to you, my sweet."

For the first time since entering the room, Arya smiled warmly and dropping the wood, slipped the dress from her shoulders and stepped out of it. Naked, she moved slowly across the floor her eyes dropped seductively low and her lips forming a sensual pout before she climbed onto his lap.

Lasairiona awoke on a stone floor in the dark. Frightened, she sat up quickly then groaned as the pain from her feet hit her. Reaching down and tentatively touching her sole she gasped as the touch of her fingers brought more pain. Moaning softly, she looked around, a small, barred window allowed a little moonlight into the room or wooden box, the space being no size at all. Behind her, the door opened and from the flickering light of a torch she saw a bowl of food and a jug of water placed on the floor, the person said nothing and as the door slammed shut again, she heard the lock click. Unable to stand, she shuffled around, tentatively feeling in the dark at the space, her hand touched something cold, and she recoiled. Reaching out again her fingers traced over metal, she recognised a dish shape, and going by the stench it was to use for her body wastes.

With fear rising in her again, she fought back the need to weep though tears of anger and perhaps hopelessness spilled down her cheeks as she reasoned her situation. Was she doomed to die in here else dragged out only to be beaten or raped? Why should Baldor come for her? Yes, he'd lain with her and they'd enjoyed a relationship of sorts but he hadn't professed his love for her, she was his slave, his concubine at best but not a wife. With the slave market overflowing and many beautiful women available for those prepared to pay, why would he even consider looking for her?

What to do? She would have worked to stay alive. Slavery, as demeaning and hard as it was, was preferable to death but she would kill herself before she would let a man rape her. Going by her treatment that was obliviously what Thaddeus intended, she was not to be left just to work as a slave in his house. Furthermore, the man was obliviously content to spend time breaking her until she could no longer resist and she knew she couldn't take much more like the beating she'd received from this Arya. She knew her work, knew how to inflict the maximum amount of pain slowly and cleverly, leaving the victim intact for more of the same. Death by her own hand was preferable to the beatings and rape that she knew would surely follow.

Cuffing at the tears she cursed herself for giving into her weakness, she was royalty, she was Cenomani and no one but she would determine her fate. She began tracing her hands over the wooden walls but found them smooth with no splinters that could be used to open her veins. Picking up the plate and jug, she felt them heavy but not made of clay that could be broken into shards but made of metal, heavy metal, not something that could be bent or squashed into a sharp point or edge. Checking the waste dish she found the same, her captors it seemed well aware of all possibilities had taken careful steps to keep their troublesome slaves alive until they deemed otherwise. However, she would watch for any opportunity, any chance to take her life and before she suffered further at the hands of Thaddeus and Arya.

Days passed, she wasn't sure how many though she was fed and watered regularly. She suffered as her small cell absorbed the heat by day, beading her skin in sweat and stifling the air making it difficult to breathe. The early evening brought a refreshing coolness but which changed to a chilling cold as the dew fell in the early morning. Unable to stand or stretch she was in agony for the need to flex her limbs. Weary for the want of a pain free sleep she was covered in her own filth though she'd long since ceased to worry about such. She heard voices nearby but not the usual chatter of slaves but a measured, commanding tone, a woman's voice.

"I don't care what my husband said, open the door and let me see who's in there, now!" The door opened wide, Lasairiona having to shield her eyes from the bright sun. A women bent to peer in then putting her hand over her mouth stepped quickly back from the smell. "Pull her out of there!"

Strong hands hauled on Lasairiona's legs as she was roughly dragged out into the sunlight. Closing her eyes against the brightness, she tried to stretch her limbs and whimpered as the unused muscles and tight tendons objected. There was silence while the woman used her stick to examine Lasairiona, she too weak and past caring to object. Lifting the matted hair, the woman studied the grime covered face then gently prodded at her breasts barely held within the remains of the thin dress. Nodding to herself, she lifted the slit of the dress to one side exposing filth covered but beautifully shaped legs.

"Huh! Just as I thought. Can you stand girl?" Lasairiona tried to rise but whimpered again when her limbs objected to the stretch, the tendons sleepy and tight from days of restriction reacting painfully to the movement. "You! You! Take her to the women's quarters and have her washed, dressed, decently fed and then brought to me in my rooms."

It was late in the evening when Lasairiona was taken to the Lady of the house's private rooms, her hair and body washed and she dressed now in clean and less revealing attire. She still walked carefully, her limbs remaining stiff from the confinement and her soles still tender. The older woman looked her up and down then pointed to a chair, Lasairiona perched nervously and took a moment to look at her potential saviour. Looking past the years, she could see the woman had been a beauty herself and though she still maintained a fine figure, time was seeing grey creep into her hair and fine lines besetting her mouth and eyes.

"I believe you suffered at the hands of that creature of my husband's?" Lasairiona just nodded. "Your beauty no doubt attracted his attentions and I take it from the beating you received that you fought back? … Don't think I show you special favour girl or that I care what happened to you, for I don't! I just will not be made a fool of in my own house. I will see that you work for me now as my body slave, that's providing you can do the job. I trust you can attend a lady, help with bathing, dressing, run errands and bind hair?" Lasairiona nodded. "They tell me you're Gallic royalty? … And don't just nod at me girl, open your mouth when I'm seeking an answer!"

"Yes … yes, I'm Cenomani, the daughter …"

The woman waved the words away. "If you do as you're bidden your life will be bearable, comfortable even, however should you displease me I will have you whipped. Do you understand me?" Lasairiona just nodded again. "I said do you understand? A yes Mistress Livia or My Lady is the response I expect."

"Yes, Mistress Livia."

"Good … you may begin now. I've already bathed so ready me for bed, take my jewellery and place it in the box over there then fetch my night attire from the chest." Lasairiona did as she was bidden and without fault. "Here!" Livia said curtly while passing a comb and a ribbon. "Comb out my hair and bind it for bed."

Lasairiona undid the fine gold chains and removed the pins that supported Livia's hair in a huge bun atop her head then gently teased and combed the hair straight, tying it back with the ribbon. After helping Livia into a beautiful nightdress, the woman stood and beckoning that she should follow, walked to a side door in the room wall.

"Here's where you sleep girl." She ushered her into the small room lit now by an oil lamp but with a high window that would allow sunlight and warmth by day. It was sparsely furnished but clean with a narrow pallet bed in the corner and a small table bearing a washbowl, a comb, a towel and items of folded clothing piled neatly on a stool close by. "If I call, you come. Otherwise, you rise with the sun and see to my breakfast, I always take it in my room. While I'm here, you may bring your own food up here should you wish and eat in your room."

"Yes, Mistress Livia."

"Go then girl and sleep; I'm sure you need it. Up at sunrise!"

"Yes Mistress."

For the first time in weeks, Lasairiona stretched out on a bed. Extinguishing the lamp, she mumbled her prayers into the darkness asking Sirona for protection while holding onto hope that Baldor would search for her. Mentally and physically exhausted, she was asleep in moments.

Part 2

It was the servant not the master, who made the lion's brood roar.

Anon

Chapter Ten

A servant rushed through the tent to the quarter where Andulas, Armaco and Baldor sat, Issa jumped up and barked at the sharp intrusion.

"My Lord! Sirs! The General, General Hannibal is here to see Captain Targa."

The men immediately rose to their feet, Armaco easing from the high seat Andulas had ordered made for him, making it easier for him to get up. Andulas gestured the servant back towards the tent door and followed him so to welcome the guest.

"General, hail!"

"Hail, Lord Andulas!" The pair shook hands as Andulas showed Hannibal through to the men's quarter, the others offering greetings and a seat, Baldor having to quieten Issa as she barked again and jumped up at the newcomer.

"Down, Issa!" Baldor said as he clicked his fingers, the pup backed away from Hannibal but stood between him and Baldor, watching."

"Another guard dog, Baldor!" Hannibal chuckled. "Not only do you have true friends but a faithful hound to boot!"

He squatted and offered his hand to Issa who cautiously sniffed it then allowed a stroke of her head, then as if accepting the newcomer went and laid on her sheepskin, watching. Andulas offered wine around then looked to Hannibal.

"How can we be of service General?"

Hannibal smiled. "It is I who hope to be of service, mainly to you, Baldor."

Baldor bowed his head. "Sir?"

"I have thought much on the promise I made you to seek your woman. When you sought leave to go I asked that you wait a little longer as I needed your men." He held up a hand to stifle Baldor's interruption. "I believe that was unfair of me, the longer you wait the harder she will be to find, so here's an offer. If you wish to go now you can take a small escort but will need to leave me your troops for as I intimated when we spoke, I think Minucius still seeks battle and I would take advantage of that, hence I need your men. Alternatively, if you wish to wait until we've taught this errant Roman his lesson you can then take your whole troop with my blessing."

All eyes turned to Baldor. "I do have a confirmed sighting of her since we spoke last sir."

"You do! Where?"

Andulas intervened. "My informer has word of her in Casilinum General, she's being held as a slave in the house of one, Thaddeus Rufus Antonius."

Hannibal sighed. "If only Capua had opened her gates to us I wager that Casilinum being close by would have followed suit, which would have made it easier."

"I would offer to buy her sir; I have the coin." Baldor looked a little sheepish remembering Hannibal had given him the silver.

"Do you want to go now?"

There was silence for a moment before Baldor, slightly embarrassed quietly committed. "Yes sir … yes I would."

"Then you shall. Here's the deal I would need. You take an escort of a dozen men or so but leave me Lord Andulas or Armaco or both to command your troop … I need good men, Baldor."

"Yes sir, I understand, totally. I could manage with that, I am hoping to just pay, nothing that should require force."

"General, if I may?" Andulas asked.

"Speak freely, Lord Andulas this is your home, I your guest." Hannibal said graciously.

"Could I accompany Baldor, General? We can contact my informer easier that way and it would fit with my plan."

"You already have a plan?" He nodded approvingly.

"Yes, it's a simple one."

"Simple is often best My Lord."

"Baldor and I will travel as a Gallic Lord with his personal retainer along with an escort such as you suggest, that would be good for appearances as well as safety. Our story, we are seeking to purchase slaves as the market is flooded and cheap, a good time to buy. Baldor, with his hair tied back, his height and command of Gallic will pass for my servant."

Hannibal smiled. "I've had him impersonate a Gaul before remember, at Victumulae?"

Armaco huffed and coughed. "What part can I play General? These two need me."

"You Armaco." Hannibal smiled. "If these two go, you I would need to command the Captain's troops for me, I need a good man that I can trust while they're gone."

Armaco seemed lost for words and just stared. "Me! You would give me command?"

Hannibal smiled and shrugged. "Why not? You have experience and Baldor speaks highly of both your bravery and competence."

"Yes … yes sir! Yes General." He spluttered.

"Good!" He swilled his wine. "It's settled then. If you will excuse me gentlemen, I'll leave you to plan further. Captain, My Lord, take the men of your choice and leave when you please. Armaco, the moment they leave you're in command." As he stood to leave the men made to rise but Hannibal gestured them back to their seats. "Baal bless and keep you all." The men bowing their heads while holding a hand over their heart.

"We can be away by dawn tomorrow." Andulas said as he stood and paced the room, his hand cupping his chin as he thought aloud. "We'll take ten of my personal guards for the escort. From my understanding, Casilinum is reachable in just over a day and a half's ride from here … no, let's say two to allow for the cart."

"The cart?" Baldor asked.

"Aye, I'll explain later. So, we could be there and back in four maybe five days at the most, depending of course on what and who we encounter."

Baldor frowned, his face serious. "Brothers … brothers! I'm flattered … flattered and grateful that you will risk all for me, for what I want." He held up a hand to prevent interruptions. "To have friends like yourselves is to be rich beyond measure and I only hope I can repay your kindness at some point."

Andulas cleared his throat and looked at both men. "I have been indebted to you both since the day you intervened and slew my enemies who were slaughtering my folk at our fishery. This is my chance to balance that debt, at least to you Baldor."

"No debt to me, Andulas. We just did what any good men would do. It is I, who owe you both. You for this undertaking tomorrow and for giving me a home and feeding me when I had nothing. And you Armaco, for always watching my back and … and saving my life more than once." He swallowed hard and cuffed at the tears as his emotions took over. "I am truly blessed."

Armaco for once had no sarcasm or glib retort to add. Looking sincere, he eyed both men. "I've never had friends, comrades like you two, never. As far as I'm concerned there are no debts between us." He bowed his head to both men then recharged the wine cups. "Friends!" There was moment's silence as the men drank.

"Brothers!" Andulas corrected.

"Brothers!" Baldor added.

"Aye, brothers it is. After all, the way I see it, teaching you both how to fight and watching your backs is what a brother does!" Armaco hid a smirk behind his wine cup.

The following morning saw Andulas and Baldor smartly attired but also well-armed though their mail shirts were hidden beneath their tunics. Leaving helmets off so to appear less martial and warlike both men had washed and bound their hair and trimmed up moustaches. Andulas, sporting thick, gold neck and wrist torcs shaped like twisted rope and looking every bit the Gallic Lord led the small party. Baldor, his face shaved except for a drooping moustache had exchanged his short Carthaginian tunic for the brightly patterned trousers of the Gauls. A plain, long black shirt belted with a Gallic broadsword and dagger on his hips completing his guise, his falcatas by necessity being left behind.

Their escort was made of Andulas's best men. All were mature warriors, large and fierce looking but like their Lord were dressed in their finest clothing but with mail shirts and helmets scoured bright, weapon hilts and metal-studded belts polished, a Lord's escort. To complete the pretence a caged prison wagon placed in the centre of the group contained two warriors, both looking ragged and unkempt playing the part of slaves. A box cunningly hidden beneath the cart floor planking holding their weapons if needed. The party was clear of the camp and heading back west just as the sun eased above the horizon behind them.

The going was easy, gently rolling hills interspersed with small copses and farms, most of which were now in ruin.

By mid-morning the late autumn sun was surprisingly hot, forcing the men to ease their pace and walk the horses before returning them to a trot. They saw few people; those that saw them disappeared quickly in the opposite direction or out of sight into the copses and cover. The land, once beautiful, showed signs of burning and destruction, the fields empty of livestock, orchards picked clean and burnt, granaries emptied. The bloated bodies of some animals still lay in the fields rotting and stinking in the autumn warmth with large clouds of buzzing black flies in attendance. The men exchanged information with their own patrols but saw no sign of Roman ones. Camping overnight, they were on their way again at daybreak, making good time without incident or altercations.

By early evening the following day they saw the walls of Casilinum crowning a small hill in the distance. The gateway and adjacent towers were of stone; plastered over and painted white, the sinking sun reflecting brightly from it. The rest of the walls however were no more than a wooden stockade, albeit tall and well built, with numerous sentries patrolling the parapets and the tower tops. Drawing closer the men eased their pace again, walking their mounts and negating any sign of urgency so not to panic the sentries, who could already be seen pointing in their direction. Reaching the gate, they were stopped by a squad of guards while in the towers above a handful of archers looked down with arrows laid ready on the string should trouble eventuate. When Andulas stated their business and mentioned Thaddeus by name the guards relaxed somewhat.

"Is Master Antonius expecting you?"

"No, though we hear he's the man to see for slaves, thus we seek an audience with him and a chance to purchase; perhaps you could tell him we are looking for him?"

"Find him yourself; I'm not his lackey or yours!"

Andulas snarled. "Watch your mouth, man or I'll cut your insolent tongue out! I'm not some peasant or lackey either! I'm Lord Andulas of the Cenomani and an ally of Rome! When I find Master Antonius I shall inform him of the way his potential clients are treated."

The big Gaul in anger was a frightening, sobering spectacle. The guard looked again at the size of Andulas and the men behind him; these were no soft city guards. Their stature and appearance told of warriors, professional warriors! Killers! If a fight started here, archers above or not, he was a dead man. Clearing his throat, he began again.

"My apologies, My Lord … I have … It's just I must be careful who I admit into the town, these are dangerous times."

"That doesn't excuse your lack of civility." Andulas growled.

"No, My Lord … no it does not." He dipped his head. "My apologies. Pontius! Go and inform Master Thaddeus of the visitors. My Lord, if you will follow Pontius, Master Thaddeus's villa is situated on the rise at the rear of the town." Andulas brushed the horse past the man making him stumble.

The town was busy and full of folk, many seeking the safety of the walls as much of the surrounding countryside had gone up in flames, the mounted party having to weave slowly through the throng. The strong odour of too many animals and people crammed into one place vied with the more pleasant smells of baking bread and food being prepared by vendors. Baldor leant close to Andulas.

"That was relatively easy at the gate!"

"Aye, except for me having to say I was Cenomani and wanting to slap that insolent bastard!" He growled and spat. "It's hard to say where these people's sympathies lie, we are in Campania but very close to Samnium and until a few decades ago there was no love lost between the Samnites and Rome." He shrugged. "However, I surmise like most folk, they're probably hedging their bets as to which side to ally with. Mind you, with our previous depredations hereabouts we've probably not endeared ourselves to most."

Ahead of the party, Pontius had stopped at a villa gateway and was conversing with the two sentries while waving Andulas and his men onward.

"My Lord, Master Thaddeus is not home until tomorrow."

Andulas nodded curtly. "Tomorrow then, tell Master Thaddeus to expect us."

"Yes, My Lord."

Andulas turned to Baldor speaking quietly. "Now we wait, come let's find this Eagle inn and lodging that Cassia told me of."

The following morning saw Baldor, Andulas and their party back at Thaddeus's gate and one of the guards on his way, hot foot to announce the visitors and their business to his master.

"A lord of the Cenomani you say?" Thaddeus gabbled, his face paling.

"Yes sir."

"Seeking who … what?" He hissed. "Quickly man!"

"Seeking slaves …"

"Looking for or seeking to buy, man? There's a difference!" He snapped. His nerves clearly on the raw.

"To buy sir."

"He's come with armed men?"

"Yes sir, ten warriors and a cart holding two slaves."

"Is there anyone that looks like a Carthaginian Captain with them?"

"No sir, the men are all Gauls."

"His name then, did this Gaul give a name?"

"Yes sir …"

"Out with-it man! Gods above!"

"Lord Andulas of the Cenomani and a companion, a Master Gestix."

"No mention of a Lugobelinos, son of Maponos, son of Teutorigos?"

"No sir."

"How old is he?"

"Mid-forties I'd say, sir."

Thaddeus thought quickly. It could be an assumed name? The man's age certainly made him old enough to be the redhead's father come seeking his daughter or was it an elder brother? However, if he refused to see the man it may arouse suspicion as slave traders were not known for turning away business. "Turn out all my guards, have them armed and ready and arrayed around the house. Send word to my wife; tell her to keep her redheaded Harpie out of sight if she wants to keep our lives safe and a roof above our heads."

"Yes sir."

"Admit this Lord Andulas and his companion but his men stay outside the gate."

"Yes sir."

"Send my Steward to the gate for the welcome and formalities."

The man bowed and left at the run while Thaddeus breathed deeply attempting to calm himself. Tidying his robes, he sought his seat; sitting would help his composure and hopefully hide his nerves and trepidations.

The reply arrived to the Gallic party along with servants bearing trays laden with wine and a well-dressed man, most likely the Steward of the house who bowed low to Andulas.

119

"Greetings My Lord, Master Thaddeus apologies for the delay and bids you most welcome, he asks that you and your companion join him within. We will bring food for your men if they'll wait outside, please."

Andulas, at his imperious best drained his wine and turned to his men. "Wait here." Giving a brief nod to the Steward, he flicked his hand that the man should lead on.

Passing through the gateway, the paved courtyard was large and edged with beautiful gardens, some late autumn blooms adding colour and a sweet scent to the air. The pair noticed the large number of armed guards at doorways and various points around the property.

"He's very rich going by the number of men he has." Baldor said under his breath.

"Aye, and very nervous!"

Slaves came to take the horses bridles and the men dismounted following in the lee of the Steward as he led them into the house. Entering a large room, the Steward announced the visitors. Thaddeus, hefting his portly frame from a throne like chair stood to receive them.

"My Lord Andulas, Master Gestix, welcome." He smiled and dipped his head. "My apologies again for the delay I wasn't expecting visitors. Come, please sit … tell me of your journey and how I can be of service, my humble home is open to you."

The room was spacious and grandly furnished with settles covered in sumptuous throws, colourful rugs scattered on the tiled floor and small occasional tables of dark hardwood, one of which was laden with a silver wine jug and more cups. The walls on the south side had windows to catch the all-day sun; the others decorated with vibrant patterns and scenes from antiquity. One wall showed a scene of a lush forest complete with hoofed and horned Satyrs, all with an erect and exaggerated phallus chasing scantily clad or naked maidens. Thaddeus clicked his fingers, and a slave filled the cups. Dismissing him, Thaddeus served the two men himself.

"It's dangerous times to be abroad, My Lord?"

"It is Master Thaddeus. However, life and commerce go on and I need slaves for my household in the north."

"The north? You're a long way from home then?"

"Aye! We're with Fabius and the army but suffering from a shortage of slaves."

"A lack of victories brings a lack of slaves … no disrespect intended My Lord." He added quickly. "This Hannibal is proving a capable and worrying adversary and we … we simple folk are caught between."

"Hence my visit, Master Thaddeus. With most of my men here at war, I need slaves for home. Winter is coming and it comes early in the north, thus I hope to send slaves home for there is much work that needs completion before the snows are upon us. However, as you said, with victory eluding us at present I must buy what I need."

"Ah! I believe I can help you there My Lord, you will be seeking male slaves I surmise?"

"Yes mainly men but some women also for there are foods to prepare, skins to tan and treat, wool to spin and blankets to weave and repair, so on and so forth."

"Young then? You will wish them young and strong?"

"Aye, good strong-backed men but the women must be young and have beauty as much as work skills for I have warriors to entertain as well."

Thaddeus smiled and clapped his hands twice; his Steward appeared within moments and bowed his head.

"Have the male merchandise paraded in the yard for My Lord Andulas and Master Gestix to view."

As the Steward bowed and disappeared, Thaddeus led his guests down to the yard where the first of the male slaves were lined up. Seating his guests, he called for a slave to bring more wine. Andulas took his time choosing from the slaves. Of those he deemed showed promise; he checked limbs, muscles and teeth before standing some aside and rejecting others. Having shortlisted ten he compared them again reducing them down to eight.

"These eight, Master Thaddeus and your price?"

The two men haggled amicably over the price while Baldor looked casually on and around seeking any sign of Lasairiona and though women came and went with more wine, she was nowhere to be seen.

With the proceedings going well, Thaddeus seemed to relax and invited the men to partake of the midday meal.

"Now My Lord." Thaddeus said excitedly. "I've saved the more pleasant merchandise until last, the women."

"Aha!" Andulas gave an excited chuckle. "Show me the very best you have Master Thaddeus."

Thaddeus watched both men's faces as he signalled for the women to be brought out; Andulas maintained his smile while Baldor betrayed an apprehensiveness. Seeing Thaddeus watching him, he managed a nod and a smile.

The women shown were many and beautiful, each being stripped for display, blondes with pale skin and blue eyes from the north, brunettes, brown eyed and swarthy skinned from the south, raven haired beauties with dark, almond shaped eyes and looks of the east and tall, elegant black girls from the lands of Nubia and Kush.

"Such beauties, Master Thaddeus! I think you tempt me so to lighten my purse further."

Thaddeus chuckled. "Purchase as many as you wish, Lord Andulas. The more you take the better the price."

"Alas, I only have room for two. With the two men I already have and the eight I have bought from you; my wagon is full." He chuckled. "Choices, choices!" He sighed.

"I admit I've been wicked; I have offered you all and the best that I have to tempt you to part with your silver and as you have troubled to visit me I've even shown you my personal favourites." He sighed then chuckled. "Still, these are uncertain times and money not my pleasure or wants is paramount."

Andulas smiled in return and selected two blonde-haired women. "These two, they remind me of home."

With business concluded and the slaves escorted to the wagon, the visitors sought their leave. Thaddeus, comfortable with the proceedings and confident the men were leaving on good terms probed Baldor, his silence throughout the afternoon making him a little suspicious.

"Are you not happy with your Lord's purchases, Master Gestix? You haven't said much?"

"It's not my place to comment, Master Thaddeus."

"Perhaps not but surely you would admire beauty, perhaps wish for some of what has been offered? Was there nothing there that you found desirable? … Can I seek something special out for you, perhaps for when you visit again?"

"Thank you, Master Thaddeus but no. I have my own wife with which I am content."

"Ah, a pillar amongst men. Would that I had your fortitude, unfortunately I find women irresistible, well beautiful women anyway." As the men rose to leave, Thaddeus probed again. "Where to from here My Lord? Back to camp?"

"Perhaps, though it's growing late in the day, so we'll likely lodge again in the town and leave tomorrow."

"That may be wise, I hope to see you again … and your silver."

Later that evening, Andulas, Baldor and their party were back in the Eagle inn near the town gate. The chilly night saw a roaring fire in the hearth, the smell of wood smoke mixing with the odour of people that crowded in for the warmth and a drink at the end of a working day. The two men were seated in a quiet, darkened corner for dinner and talking quietly over wine when a young serving woman approached, Baldor quietened immediately. Wiping down the table top she unloaded food from her tray setting it before the men while she spoke in low tones.

"I see you're empty handed of what you sought, Lord?" Baldor, surprised at the interruption looked up quickly as the woman continued quietly. "She is there Lord, I've seen her."

Andulas nodded slowly. "Aye, is he keeping her for himself perhaps? But why hide her though? All he had to do was say she was not for sale." He looked at Baldor. "This is Cassia, my eyes and ears."

The woman and Baldor exchanged a brief nod though Baldor could not hide his surprise. Cassia made a show of retying her hair while she spoke quietly.

"The rumour is out that she's Gallic royalty, Lord. Perhaps you arriving as Gauls unnerved him? I only heard the rumour this morning else I would have warned you … I'm sorry Lord." She added quickly.

He waved the apology away. "Worry not Cassia, it's not your fault. He has himself a Princess, maybe that's why he won't offer her up. Keep watching and listening for me, eh?"

The woman smiled briefly. "Yes Lord." She said under her breath before raising her voice. "Shout up when you need more drinks." She added for effect as she turned away.

"How do you know Cassia?"

"That would be telling Baldor, and a man of honour does not betray a lady's confidence."

"So, you and …"

"Hush! … Hush!" He chuckled. "Ask no secrets and you get no lies!"

"Sorry, I didn't mean to intrude."

"No problem my friend, you're too polite for that. It's just a man needs something only for himself sometimes and we've been gone from home a long time now. Suffice to say she came my way after the Trebbia fight and was gone again before we fought again at Trasimene. Cassia's a free spirit, a wanderer and a healer by profession."

"The world is a dangerous place for a woman on her own; especially a pretty one, how does she manage?"

"Very well I surmise as she's also deadly; she can fight and fight well!"

"Is she Gallic?"

"Yes, from the Boii tribe if my memory serves."

"She'll bear no love for Rome then?"

"No, like most of us Gauls she's not fared well from contact with the sons of the 'She Wolf.'"

Baldor nodded. Rome and all she stood for seemed to be a blight on the world with their seemingly insatiable greed for land and power; she was a bad or bullying neighbour to those close by and enemies to everyone. Not seeking to question Andulas further on Cassia, he changed the subject back to Thaddeus.

"So, it seems we must seek another way to Lasairiona?"

Andulas turned to Baldor and growled. "Next time it'll be force Baldor, if the fat bastard won't give her up we'll take her."

"We'll need a lot more men then, I counted two score of guards and there may be more."

"Aye, we'll bring more men and may have to wait a while as well, until the General has bested Minucius."

"It'll be bloody in there, not a lot of space to fight. You'll remember the fighting in the houses at Victumulae?" Baldor said quietly and shuddered at the grim memory. "I was hoping to just pay for her. I don't understand him; with that many women slaves what difference does selling another one make? Baal knows the ones he showed us were beautiful."

"It's all about power Baldor. He will do as he pleases because he can, well thinks he can, at least until we show him different. Furthermore, Lasairiona is both beautiful and a Princess ..."

"Your people would not term her such though!"

"No, we wouldn't. To us she certainly has high status, she's important, aristocracy if you like but to a Roman or whatever that slug of a man is, a Princess describes her and to have such under your control is obviously powerful and intoxicating for him."

"If he's touched her I'll kill the bastard." Baldor growled.

Andulas was about to reply then quickly changed tack. "Going back to needing more men, I don't think we'll need the whole troop. Those guards of his are numerous but not professional warriors, some were old and the rest had that look of soft town guards, once our lads are in amongst them they won't be too difficult to kill, there's a big difference between beating slaves and fighting warriors."

"It's getting in there that could be costly."

Andulas smiled. "Leave that with me, I have another plan for that. We've tried a peaceful solution, next time … well, next time we'll do something different."

"What's the plan?"

He tapped his nose with his finger, chuckled and pushed his empty plate away. "I'll tell you tomorrow on the way back to camp. Right now, I need some sleep."

Baldor placed a hand across Andulas's forearm. "Thank you for all the help, for everything!"

"No need to thank me Baldor, we're brothers remember and like you I want to even the score with this Thaddeus. Those girls I bought today are Lingone, my people, and that fat bastard is going to pay. No one enslaves my people."

Chapter Eleven

Thaddeus heaved Arya off his lap. His overweight frame damp with sweat from the exertions of pleasure, she displaying a petulant pout at hers being cut short.

"Gods above girl you're Siren … a witch, another Circe!" He gasped.

"How so, My Lord." She purred while lowering her eyes seductively. "I don't sing, and I don't have my own island." She laughed softly.

He mopped at his sweat-beaded brow with her discarded dress. "You're insatiable! A damned temptress! A Harpie with a Nymph's body and thus I cannot let you be. You'll be the death of me!"

"But you have the choice of any woman in the house, and many are beautiful are they not? I know a certain redhead has caught your eye?" Her lip curled into a slight snarl.

Thaddeus sneered. "Maybe but she needs breaking first, I'm too old to be fighting and struggling with her before I plough her, I'm not a young man anymore."

"You know I can help you with that."

"Yes, my dear I know you can, and you will. We'll have some fun with our Gallic Princess; your talent for inflicting pain is almost as intoxicating as your body, almost!"

"When?" She asked, giving a seductive pout and trying to climb back on his lap.

He pushed her off. "When I say girl and when I can get our Princess away from my wife."

Arya went quiet at the mention of Thaddeus's wife though her face darkened into a mask of hatred. She collected the dress from the settle, her passion gone cold. "If you're done with me sir, may I have your leave to go?"

"No! You may not have my leave to go. Come here …" He patted the settle next to him. "And leave your dress off." Arya dropped the dress and sat; he pulled her close across his chest enjoying the smell of the perfume on her heated skin. "Now, my little Syrian demon, what are we going to do about my wife?"

Arya looked up, puzzled. "Your wife?"

"Yes, the wizened, cold bitch needs to go."

"Go?"

"Yes! Go … go away, die!" He said matter-of-factly. "She's preventing our pleasures, well some of them." He slapped at her buttocks playfully. "And if she catches you with me again I think that last whipping she gave you will pale to insignificance to what she will do to you then."

"Surely … surely you would protect me?"

"Oh, I would like to but she's fierce! Too fierce for me." He chuckled, feigning fear. "Which is why I need your help, your knowledge."

"Help? Help for what?" She asked quietly.

"To get rid of my wife."

Arya sat bolt upright and looked around the room, her fear reducing her words to a whispered hiss. "But … but I have no knowledge of such things! My knowledge, my skills are of inflicting pain, not …"

Thaddeus hooted and chuckled. "Come Arya; don't be so modest! Anyone who can inflict pain like you will know of ways to go a step further."

"But … that would be murder!"

"No Arya, not murder just removal of a pest." He said nonchalantly. "And Jupiter knows these last few years has seen my dear wife assuming that role. What was once a beautiful, seductive woman has now become an angry, frigid old bitch, a pest! A pest that forces me to seek my pleasure elsewhere and even then tries to prevent it! So Arya, how do we remove our pest?"

"Sir, I will do anything for you but this, this is …"

"Necessary! For I will not give you up … well, until I choose to, or my wife deals with you." He chuckled as he saw Arya's eyes widen in fear. "I wager it's only a matter of time before she catches you in my rooms again and then … well?" He raised his eyebrows and sighed. "Still, it's your hide I suppose?"

Arya shuddered as she remembered the whipping, the whipping that had seen her screaming and begging for mercy and which had only ceased when the older women was exhausted. Perhaps next time Thaddeus's wife might just have her killed, for she was no concubine and the Lady was clearly not going to be embarrassed again. She had no status being just a slave herself, albeit a highly privileged one but only as long as her Master found her useful or until he tired of her. Feeling trapped between a rock and a hard place she quickly considered her options. If she didn't help, the very least outcome could see her fall from favour and end up back in the communal slave quarters where she was hated. Hated, for the punishments she devised and inflicted on the other slaves to please her Master when he deemed they required reprimanding. Slaves, she knew had their own ways of settling scores. At worst, Thaddeus could just have her quietly killed and as she now knew of his intentions towards his wife that was the most probable outcome. Her only option it seemed, as risky as it was, was to assist him.

"Sir, I …"

"Yes! Go on."

"I … I think …" She struggled trying to find the words that wouldn't make it seem like her suggestion before speaking in a whisper. "Poison … poison is a common, usually untraceable method; I've seen it used in my homeland."

"H'mm, it's quick I presume? I'm not a cruel man Arya; I wouldn't want the old hag to suffer … much!" He chuckled.

"It can be very quick yes, else done slowly over time if you are patient."

"I'm not a patient man, Arya."

"But people talk sir, slaves especially! Moreover, most here are well aware of why your wife whipped me. Talk would become suspicion, especially if the lady is seen well one day then dead the next and as I intimated, many in the house are aware that you and she are estranged."

"Estranged eh? No, I just hate the bitch!" Arya paled at the venom in his voice. "Go on!" He snapped.

"However, …" Her voice dried in her throat. "However, if a small, careful dose is given over time it brings sickness and debilitation and forces the victim to take to their bed; it can then look like a natural illness."

"So, either the original dose does its work slowly or extra doses are applied if needed."

"Yes sir."

"See Arya! You do have the knowledge! I knew you would know." He patted her shoulder commendably. "Now, which poison and how much?"

Arya, dropping her reluctance committed. "There are many sir, most are obtainable from simple everyday plants or flowers, being beautiful blooms to look at doesn't mean they are not deadly."

"Not unlike yourself, Arya." He smiled. "Go on ... which plant, where from, how large a dose and when?"

"Some grow here in your garden; there is Arum, Foxglove, Hemlock, and Aconitum and ..."

"My, my Arya, you are quite the expert! I shall have to be careful around you, who knows? You may seek to poison me instead?"

Arya almost choked. "Never sir, no, no ... I wouldn't think ..."

"No, and you'd better not my dear. For should I fall ill I will see to it that you accompany me to the grave." He twisted his hand in her hair making her wince then kissed her head. "Which one is best, untraceable?"

"Aconitum is the deadliest so maybe too quick. I would use Arum in small doses over time."

"How long?"

"I don't know." He twisted her hair again making her gasp then move as he dragged her close. "I don't know sir, I'm sorry I don't know."

"Ah well, we shall find out." He said resignedly. "How?"

"I would add it to food, honey or garum are both good choices."

Thaddeus laughed lightly. "Garum, how ironic! Some say that garum has healing properties. Put it in either then for my wife enjoys both. Will the dose be liquid or powder form?"

"The Arum flowers are gone with the summer otherwise I would have steeped the petals and taken the juice. Autumn has brought the berries, if I harvest those and take the seeds they can be dried and ground up very finely; the powder can be hidden easily within the food and the sweet or strong flavours will help mask any taste."

"Excellent Arya, excellent! Your wickedness always gives me an appetite, now come show me some of your other skill." He pulled her roughly onto his lap again. "Come Circe, pleasure me!"

****

Cornelius frowned and shook his head as Gaius relayed the news that had arrived in camp along with the return of Fabius.

"Can the senate do that, appoint Minucius a joint Dictator? Anyway, what's the point? It sounds just like the usual two Consul command again!"

Gaius shrugged. "They can't remove the title of Dictator from Fabius during his term of office. However, they see that last action by Minucius outside Geronium as a victory, so the same army with a different General has produced a better result, hence this promotion."

"Playing bloody politics more like! Useless, lard-arsed bastards!" Cornelius spat.

"Hey lad! Show some respect! There are some old soldiers, good men amongst them not all are timeservers, and politics or not we need to keep trying things. Moreover, and think on; between Fabius and Minucius we have caution tempered with opportunism."

"Do we? This sounds just like what has gone before."

"No, I disagree I think Minucius is a trier and he's not reckless like Tiberius or rash like Flaminius turned out to be. The way I see it, Minucius is trying when he thinks he has opportunity and as you saw he came very close to good success outside Geronium. Furthermore, Fabius will fight if the conditions and time are right, for as I told you before he's no milksop."

"I'm not arguing that Gaius, it's this business of two commanders that I don't understand. Very seldom will two men act as one, especially when prestige or glory are waiting for the victor."

"Well, that's the way it is, always has been."

"Why? Because the senate fears that one man may overreach himself?"

"Maybe? Probably!" He answered tetchily. "We … Rome will not tolerate the rule of Kings, you know that!" Fast growing weary of debating issues outside his control his tone was growing terse.

"It was a bold move electing a Dictator then, if Fabius had destroyed Hannibal what would they have done then, remove him, ere success went to his head? Is he just left in place now to control Minucius should he become successful and over mighty?"

Gaius just sighed. "I don't know Cornelius! I'm a bloody soldier not a politician or a thinker I just do my job as best I can."

Cornelius, lost in his own concerns and frustration grumbled on. "Can it get any worse?"

"Humph! It might."

"How so?"

"Well … just like two Consuls, Fabius and Minucius have the choice of alternate daily command or splitting the army into two. Minucius has opted to split.

"No! No! Oh, for the love of …"

Gaius held up his hand to quieten Cornelius, his patience worn thin from the younger man's pessimism and grumbles. "That aside! Our orders are we, being the second legion plus the third legion, along with two auxiliary legions are with Minucius, legions one and four and the other two auxiliary legions are with Fabius. We march now to separate camps."

"Gods above! Dividing an army in the face of your enemy, Hannibal will love that; he'll chop us into carrion food!"

"Enough of that talk, Centurion!" Gaius growled. "We didn't have the whole army deployed at Geronium and that fight was a close-run thing … and you know that as well as I do! Furthermore, I've told you before Hannibal did not and will not prove infallible. If the Carthaginian reinforcements hadn't arrived we would have been through their lines and into Geronium, Minucius was just unlucky."

Cornelius, seemingly oblivious to the warning signs of his friend and superior officer's rising ire blundered on. "He should have forced the issue quicker then."

"Bloody easy to say lad! However, there's a huge difference between commanding a century and commanding an army."

Cornelius persisted. "Maybe but splitting the army! It's bloody madness! It's …"

"It is what it is, Centurion." Gaius shouted. "Damn you man! And damn your bloody pessimism!" He slammed his fist hard onto the small table, tumbling wine cups and making Cornelius jump.

Cornelius, finally recognising he was overstepping the mark of military protocol immediately deferred to his senior officer.

"My apologies sir, our orders?"

Gaius took a moment to calm himself and lower his voice. "We have a short march south at midday for a mile and a half or so then we will set up camp. That way, one camp can quickly offer support to the other should the Carthaginians come calling."

"Yes sir." Cornelius was on his feet now and at attention.

"You have men to see to get to it!"

"Yes sir." Cornelius saluted and turned to go then stopped and turned back. Gaius just glowered at him.

"Yes!"

"Sir, I'm sorry. I forget myself sometimes."

"That you do! And regardless of being young, frustrated with events and of good family does not excuse you!"

"Yes sir, I mean no sir, it does not. My apologies again sir."

"I'll see you on the march, dismissed!"

****

The moment Baldor dismounted, Issa was at his feet her tail wagging and body swaying in excitement.

"Steady girl, steady!" He said, squatting to stroke and ruffle her head and ears.

"You were quick, all good?" Armaco asked anxiously as he stepped out of the tent, his eyes scanning and counting the arriving men and folk in the cart.

"All good, just empty handed." Baldor replied while patting Issa as she continued pushing against his legs seeking fuss.

"Where's the lady? Where's Andulas?"

Baldor shook his head. "Lasairiona is still in Casilinum, Andulas won't be long." Placing his arm over Armaco's shoulder, he steered him back into the tent. "We need to think anew and Andulas has another plan. What of yourself, any changes since I left?"

"I was summoned this morning to a meeting at the General's tent. Battle's coming and I think within a day or two at the very most as there's been decisive developments in the Roman command."

"We're involved?"

"Oh yes! And playing a prime role."

Baldor smiled mischievously. "Has our return robbed you of your chance to show your mettle?"

Armaco however, remained serious. "If I'm honest, I'm glad you're back."

"Come on Armaco, you're a better warrior than I and your experience much greater!"

"More battle experience perhaps but I've never commanded this number of men before."

"Hannibal obviously doesn't doubt you otherwise he wouldn't have offered you the command."

"It's not so much the number of men I suppose; it's more the nature of what we he wants us to do."

"Which is what?"

"He's baiting a trap for Minucius." Armaco flicked his head towards the table then steered Baldor to a large map showing the surrounding terrain. "Here's our camp." He pointed. "Fabius's camp is here and Minucius's here, I'll explain that later. The proposed battle site or area of entrapment is here and isn't far from either Roman camp or ours. The General is using five thousand infantry and our whole troop of horse, of which he said he'd make up to our usual strength of five hundred owing to our wounded and sickness numbers. We'll spring the trap from here." He traced a finger over places and features on the map. "He's placing a contingent of light infantry on this small hill here as bait and he wants us here!" His finger traced to either side of the proposed light infantry's position.

"What's so important about the light infantry? What's the attraction of them as bait?"

"This slightly elevated position lets them oversee Minucius's camp and all that goes on. The General thinks it's bound to enrage him and as they're only light infantry and seemingly unsupported, they'll look like easy meat. Apparently, our lads coming too close to the Roman camp is what set off that last fight."

"Where do we fit in and where do we hide? There's no forest marked here that I can see."

Armaco chuckled and tapped his nose. "You'll see."

Baldor looked at the map and the features marked on it, while listening carefully without further interruption as Armaco outlined the plan of action.

"H'mm. I like it!" He said as Armaco finished. "And the weather is still kind, not too cold … You would have managed this all right!" He said confidently while placing his hand on Armaco's shoulder.

"Maybe? However, you know me; I'm the warrior that's in your face, head on, I don't think I'd be much good at this covert waiting game."

"Armaco, you're one of the bravest, fiercest warriors I've seen, you lead your contingent well, very well."

"Maybe, but action, impulse, the fight is what I crave and can handle but I swear my nerves would struggle with this."

"Don't doubt yourself brother, no one else does. We all prefer and love the outspoken belligerent, Armaco."

"All the same, I'm glad you're back and can take command again."

"Do I need to see Hannibal at all?"

"No, he said if you returned in time I was to brief you and hand over command, if you didn't I was to carry on."

"See Armaco, that's trust!" Armaco blushed slightly making Baldor chuckle. "You'll be with us though, yes."

"Of course!" He snapped then smiled. "I'm your guard dog remember."

Baldor smiled. "Aye, you're that all right. Baal bless you brother!"

"Don't you mention my misgivings to Andulas?" He said aggressively.

Baldor smiled again. "No, I wouldn't dare, you'd thump me!"

Armaco sniggered. "Where is he anyway?"

"Seeing to the slaves we bought." He sighed. "It's been an expensive exercise and with no real result, well apart from two of the women who turned out to be Lingone, so Andulas is pleased their freedom is secured."

"His heart is as big as he is!"

"True, his anger is also fearsome to see."

"I know I've seen him in battle."

"No, I don't mean that kind of anger."

"How mean you then?"

"Well, as we talked and planned on the way back to camp and he expounded his idea for another attempt to release Lasairiona, I could see his mind was elsewhere. When I probed, the way he answered made my blood run cold."

Armaco stepped close. "Why, what did he say?"

"It wasn't so much what he said but how he said it. There was no hot, angry promise to kill this Thaddeus; instead, he spoke quietly but with a chilling, cold finality. Honestly Armaco, the words felt colder, harsher than a stone tomb, it's how I imagine a vengeful ghost or demon would speak if they came to wreak havoc on the living."

"What's irked him so badly?"

"It seems this Thaddeus is a dead man for making slaves of Andulas's people and for him having to play the part of a Cenomani Lord."

Armaco frowned seeming confused. "But it's just a tribal name! Granted it's a bad one, especially when you are Lingone but? … And slavery is well, common!"

"I know but I tell you it's gotten to him. You and I have heard and seen many angry men, heard many threats but this; this cold, hard anger was more frightening. I tell you; I wouldn't want to be in this Thaddeus's shoes."

Armaco shook his head slightly. "Gauls usually go battle mad, they don't care, that's un-nerving enough."

"Exactly Armaco but if you'd heard him." Baldor shuddered.

"He's all right now?"

"Yes, he seemed to come back from wherever his mind was, the coldness went and he was like the Andulas we know and love again. Full of plans and ideas, good company."

"What's his plan this time?"

"Pour me a drink then I'll tell you, I won't be long."

"Baal Almighty! Where are you going now, you've just got back?"

"Issa will need a quick walk, or she'll be pissing on your gear again."

"Already done."

"What?"

"Issa and I have been out twice this morning."

"But you said …"

"That she's not just your dog! … Are you Issa?"

The two men laughed while Issa looked on wagging her tail before running to her bed and bringing a short, knotted rope to the men so to play. Baldor indulged her as he drank, she tugging hard on the rope and emitting playful growls while he explained Andulas's plan to Armaco.

The following evening just as twilight came Harbro, Malo and one hundred and ninety cavalrymen appeared outside Andulas's tent, Harbro dismounted and embraced Baldor.

"The General sent us to make up numbers!" Harbro laughed as he offered his hand to Armaco and Andulas. Malo, still atop his horse held his hand over his heart and bowed his head while muttering a blessing.

"Welcome brothers, welcome!" Baldor smiled warmly. "We're ready, we'll collect my lads at the camp gate and follow you shortly. He slipped his helmet on, it purposely smoke blackened to reduce any glare, his nose and cheekbones blackened with soot to darken his face.

An infantry detachment came past at broken step. They like their cavalry brothers, dressed in dark clothing with bare skin blackened and weapon hilts and shields wrapped in cloth to guard against rattles and scrapes.

"That's the fourth lot we've seen go past." Andulas said.

"The General's releasing them in small detachments throughout the night. Five thousand men plus us is a lot to move into position before sun-up." Armaco replied as he pulled himself onto his mount.

"Aye, let's thank the Gods for these longer autumn nights; we wouldn't have managed this manoeuvre in the summer … but at least it'll be warmer than the last time you did this, Baldor?" Harbro chuckled.

Baldor grimaced. "Aye, that winter's night by the Trebia, brrr! But let's hope it works as well as last time."

"The numbers against us are much less methinks? The General thinks we'll only have Minucius and his legions to contend with as Fabius will hopefully again do nothing."

"As long as the Romans keep dividing their legions I'm a happy man." Baldor replied as he reached for his horse's reins.

"Baal bless and keep you all." Harbro said as he mounted. "If you don't find us on the field in this murk we'll see you in the morn."

Returning the blessing, Baldor watched Harbro's men move off, their horse's hooves covered in cloth or sacking the animal's steps nothing more than a muffled drone.

Chapter Twelve

The night was cloudless and clear with only a faint light from a pale, crescent moon and the sky studded with stars. The day's warmth had disappeared soon after sunset and the temperature was dropping, thankfully, it was dry and looked to remain that way. A low voice spoke out of the dark and Baldor instinctively snatched for a falcata, a scout appeared and stepped close while muttering the password and Baldor relaxed.

"This way sir." He whispered and reached to take the bridle of Baldor's mount.

The man led off, steering the horse away from the dirt track they'd been following with Baldor's men close behind. He led faultlessly, with no pauses or backtracking, Baldor quietly marvelling at the man's uncanny ability to navigate in the dark. The ground began to rise gently becoming rougher and broken in places where wind and water erosion had scarred it, huge rocks poked out of the ground here and there like broken teeth. The silhouettes of stunted bushes, gorse, bramble and scrub dotted the darkened sward, some patches large and dense enough to force the horses to walk around. The scout led them sharply to one side skirting a large and deep depression in the grass, Baldor looked down into the hole's blackness and became aware of the dim shapes of men, all laid flat on their bellies and lining the sides of it, within moments he'd passed four more similar features, also full of men. Weaving around more and more of the features he recognised these holes or natural drains as the symbols he'd seen marked on Armaco's map; they dotted the ground like pockmarks on a disease-ravaged face. Most were quite deep, twice the height of a man and some held water, now thankfully shallow owing to the long hot summer and very dry autumn. The infantrymen were packed into these features, each holding as many men as possible and who would remain undetectable unless you were at the very edge of the drain hole.

The scout led on and up a gentle incline to a flat crest, some of the horses stumbling and slipping as their sack-covered hooves struggled to find purchase on the night-dampened grass. He turned sharply to one side again into a deep scar that ran at a right angle down the edge of the opposite slope away from the crest. This deep gouge, naturally formed by millennia of wind and draining water tilted slightly back from the hillside like a cambered roadway. Urging Baldor to dismount, the scout walked the horse a few paces into it, stopping as its nose neared the bankside rising again in front of them. Above them, the top edge formed a small, scrub-lined overhang blocking some of the view of the night sky. This recess, just higher than a fighting spear cut into and down the contour of the slope for just over a stade, the men and horses following Baldor filed past and settled into it as if it was a long stable, the feature like a one-walled corridor cut into the hillside.

"This is you, Captain. You can't be seen from above, in fact unless someone comes right over and looks in, they won't be able to see you at all. It runs down this slope for two hundred paces or so and should shelter all your men, Captain Harbro's men are in a rocky defile directly opposite you, the infantry bait will be above and between you on the crest." He pointed off into the darkness. "As you've seen, the reserve infantry are scattered in the drains and hidden in the rocks behind you on this side of the hill with more secreted close to Captain Harbro's men."

Baldor sought the man's hand, shaking it. "Thank you that was well led!"

"No problem sir, will you excuse me while I go back for the others, we still have a great deal to do before sunup."

Baldor clapped the man on the shoulder then quietly passed the order for his men to settle in, sending Andulas along the line to count all were present, he had Armaco set the watch roster.

Andulas, finding the men closely packed but settling quietly to wait was back quickly reporting that all were present and surprisingly without injury. Stepping cautiously in the gloom, he unfastened a bag from his horse's tack and eased down alongside Baldor and Armaco while giving a sigh as his back found support against the dirt wall.

"Struggling a bit, old man?" Armaco quipped and he and Baldor chuckled.

"Aye, it's from carrying you two on my back all the time!"

"Oh! He's sharp for a Gallic farmer." Armaco retorted.

"Sharp enough to bring extra food and drink too! It's going to be a long night." Andulas opened a package containing cold meats and fresh bread that still held a hint of warmth and smell. "And an even longer time until we get fed again methinks; I imagine breakfast may be cancelled?"

"I've got dry meat sticks." Baldor chirped.

Armaco was quiet. The silence finally prompting him to speak. "I ate before we left."

"Well!" Andulas said smoothly. "Baldor, enjoy your meat sticks, Armaco, enjoy your full belly. And here's me thinking you two would have brought food to share. Ah well! Seeing as you're both replete it looks like the old man dines alone!" The two men swore softly as Andulas began to eat. "H'mm delicious!" He smacked his lips appreciatively. "So, let me see, what skills do we have between us and our return to camp? Baldor has command and jerked meat while Armaco isn't hungry but will teach us how to fight. However, it seems that Andulas the farmer came prepared and knows how to dine. And see, there's wine too! Watered maybe but it's nicer than just plain water I'll warrant. Still, seeing as you are both comfortable I may as well slip these other two cups back into my pack." He let the silence prevail for a while as he chewed and gave satisfactory sighs then another exaggerated smack of the lips after taking a draught of wine. Eventually, unable to hold his mirth any longer he chuckled then laughed. "Here! You pair of bloody miscreants, help yourselves, I've enough here for the three of us. If we fight tomorrow, at least it won't be on empty stomachs, the old man will provide." Eager hands reached into the package while Andulas chuckled again. "Apparently age brings not only wisdom but food and wine as well!"

After eating, the men stretched out as best they could and sought sleep or at least rest. The night was quiet other than the natural noises of nocturnal animals going about their business. In the distance, a fox barked then a rooting boar passed close by, all grunts and snuffles, its scent unsettling the horses until it moved on. A screech owl flew overhead on noiseless wings, its sudden piercing shriek making men jump. Men slept or talked in low whispers as they waited for dawn to come, their hand or foot keeping a hold on their mount's reins. Well before dawn, the temperature dropped again and the dewfall whitened becoming frost and crisping the grass. Men huddled closer together and nearer to the bankside while wrapping themselves in heavy cloaks against the cold, those with gloves slipped them on.

Dawn broke with a watery sunrise and cloudless skies, the air sharp and cold, the surrounding area heavily dusted in white frost. Breath from both horses and men made bloated, white vapour clouds that dissipated only slowly as the morning was windless and still. Men groaned softly as they stood to stretch and relieve cold, cramped limbs. Some, needing to piss did it where they stood ensuring they kept well within the cover of the scar, others were already seeking their cold breakfast. Baldor cast his eyes across the area and could see no one, just the occasional vapour cloud rising from the drains or broken areas where men laid hidden. His concern at that being seen was quickly allayed when he noticed the small stream also emitted a constant vapour as the sun slowly began to warm the land. Movement to their rear caught his eye and he nudged Andulas and Armaco and nodded in the direction.

"Here's the bait coming."

A regiment of Spanish caetrati approached, advancing at double step and making for the hillcrest above and between Baldor and Harbro's positions and the hidden pockets of infantry. A huge cloud of vapour hung above them as their hard worked lungs and bodies sent hot breath and sweated steam into the frigid morning air.

"Let's see what Minucius does now, anyone keen for a wager?" Andulas said quietly.

"Let's hope he does something; I wouldn't like to think we've laid here all night for nothing." Armaco grumbled as he rubbed his hands together briskly.

"We'll know soon enough I reckon." Baldor added. "And I'll take a wager Andulas, that Minucius reacts quickly as he finally has the unrestrained power he's sought and here's the opportunity to use it."

The three men watched as the Spaniards wove their way through the rocks and around the drains and broken ground to begin ascending the gently rising hill. The men were a blaze of colour against the frost-white grass, their heads covered in leather hoods topped with scarlet horsehair crests, tunic's bright white and edged with a wide, crimson or blue stripe. They carried small, brightly painted shields and a handful of javelins, their banners and standards waving above their heads.

"It's a good show; the Romans will see them all right."

"Aye, Andulas and they're wicked buggers too, fast and deadly, I was certainly impressed with them that night on the saddle. They might have little armour, but they are well armed with javelins, sword and shield, give me a Spanish caetratus over a Roman velite any day."

"They're still only light troops though; let's hope Minucius doesn't send legionaries to move them."

"Why would he, Armaco? The ground is not ideal for heavy infantry and apparently he doesn't rate us as warriors anyway, he'll send his velites to try and move them."

The Spaniards reached the crown of the hill between Baldor and Harbro's men and crowded across it, their banners planted in full view for all to see. The sun rose behind them glinting off metal and highlighting the colourfully dressed warriors against the whitened grass. A drone of trumpets from the Roman camp had the three men look at each other and smile.

"Gods above! That hasn't taken long, Minucius is hungry all right. I wonder what his plan of attack is. What if he sends equites or auxiliary cavalry to try to move the Spaniards rather than velites? They would be quick and Minucius will know the Spaniards don't fight in close order?" Andulas ventured.

"He might, for the ground isn't steep at all for cavalry but it's well broken so he'd have to throw in some infantry support. No, my money's still on velites, it's what he does from there that's going to be interesting."

"Well, whatever's coming it'll be coming quick so we'd best eat while we can … Oh! No comments lads?" Andulas chuckled as he refilled the three small wine cups again and opened his pack offering food once more. "Best way I suppose. As my mother always says, let your meat stop your mouth!"

The usual pre-battle fidget began amongst the men. Some ate and drank; some quietly prayed while others began checking their weapons. Baldor, remembering advice from Gestix about frosty weather and sticking sword blades, slid each falcata a hand's breadth in and out of their scabbards then tried his dagger checking their removal remained smooth.

"I think we may have some time to wait yet if Hannibal wants the whole of Minucius's army engaged." Baldor said as he pulled and chewed without enjoyment on a piece of hardening bread. "I don't imagine he'll send all his men just to move the Spaniards so it may be a long wait?"

Andulas immediately pulled the wine and food away. "If we aren't going to be home for the midday meal I'd better keep this lot for myself!" He chuckled as he saw momentary disappointment on Armaco and Baldor's faces. "An old man has to keep his strength up you know." Then immediately offered the food back. "Eat up brothers, don't be hungry, you can't fight on empty bellies."

Armaco growled his thanks while tearing at the meat and the now hardening bread, Baldor politely refusing any more food as he felt his guts begin to heave, his appetite suddenly gone, though he reached for another cup of wine.

Before long, the men heard the Spaniards begin to shout their battle cries. The singular yells gradually changing to a chanted crescendo with weapons hammered on shields in time to it. A responding roar told of the enemy advancing to the attack, the air suddenly filled with the whoosh of javelins as they loosed in their hundreds. Before the exchange of javelins was exhausted and battle proper commenced, Baldor and his men saw more regiments of light infantry already making their way to support the Spaniards from the rear.

"It would be good to see what's happening." Armaco grumbled. "I'm not keen on this hiding away and waiting thing, especially when I can't see those Roman bastards!"

The battle noise changed to the clash of metal and the dull thump and thud of weapons hitting shields, punctuated with shouts and screams as the two sides went hand to hand. As the first of the reinforcements joined the Spaniards and swelled their ranks there was another huge roar and the fighting clamour slowly moved off and away, the noise diminishing.

"I guess that's the velites pushed back." Andulas smiled.

The shouts and sounds of battle faded then stopped. The Spaniards and their reinforcements, after seeing the velites off, moved back to their original position atop the crest, where they took a moment to rest and drink and to see to their wounded. Moments later, there was commotion and surprised shouts from the far end of the line of Baldor's men. Dropping the cup and cursing, he dashed in the direction of the noise drawing a falcata as he went. He arrived just as three velites went down to multiple stab wounds from a group of his men, one of them holding their hand over the last velite's mouth as he died under half-a-dozen savage blade thrusts.

"What in Baal's name happened?" Baldor snapped as he stared at the bloodied bodies laid in the grass. "Where did they come from?"

"They just appeared Captain; they must have been looking to hide when they were pushed back by the Spaniards."

"Did any get away, did any others see you?" He asked anxiously.

"We don't think so sir, we just heard fast footfalls then these three appeared around the end of the scar. They seemed totally surprised to find us here but we killed them quick enough."

Baldor stepped around the bodies then dropped to his belly cautiously peering around the edge of the scar. There was no one close; the velites were already some distance away and still falling back, with no sign of any others close to the Carthaginian position. Easing back out of sight, he stood and called his men close.

"There'll be more attacks coming and we may not move for a while yet, stay vigilant and be ready should any others seek to hide, we must, remain undetected."

A chorus of quiet 'yes sir' came back at him.

"Well done, lads!" He patted the two men nearest him on the shoulders then somewhat relieved made his way back towards Andulas and Armaco. Before long, trumpets blew again and the Spaniards took up their weapons once more as orders to 'Stand-to' rapped out, the Romans were coming again and this time the rumble of hooves could be heard.

Back at his position, Baldor could feel the unrest in his men; the quiet talk had stopped as men listened to the fighting beginning again in front of them but out of sight. The horses picked up on the men's trepidation and showed it with stomping and head tossing, some even pulling hard on their reins and having to be calmed, they too it seemed keen to move. He too was becoming edgy; this waiting did nothing for the nerves. Far better to be in action he thought, when the fear was replaced by a fierce need to survive, when all you thought about was the fight. When would they be called to help?

"Look!" Andulas said and nodded to their rear. "Things are moving fast."

Regiments of Numidian light horse were now racing towards the Spaniards and in their wake came the heavy Libyan cavalry.

"When do we move?" Armaco growled.

"No word yet."

"Gods above! How much bloody longer." He groaned and spat.

A lone horseman broke off from the heavy cavalry, it was the scout who'd brought them to the scar the night before, he reined up in front of Baldor.

"General's compliments sir …"

"Are we to go?" Baldor interrupted anxiously.

"No, not yet sir. The General asks that you remain hidden for the moment, the Romans have dispatched their cavalry, you probably heard them coming towards the Spaniards and we are responding." He pointed to the Carthaginian cavalry. "We'll fight them to a stalemate else hurl them back as the General wants their legions to come up in support before he releases you. When your men and the infantry erupt from the sides of the battlefield and hit their flanks, he's sure the Romans will panic, and then we can destroy them."

"What of Fabius though, is he making any move to intervene?"

"Not that we've seen sir, his camp has gone on alert and his men are marshalling but that's it. We can see Minucius assembling his legions and as I said the General's hopeful he'll push them forward in support of the cavalry."

Baldor nodded and raised his hands waving his expectant men back into cover of the scar.

"Andulas, pass the word it won't be too long before we move, we are just waiting on the rest of the Roman army arriving." He sobered as he realised what he'd said. This battle was growing and looking to become a race as well as a gamble. Hannibal, cunning as ever had fed just sufficient men to fight the Romans to an impasse or push them back and to which Minucius had responded with more troops, the two sides counter moving. Now, Hannibal had to hope Minucius's ego would see him release the legions to attack so the trap could be sprung, while also gambling that Fabius would once again do nothing. The scout drew Baldor's attention back.

"I'll come for you sir the moment it's time."

Baldor nodded and stepped back into the scar, his nerves on the raw. His men were quiet again, many now at their prayers. Andulas crouched, his eyes closed and his fingers gently rubbing a small bronze figurine of a lady on a horse. Baldor heard him quietly intoning his pleas to Epona to spare him and his friends in the battle to come. Armaco was looking skyward and mumbling softly though he spoke too quietly for Baldor to hear what he said.

With the risk of mortality coming close it brought a forlorn emptiness for him as he had no devotions to make, his anger at the divine still strong. It brought along with it a pang of guilt as he had no prayers to offer for his friend's lives, yet he knew they would be praying for him. Should he pray for them regardless? After all, it was his fight. His anger alone at the Gods for what had gone before not theirs, but would the Gods judge him a charlatan? As he thought, he fingered the cameo at his neck then lifted it to kiss it. His mind then thought of Lasairiona, how was she faring, was she even still alive? Was he being false to the memory of his dead wife by thinking of this new woman? He groaned inwardly and swore under his breath. Alone and with no answers to either dilemma, he sneered at himself then moved his thoughts to the fight.

He knew that surprised or not, fighting legionaries would not be easy. If their formations were not disrupted by the terrain and remained solid, he'd need his infantry comrades to smash holes in their ranks to let his cavalrymen through. Still, he thought, the ground is not the best, being an incline, rough and broken and all soldiers feared being attacked in the flank, especially when you have the enemy in front of you as well. Once the command came to go, the Romans would be attacked in both flanks by infantry and cavalry but would it be enough?

It was midmorning before the scout appeared again. He came at the gallop, reins lashing either side of the mount's flanks for speed.

"Captain! … Captain! Now's your time!" He called before he reached Baldor's position.

As anxious as he was, Baldor took some comfort that action was here at last.

"Mount up! … Mount up!" He called as he dashed a few paces from his position making sure his orders were heard and passed on. Grabbing for his mount's reins, he had Andulas's hand pushed forward seeking his.

"Epona keep you Baldor." The big Gaul smiled and dipped his head.

Grasping the hand and feeling thoughtless for not wishing his friend well, Baldor dropped his reins and threw his arms over the Gaul's shoulders. "And you brother, Epona and Baal keep you safe." Turning, he sought Armaco and hugged him close, not caring that his rough mannered friend found affection awkward. "Baal and Tannith bless you, brother."

"And you Baldor."

The three managed tight smiles then mounted, each calling for his unit. The scar emptied like a city's cavalry barracks on parade day as men and horses sought their officer and assembled behind him, the atmosphere a mixture of tension and fear tempered with release, the horses skittish, stomping and jostling nervously. All over the field and hillside men appeared as if by magic. The holes, drains and rocks in the field spewed infantry as hundreds of men climbed out of the ground and from hidden crevices, their officers leading them off the moment a unit was complete.

With battle cries and roars filling the air, the secreted infantry burst into view of the embattled Romans and charged the legions flanks. Attacking from both sides and with more and more men arriving they flowed around the Roman rear enveloping them.

Cornelius and his century were not yet engaged but pressing forward towards the Spaniards on the hillcrest directly in front of them, the numbers of which seemed to be multiplying alarmingly. Hearing a huge roar to his left like an approaching thunderstorm, he turned to see masses of Carthaginian infantry charging towards his flank, he seized his trumpeter.

"Left face! Left face!" He screamed as he pointed and pulled the man around to see. The trumpeter's eyes went wide as he saw hundreds then thousands of the enemy running towards them as he filled his cheeks to blow. Cornelius was already bellowing the command to his men. "Left face! Shields up! … Close up!"

Javelins landed amongst his men hitting many before they could raise their shields or even realise what was happening. His voice was lost in the noise and the trumpet blast and then the Carthaginian infantry hit his flank. The charge forced into gaps torn in the Roman line by the javelins destroying order and cohesion in the ranks. With their lines punctured the legionaries grouped together where they could, standing shoulder to shoulder or back-to-back as the Carthaginians swarmed around them. Cornelius looked past the infantry and saw cavalry appearing close behind.

"Juno, mother of us all, have mercy!"

The cavalry followed their infantry riding into and widening any gaps in the decimated Roman lines.

A huge roar from the Roman right flank saw more Carthaginian infantry and cavalry appear as if from nowhere and launch themselves at the Roman lines. Cornelius's head flicked cockerel like. The Carthaginians were everywhere, at the Roman front, the flanks and spilling around the rear and seemed to be increasing in numbers, the sons of the 'She Wolf' were trapped again. Horrified at the chaos unfolding around him he fought the panic rising in his chest and seized his standard-bearer, pushing him next to the trumpeter while calling to the men closest to him.

"Back! … Back! Protect the Signum! … Sound the stand! … Stand!" He yelled at the trumpeter.

The man began to blow, the notes cut abruptly short as a javelin hit him in the chest knocking him backwards. The few men in earshot of Cornelius dropped back, raising their shields and ringing the standard, he also looking to defend it and himself as the enemy closed in. Glancing to his rear he saw some men had fought free of the enveloping Carthaginians and were fleeing in the direction of the Roman camp, the enemy cavalry whooping, chasing and killing.

'Was this it? Was this to be the end of him and his men?' He thought bitterly. 'Were they fated to die on this piece of insignificant broken ground? Victims once again to the vanity and foolishness of supposedly greater men and a clever enemy?'

Quickly raising his shield to deflect a javelin snapped him from his thoughts, another following close behind went wide of him and hit the standard-bearer, the man letting go of the Signum and collapsing.

"Close up! … Close up! Shields! Plant that Signum! Defend it!" He bellowed.

A legionary snatched the fallen standard from the ground just as the enemy began hacking and banging on the nearby Roman shields turning the immediate area to bloody chaos. Pushing back with his shield, Cornelius thrust his gladius low and felt it puncture flesh. Swords rattled off his shield while javelins and spears thrust at him, he ducking low and stabbing again. Fingers hooked over his shield rim pulling it forward and down. Lifting his gladius, he thrust it in the direction of the hand and roared his hate; he was hit in the face by a spurt of hot blood as the blade took the man in the throat. Blinking, he heaved the shield back into place as the man collapsed. He was pushed back a pace as the Carthaginians pressed forward, his small group forced ever closer together as the pressure grew. Pushing back and stabbing furiously, he ducked down behind his shield again. Frightened and angry he grunted and fought while his prayers slipped quickly across his lips.

"Juno, mother please accept your son!" He was going to die here.

Hannibal and his command group watched the battle from the edge of the field, the ground itself seeming to roll and heave like the ocean swell as men fought, pushed or tried to run. The roar and the cries were that of a huge crowd accompanied with the clang of metal. There was little order now as the cavalry mixed through with the infantry but the result was what he'd hoped for, the Romans were almost enveloped and being slowly crushed as his men pressed in on all sides.

"We have them sir." Maharbal chuckled.

"Aye, as long as Fabius doesn't mobilise to support for we haven't the men to take on both armies at once, especially if one comes fresh to the field."

"It will be the first time for Fabius if he does."

"True, but never say never."

The battle raged on for some time, the Roman ranks slowly diminishing. Then a blare of trumpets sounded in the distance, paused and then came again."

"Aha! That cloud on the mountains has broken in storm at last!"

Hannibal said and pointed as the trumpets sounded again. Cavalry turmaes and legionary maniples could be seen exiting from Fabius's camp.

"Hah, Fabius! … The old goat has finally grown a pair of balls!" Maharbal grunted.

Hannibal smiled. "No matter. We've rubbed their noses in the mire once more and have all but decimated Minucius's command, which is what I wanted. Recall and reform the men then screen our frontage with skirmishers."

"Yes sir, do we carry on the fight?"

"Not unless Fabius forces the issue and despite his men being fresh and ours tired I don't think he will. I'll take what we've won and be thankful but we'll stand awhile and see what he does, we can't have him claiming a rescue and a victory." He smiled. "Come, let's walk the lines and cheer our men while we wait on the old delayer." He chuckled as he led his party forward.

Chapter Thirteen

Across the field Carthaginian trumpets and horns blared three short blasts to recall troops. There was no immediate cease in the fighting, as always, with bloodlust up and adrenalin coursing through men's bodies the combat took time to slow and stop. Slowly, the Carthaginians began to disengage, some men having to be physically pulled away by their comrades as pending victory brought euphoria and they still sought Roman blood.

Cornelius barked orders for his men to 'Stand-to' while gazing in disbelief as the enemy slowly backed away. Was this just a regroup for the final push by the Carthaginians? If it was, this lull was merely a respite from certain death for he knew he and his men could not take much more before being overwhelmed. His battered mind went over his training; regroup, clear the dead and the wounded from the lines; weapon checks ... His thoughts were interrupted by his Optio shouting and pointing excitedly to their rear.

"Sir! ... Sir! Fabius has come!"

Cornelius looked to where the Optio pointed and saw Fabius's legions deploying into line by maniple with turmaes of equites assembling on the wings. Not quite believing his eyes, he looked again at the colourful, impressive array and saw the lines begin to advance. A trumpet blared nearby, ragged and forlorn sounding, calling for men to fall back and regroup. Shouting orders to his Optio, they moved amongst their men attempting to make order out of chaos while commencing an orderly withdrawal and regroup. Herding his men, he muttered a heartfelt prayer under his breath to Juno for deliverance.

"Juno, Goddess, thank you! With all my heart, I thank you!" Tears of relief spilled down his cheeks, emotion stealing his breath.

Across the field troops on both sides were regrouping. The battered remnants of Minucius's command slowly coming to order as they eased back and away towards their advancing comrades while keeping their eyes front watching the enemy. Cornelius heard shouts then cheering growing in volume and paused to look. The enemy ranks cheered while raising spears and shields in salute as the Carthaginian command group made its way across their line's frontage. The man riding at the front of the small cavalcade, with a purple diadem in his hair raising a hand to his men acknowledging their cheers. It had to be Hannibal, but he was so young! And very much junior to the men that rode with him, they being middle-aged or older. How could this man of still early years set an empire by its ears, destroy armies, defeat and outmanoeuvre men who'd been at war longer than he'd been alive? Was this young man the monster? The eater of Roman children? The leader of the 'Lion's Brood', come to destroy Rome? Still watching, he looked briefly for Baldor's black plumed helmet amongst the group then dismissed the thought, Baldor like himself, was not of sufficient rank to ride with such. So, no meeting with Baldor this time, was he on the field or dead upon it? Had the Gods finally wearied of the game they had playing out between the pair of them? The Optio interrupted his thoughts again.

"Sir, we're falling back."

"Thank you Optio, carry on."

Begrudgingly in awe of Hannibal for both his abilities and accomplishments, he dipped his head in respect then turned to follow his men.

Fabius advanced his legions right up to the combat area, Minucius's men filtering in and being absorbed into the ranks, the army slowly becoming one again. However, when the velites deployed and looked to skirmish again, Hannibal countered it with swift and exaggerated force hurling them savagely back. The message clear that reinforcements arrived or not, the Carthaginians remained Kings of the hill and were still full of fight.

It was now early afternoon and growing late in the day for battle anew. The two sides stood off, watching each other across the field of dead left from the morning's battle, the atmosphere tense. An un-natural silence reigned; the aura of grim anticipation had men sweat and fidget waiting for the bloodletting to begin again. The lull brought the first of the carrion birds, the few quickly becoming a multitude that landed boldly on the dead to pick and tear just paces from the waiting ranks, a grisly reminder of what awaited those who would fall. It was grimly obvious that most of the bodies on the field were Roman and also very clear that the Carthaginians still held the vantage point on the low hill. Their ambush parties of infantry and cavalry remained on the wings, their thick lines curving away from their comrades on the hillcrest like the tips of a crescent moon or a scorpion's open pincer, ready to close and nip the Roman flanks. However, it seemed neither side was keen to commit to further action and men just stared, then a horseman trotted from the Carthaginian lines, staying out of javelin range he bowed from his mount's back.

"My Lord Fabius, you may take your dead."

As he turned and rode back to his lines, the silence that hung over the field changed to a dull rattle of wood and metal as men on both sides firmed their grip on their weapons. If further battle was coming it would come now, for that message could be interpreted as either an insult or polite respect. The moment seemed to stretch; only the occasional whicker from a horse and the cackle of the birds disturbing the silence, men watched, and quiet prayers were mumbled but no one moved. The Roman command group looked to Fabius who maintained an impassive stare at the men crowding the hill.

Time passed and the carrion grew in numbers when the kites joined the crows and ravens to feast amongst the dead. A Carthaginian trumpet blew sounding withdrawal though the notes were lazy and without the urgency associated with a retreat. Cavalry slowly turned their mounts and walked off, the infantry units following and marching off one by one. On the Roman side, orderlies and their assistants stepped forward searching amongst the dead and wounded seeking to save those they could. As the Carthaginians continued to disperse the legionaries moved in, searching for injured or dead comrades and helping carry them back towards the camp. Cornelius helped with his wounded men and then when his Optio presented him with a situation report of his century's dead and wounded, he went in search of Gaius to report. Gaius and his men had been alongside during the battle; however, with no sign of him since, Cornelius hailed an Optio seeking news of his whereabouts.

"He went down sir, a ..."

"What?" Cornelius snatched the Optio by his mail shirt pulling him close. "What happened? Is he dead? Injured?"

"Badly injured sir, he took a javelin in the chest and then a sword slash to his thigh. An orderly has taken him back to camp and the medical tent, he needs care and quickly."

Cornelius cursed. His stomach felt as if he'd swallowed a stone and he flushed hotly in worry for his friend. Gaius had only just recovered from a shoulder wound taken earlier in the summer at the battle at Trasimene, was his friend running out of luck? Turning back to his own men, he badgered them on, keen to be off the field and back to camp. Once his men were safe and the injured under care he could look for Gaius. A messenger interrupted his work.

"Centurion Scipio?"

"Yes soldier?"

"Sir, with Senior Centurion Gaius Laelius incapacitated, you are commanded to report in his stead. There's a briefing at the Dictator's tent before the evening meal."

Cornelius groaned inwardly as he acknowledged the orders.

Fabius's tent was full of officers from senior Centurions upwards and Cornelius felt distinctly out of place and ill at ease as he expected trouble between Fabius and Minucius. Others must have suspected similar as the atmosphere remained tense, men had little to say to one another, the few words exchanged being had in low tones. Minucius and the officers from his command, including Cornelius, were still attired as they'd come from battle, blood stained and filthy, having managed nothing more than a wash of their hands as they entered the tent. With so many men gathered inside, the stink of stale sweat was sharp and vied with the smell of the bread and roasted meat that slaves deposited on the table. A bang on the table from a goblet drew men's attention and Fabius called the meeting to order. Before he could continue, Minucius stepped forward and the air became charged, the silence ominous as men held their breath and watched. Fabius frowned, clearly ready to subdue any outburst from Minucius. However, he was left speechless as the man bowed his head and placed his hand over his heart.

"Sir, the title and state of a father is a noble one. My father gave me life but today sir you saved my life, you are my second father. As your son, I recognize your superior abilities as a commander, my commander. My men and I are at your disposal. Hail father, Hail Fabius."

Other than some sharp intakes of breath, the tent remained quiet as men waited for Fabius's response. The older man didn't reply immediately but slowly moved his hand placing it gently on Minucius's bowed head.

"Marcus Minucius Rufus … a brave and valiant son of Rome … my son. As your second father I welcome you home."

There was an audible sigh of relief in the tent. Men looked on dumbfounded, the expected bitter fight between the two men seemingly dissolved into friendship or at least respect. Cornelius closed his eyes and mumbled a prayer of thanks to Jupiter for the accord between the pair following it quickly with a prayer for Gaius. Ignoring the offered meal, he sought Fabius's Adjutant and asked to be excused while offering his report by way of a wax tablet denoting his and Gaius's list of their able, wounded and dead legionaries. Not classed as the great or the good he was readily released and made his way at speed across the camp to the field hospital.

To access the tent, he had to make his way around the queues of men awaiting treatment for flesh wounds and less serious injuries. As he neared the front of the queue, the stink of blood and cauterised flesh fouled the air, the buzz of flies became louder and the injuries more serious, here men were supported by comrades or laid down awaiting their turn with the surgeons. Stopped at the tent entrance, he was directed to a clerk seated behind a rough wooden bench that passed for a desk, the top covered in parchments and small wax tablets.

"Whom do you seek Centurion?" The clerk asked while looking back at the parchments.

"Senior Centurion Gaius Laelius, second legion, first cohort."

The man picked up a parchment and ran an ink-stained finger down the list, putting it down he picked up another and then another.

"Sorry sir, the list for the second is extensive." He said quietly and looked up briefly at Cornelius whose face was aghast at the long list of casualties. Reaching for yet another parchment the clerk's finger paused halfway down the list and clearing his throat said. "He's here sir, he's been treated and is in the far tent." The clerk stood and pointed. Cornelius grunted his thanks and took off apace.

Stopped again at the tent entrance he growled savagely at the sentry who quickly stepped to one side. Pushing into the gloom of the tent, he paced up and down, quickly checking the men laid in neat rows on the ground seeking his friend. Many were badly hurt and swathed in bandages, some of which showed fresh bloodstaining; others had stumps where limbs had once been. There were low moans of pain mixed through with whispered prayers while one or two men called for orderlies to bring water or more pain relief.

"Can I help you sir?" An orderly asked with quiet respect.

"I'm looking for Senior Centurion Gaius Laelius, second …"

"This way sir." The man replied quietly while beckoning Cornelius to follow him. "He's been treated and will hopefully survive."

Cornelius snatched roughly at the orderly's tunic stopping him and pulling him close. "What do you mean hopefully?"

The orderly retained his composure while gently removing Cornelius's hand from his tunic and replied quietly, his voice steady. "He's lost a lot of blood sir, his top ribs are broken from the javelin and the wound's deep, mercifully though it missed his lungs. The leg wound is also deep and may have complications as it chopped someway into his thighbone. Thankfully, it doesn't appear the marrow has entered the blood and …"

"How bad is it?"

A surgeon, hearing the conversation rose from treating a nearby patient and wiping bloodied hands on a clean rag stepped forward. He nodded in greeting to Cornelius while quietly sending the orderly on his way.

"We won't know for a day or two sir; we've done the best we can but he's in the hands of the Gods now."

Cornelius paled and his head dropped. "Yes … yes, I'm sure you have, thank you. Can I see him?"

"Yes sir, though he was still unconscious last time I checked him, we gave him quite a draught of Opium to numb the pain. This way please."

"Can I do anything? Help or …"

"He really needs special care sir; I've done what I can in the time I had but he needs almost constant one on one care really."

"I'll pay you, whatever you wish, just …"

"It's not the money sir, it's the time. I'm paid to care for the mess you soldiers make of yourselves, but I cannot devote the sole time he needs for his recovery. As you can see, we have plenty work." Seeing Cornelius's angst and frustration, he continued. "I'm sorry sir, we've done our best. However, if you could get him to Casilinum I have a friend there, a good man and a gifted physician, you would have to pay but he would be able to care for your friend."

"How … how am I going to be able to do that?" Cornelius's head dropped in despair.

"I don't know sir but if you can manage it come and see me and I will give you the name and residence of my friend." The surgeon stopped walking at the end of the row. "Here he is sir; I'll leave you with him. As I said, I don't think he'll know you're here but if he comes to, seeing you will be a comfort."

"Thank you … thank you? …"

"Titus Quintus Regulus. You're welcome, sir." The man dipped his head and moved off.

Cornelius stared at his friend, a lump forming in his throat, his heart beginning to race in his chest. He squatted alongside Gaius and placed a hand gently on his good arm.

"Gaius … Gaius!" He whispered.

Gaius didn't respond. His injured leg was elevated on a wooden block, his chest and arm swathed in tight bandages, his upper body slightly raised by folded blankets placed under his back. Cornelius looked at the bandages and the patches of blood that had leaked from the wound area. Gaius's skin was pale, his lips a faint blue smear, his breathing shallow and barely audible.

"Gaius! … Gaius! It's me, Cornelius." His voice urgent, his hand gently shaking Gaius's good arm.

With no response, Cornelius settled himself beside Gaius, watching and quietly worrying and wondering at the madness of it all.

****

"Don't you have a tongue in your head, girl? A greeting, whether it's meant or not is preferable to silence."

Lasairiona lowered the tray of food onto Livia's lap then dipped her head. "Good morning, Mistress Livia."

"There! That didn't hurt too much did it?'

"No, Mistress Livia."

"If I'm to keep you from my husband and his creature's clutches I expect a modicum of pleasantness. Slavery is hard and likely harder for the likes of you, but lives and times change and here you are."

Lasairiona cringed inwardly at the mention of Thaddeus and Arya. "Apologies Mistress, I'm trying to find my place."

"Your place is caring for my whims and needs while being respectful and pleasant."

"Yes, Mistress."

"Good! After I've eaten you can dress me, meanwhile tell me of yourself and where you come from, you barbarians intrigue me."

Lasairiona quietly relayed her tale from the fall of Victumulae to being kidnapped and sold but left out details of Baldor, passing him off as her owner rather than her lover. Livia listened as she picked through the plate of poached fish, onions and garlic garnished in garum before throwing down the fork and fanning her open mouth.

"Tell the cook to put fewer onions in the food, my mouth is on fire!" Pushing the plate to one side, she rose from the bed intimating she could be dressed. "It seems Fortuna has not favoured you, girl. However, keeping my favour ensures your safety, mind it."

"Yes, Mistress."

"I'm visiting the gold market this morning and you'll accompany me. We will go as sophisticated people, a lady with her body slave. However, I'll warn you now, if you disappear or run, when they catch you, I'll hand you back to my husband, is that clear?"

"Yes, Mistress."

"Good! Now, finish my hair then tidy yourself up. Tie your hair back and put on that long dress, we can't have you displaying those legs of yours to all."

"Yes Mistress."

To be outside of the villa was a welcome feeling for Lasairiona. Despite the noise of the town and the bustling, crowded streets, it was good to be away from the enclosing walls and rooms and the feeling of dread that they held. Walking a respectful pace behind Livia, she was in awe of the paved streets and orderly buildings that rose to two and sometimes three storeys in height. She'd never been so close to people she didn't know as they pushed or squeezed past her without a care, the air heavy with a mixture of food smells, perfume and human sweat. She noticed that Livia never once looked back to see if she was following, but why would she? Where was there to run?

She followed Livia past two heavily armed guards who flanked the doorway into a shop. Inside was another guard and a shopkeeper who bowed low to Livia bidding her a cordial good morning while gesturing her to a counter and producing a tray of gold bracelets.

"These have just arrived from the east My Lady; they're quite delicate and very different, see the turquoise worked into the gold for the animal's heads."

Livia picked the bracelet up; it was heavy but beautifully made, the ends of the metal coming together as two small birds facing each other, their chests and heads inlaid with turquoise and giving colourful relief to the gold. She tried it on her wrist.

"Love birds, My Lady." The man said smoothly.

Livia removed the bracelet quickly her lips betraying a sneer.

"No, no!" She said with finality. "That won't do Cyrus. It won't do at all!"

Cyrus saw the sneer and heard the bitterness and moved on quickly picking up another bracelet showing two, horned animal heads, all wrought in chased gold and coming together again face to face, with red garnets for their eyes.

Livia gave a sarcastic laugh. "Now that does remind me of myself and my husband! No ... no I'm looking for something more delicate, something more feminine. However, before we go further can you bring me some water, I have a raging thirst." She ran her hand over her mouth and throat.

The man clicked his fingers to a servant who quickly went in search of water and a cup while Cyrus produced another tray, this one full of gold and silver torcs and sized for both the neck and wrist. Livia picked up a neck torc of twisted gold strands, the ends fused into golden orbs with patterned relief engraved into them.

"Help me girl!" She said while holding the gold to her neck. Lasairiona opened the ends and slipped it around Livia's neck while Cyrus produced a bronze mirror passing it to Lasairiona so to show her Mistress. Livia turned her head, trying the torc for comfort and weight.

"That will be fine, Cyrus. Thank you."

After haggling the price, the women left the shop making their way back to the villa when Lasairiona noticed a slowing in Livia's walk. Eventually she stopped. With one hand supporting herself on the wall, she bent over holding her stomach while retching drily.

"Mistress! Are you all right?"

Livia pushed Lasairiona away as she came alongside seeking to help.

"Just get me home girl, quickly!" Recovering a little, Livia walked on before the cramps came again forcing her to stop once more. This time it seemed worse, and she snatched for support from Lasairiona, she groaned as the pain intensified, her fingers claw like on Lasairiona's arm. "Home!" She gasped. "Before my bowels empty!"

This time she held onto Lasairiona, her legs weak, her face drawn tight in agony, her eyes closed tight, her skin breaking out in beads of sweat. As they tried to walk on Livia seemed to wilt, Lasairiona holding her while struggling to the side of the street and easing her down against the wall. Some people stopped to stare others just ignored them and moved on. A fleeting thought to run crossed Lasairiona's mind though it disappeared as quickly, for she had no idea where to run to. Escaping the town would be difficult enough but then where?

"Water! Water!" Livia implored.

"Water!" Lasairiona shouted desperately at passers-by while holding Livia as she vomited. A man approached the two women. "Water! Have you any water?"

He squatted as if to help and then made a sudden grab for the torc on Livia's neck. Being closed snugly it didn't come off easily and he heaved hard, dragging Livia across the street like a rag doll, her screams cut off by the force of the pull. Lasairiona jumped up to stop him while shouting for help and he swung a punch at her. The punch was wild and hit the top of her arm hard; glancing off, it caught her face, the force of the blow was much reduced though a heavy ring cut her cheek deeply. Fighting back, her punch landed on his ear, she followed it quickly with another that hit the side of his jaw. Letting go of Livia to defend himself he grabbed a knife from his belt. People were shouting for the Watch now and attention was focusing on the fight. Shocked at the ferocity and strength from Lasairiona, he brandished the knife to keep her away then turned and ran.

Lasairiona eased Livia up from the street just as the Watch appeared. The soldiers, recognising the wealth and class of Livia seized Lasairiona thinking she was the thug; dragging her roughly to one side, one of the men punched her head as she shouted and tried to shake loose from his grip. After moments of shouting and chaos, folk that had seen the altercation explained to the guards and Lasairiona was finally released and helped.

Escorted back to the villa by the guards, both were taken to Livia's rooms. Thaddeus, informed of the incident lethargically organising slaves to assist while firmly dismissing any calls or need to send for a physician. While slaves fussed over Livia, Lasairiona was left to see to herself. When Livia regained consciousness and command of her senses, she demanded water while asking for a physician, when told none had been sent for, she commanded, Thaddeus reluctantly acquiescing. Passing Lasairiona, he chuckled.

"Not so pretty now Princess, are you?"

Lasairiona said nothing but held a cloth to her bloodied cheek, her arm aching, tender and already colouring from the blow, her head throbbing. After taking a salted drink and vomiting again, Livia felt better. While the physician treated her cuts and bruises from the dragging, she gleaned the happenings from the Steward who had received details from the guardsmen. The physician finished up, advising that she'd suffered from bad food or picked up a contagion from the streets, she was to rest and if the stomach pain persisted, take more saline infusions until she vomited again. Turning to go, Livia pointed him to Lasairiona.

"Before you leave, see to my slave … I'll pay." She added when he looked bewildered.

Opening his bag again, he requested more clean water and examined Lasairiona's cut, then taking fresh linen swabs dipped in hot vinegar-water, he cleaned the wound.

"It's deep Mistress Flavia, it really requires stitching."

"Then do it man!" She snapped irritably. "And make sure the stitches are tiny and neat, it's a woman's face."

"That will take time Mistress and it'll be quite an expense for just a slave."

"That slave just saved my life so get to it! And slave or not, make it your best work, the best! … Do you hear?"

"Yes, Mistress Flavia."

"And use silk! Make it good and I'll double your bill."

With a sudden renewed interest, the man set to work. Apart from minor flinches as the fine bone needle entered the flesh, Lasairiona didn't whimper, though a solitary tear rolled down her cheek.

"Good work Arya, good work! That fool physician thinks the old bitch has eaten a bad oyster else picked up filth from the streets." He chuckled. "Now! When for the second dose?"

"We must be careful sir, small and not too regular is the answer. The poison will take hold and the illness will worsen each time, done right it should look like an affliction of the stomach a natural thing that won't arouse suspicion."

Thaddeus growled in his throat. "Well until she's gone you must run the risk of being caught with me."

"Can we not wait until your wife is dead sir?" She pleaded, the fearful memory of the savage whipping still fresh. "We must be careful sir, it will happen soon enough, the Arum will kill her."

"Soon enough is not quick enough, my dear." He replied flatly then shrugged. "However, as I said before, it's your hide." Taking her by the hair, he pulled her roughly towards the bed. "You have a month and I want her dead and gone."

"But sir, that's not a long time for a fatal illness."

"A month Arya." He said as he lifted her dress over her buttocks and opened his robe. "A month, after which I'll let you loose on our Princess again for she no longer interests me as that's an ugly scar she carries now, and I abhor ugliness."

Chapter Fourteen

The men tied their mounts off at the horse line removing their riding blanket and gear before rubbing and brushing the horses down then watering them.

"What do you make of that then? Was it a victory or stalemate?" Armaco asked.

"I'd say a victory; there was plenty of them laid dead on the field." Baldor replied while continuing to comb cots out of his mount's tail.

"We still left Fabius in command of it though."

"I don't think so, we threw their velites back and he didn't respond further, despite his numbers."

"H'mm, I suppose so." He shrugged, then bent to lift each of his mount's hooves in turn, inspecting and cleaning as required.

"I thought the General's offer for him to take his dead was clever." Andulas added. "Taken as respect it gave Fabius an out from having to assault our lads on the crest for with us waiting on the wings he wasn't in a favourable position. Also ..." He pre-empted Armaco's next question. "Also, it gave us an out too. Many of our men had fought since early morning while he had plenty of fresh legionaries to throw at us. I doubt he would have chased us off the field but if he'd tried, it would have been bloody for both sides. Thankfully he's a cautious man."

"Aye, you're right about them coming fresh and still outnumbering us, at least we gave that arrogant bastard Minucius a good thumping." Armaco said and chuckled. "I love it when we bring another arrogant Roman low. Haughty, overconfident bastards the lot of them and that's how many now? Scipio, Sempronius, Flaminius, Geminus and now Minucius." He finished up on the hooves and leant over his horse's back while wiping dirt from the blunted knife on his sleeve. "They don't look like they're giving up yet though, they keep fighting … bastards!" He added solemnly.

Andulas sighed. "Land, hearth and home, Armaco, that's what's behind it all. It'll be really bloody before they finally give in. I know them of old; they're a resilient, persistent people."

"They're a bastard people!" He growled. "They have to give in eventually, surely? The Trebbia and Trasimene fights killed thousands of them, and you can add a few thousand more to that tally now for this morning."

"What about the last war Armaco? Twenty years or more with untold thousands dead and they didn't give up." Baldor added grimly.

"Baal Almighty! Andulas will be a grey beard if it goes on that long!" He chuckled and looked at Baldor who tried to hide a smirk. "Looking on the bright side though you might just have learned something about soldiering by then …"

"And you will be how old? Should you live that long?" Andulas smiled and shook his fist.

"And right now, that's not looking very likely." Baldor chirped and sniggered while raising his own fist.

"By then, My Lord Andulas and Baldor the peasant, by then, I will have a piece of this country for myself. Methinks Lord Armaco of Campania has a ring to it."

"What if we just ring your neck?" Baldor added and the three laughed.

"Come on, let's wash and eat while we plan." Andulas said as he threw his arms over the other's shoulders pulling them close.

"Plan what?"

"Getting Lasairiona back and killing that bastard, Thaddeus."

Almost back at the tent they were met by an excited Issa who ran at them full speed, barrelling into their legs and barking. Baldor squatted to stroke and pat her; she licking his face and whimpering, her body all of a shake, her tail flailing.

"There girl, there." He said as he ruffled her ears.

Issa took off back to the tent and reappeared with her chew before running towards the men and teasing by coming close then backing off before they could grab it from her.

Stripping off armour and washing, the men sought rest and dinner. With dinner served, Andulas dismissed the servants then lowered his voice.

"Can you see the General for leave to take the men again, Baldor? And we'll pay Thaddeus another but final visit."

"Yes, I …"

"Make sure I can come this time!" Armaco growled.

"I'll see what he says though I imagine he'll be fine with it now that Minucius has been humbled. I surmise the Romans will be looking to regroup and with winter coming on I think offensive operations will ease."

"Good. Ask him for a turma's worth." Andulas said as he tore meat off a goose leg.

Both men looked up from their plates.

"A turma? That's just thirty men?" Armaco grunted and frowned.

"Aye, thirty just, plus us of course."

"Why only thirty and what's with the turma?"

"We're going to Casilinum as a Roman auxiliary cavalry unit."

"What?"

"Well, think on it. We have access to plenty Roman equipment and as an auxiliary unit arriving at a town that appears to be still allied to Rome or at least sympathetic to their rule; we shouldn't raise too many questions. More importantly it should get us through the gate without a fight."

"Will thirty men be enough?"

"I reckon so. As I said to Baldor, Thaddeus's men had the look of soft city guards; you know the type; lethargic, too well-fed bully boys and thugs most likely, and no match for our lads."

"Fair enough."

"If we are quick taking the villa and finding Lasairiona we could be on our way out by the time an alarm is raised and even when it is, we'll look like we are on the right side."

"Do we burn it?"

"Yes, that will add to the confusion and draw men to fight the fire."

Armaco beamed a smile. "I love it when we burn Roman property, you'll have no objections this time, Baldor."

"None! I'll burn that fat bastard Thaddeus with it if he's harmed Lasairiona."

"You can burn him after I've killed him, Baldor."

Both men looked up quickly as Andulas's tone had dropped low and menacingly cold. "No man makes slaves of my people and he'll know before I end his life that it is a Lingone Lord that kills him and not a Cenomani one.”

Neither man looked to argue.

A servant made a tentative entrance and broke the silence. Issa jumped up at the sudden interruption and barked fiercely, Baldor having to settle her.

“Sorry to intrude My Lord but there’s a man to see Hypolokhagos Armaco.”

“Send him in.”

The servant ushered a warrior into the main tent, Issa still growling low in her throat. The man looked around nervously before speaking. Armaco pre-empted him.”

“Hattam! You have news?”

“Yes sir.” The man answered while dipping his head respectfully to Andulas and Baldor. “I believe I’ve found or rather seen the falcata you seek, sir.”

All three men stared then Baldor jumped up from his seat. “Who, where?’

“A Libyan cavalry Hypolokhagos called Amanar has it, sir.”

“Are you sure it’s the right one?” Armaco asked.

“As best as I can tell sir, ivory hilted with gold wire twisted thorough the hilt, a horse’s head in gold forming the curve of the handle and a patterned cross guard.” The man looked at Baldor for reassurance.

“Aye, that sounds like it.”

“Do you know anything of this Amanar?” Andulas asked.

“Not much My Lord but from the little I have heard it seems he’s a decent man.”

“A decent man doesn’t buy stolen goods!” Armaco quipped.

“Who says he isn’t a decent man? Did he buy it in good faith, did he find it or was it given to him?” Andulas smiled and put a hand on Armaco’s arm seeking his silence. “I suggest we rest now and go and see this Amanar tomorrow and ask him politely about the sword.” He squeezed Armaco’s arm as he tried again to interrupt. “The man’s answer will determine what we do from there.”

Armaco nodded then turned to Hattam “Is there news of anything else, the dagger or the helmet?”

“Nothing certain yet sir, though I have another lead to a Greek who goes by the name of Haemon.”

Armaco patted the man on the shoulder. “That’s good work anyway

Hattam, thank you."

The man saluted, dipped his head to Andulas and Baldor then left.

"Well, I suggest we get some sleep, it's been a long day." Andulas yawned and stretched his shoulders.

"Can I say something before we retire?" Baldor asked quietly, the men acquiescing by turning to listen. "If there is trouble tomorrow you two should not be involved, this is my issue."

"I don't think so!" Armaco grunted. "You're my friend and some bastard hurt you and robbed you, which makes it my issue as well."

"Agreed Armaco." Andulas added. "However, there will be no trouble tomorrow; we are asking questions is all."

"Yes but ..."

"But! ... If we don't get the answers we need, then there will be trouble. However, not tomorrow and not in the camp, we do things carefully."

"Yes!" Baldor added. "None of us are risking crucifixion over things which can be replaced." Armaco nodded and raised his hands as if to say fair enough. Baldor placed a hand on each man's shoulder. "Thank you, thank you both. I'm rich in friends if nothing else."

****

Cornelius mulled over his decision as he walked, his hand holding the harness of the mule pulling a small cart as he led it down the grass track. After the fight near Geronium, Fabius had dismissed Minucius's units who had suffered heavy casualties sending them back to Rome to rest and recover. With winter fast approaching and the campaign season ending, he judged he had sufficient men to keep Hannibal under watch until spring. Cornelius and his badly mauled century had been released and he, taking the advice from the surgeon, had opted to take Gaius to Casilinum seeking immediate treatment from the physician there rather than risk delay with the long road back to Rome. Now, he and ten legionary volunteers were making their way there with Gaius bandaged and bundled on the small cart.

He stopped the mule and walked back to peer over the cart side to check on his charge the ten legionaries he had with him halting behind the cart as it stopped. Despite the blankets rolled as padding and supports the motion of the cart had moved Gaius, and Cornelius set about rearranging them and securing his friend again while calling to the men.

"Rest stop! Take a drink but keep your eyes open for Carthaginian patrols."

Gaius was sleeping or unconscious, his face and arms still pale. Suffering a moment of panic, Cornelius quickly felt his skin and was relieved to find it warm to the touch and on checking the bandages he saw the chest was dry but the thigh wound was leaking blood. It wasn't a great amount but he called for a hand to lift the leg while he checked beneath the wrapping. Exposing the wound, he found it clean, and sniffing it, found no taint of rot though some of the stitches had burst with jolts from the cart bringing on bleeding from the torn flesh. Applying a clean, new pad from his pack, he bound the leg tightly with the bandage again and arranged blankets to keep the limb elevated. Ensuring it couldn't move, he stuffed more blankets firmly around his friend trying to pad him against the movements of the cart then producing his water bottle, he eased Gaius's head up.

"Here Gaius, drink … drink, I have to keep putting fluid into you." The water washed over Gaius's lips and down his chin before he opened his mouth and managed to take some in. He coughed and choked when some caught in his windpipe and his eyes opened. "I'm sorry my friend but you need to drink."

"Get … get me … some wine then!" He managed in a hoarse whisper, a sad smile teasing his lips as Cornelius put more water into him before he faded back to sleep or unconsciousness.

Finishing up, Cornelius took a drink himself then shook his head slowly, his heart heavy at the state of his friend. Would he survive the journey? He gave an involuntary shiver when he thought of history repeating itself, here they were again, Gaius badly injured and they having to travel to have him treated. At least they weren't on their own this time and Casilinum was only another day or so away, he didn't think Gaius would have survived the journey as far as Rome.

Early evening of the next day brought them in sight of Casilinum's walls and Cornelius's hopes raised a little. Stopped at the gate by the guards brought questions, albeit respectful ones when they recognised Cornelius's rank. The guards were nervous and seeking news regarding the battle and Carthaginian troop whereabouts.

Cornelius however, weary from the journey and with his patience short rapped out curt replies doing little to soothe the guards' nerves.

"Now, if you are done questioning me, tell me where I can find the physician, Atticus Linus Silvanus."

A guard stepped a pace or two through the gateway beckoning Cornelius to follow him.

"Follow this road to the marketplace sir, then take the first road off to your right and his house is on the right, you'll see the sign outside his door."

"Thank you." Taking the mule's bridle, he walked the animal on.

Arriving at the house, he used his vine stick to hammer on the door. Impatient at the delay in answering, he hammered again. The door opened forcefully and an old, tired looking man with wild grey hair and dressed in a tattered, grubby tunic thrust his head out, his face wrinkling into a frown.

"What do you want?" He snapped, as he looked Cornelius up and down. "Are you trying to break my door down with your hammering?"

"Is this the house of Atticus Linus Silvanus?"

"That's what it says on there! I thought Centurions could read?" The man shook his head while pointing to the sign.

"You're Atticus?"

"Who are you?"

"Centurion Cornelius …"

"What do you want? I'm busy!"

"Are you Atticus or his damned impudent servant?" Cornelius growled as his patience gave out.

"I'm Atticus, now what do you want?"

Cornelius sighed deeply and took a moment to control his temper. "Sir, I have a wounded man that needs your help."

"A soldier?"

"A Centurion, a senior Centurion."

"And you'll pay me what?"

"I'll pay you whatever you ask." Cornelius said flatly.

Atticus, taken aback stared and frowned again. "The legions have their own physicians and surgeons, see them! I'm busy."

Fighting an urge to seize Atticus by the throat, Cornelius held his temper. "It was one of our surgeons that sent me to you, he said you would help."

"Who said that?"

"Titus Quintus Regulus."

"Titus!" Atticus's face went from a heavy frown to a wide grin.

"Titus! How is the boy?" His words suddenly kind.

"He's fine, he said you would help."

"Good, good! … Of course I'll help, why didn't you say? Titus, my best, most learned pupil." He smiled warmly at the memory.

"So you'll help?"

"Of course! Of course! Didn't I just say I would! Are you deaf as well as stupid?" Cornelius bit his tongue but glared at the angry little man. "Well! Are you going to stand there all day?" Atticus shook his head in dismay. "Centurions, legionaries, you're all idiots! Bring your man in, quickly. Cassia! Cassia!" He shouted back into the house. "Show these fools where to put their man, I must wash. Damn you boy!" He growled at Cornelius. "Now my garden will have to wait."

Atticus disappeared back into the house, passing Cassia on her way to the door.

"Bring him this way." She beckoned Cornelius onwards who in turn signalled the men to bring Gaius.

Laying Gaius on a scrubbed table, they stripped him to his loincloth while Cassia quickly peeled off the bandages and was examining the wounds when Atticus reappeared. He, washed, his hair combed and tied back and dressed in a clean tunic.

"What's your diagnosis girl?" He asked Cassia as he pushed past Cornelius. "Out of the way man!" He snapped.

"The top ribs are broken but the wounds are clean with no sign of infection though drying out a little. I'm not sure if the leg wound has begun to knit together and tightened the stitches and they've torn or if they've snapped from movement." She pointed. "We need to check that, clean the wounds again then re-stitch and apply new dressings I'll fetch what we need."

Atticus scanned the wounds then probed the areas gently with his fingers. "You! Centurion whatever your name is, what did Titus tell you? Did the weapon pierce the vitals at all?"

"No, both wounds are deep but the javelin missed the lungs and the slash to the thigh didn't sever the main artery."

"Of course it didn't! Otherwise, he'd be dead, you wouldn't be here and I would be getting on with my garden!"

Cornelius bit his tongue again at Atticus's sharp retort, reasoning that being snarled at was a small price to pay if Gaius could be helped. Cassia appeared with a tray laden with medical instruments, fresh bandages and a bowl of steaming water. Atticus, despite his previous irritation and ire at Cornelius, smiled at Cassia.

"Thank you my dear. Clean then sluice the wounds with that vinegar-water and we'll begin."

Cassia dabbed the wounds gently, cleaning any dry blood then squeezed a cloth to dribble the solution over the stitches before patting the surface dry with a clean pad.

"Now Cassia, look closely. As you said, the wounds are clean with no sign of infection and where the skin is torn here and here, it needs re-stitching and that will be tricky." He looked at Gaius then pinched his ankle hard; with no movement or pain recognition evident, he nodded. "No need for Opium he's still unconscious. If we're quick, we can be done before he wakes. Remove those damaged stitches and I'll show you how to join the new to the old."

Cassia reached for a tiny, hooked knife and began carefully slicing the broken stitches before teasing them out of the skin with tweezers.

"You're letting her do it?" Cornelius growled.

"Are you still here?" Atticus snapped without looking up from the work.

"Yes! And I'm paying for your skill, not hers!"

"You're paying for my knowledge, boy! Cassia's fingers will make a finer job than mine. Not that it's any business of yours, now be quiet or get out! … Get out anyway, we're busy!"

"I'm paying so I'm staying."

Atticus gurned his lip. "Not another word then!" He snarled. His manner then changed to a low, warm tone. "That's it, Cassia excellent, excellent. Now, if we join to the old, good stitches here, the knot won't pull through the skin. Before we do that though, wash it again with the vinegar water."

Cornelius remained silent as the pair worked, quite amazed at their speed but also their care. With the thigh wound cleaned and re-stitched, they applied a smear of honey over the wound. Cassia reached for a fresh pad but dipped it in a clear oil then wrung it out before applying it.

"Good, good." Atticus purred. "The honey will keep infection out and the oil will keep the pad moist and stop it sticking to the wound."

With Gaius bandaged Cassia disappeared again, returning with a small jug complete with a wax seal. Meanwhile Atticus wafted a tiny glass bottle under Gaius's nose until his head twitched and moved away from the smell; Atticus repeated it twice more until Gaius opened his eyes.

"Is that Hammoniacus sal?" Cornelius asked as he peered over

Atticus's shoulder.

"Yes! And that, before you ask, is colostrum." Atticus answered and pointed to the sealed jug then added. "That's mother's milk to simple folk like yourself."

Cassia tried to stifle a giggle and failed.

"Mother's milk!"

"Yes, from a nursing mother of a male child."

"What? But that's …"

"Expensive! Is all you need to know, as she doesn't have a lot to spare."

"What in Hades does that do?"

Atticus sighed. "Jupiter save me from half-wits and Centurions though it appears there is little difference! Colostrum boy, helps minimise the risk of infection, it'll be added to your bill along with the fortified wine, special diet and nursing care that your friend needs if he is to recover."

"Special diet?"

"Aye, he's lost a lot of blood so will need to replenish it, he needs cabbage, kale, garlic, good fish, red meat, pepper and of course rest and care. None of which is cheap!"

Cornelius reached for his purse and placed a silver denarius on the table. "Will that cover the work so far and some of the care?"

Atticus's eyes lit up and he snatched the coin though he still growled at Cornelius. "Keep the coin off my table! Nothing goes on the table except the patient and sterilised implements." He tut-tutted. "Soldiers! Fools with as much sense as a cabbage! … Yes, yes that will do for now, you can pay the balance in seven days or so."

"How long!"

"Are you deaf as well as stupid? Seven days or so! Your friend has lost a lot of blood …"

"Yes, I understand, completely." He said resignedly.

"Thank the Gods for that then! Now, out you go."

"But …"

"Out! There's nothing more you can do except get under my feet; your friend will receive the best care we can give him." Atticus hustled Cornelius to the door. "Come back tomorrow but only if you must."

Cornelius found himself in the street and the door slammed behind him. His men came to attention as he approached.

"Orders sir?"

"We need to find lodging; we are going to be here for a few days."

****

Lasairiona held the dish under Livia's chin as she vomited again then fell back on her pillows breathless. Moving the dish away, Lasairiona mopped at Livia's brow and neck with a damp cloth, the woman closing her eyes as the coolness brought some relief while wiping away the sticky beads of sweat from her skin.

"I thought … I thought, I was recovering but the cramps seem to be growing worse and my mouth still burns."

"Shall I mix another infusion, Mistress?"

"Yes, yes I'll try that but I'm so hungry, yet I can't keep anything down."

"Maybe starving a day or two more will help? If there's nothing in your stomach for the sickness to feed upon, whatever it is causing the vomiting may ease?"

"Everything I've eaten these last few days has come back up; surely there can't be anything left?"

Lasairiona lifted Livia's head from the pillow and helped her drink the bitter infusion.

"This will likely make you vomit again but at least it should purge what's in there. Here, take some water that will help dilute the taste."

Livia drank willingly her thirst still strong and then laid back again.

"I need to sleep, I'm so tired, so …" Her eyes closed.

Lasairiona pulled the sheet up over her and went to empty the bowl. The stink from the vomit was pungent but different to the normal sharp, nasal piercing smell of part digested food, glancing at it she saw it was dark in colour with flecks of blood mixed though it. She wondered at that, for Livia had eaten very little and what she had managed had come almost straight back up. By now she would have expected just clear liquid.

When she returned she was startled to find Thaddeus in the room.

"I trust you are caring for my wife!" He said fiercely and before Lasairiona could reply, he continued. "It's strange is it not? How she was well until you became her slave."

Lasairiona paled at the insinuation though she answered firmly. "I do my work and Mistress Livia has no complaints."

"She's almost unable to complain now." He sneered.

"Why would I wish to hurt her? I helped her when we were attacked."

"Ah! My brave Princess, how touching." He replied with smooth sarcasm. "We'll both be praying for her recovery then?"

"Yes I will, for the lady is good to me."

"I could have been better but you made your choice."

"You were going to rape me!"

He raised his arms and shrugged matter-of-factly. "You're a slave so there for the use of. You chose to resist!" He turned for the door. "If she doesn't recover soon I will be asking questions."

Lasairiona felt the panic twist her stomach. "I'm not a physician, not a healer; call them if you're worried!"

Thaddeus rounded on her and slapped her hard across the face, the force sending her stumbling off balance. "Don't raise your voice to me, bitch!" He snarled, and then lowered his voice, the tone flippant. "My wife called her physician; so it's no business of mine to interfere. Tell her when she awakens I was asking kindly for her." With that, he was gone, leaving Lasairiona to collect herself.

Rubbing the skin and massaging her jaw, she took a moment to clear her head, it still ringing from the heavy blow, she thankful it was not the side that was stitched. Going to the bed she found Livia still asleep, feeling her brow she found the skin hot and wet again with sweat, her breathing shallow and laboured. Pulling up a small stool alongside the bed, she sat to think. Whatever was wrong with Livia it seemed Thaddeus was going to blame her for it, if Livia was to recover she was sure the lady would protect her, however what if she died? Just then, Livia stirred again, began to retch and cough, and with a loud groan vomited before Lasairiona could reach for the dish.

Chapter Fifteen

The following morning the three men made their way through the camp in search of the Libyan cavalry unit and Amanar. The air was filled with the aroma of fresh baking bread as folk prepared breakfast and despite having just eaten, Andulas sniffed hard.

"Makes you hungry again doesn't it?"

"Aye, it does." Baldor answered. "Hot bread with fresh butter! You can't beat it. What do you say Armaco?"

"Do you two ever stop thinking about your stomachs?" Armaco grumbled into his furs and pulled them tight about him for the cold, cloudless night had dropped the temperature and left the grass dusted in heavy frost, the air clear and ice cold. Clouds of hot breath vapour accompanied them as they rode. "Winter's coming." He growled.

"Nonsense, it's a nice fresh morning the real winter is a month or two away yet." Andulas countered.

"Are you always happy?"

"As much as I can be for life can be awfully short."

"I hate the cold and the bad weather."

"There's no such thing as bad weather Armaco, just badly dressed."

"You could have stayed at the tent and kept warm by the brazier, that's what cold, old men do isn't it?" Baldor added and smirked.

"Huh! Gallic philosophy and a smart-arsed boy at this time of the morning, I'd get more sense talking to the dog."

"Bad headache is it?" Baldor asked and chuckled.

"Just bad wine and the money I can't bloody find, I think that whore must have taken coins from my purse when I fell asleep."

"You paid for a whore then fall asleep." Baldor laughed. "Baal Almighty! You are getting old!"

"She plied me with wine."

"If you're going to drink, then drink, if you're looking to hump …"

"Yes, yes Andulas! I'd already humped her once but the wine …"

"Old age is not coming itself!" Baldor quipped.

"Less of the old, boy, you should live so long!"

Andulas, still chuckling interrupted the tetchy diatribe and pointed. "I think that's them over there."

They found the Libyans exercising their horses and practicing manoeuvres on the flat sward outside the camp, casual enquiries with resting troops led them to Amanar. Alerted to their presence, Amanar turned his mount from the activity and trotted over. He was immaculately dressed in clean leather and canvas armour with a scarlet crested bronze helm, the tail of which laid half down his back. Despite the cold, his skin was flushed and sheened in sweat from the exercise.

"Good morning Captain, gentlemen, how can I be of assistance?" He dipped his head and saluted.

Baldor returned the salute and offered his hand. "Good morning sir, I'm Captain Baldor Targa, we were wondering if you could help us with an enquiry?"

Amanar shook hands but gave a puzzled look. "Certainly Captain, if I can?"

"It's a delicate matter and not one we wish you to take offence to but I'll cut to the chase."

"Ask away Captain, as I said, if I can help you I will?"

Baldor cleared his throat. "Your falcata, may I see it."

"Surely." He drew the blade and passed it over. "I bought it for parade days, it was an extravagance but its beautiful work is it not, Spanish I think?"

"Yes, it is." Baldor replied while examining it closely, he cleared his throat again while passing it back. "Can I ask how you came by it?"

Amanar's facial expression hardened. "Yes you can but why."

"It's actually mine. It was willed to me from my former Captain, he was killed after Trasimene."

"What?" Amanar frowned but gave a small laugh. "I don't think so; I purchased it in good faith."

"Fair enough, can I buy it back from you?"

"I'm sorry, no. I like it."

"Would you tell me who sold it to you then?"

"What's this about?"

"We're trying to ..."

"What the Captain is too polite to say is it was stolen from him." Armaco interrupted while Andulas growled at him under his breath to be quiet.

"Stolen!" Amanar motioned his horse close to Armaco. "Are you accusing me of stealing it?"

"No, he isn't, are you Armaco?" Andulas said forcefully.

Amanar however was not to be easily placated, ignoring Andulas he stared at Armaco. "I've never stolen anything in my life."

"You'll have no problem when we take the sword and you to the General then?"

"No problem at all! Shall we go now?" Armaco suddenly looked uncertain. "However! You ... whoever you are?" He snarled contemptuously. "Are calling me a thief so…"

Andulas interrupted. "No, no he isn't." He said calmly, trying to diffuse the rising tension.

Amanar ignored Andulas and stared at Armaco while leaning in closer. "I'm a law-abiding man and no one calls me a thief, so shall we settle this away from the camp? Let's see if your blade is as fast as your mouth."

Before Armaco could reply, Baldor pushed between them. "Brothers!" He said firmly. "Brothers please, enough! We can talk like civilised men." When the two men did not back down, Baldor asserted his authority. "Damn you both! Stand-down now!" The voice of command brought some calm and Baldor carried on. "Hypolokhagos Amanar! Clearly, you're an honest and upstanding man with nothing to hide and as I intimated earlier this is a delicate matter and no insult or accusation was intended towards you."

"I'll fight him if he wants!" Armaco blurted.

Baldor turned on him. "No one is fighting anyone! Now, I suggest ... no, I'm ordering, that we all calm down take a cup of wine and become acquainted while Amanar tells us his tale. It's obvious the sword has changed hands, possibly many times, we need to track it back is all." With no answer and Amanar, and Armaco still glaring at one another Baldor snapped. "Am I clear?"

Reluctant agreements were given and Baldor led off, seeking the wine merchants tents that passed for portable inns within the camp. Eventually they found one with a cleared area littered with odd tables, benches and stools placed around a fire and that doubled as an inn room.

A tent at the rear held wine and ale stock with two barrels topped by long planks in front making a counter as well as barring entry to the tent. Still early in the day, it was easy to find an empty table and some stools by the fire and the men settled. Baldor took the lead and ordered mulled wine from a weary looking slave girl then attempted to clear the air.

"You two!" He said sternly, jabbing a finger at Armaco and Amanar. "Save your anger for the Romans we're all friends here. Armaco, your friendship is precious to me and your loyalty I appreciate but in this case it's misplaced. Amanar, you are clearly above reproach and I admire your honesty." He softened his tone. "Now, this is my trouble and my fight and I won't have two good men spilling blood over it so we'll start again." He gestured to each man in turn. "Amanar this is Armaco. Armaco, Amanar."

With hesitation still evident between the pair, Andulas unseen, kicked Armaco under the table. Armaco hid it well and taking the hint offered his hand across the table.

"I'm rough and intemperate but I have to look after him, I promised." Was as much of an apology as Amanar was going to get, however the man took the offered hand while speaking to Baldor.

"It seems you are blessed with good friends, Captain." He managed a mischievous smile. "Now, how can I help?" Baldor relayed the tale of the robbery and abduction, Amanar shook his head. "Scum! I am sorry for your trouble, if I can help you find them I will. I purchased the blade from Alvaro the Spanish Smith; I can show you where he works from as he does weapon and mail repairs for me and my men. He told me he'd recognised the blade as Spanish work and wanted it for himself. His gambling however, then forced him to offer it for sale in order to settle his debts so I bought it from him in good faith."

"What's this Alvaro like as a man?"

"He's hot-tempered and difficult to bargain with and he charges like a wounded bull for his repairs, but his work is good."

"Honest, you think?"

"I would say yes. He's a hard man but it would seem a fair one, he's never tried to cheat me or any of my men and he talks straight."

Baldor chewed his lip as he thought. "So, we'll need to visit Alvaro the Smith, I wonder where he got the blade from?"

There was silence for a moment as the men digested the information. Amanar lifted the baldric from his shoulder and unhooked the falcata and sheath from it laying it on the table.

"Here Captain, this is rightfully yours and a willed gift is a precious thing. However, I paid for it fairly and it wasn't cheap so I have to ask that you reimburse me as I cannot afford the loss of both weapon and coin."

Baldor smiled and reached into his purse. "Thank you."

"You can check the price I paid when you talk to Alvaro."

"You strike me as an honest man Amanar, give me your price and your word will be good enough."

Amanar dipped his head and smiled. "No Captain, when we finish our wine I'll show you the way to Alvaro's Smithy so you can hear the price I paid for yourself."

Warmed by the wine and with the sun high enough to give a gentle warmth the men made their way in search of the Smith, Baldor and Amanar riding out front, Andulas and Armaco following on. Andulas leaned across to speak quietly to Armaco.

"Hey, grumpy!" Armaco just scowled back from his furs. "Please, let's not start a fight with this Smith eh?"

"No promises, two honest men in less than one morning, I'll believe that when I see it and by the way my bloody leg hurts!"

"Your head will match it if you don't behave! And I'll put you out of the tent on your ear." He raised his fist in mock threat.

"You wouldn't do that, would you?" Armaco asked earnestly.

Andulas chuckled. "Put you out, never! You're my brother. However, I will thump your head if you start trouble without good reason." When Armaco looked as if he would give a quick retort, Andulas held a finger over his smile and whispered. "Shush! Silence is a tool of a wise man."

The men rode for a while weaving their way through the haphazard camp, in the tent shadows where the sun didn't reach the frost remained white and hard, winter was almost upon them. Amanar stopped them outside a large tent where a huge tree stump with a crude anvil on top of it stood to one side of a stone and clay forge. A young boy worked the bellows driving air into the charcoal fanning the low flames red-white, while two swords rested their tips in the centre of the heat. Further back, a huge man sat astride a wooden framed grinding wheel raising orange sparks as he ran a spatha blade across the moving stone. Amanar dismounted.

"Alvaro!"

"Aye! Who's asking?" The man growled without looking up from his work.

"Amanar."

"If it's more repairs you'll have to wait, I'm busy."

"Not this time my friend. These men would like to talk to you if you will spare us a moment."

"What do they want?" He asked, again without looking up. "You can see I'm busy. Keep turning that handle boy! I need a steady speed for the grind." He growled at the young boy who had two hands on a handle turning the large stone disc. Alvaro looked up briefly at the forge and the other boy working the bellows. "Pump those bellows you lazy little bastard! Put some heat into those blade tips so I can rework them."

"That ivory hilted falcata I bought from you …"

"That twenty denarii was a fair price, that blade is quality!" Alvaro interrupted gruffly. "And I can't afford to buy it back yet if that's what you're after? That damned Numidian I play with uses loaded dice, I'm sure of it."

On hearing the price Armaco's eye went wide, and he whistled softly then whispered to Andulas. "Twenty denarii! That's about two month's wages or so for a bloody legionary!"

Andulas chuckled. "Well that would make it cheap at twice the price, those bastards aren't worth much." The comment drawing a snort and finally a chuckle from Armaco.

"No Alvaro, I don't want to sell the falcata back to you but can you tell me or rather us where you bought it?" Amanar continued.

"I might, though information usually costs money."

Armaco's lip twisted into a snarl and a low growl started in his throat, Andulas shushed him quickly.

Alvaro sighed and putting the blade down stood up from the wheel, wiping his hands on his apron he finally looked at the group of men. The man was huge, his thick arms all corded muscle, his broad chest shirtless and barely constrained within the leather apron. A thick layer of black hair covered his shoulders and arms like a fur pelt, his face almost covered to his eyes in a wild black beard.

Baldor dismounted and stepped forward. "Fair enough friend, I'll pay for your knowledge of the blade."

Armaco groaned and muttered under his breath.

The big man looked at Baldor. "Tell you what, Captain. I'll riddle you for the information, if I win you pay me, if I lose, I'll tell you for free."

"Fair enough. Let's hear it."

Alvaro looked up as if seeking inspiration. "H'mm let me see, aha! I have it. What kind of animal begins life with four legs then changes to two and then back to three?"

Baldor took a moment and then smiled as if recollecting. "That my friend is not an animal but a man. As a baby, a man crawls on hands and knees, thus four legs. As he grows, he learns to walk on two legs but in old age he uses a walking stick so three legs."

Alvaro huffed. "Do I get a chance to win my money back?"

Armaco laughed and blurted. "You haven't spent any bloody money! What you mean is do you get another go."

"Same thing!" The big man growled.

"No, it …"

"All right Alvaro." Baldor said quickly cutting Armaco short. "I'll riddle you this. There is a house, you enter it blind but come out of it seeing, what is it?"

The big man's face showed his emotions as he frowned then smiled as if to speak, then frowned again and gurned. "How many guesses do I have?"

Baldor laughed. "Only one, the same as you gave me."

"Play fair Alvaro." Amanar chuckled.

Alvaro paced, tugging at his beard as he thought, after waiting a considerable while, Armaco quipped. "Then along came the summer."

Alvaro glared at him then threw his hands in the air. "All right, I don't know and don't have all day to play bloody games! What is it?"

Baldor smiled. "A schoolhouse."

"A schoolhouse!"

"Yes, you enter it blind to knowledge but when you leave your eyes have been opened to learning."

Alvaro snarled and snorted his face sour. Armaco, expecting trouble eased his hand beneath his furs to his falcata hilt. Moments later the big man burst out laughing. "A schoolhouse! A bloody schoolhouse … I'll remember that one, I'll win some coin with that."

"So I win my information?"

"You do Captain, you do! I won the sword in a game of knucklebones. There's a regular group of players that meet most nights at Sabo's wine tent or hostelry as he terms it, it's over on the east side of the camp. You can't miss it as it's quite large, there are many tables to drink and gamble at. The man I won the blade from was a Numidian called Hiempsal, he was short of coin that night so offered the blade as a wager."

"Thank you, Alvaro."

"A word to the wise Captain, he's an angry, bad-tempered bastard and he wasn't happy giving the blade up. I think my size gave him pause to argue, though I did watch my back for a while."

"Thank you, I'll tread carefully." Baldor mounted and turned his horse away and back in the direction of Andulas's tent but stopped to offer his hand and some silver to Amanar. "Thank you Amanar, I'm a step closer to finding who robbed me, we'll call upon this Hiempsal and ask him the question."

"If you need me anymore Captain, you know where I am." He shook Baldor's hand warmly and nodded to the others then turned his mount back the way they'd come.

With the three men alone again, Andulas ventured. "Tonight, Baldor?"

"Yes, tonight."

"Where did you learn all that riddle shit?" Armaco grumbled.

"A former life Armaco, before the war."

"Before the war you were just a boy! Still are!" He chuckled.

"Exactly! And my father, determined that I was to be educated had me tutored, I thought it a pain and a waste of time but there you go."

"Is there anything you're not good at? You speak Gallic, Greek and some Roman rubbish and …"

"He can fight too." Andulas interrupted while smiling at Armaco's rant. "And fight well!"

"He's learning!" Armaco smiled and started to laugh, "Just like you but the pair of you still have a lot to learn, don't worry though, I'll tutor you!"

Baldor spoke over the laughter. "There was one thing I was always slow at until I met you."

"Yes, fighting, I said that!"

"No, finding good, loyal and true friends. When Gestix was slain I was lost, you two have since filled a huge gap."

Armaco just stared, expecting a catch or to be the butt of the joke he continued to gawp.

"Gods above Baldor!" Andulas exclaimed with great exaggeration. "That's another gift to add to your list, you've managed to shut Armaco up!"

Later and at Andulas's insistence, after dinner. The three men made their way across the camp once more, this time to seek Sabo's wine hostelry. The camp was a different place after dark, fires burned outside most tents with folk collecting about them seeking company and warmth from the cold autumn night. The daytime bustle replaced by a low buzz of talk interjected with laughter and the occasional cheer as someone won a wager. The sounds of a reed flute drifted on the still air and a woman's voice sang a beautiful but haunting tune of home. Baldor's quiet reminiscence of Lasairiona playing the flute was brief for as they rode past one of the camp brothels, Andulas asked loudly.

"Going in for a sleep, Armaco?"

"I might on the way back as no doubt it'll be me that has to sort out any trouble or thumping that may be required at this Sabo's."

Andulas laughed but Baldor cut through it, his tone sharp. "There'll be no trouble we are asking questions is all."

"This Hiempsal could be a handful Baldor, you heard what the Smith said, he's an angry man."

"Aye I did Armaco, so all the more reason for us to be calm."

"Fair enough but I tell you, I have a bad feeling about this."

"There's no need, I've brought no weapons and you two will leave yours with the horses. Did you hear that Armaco?"

"Yes Captain, I'll be good." He said with slow sarcasm.

Becoming lost in the dark vastness of the camp the men had to ask directions, eventually their ears picked up the wine and ale-fuelled noise associated with an inn and men taken with drink. The area was quite large and lit by tall, burning torches stuck in the ground just as Alvaro had described. Men stood about drinking and talking else settled at tables playing dice, knucklebones or engaged in games of tabula, many with a woman or two on their knee. Some of the women took throws for the men, blowing on the dice, kissing them or rubbing them on barley-concealed breasts in a show of bringing luck. Others gave mock screams as they were pawed by their drink taken customers while some were already taking their man by the hand and leading him towards another tent, it less well-lit and set alongside that which provided the drinks. Making their way through the throng to the counter, Baldor paid for wine for the three of them, drinks in hand they began to circulate seeking Hiempsal the Numidian.

A loud disturbance at a table drew their attention and that of Sabo's house guards.

"Let him go Hiempsal!" One of them shouted as he and his comrade pulled the Numidian off another man who Hiempsal was dragging over the table by his throat. "Let him go or you're out!"

The Numidian hissed something from between clenched teeth but let the man go while raising open hands.

"Enough Hiempsal! This is your last warning." One of the men brandished a club and the Numidian sat back down.

"He tried to cheat me!"

A chorus of denials quietened quickly as the Numidian glared around the table. Some men lowered their gaze, others got up and walked away shaking their heads and refusing Hiempsal's calls to return to the game.

"Next time you're out!" One of the guards snarled while pointing at Hiempsal with the club.

The men still around the table were quiet, Hiempsal hiding his anger in his wine cup before shoving the dice beaker across the table and gesturing that the game should begin again.

Andulas leaned to Baldor's ear and whispered. "I think we should leave it for tonight, let's talk to him when he's sober."

"Let him finish his game; if he wins he may be in a better frame of mind, if not I'll ask him anyway we've come this far."

The three men stood back watching the game from a distance patiently waiting for it to finish. As players lost and removed themselves it left only Hiempsal and one other. Hiempsal threw the dice then cursed and slammed his fist into the table, snarling, he stood quickly throwing the dice to one side then moved away from the table.

"Can I have a word, friend?" Baldor asked amicably.

"What? Who are you?" Hiempsal growled while draining his cup before snatching a jug from the table and refilling it.

"Captain Targa."

"What do you want?"

Baldor ignored the man's lack of respect to his rank and remained calm. "Just some information, please."

"And if I don't choose to give it?"

Andulas threw his arm quickly over Armaco and shushed him while Baldor sighed. "Look, all I want to know is who you bought the ivory hilted falcata from, the one that you lost in a game to the Spanish Smith."

"What's it to you?"

"It was mine."

Hiempsal, clearly drunk stared at Baldor and sneered. "What's a boy doing with a blade like that?"

Armaco threw Andulas's restraining arm off and stepped closer, his ruined legs moving awkwardly. "You'll answer the Captain respectfully you drunken piece of shit! Else we take the matter and you to the General."

Hiempsal looked Armaco up and down then gave a contemptuous laugh before throwing the wine in his face and grabbing a knife from his belt. Armaco, veteran of many a drunken brawl did not waste time trying to wipe his eyes but threw a jab that caught the man in the solar plexus taking the wind from him and bending him double. Shaking the wine from his face like a dog shedding water, he stepped closer delivering a vicious uppercut to Hiempsal's downturned face. The blow knocked him backwards onto the table smashing it to matchwood and scattering wine jugs and cups. Unconscious, he fell onto his back the knife flying from his hand, his nose and mouth a bloody mess. As Sabo's guards rushed over, Armaco stepped back and raised open, empty hands.

"The piece of shit was going for a blade." He pointed to the knife laid in the grass.

Sabo's men, brandishing clubs hustled Armaco to one side checking his belt for weapons while Baldor cursed under his breath and stepped in calling for calm.

"We're unarmed …"

"What's the commotion about?" A guard growled.

"Captain!" Baldor affirmed.

The man immediately dropped his attitude. "Sorry Captain, please could you explain?"

"I merely wished to ask this man some questions." He pointed to the unconscious Hiempsal. "He was drunk, disrespectful and my Hypolokhagos here took exception to his manners. The drunken fool then lashed out and went for a knife."

One of the guards picked up the knife and tried it into the empty sheath at Hiempsal's belt. "Aye, the Captain's right, it's the Numidian's blade alright."

"None of you are armed?" Another guard asked civilly.

All three men raised their hands while turning to show belts free of daggers.

"Fair enough! Thank you Captain, gentlemen. Clearly we don't need to involve the Watch as no one is cut or wounded … unless you wish to do so, Captain?" He added quickly.

"No there's no need for a formal complaint, we've all been the worse for drink at some time but have him locked up until he cools off and sobers up. All I want is an answer to my question."

"Who pays for the damage Captain? Master Sabo will need to know."

"Ask the Numidian, he started the trouble."

"Yes sir." The man signalled to his comrades to remove the still unconscious Hiempsal. "Can you leave us your name though; we have to report any disturbances and damage to Master Sabo."

"Captain Targa, Captain Baldor Targa."

"Thank you sir. Can we offer you a table and a jug on the house?"

"No thank you. Make sure the Watch don't let him out until I've spoken to him tomorrow."

"Yes sir."

Baldor turned to Andulas and Armaco ushering them back in the direction of the horses.

"That went well." Andulas muttered.

"What's wrong with folk? I only wanted to talk to him!" Baldor asked.

"Drinking and losing at the game does not a happy man make." Armaco ventured.

Andulas chuckled. "I have to say, that was a fast move Armaco. He expected you to wipe your eyes."

"Huh! You need to get up early of a morning to teach me a thing or two about a brawl."

"That could have been ugly Armaco." Baldor said reprovingly. "If you hadn't dropped him quick, he was going to be at you with that knife."

Armaco reached to his throat and a snugly fitting leather cord tied around a small silver disc with a lightning bolt embossed on it. Running his fingers around it to the nape of his neck, he slipped a very thin, short-bladed knife from a sheath hidden under his tunic. "As I said, you need to get up early to teach me about brawling."

Andulas smirked then laughed. Baldor just shook his head in dismay while mimicking Armaco. "Yes Captain, I'll be good."

"What? … Well, I was good, wasn't I?" He exclaimed in mock respect. "I didn't stick the bastard did I?"

"No Armaco, you're a pillar of obedience." Baldor said but couldn't hide a chuckle.

Chapter Sixteen

The following morning brought leaden skies and hailstones that battered the tent like tiny slingshot and waking the men early. Issa barked loudly when she heard a strange voice at the tent door. Andulas grumbled into his breakfast.

"Who now? Can we not have breakfast in peace?"

A servant returning from the door dipped his head. "A message for the Captain, My Lord. He's to report to the General's tent immediately."

Baldor pushed his plate to one side and stood. "Finish your breakfast lads; I'll see what's afoot."

"Well, it can't be Romans; they've stood a good amount of their men down for the winter." Andulas muttered.

"It can't be about last night either, nobody was stabbed." Armco chuckled.

Baldor was already lacing his boots while looking around for a clean tunic and didn't reply, Issa not helping by tugging at the laces and growling playfully. With the hail not easing, Baldor grabbed a heavy cloak and donned his helmet for further protection then dashed out making his way across the camp at speed. The ground already had a light carpet of white with the roads almost clear of people as they sought shelter from the hail making his progress quick and unhindered. He did wonder what was afoot as both men had been correct in their assumptions, so why the summons and why so early?

Reporting to Hannibal's guards, he was shown through to the meeting area.

"Captain Targa, good morning." Hannibal said formally.

"Good morning, sir."

Hannibal gestured to others in the tent. "This is Prince Massinissa of

185

the Numidian Massylii. His father, King Gala having already supplied us with our formidable Numidian light cavalry sends him to us to aid in our war against Rome. He commands the Numidian cavalry with General Maharbal, Lord Sakarbaal you already know."

"Your majesty." He bowed his head while holding a hand over his heart then turned and dipped his head to Sakarbaal. "Lord Sakarbaal."

Massinissa was as tall as Baldor but much darker skinned. His hair and beard, as black as ebony were shaped and trimmed flawlessly as if for attendance at court, his tunic though remained simple, yet spoke of high quality. A gold chain as thick as a man's forefinger hung around his neck denoting his Princely worth. Heavier built than Baldor, his arm muscles were large and well defined his thighs thick and strong from years of riding. His carriage, as Hannibal gestured the men to the table and seats was regal and unhurried. Hannibal turned to Baldor.

"The Prince is seeking a Captain of his, a Captain Hiempsal? It would appear you have him locked up along with his broken nose and loosened teeth."

Baldor cleared his throat. "That's correct sir."

"Would you care to explain?"

"Yes sir, I can and willingly."

Massinissa rested his chin on his hand and gave Baldor a long stare across the table, Baldor dipped his head then returned a level but respectful gaze. Hannibal seeing the looks interjected.

"Lord Sakarbaal is here as he was a breakfast guest of the Prince; he was also supposed to hand over patrol responsibilities to Captain Hiempsal."

"Yes sir."

"Over to you, Captain."

Baldor relayed the events of the previous night and was left to speak without interruption. When he'd finished he did notice that Hannibal's face had lightened, Massinissa however continued to stare at him. When the Prince spoke, it was moderate in tone but with a confidence of a man used to giving commands.

"You have no right to imprison my men Captain; let alone strike them; you were not part of the camp guard patrols and nothing to do with the guards at this wine shop."

"That's true your majesty. However, as you heard I was civil in my approach and unarmed as were my men. However, when Captain Hiempsal took a blade to my man I believe the resulting actions to be justified."

A brief flicker of doubt slipped across Massinissa's face though he hid it well. "If you have a problem with my men Captain, you come to me."

"Yes, your majesty I will, though in this case I did not think it pertinent to bother you over a drunken man, Captain or not."

"Captain Hiempsal admits to being drunk but claims you were neither civil nor restrained in your approach or actions and that you and two of your men attacked him. His only mention of a knife was that in the hand of one of your men?"

"Then your majesty, the man is a liar as well as a drunk." Baldor answered levelly. The tension at the table heightened.

Before Massinissa could reply, Sakarbaal interrupted the conversation.

"Your majesty, if I may comment?" Baldor's gaze moved quickly to Sakarbaal, his brow beginning to furrow, Hannibal's countenance also changed from impassive to concern though his tone remained polite.

"Lord Sakarbaal, I don't believe you were there or involved so surely can have nothing to add in regard to this altercation."

"That's true, General but I can speak in support of Captain Targa." Hannibal's face showed a brief moment of surprise which he quickly changed back to the impassive look of before; Baldor however looked on in shock. "If I may, General?"

Hannibal raised open hands. "As you wish, My Lord."

"Majesty?" Massinissa gestured he could continue. "Majesty, General, I don't know Captain Hiempsal for to comment on his actions or the strength of his word but I do know Captain Targa. In fact, I know him very well, all the way back to when we were children and can vouch that he's a man of truth and honour."

Hannibal continued hiding his thoughts though Baldor looked bashful. Massinissa turned to Sakarbaal.

"So you don't believe Captain Targa started the fight?"

"No majesty, if he says not then that is the truth of it."

"And this knife?"

Sakarbaal shrugged. "As the General said I wasn't there so don't know the facts. However, I do know the Captain would not take to an unarmed man with a weapon."

Massinissa took a moment and looked intently at Sakarbaal before speaking.

"So, you are a friend of Captain Targa?"

"No majesty, I cannot presume that privilege for until very recently Captain Targa was my enemy."

Massinissa raised his eyebrows. "And now you vouch for him?"

"Yes majesty, I grievously misjudged him and by his grace I am still here to tell the tale. He is a fair and honest man."

Massinissa nodded slowly then turned to Baldor. "Captain Targa, it would seem I was not given the full story by Captain Hiempsal. That is a weighty commendation from a former enemy … also; Lord Sakarbaal's words bear out the story I heard from this wine shop's guards. I thought they just wished to apportion blame to the man they had incarcerated as it was easier but with Lord Sakarbaal vouching for you and the honesty I see on your face; I believe I have been misled."

Baldor dipped his head slightly. "Thank you, majesty."

"However Captain, I insist that in the future you approach me for matters regarding my men, drunk or not, am I understood?"

"Yes, majesty."

Massinissa gave a curt nod and turned to Hannibal. "Thank you General, I won't trouble you further and can deal with this matter from here. I will bid you good day." He was about to rise from the table when Baldor spoke.

"Majesty, as you've heard, I only wished to ask a question of Captain Hiempsal, I …"

Massinissa cut him short his tone brisk. "He will be asked Captain and an answer sent to you."

Baldor rose quickly and bowed, Hannibal and Sakarbaal in his lee. "Thank you, majesty I am sorry you were troubled with this."

Massinissa never looked back. "Come My Lord."

With both men gone, Baldor pushed his chair under the table. "Sir, may I go?"

"No, you may not." Expecting a reprove, Baldor tensed. "Have you breakfasted?"

"No sir … well, I had half …"

"Then sit back down and we'll eat."

"Thank you, sir."

"You don't need any more powerful enemies Baldor and I am thankful that you could explain. I admit I was worried to begin with, as I thought your temper had once more come to the fore. Also, and more importantly, from a military point of view we cannot afford to upset our allies and especially a Prince."

"I promised you I would abide by the laws of the camp sir and Baal knows I wasn't seeking trouble; I only wanted to ask this Hiempsal a question."

Hannibal smiled. "Yes, I think trouble was averted this time and as you said Baal knows, and I think in this case, Baal smiled upon you." He chuckled at his prod at Baldor's lack of piety.

Baldor half-smiled. "Why do you say that sir?"

"Well, I think the answer to your question of who the sword was purchased from will be quickly forthcoming."

"You do?"

"Oh yes! Prince Massinissa was embarrassed for not securing the whole story, especially when it appears this Hiempsal has not been truthful." He shook his head slightly. "I'm glad I'm not Hiempsal for embarrassing royalty is a dangerous game, more so with a proud young man like Massinissa."

"I guess I've gained an enemy in Hiempsal then."

"I wouldn't worry too much about it Baldor." He said dismissively then smiled. "Moreover, what of this support from the Lord Sakarbaal? I near swallowed my tongue when he came out with that."

"I couldn't believe my ears sir."

"Well, it must be no more than you deserve, that is much respect from a man who wanted you dead but a short while ago. I think the Gods are smiling once more upon Baldor Targa." He grinned mischievously.

Baldor gave another half-smile. "Sir, if I can get Lasairiona back, retrieve the dagger you gave me and see the guilty men dead then yes, I might believe I am at last back in favour with the Gods."

"Pray for it then Baldor and I'm sure you will receive what you wish." He held up a hand to stifle Baldor's reply. "Meanwhile, I shall pray for it for you, but then … then, when it comes to pass I ask that you pray and give thanks to the Gods with me."

Baldor took a moment before replying and Hannibal didn't badger. Remembering Gestix's words not to blame the Gods for his misfortunes and Hannibal's urgings in a similar vein earlier in their relationship, he sighed deeply then dipped his head to Hannibal.

"Very well, sir. If it comes to pass, I will do as you ask."

Hannibal, being deeply religious beamed a smile. "Excellent Baldor! Excellent! Both the Lord Baal Hammon and I will cherish you for it.

Now, business done it's time for breakfast and as we are alone its, Hannibal and Baldor."

When Hannibal called for his servant requesting breakfast and received no reply, he rose and went seeking him while threatening a whipping if breakfast was not forthcoming and quickly. Baldor sat back in his chair, quietly relieved at the outcome of the conversation with the Prince. He still had Hannibal's friendship, he had no new trouble and it seemed no new enemies, well perhaps Hiempsal, despite Hannibal's assurances to the contrary. Hannibal returned holding an apologetic, bumbling servant by the ear bearing plates and promising food would be forthcoming in a moment.

Before long fresh bread, boiled eggs, fruit, porridge and watered wine appeared in abundance and the men sat to partake. Both were hungry and Hannibal talked as he ate.

"Where to from here Baldor? You have my leave to seek your woman but what of these thieves, what to do about them?"

"I'll have to follow the trail further, as you've heard I've traced it back from Amanar to Alvaro to this Hiempsal, who knows how many more yet?"

"Go steady my friend as you ask."

"I will, I promised you I would abide by the law within the camp."

"Yes, and I know you will, what I'm saying is watch out for others as I have no doubt the closer you come to the thief the more dangerous your questions will be for the guilty."

"Yes, I thought by Hiempsal's reaction he had something to hide."

"We'll soon know."

"You think the Prince will take him to task?"

"I'd wager on it."

"Well, I'll see what transpires and search from there."

"I think you'll have time for both endeavours. For as you've likely seen or heard, Fabius has released many of his men to winter quarters leaving only a token force to keep an eye on us."

"No more fighting until spring then?"

"I guess not. In truth, I'm happy to leave things quiet, we have provisions enough for a good while and both men and animals would benefit from a rest. When we do choose to move I think Fabius will do no more than follow us anyway."

"How much longer is his period of office?"

"My spies tell me it ends with the dying of the year."

"A month or two at most then?"

"Yes, which will take us to midwinter, so any new hot-head that takes the post will be handicapped by the weather."

"Aye and perhaps the memory of last midwinter and their disaster at the Trebbia will also give them pause." Baldor chuckled.

Hannibal laughed lightly. "Yes, I don't think they'll venture there again." He gave a mock shiver. "Wading over an icy river in a hailstorm, they must have had some balls."

"Maybe they had none at all and didn't feel the cold."

Hannibal almost choked on his food as he burst out laughing, his calamity making Baldor laugh while slapping his back to help. Finally, after taking a moment Hannibal managed to resume his breakfast.

With breakfast complete, Baldor took his leave and was about to depart when a Numidian infantry Captain appeared seeking an audience with Hannibal. Calling Baldor back to the table, Hannibal accepted the visit, the officer saluted and turned back to the door and clicked his fingers. A warrior appeared with a basket in hand. The officer bowed to Hannibal and Baldor.

"General, Captain, Prince Massinissa asked me to relay a message regarding this morning's conversation."

"Say on." Hannibal gestured.

The man lifted the basket lid and pulled out a head by the hair.

"Captain Hiempsal!" Baldor exclaimed.

"Yes sir, as was."

Hiempsal's eyes were missing leaving nothing more than cavernous empty sockets, beneath a flattened nose his bloodied mouth had a piece of parchment stuck in it bearing some words scribed in black ink and held in place with a gag. The officer, seeing both men looking at the parchment and gag explained.

"Captain Hiempsal was a liar and a drunk and brought disgrace upon the Numidian people, now he will eat his false words and drink no more while wandering in the dark seeking the afterlife. Before he died, he named a Haemon the Greek as the man he bought the sword from, the Prince hopes this information will help you find the man you seek."

"Please convey my thanks to his majesty for the swift conclusion to the matter and for the information."

"Yes General. Do you wish the head or can I deposit it in the camp midden?"

Hannibal looked to Baldor who shocked as he was, managed with a level of calmness to say the head could be discarded. The man placed the head back in the basket then bowed and left. Once the men were gone, Hannibal turned to Baldor, his tone matter of fact.

"Lying is grievous at any time but lying to a Prince is both grievous and foolish."

"You knew this would happen?"

"Yes, the Prince was embarrassed this morning, so the liar pays the price. You would notice you received no verbal apology from him?"

"Yes."

"Well, he's a Prince and they don't do apologies this however is his way of apology to you."

"That's why you weren't concerned about Hiempsal becoming another enemy?"

"Yes, once Lord Sakarbaal backed your version of events with your character traits, Captain Hiempsal was a dead man."

"Surely though, a flogging or a flogging and a hot branding as a liar would have sufficed?"

"Not when you embarrass a Prince."

Baldor just shook his head. "I guess not."

"I'm glad the head didn't arrive during breakfast." Hannibal chuckled. Baldor, still somewhat shocked at the speed and result of the event said nothing. "So Baldor, what's first? Do you follow the trail to this Haemon the Greek, or do you try for your woman?"

"I'll leave Armaco's man to make some more discreet enquiries for the whereabouts of this Greek while I seek Lasairiona."

"That's wise methinks for she has been gone a while now."

"Yes, over four moons."

"What do you need?"

"Thirty men, myself, Andulas and Armaco."

"Only thirty?"

"Yes, Andulas says thirty will suffice but I was thinking if I could also take Malo."

"Malo?"

"The Nubian archer in Captain Harbro's command, I think a bowman could be useful."

"Aha! I remember, the hunter, a good man. Yes, of course, just see Captain Harbro, you know him well enough so I will leave it to you to arrange."

"Thank you."

"No thanks needed Baldor; I promised you. All I ask is that you don't get yourself killed in a small fight with some slave trader, I need you."

As ever, Baldor coloured under the sentiment. "I won't, I promise."

Hannibal smiled warmly. "How long will you be gone?"

"Four, maybe five days at the most."

"Do you think this small operation will work better than a large force? I can give you all your troop and more besides if you wish?"

"Thank you but this Thaddeus hid Lasairiona from us the last time, if we go in like a sledgehammer cracking a nut we think he'll escape in the confusion. We think stealth is the answer."

Hannibal smiled and nodded while offering his hand. "Fair enough, if My Lord Andulas has it all planned and thinks thirty men will suffice it will be so."

****

"The dish girl, quickly!" Livia groaned as she sat up sharply while holding her stomach. Lasairiona held a dish as she vomited hard though little came up. As the woman laid back on the pillows exhausted, Lasairiona reached for the water bowl and rinsing a cloth applied it to Livia's forehead and neck. Livia sighed softly as the coolness helped take some of the burning from her skin.

"Can I get you something Mistress? A drink?"

"Yes, some watered wine." She gasped. "I'm so thirsty and hungry but nothing will stay down! ... Why, why am I being sick when I have barely eaten for days?"

"I don't know Mistress; shall I send for the physician again?"

Livia shook her head. "He wants me dead!"

"Who Mistress?"

"My husband, Thaddeus." When Lasairiona looked taken aback, Livia continued though her voice grew quieter and weaker. "With me gone he can run the house as he pleases and bed whom he pleases ... I curb his excesses when I can but I'm in his way ... I know he hates me but this, this, I didn't think he dared." Her eyes filled as she spoke.

"Dared what, Mistress?"

"Poison! ... I think he's poisoning me!"

Lasairiona paled at what she heard, her stomach knotted as fear took hold for Livia was the only person between her and Thaddeus and without her protection she was doomed. Fighting back her fear, she bathed Livia's brow again.

"Shall we try some milk and chalk Mistress? The milk will help line your stomach and also feed you, I have heard that chalk can help by binding any badness in your stomach to it and you pass it out in the usual way."

"Yes, yes I'll try …" Livia's eyes closed as she drifted into a fitful, twitching sleep.

Lasairiona turned her onto her side in case she vomited again and went in search of milk and chalk.

Having secured a jug of milk from the kitchen, she made her way to the laundry and asked there for chalk, a slave; busy whitening a toga offered a cup full. Returning to Livia, she found her sitting up and her face all swollen and puffed-up, when Livia tried to speak her enlarged tongue mangled her words. The little Lasairiona knew of illness and afflictions was enough to know Livia had been poisoned; first, the stomach cramps then the sickness and diarrhoea and now the face swelling. However, sniffing at the meal that Livia had left virtually untouched on the bed, she couldn't detect any taint. However, when Livia mumbled at her and pointed again to the plate Lasairiona took a deep breath and committed.

"Mistress, I think you're right, there is or has been something in your food and not just something that doesn't agree with you." Livia looked at her wide-eyed, nodded and tried to speak, the words however, hard to understand. "I have milk and chalk, I'll mix them together, see if you can manage to get it down. It will be difficult to swallow and won't be pleasant as it's like a watery paste, but I think it may help."

Livia just nodded ascent. Lasairiona noticed her condition had deteriorated further since she went for the milk, her eyes seemed more sunken and her pallor a ghostly grey-white, her skin taut and stretched from the swelling. Mixing the chalk and milk to a drinkable consistency, she eased Livia up and helped her drink. It was difficult and slow owing to the swelling and Livia gagged and choked spilling some onto the bed. Lasairiona persevered and managed to get most of the liquid into Livia then eased her back to her pillows but propping her upright in case she vomited again and then cleaned up the spillage. As Livia fell asleep, Lasairiona examined the plate of food again, breaking the fish up with a knife and sniffing at it, she still couldn't detect a taint the garum sauce being too strong. Dipping her finger into the sauce, she smeared a little on her lip but other than the taste of fish there was nothing, however, after waiting a while she found her lip began to tingle and heat up, was it just the spice of the sauce? Reaching for the remainder of the milk, she smeared her lips liberally with it; her lips continued to tingle and then eased. Her mind raced at what to do; somehow, she needed to keep Livia alive in order to survive herself.

Livia slept quietly into the evening without vomiting, Lasairiona sitting close by her bed. When she awoke, it was with a hint of energy and a ready hunger.

"I need food and drink, girl." Her voice commanding though still small.

"Yes, Mistress but I think I should get it, make it in fact, at least until you are well again."

Chapter Seventeen

Cornelius was back at Atticus's door the following day, the loud rapping with his stick brought a servant and Atticus's distant voice that echoed down the passage as she opened it.

"If it's that damn fool Centurion, tell him to begone!"

"The fool Centurion wishes to see his colleague!" Cornelius shouted back and pushed past the servant while mumbling a curt. "Excuse me."

Striding along the corridor the servant ran after him and steered him into a side room. Gaius was propped up on the bed half-awake with Cassia feeding him and Atticus carefully examining his wounds. Gaius, seeing Cornelius gave a small, tired smile though his eyes shone warmly before closing again as sleep took him.

Atticus looked up briefly, scowled and tutted. "Well! You've seen him, now begone!" Ignoring Cornelius further, he continued his examination while questioning Cassia. "Has he had a bowel movement this morning?"

"Yes sir."

"And it's of regular consistency?"

"Yes sir."

"And his piss?"

"Concentrated, dark and smelling strongly so I've upped his fluid intake on top of the wine and colostrum."

"Good, good!" Atticus muttered. "The wounds are looking good; he just needs time to rest and build his strength now." He stepped away from the bed and went to wash his hands in the water bowl, seeing Cornelius he growled. "Are you still here?"

"Yes! And I'm staying until I've had some time with my friend."

"He needs rest not you yapping in his ear!"

Cornelius bit back the sharp retort and tried a different tack. "I just want to see him and let him know I'm here and will be until he's recovered."

"Well! You've seen him and he's recovering so begone."

Clearing up from feeding Gaius, Cassia placed an arm gently on Atticus's shoulder and ventured. "I have noticed that patients can benefit from a visit of a friend, it helps their mental state which you told me is as important to their recovery as their general wellbeing."

"Is it now? ... Did I?" He frowned looked unsure then scowled. "And what of the filth they bring with them eh? And soldiers, hah! Worst of all! Filthy creatures! ... But what do I know?" He threw his arms in the air. "I'm just the fool physician that has to treat them."

"No Atticus, you are the good physician that cares deeply about his charges but needs his breakfast." Cassia smiled warmly. "You've checked the patient's wounds and I've fed him what if you take your breakfast while the Centurion has a moment or two with his friend? I can smell the bread and ..."

Atticus sniffed. "Yes, yes breakfast." He nodded appreciatively then glared at Cornelius. "Not too long and then begone! It's best if you don't touch him. However, if you must; wash your damned hands first." He stormed off.

Cornelius watched him go then turned to Cassia. "Thank you."

"He's a good man Centurion and a fine physician perhaps the best I have seen and studied under; he'll make sure your friend will recover."

Cornelius nodded and stepped closer to Gaius who was still sleeping. Beneath the stubble of whiskers, he could see the skin was clean and had gained a little colour from the deathly white of the previous day. His eyes were still darkly ringed and he looked exhausted but the fraught pain lines and grimness had gone. He reached out to touch him then stopped himself.

"Get well old friend you're in good hands." Content at what he saw he turned to Cassia. "Please remind him I was here will you? I'll come back in a few days; I can see now that he'll recover so won't antagonise Atticus with a visit before then. Will you give him my thanks; I don't think he will take it from me."

Cassia smiled and nodded. "Yes, I will. It's not personal you know; he doesn't dislike you it's just he gets frustrated with the damage you soldiers do to one another."

"Surely his sympathies lie with Rome though?"

She shrugged. "He's proudly Capuan he tells me and his sympathies lie with anyone at all who is injured or needing help, as do mine."

Cornelius nodded slowly. "And yourself, are from where?"

"From the mountains in the north."

"You're a Gaul by your height and colouring and a long way from home?"

"I am and though I bear no love for Rome, just like Atticus I bear an injured man no ill will."

"Yes … yes, I can see that. I'll bid you good day …?"

"Cassia."

"Good day Cassia." He smiled warmly at her and turned to go.

****

"Make sure everything you have is Roman, we don't want to give the game away." Andulas said as the three men rummaged through a pile of Roman equipment on the tent floor, Issa stepped amongst it sniffing and then trying to lick the men's faces.

"Come on girl, out of the way." Baldor said as he gently pushed her to one side, Issa, thinking it was a game came straight back and grabbed his arm bracer pulling hard. "Issa, stop!" When she carried on, he tapped her on the nose and she let go, backing off to settle on her sheepskin she watched the men while looking sad.

Armaco picked her up and stroked her. "She just wants to play! Give her something to chew! Don't you two know anything at all about dogs?"

Baldor and Andulas stared at him in amazement.

"Epona help us! Now he's a dog expert." Andulas chuckled. "Can we concentrate on what we are doing here, never mind the dog?"

"I can do two things at once, ask Helena at the whorehouse."

"We'd rather not." Andulas sniggered and passed Issa her chew.

Armaco smirked mischievously. "Anyway, what about that moustache? It doesn't look very Roman to me."

"What about it? We just have to dress in Roman equipment, I didn't say we have to be Roman, we're auxiliaries remember."

"What if this Thaddeus recognises you?"

"By the time he does it'll be too late, I just want to get us past the guards at the gate and into the town without trouble. Baldor, you'll have to leave your falcatas here again, take a spatha and pugio only."

Baldor nodded while drawing a spatha from its scabbard and sighting the edge then giving a swing or two.

"It's going to be different; I'm used to the weight of the falcata, and this spatha is light." He continued trying practice swings then unsheathed the pugio and held it up admiring the broad blade. "That's quite a dagger, I like it … what about Malo? We could do with him there, but he won't fit into the plan as there are no Nubian auxiliaries that I've seen?"

"Not to worry, he's already left."

"What?"

"It gives him a chance to have a look around and he'll meet us inside the town. He'll enter as a hunter, arriving singly with just his knife and bow and some dead game so a spare sword, spear and shield for him will go with us."

Armaco dumped his borrowed gear and reached for the wine jug. Andulas stopped him when the cup was half-full and topped it up with water.

"Clear head tomorrow brother we'll need our wits about us."

"Fair enough." He grumbled. "Baldor! You can buy me a jug of the expensive stuff when we get back."

Baldor smiled. "Willingly brother, I'll buy you two if everything works out."

Armaco groaned. "I hate it when he doesn't bite!"

Andulas chuckled and looked at his two comrades. "Right, here's the plan. We leave after dark tomorrow …"

"After dark?" Armaco interrupted.

"Yes, the least folk that see us the better. Remember, we are dressed as Roman auxiliaries so I've arranged an escort from some of our men who will see us safely away from the camp; we don't want to be attacked by our own side do we? Once we are well clear we are on our own.

Now, we can likely make Casilinum in a day and a half but we'll time our arrival to just before dark. The less we're seen, the better I think our chances. Also, arriving at the town gate just before nightfall should save protracted questions as to who we are and where we are from as the guards will be anxious to close up."

"And then?" Baldor asked.

"Then comes the tricky part, we'll take lodging for the night and lie up during the following day until evening."

"Why take the risk of being there so long? Once we are in the town why don't we just attack?"

"Several reasons Armaco. One, the horses will need a rest especially if we are looking to make a fast exit after securing Lasairiona. Two, the lie up day gives you and some of the men a chance to look around and familiarise yourself with the town, so we know where we are going when it's dark. Three, we'll have an advantage if we attack Thaddeus's villa just before it's locked up on dark as his guards will be less attentive and seeking their evening meal. Lastly, if we were to be pursued it will be in the dark which will make it more difficult."

"And for us!"

"We can't have everything Armaco!" Andulas chuckled. "Anyway, if you raise us a good fire at the villa I think that along with their shock at the attack will give them plenty to think about."

"And the town gate?"

"We'll try and bluff our way out, we tell the guards that Carthaginian raiders have come over the walls, robbed and burned the villa then fled when we appeared, and we are to give chase."

Baldor nodded. "That would also help explain the noise of the fighting coming from the villa."

"Hold on, we'll have Lasairiona with us, she isn't going to look like a Roman auxiliary."

"True Armaco. However, if we give her a helmet, spear and shield and place her in the middle of the men I think we'll get away with it. Remember, it'll be dark and the guards should be panicking as chaos will have ensued."

"And if they don't open the town gate."

Andulas shrugged and smiled. "We rush it and kill the bastards."

Armaco nodded approvingly.

"The plan sounds good Andulas; it seems you have every eventuality covered." Baldor said quietly.

"Why do you look so worried then?" He asked kindly.

"Because … because this is all about what I want, I'm asking you both and the men to put your lives on the line for me."

"We're soldiers, it's what we do."

"In battle yes but this is different. You don't have to go to Casilinum?"

"No, we don't but we choose to because you're our friend and brother and the men are all volunteers, none are going by command but out of respect for you."

"And I need to look after you both." Armaco interrupted and broke some of the seriousness from the conversation.

Baldor, still sombre carried on. "As I have said before I am much blessed and rich in friends."

"Just remember the two jugs of expensive stuff you promised me."

Baldor stepped across and much to Armaco's discomfort hugged him close. "I won't forget; you're a bloody good man Armaco Salamar."

"You're not so bad yourself." Was the best he could manage along with tentative slaps on Baldor's back.

Baldor moved towards Andulas and hugged him. "Thank you Andulas, for everything."

The big Gaul, as easy with his feelings as Baldor hugged him back. "You would do the same for either of us Baldor."

"Yes, but …"

"A good man should have good friends." He smiled warmly. "Come; let's grab some sleep before we have to leave, it's going to be a long night followed by a long day with a cold sleep outside tomorrow."

Baldor lay awake quietly contemplating the next few days. Armaco's snores made him smile, even more so when he saw Issa curled up asleep on the bed with him. His thoughts were interrupted by Andulas offering him a cup of hot water and honey.

"How does he do it Andulas, sleep like that?"

Andulas chuckled. "Only a man of clear conscience can sleep like that."

"For Baal's sake don't tell him that we'll never hear the last of it."

The men dressed and armed themselves quietly as they drank, Issa opened one eye and watched then went back to sleep. They had to wake Armaco who came to with instant recognition of what was happening and was immediately on the move.

The gentle thump of hooves told of their men assembling outside the tent and the three made their way out into the cold darkness. Flanked by the normally attired Gauls the 'would be' Roman turma moved quietly out of camp and turned southwest back towards Casilinum. As they entered the hills, the escort took their leave and headed back to camp. The moon rose silver-white and full faced casting a ghost light and helping light the road. Andulas tapped Baldor's arm and pointed.

"How's that for a sign? Reannon our Goddess of the moon is lighting our way."

Almost hidden beneath a wolfskin stole Baldor managed a hesitant chuckle. "A girl called Reannon asked me to marry her once."

"Perhaps she was the Goddess in human form and now she lights your way?"

Baldor smiled warmly at the memory. "Maybe, she was certainly beautiful."

"And you weren't tempted?"

Baldor swallowed hard. "No, my heart was still broken from the death of my wife but I made a pig's ear out of turning her proposal down, Gestix wasn't too pleased with me."

"Ah Gestix, your good friend and brother."

"Aye, Epona bless and keep him." He managed a smile.

"Was he angry because you turned her down?"

"More for my rudeness and lack of manners."

"You, rude!"

"Aye …"

"Don't sound so surprised Andulas; he does have a hole in his arse." Armaco muttered.

"Ah, my conscience speaks!"

The three chuckled among themselves. "Come, let's see if we can increase the pace a little and put some warmth in our bones." Andulas said as he kicked his mount on.

The first glow of dawn breaking behind the small column showed a white, frost hardened landscape. The grass crunched beneath the horses' hooves and the breath of both men and mounts rose in clouds, the animals' coats gently steaming in the clear, sharp air. The sun was still invisible, hidden by the surrounding hills as the men made their way along a shadowy valley floor. No one spoke much, all were gloved and fur wrapped against the cold for winter it seemed was coming early.

As the sun climbed throughout the day, some warmth filtered down to the men though it remained too low to give any real heat, some places remained in permanent shadow and here the ground stayed white, bright and stone hard. Late afternoon saw Andulas call a halt. Having found an elevated, sunny knoll that caught the last of the sinking sun but screened by large boulders the group made camp. Judging they were far enough from both army camps and thus roving patrols the weary men set small fires and managed some hot food before producing bedrolls, furs and blankets looking to sleep.

"I reckon we'll be in sight of Casilinum by early afternoon tomorrow but as planned we'll wait until just before dark before we try the gate." Andulas nodded southwest as he spoke.

Without further discussion the men settled, huddling close to one another for warmth and as near to the fires as they dared. The night brought a clear, star-studded sky with near freezing temperatures and most men slept fitfully when the fires burned low and the cold crept into their bones. Before dawn broke the following morning most were up and about seeking a hot drink and food, talk was still scarce though Armaco managed a grumble.

"Baal Almighty! It's as cold as a witch's tit out here!"

"It's not nearly as cold as that night I spent down by the Trebbia River." Baldor said before taking a mouthful of steaming honey-water. "You think this is cold but believe me that night was colder than Hades it killed a few lads and nearly did for Malo. Thank Baal for the river rocks."

"River rocks?" Andulas asked.

"Aye, we were told to each heat a river rock in the fire and place it in our pack, they kept us warm for a while but they didn't last all night."

"Why have we not got river rocks Andulas?" Armaco asked sarcastically.

"Because you blow enough hot air to keep us all warm."

The sniggers and snorts from the men nearby had Armaco sneer then chuckle good naturedly while grumbling. "Baal save us from smart arsed Gauls. Oh! And Captains." When he saw Baldor trying to supress a laughing fit.

The men broke camp and moved on while Andulas dispatched scouts wishing ample warning of sighting Casilinum.

The scouts returned quickly and at speed. Seeing them, Andulas halted the column while men immediately checked their weapons; this must be trouble. Baldor, instinctively reaching for his falcatas felt naked by their removal and slid the spatha in and out of its scabbard instead. A moment later one of the scouts reined in.

"My Lord, there's a large Numidian patrol up ahead though they look to be moving directly south."

"Huh! If they see the Roman garb they won't wait to ask questions." Armaco snarled.

"True, we'll give them a wide berth and head west then swing back southwest, it'll add to our time but no matter, better that than an unnecessary fight with our own side. Let's hope they keep going south for if they come this way and see our tracks they're likely to follow us."

Sending a man to watch the Numidians, Andulas waved the column on. The detour swung them wide of Casilinum but kept them out of sight of the Numidians.

Coming closer to the town brought signs of human habitation with small farms, gardens and orchards and as before the familiar signs of a rapacious army. The buildings burned and blackened from smoke, tiled roofs caved in as the supporting trusses had burned through, the thatched buildings left with charred, skeletal timbers pointing skyward as the fired reeds had burned off. Orchards stripped of their autumn fruit and the smaller trees smashed, the gardens with their vegetables dug up and anything unripe being trampled and destroyed and covered now by the thick frost. The bodies of old or lame animals lay where they had been slaughtered their legs sticking out rigidly from bloated bodies as they slowly rotted; interspersed amongst the carnage was the odd human body.

Baldor looked at the grim spectacle then shook his head before pulling his furs over his mouth and nose as the waft of decay caught on the breeze. "We're consistent and efficient if nothing else." He said quietly.

Andulas nodded as he scanned the carnage. "The face of war I suppose. However, apart from the need to eat I'm not sure the end justifies the means and despite Rome doing nothing to defend these folk I don't see many of them coming over to us." When the scouts returned and announced Casilinum to be over the next rise, Andulas looked around for a place to lay up and wait for evening. "We need to find a place upwind of this." He said from beneath a scarf covered face and waved the column further on.

Finding the remains of a large empty barn where fire had only destroyed half of the roof and left three of the walls almost intact, the group dismounted and settled. The stink of charred timber, old dung and burned hay was still strong but thankfully free of the stench of rotted flesh. Seeking water for the horses two men went to check the small well in the courtyard but returned quickly with shaking heads, the well a grave to a number of bodies.

As the sun dipped low the column was on the move again, this time displaying a banner denoting the turma name and number.

Approaching the town, they saw the usual hurried activity on the walls above the gate before one-half was pushed closed with the guards moving in front of the remaining entrance. Andulas slowed the canter to a walk while he and Baldor dropped casually back within the column leaving Armaco and a Gaul to lead.

"Now we'll see how nervous they are, they can see the turma banner so hopefully that'll calm them a little." Andulas whispered to Baldor.

A guard stepped ahead of his colleagues and raised his hand to halt the column. As he approached, the Gaul next to Armaco took the lead.

"Gallic auxiliary cavalry attached to the first legion, we're stood down for the winter and heading home."

The guard scowled and looked nervously at the man then at the column behind him. "You can't winter here; we're short of provisions as it is."

"We're just passing through; we need to rest and we'll begone in a day or two. We have coin to pay."

The guard took another look at the men and decided he didn't need any aggravation, stepping back he flicked his head towards the gate while shouting to his colleagues to stand aside. As the men passed under the gate arch Andulas winked at Baldor. With evening coming on the streets were growing quiet, a few remaining stallholders were packing up while dealing with late come customers; a Watchman was walking the streets lighting torches. Armaco split the column into three sections of ten men to seek lodging but with instructions for one man from each to report to the command group at the Eagle inn.

****

"She's saying what?"

"Insisting that she alone prepares Mistress Livia's meals from now on, sir. She told the cook that was the Mistress's orders."

Thaddeus scowled and his face clouded darkly as his temper rose. "Did she now? The insolent bitch!" Then as suddenly as his anger had surfaced, it disappeared, replaced by a vicious smile. "Yes and why not?" He chuckled quietly while Arya looked on confused. "Perfect, perfect! Now all you have to do is add your potion to the meal that she prepares and the Princess can be easily blamed when Livia dies."

"But that might not be possible sir, she …"

Thaddeus grabbed Arya's hair forcing her head back. "Then make it possible!" He hissed sharply, before softening his tone. "I'm sure someone of your intelligence and guile will manage." When Arya didn't answer, he twisted harder making her yelp then spoke quietly into her ear. "Don't fail me now Arya, for if you do … well, as you said yourself the house is full of many beautiful women."

"I'll see to it sir." She managed as he continued to hurt her.

"Good, good I thought that's what you said." Spinning her around by her hair, he forced her over the end of the bed. "Your wickedness gives me such an appetite."

"Yes sir." She managed while lifting her dress.

Thaddeus pulled his robe to one side as he talked. "Just one last dose and the work is done then I'll be happy and you'll be safe, no more whippings from Livia."

"Yes sir."

"Make it a fatal dose Arya and then we blame the Princess."

Chapter Eighteen

"It's not the best inn I've stayed at." Armaco grumbled, his nose twitching at the smell of sour wine, spilled ale and wood smoke that filled the room, his boot soles sticky from spills on the worn wooden floor. "Can't they afford oil lamps? It's darker than Hades in here!"

"I'm sorry it's not up to your usual standard majesty." Andulas teased. "However, it's dry, warm and reasonably clean and perfect for our needs, so you'll just have to suffer it."

"It'll do I suppose." He said with mock imperiousness and smirked. "The things I do for you Baldor." He grinned while poking Baldor in the ribs playfully.

"Thank you." Baldor replied seriously.

"I do hate it when you don't bite!" He smiled.

"I just want this over, with as few of us injured as possible."

"It will be. I'm here this time."

"Yes, that's what's worrying us." Andulas quipped and finally drew a chuckle from Baldor.

"My Lord?" Cassia muttered beneath her breath. Completely surprised at seeing Andulas she snatched her tray and a jug of wine and headed across the room towards where he, Armaco and Baldor sat. "My Lord!" She gasped as she came closer while looking about the inn quickly at the few patrons and Andulas's men.

"Cassia!"

"My Lord, I didn't know you were coming." She hissed quietly while still casting her eyes about the room.

"No matter." He said calmly while looking around himself. "What's to do?"

"There are Romans here, Lord."

"Here?" All three men glanced around while hands instinctively reached for their swords.

"In the town somewhere but I don't know where they're lodging." She whispered while recharging the cups.

"How many?"

"I only saw a few, they came to the physician's house where I work and study during the day and there's a Centurion with them, he left a badly wounded colleague, another Centurion, in the care of my mentor Atticus."

"That could mean a century or so of the bastards at least! Maybe two, if there's two Centurions." Armaco growled.

Baldor paled and Andulas looked concerned before collecting himself and speaking calmly. "Remember, we're dressed as the same side and as we're auxiliaries I don't think legionaries will want much to do with us."

"What if trouble starts? … You know; the old regimental rivalries that start once the wine and ale are flowing?" Armaco muttered.

"H'mm, seeing as we are out of camp and as you say, with the usual mix of wine, ale and hot-heads it might. However, if it does and as you mentioned we could pass it off as divisional rivalry nothing more; it doesn't have to lead to bloodshed. Furthermore, if a fight starts I would think a Centurion would be duty bound to stop it." Andulas reasoned.

"So would you, Decurion Armaco!" Baldor added and managed a smirk.

"True." Andulas smirked.

"A fist fight with legionaries but then not killing the bastards?" Armaco frowned.

"No Armaco! No fighting at all if we can help it. Save the killing for Thaddeus and his guards. Cassia, keep your ears and eyes open for me."

"Yes Lord."

"And can we have dinner?" He smiled as she nodded and taking the empty jug headed to the kitchen.

"Who's that?" Armaco grunted appreciatively.

"That Armaco; is my information man."

"She's pretty for a man! That long blonde hair and blue eyes." Armaco gave Cassia's departing back and shapely buttocks a licentious look.

"Aye, she is but you're here to work not chase the serving girls." Andulas said a little too harshly.

"Fair enough! I'm just admiring is all. I'll behave."

Appeased, Andulas moved onto the plan. "Now, the other lads will report in later tonight, as for tomorrow while the others take a walk around us three will stay here and behave, no serious drinking!"

"Where's Malo?" Baldor asked.

"Somewhere in the town. It wouldn't look right if a hunter was mixing with soldiers so he's keeping his distance but will be watching and ready for tomorrow night."

The following morning Andulas sent men in small groups to explore and casually walk around the town to familiarise themselves with the layout ready for the coming night's action. Having warned them again against heavy drinking and trouble, he Armaco and Baldor relaxed in the inn amusing themselves with dice and board games of tabula and latrones.

Just after midday the inn was quiet, one or two patrons had taken their meals there then left to continue with their day's business leaving the three men alone again and in peace. Sitting at a small table, Baldor had his back to the door while the other two faced it; they were finishing their meal when Andulas picked up his cup and using it to hide his mouth, whispered.

"Roman Centurion at the counter."

Baldor's immediate reaction was to turn and look but Armaco, moving lightning fast kicked Baldor's legs beneath the table drawing his attention back. Reaching for the jug with one hand and Baldor's forearm with the other, he hissed. "Don't look!"

While the Centurion ordered a drink from the innkeeper, Cassia came over to the men's table with a cloth. Keeping her back to the Roman, she began clearing plates and wiping the table while whispering beneath her breath.

"That's the man that came to Atticus's house."

The men settled back to their games while the Centurion looked casually around the inn and at the three men. Recognising Roman garb, he picked up his drink and made his way over. As Cassia lifted the plates and turned around, she bumped into him sending him stumbling backwards.

"Cassia!"

"Yes sir." She smiled.

"I thought you worked for Atticus?" He asked kindly.

"I do sir but I lodge here and work off some of my bill by helping out when Atticus doesn't need me."

"I see. How is my friend today, have you seen him?"

"Yes, he managed a decent breakfast sir, a good sign. I'm back there later this afternoon I'll tell him you were asking for him."

"Thank you. Can I order some food?"

"Certainly sir, I'm afraid it's only simple fare owing to the war affecting supplies."

"No matter, I'll take what you have, thank you."

Baldor, hearing the familiar voice and still with his back to the Centurion felt his skin flush hotly, Cornelius! His heart leapt in his chest pounding fast and stealing his breath, his nerves on the raw. As Cassia moved off, Cornelius looked again at the three men and raised his vine stick in salute. Andulas, looking up managed a nod of his head.

Cornelius, noting Armaco's rank smiled amicably and called. "Hello Decurion." Armaco looked up and dipped his head while grunting a non-descript greeting. "Are you lads stood down as well? Who are you with?" He asked politely.

Andulas intervened casually in Gallic. "First legion auxiliary, third turma."

Cornelius took a moment while processing the language. "The First legion? But you're still with Fabius … what are you doing here?" There was a moment of tense silence then he dropped his stick and went for his gladius. "Deserters! You're …"

Baldor leapt up and spun round knocking the stool over, one hand grabbing Cornelius's throat the other slapping the Roman's hand aside from his gladius hilt before snatching the pugio from his belt. Knocking chairs and tables aside, he forced Cornelius back hard against the wall while bringing the dagger point up under his chin.

"Cornelius!" He hissed.

Cornelius, shocked at the blur of speed stared, his eyes wide, his mouth opening but his words unintelligible as Baldor squeezed his throat hard. Andulas and Armaco were also on their feet, Armaco looking around to see who'd seen the disturbance while Andulas made to question Baldor, who pre-empted him.

"It's Cornelius!"

"Who?" Andulas asked.

"What in …?" Armaco growled.

"Cornelius Scipio!" Baldor hissed. "I'd know his voice anywhere and he knows me!"

Cornelius tried to push his head back further as Baldor's dagger was already cutting the skin.

"Hey! Enough there! No fighting in here." The innkeeper bellowed as he stepped from behind the counter. He looked nervously at the men while brandishing a lead weighted club.

Andulas intervened, easing Baldor's dagger hand from Cornelius's throat and telling them all to sit down; Armaco pushed Cornelius roughly between himself and Baldor while Andulas raised open hands.

"All sorted good sir! A disagreement over the game and money is all."

The innkeeper, relieved at the ready climb down nodded and lowered the club. "Keep it civil lads, eh?" Then turned back to the front room of the inn.

"We will, I promise." Andulas replied to the man's departing back while praying that Cornelius didn't cry wolf. With peace seemingly restored he sought his seat, though wondering why Cornelius had remained silent until he saw Armaco's hand that rested on the Centurion's shoulder held a small blade against his neck.

Baldor stared, not believing his eyes. "You! … Here?"

Cornelius, in shock himself also stared. "What … what are you doing in auxiliary uniform?"

"Quiet!" Armaco jabbed the blade lightly making Cornelius flinch.

The men continued to stare, the tension palpable.

"If you shout out, the words will be your last." Baldor said while nodding towards Armaco and his blade. Cornelius slowly raised his hands.

"Put your damn hands down and sit still." Armaco growled.

"Take him to our room." Andulas said and flicked his head to the rear door leading to the upstairs rooms. "I'll stay here."

Picking up the fallen stick they escorted Cornelius through the door then pushed him towards the stairs. Once in the room and the window shutters and door were closed, Baldor disarmed him while Armaco drew his dagger.

"I'll kill him now; we can wrap his body in a sheet and leave it under the bed; they won't find him until tomorrow when we're gone."

"No!"

"Do you want to kill him then?"

"No, we'll not do murder!"

"It's not murder, he's a bastard Roman!"

"No!"

"Baal Almighty, Baldor!"

"I said no!" He snapped then lowered his voice while shaking his head. "I cannot …"

"That's all right I'll kill him then."

Cornelius just watched calmly as the men argued.

"No, Armaco. Please!" Baldor said quietly. "Will you give us a moment?" He gestured to the door.

"What!"

"Ask Cassia to bring us some wine and cups"

Armaco almost choked. "You're going to drink with the bastard! Have you gone soft in the head?"

Baldor just smiled sadly and answered quietly. "No … no I don't think so, confused and lost maybe … please?" He gestured to the door again.

Armaco sheathed the dagger, snorted and stormed out of the room muttering and cursing. Baldor closed the door behind him and turned to Cornelius.

"So, what do I do with you?"

"Obviously as you please, though I think your friend wants me dead."

Baldor ignored the comment and instead lifted Cornelius's arm looking at the simple copper and brass twisted bracelet fitted snugly around his wrist. "You still have it!"

"Yes, I won it from you, remember? All those years ago when we were just boys. I see you still wear the marble I gave you." He pointed to the marble wrapped in gold filigree netting and hanging from Baldor's neck.

"I earned that when I saved your life!" He couldn't hide a wry smile.

"So now you'll take back the life you gave?"

"Don't be stupid Cornelius if I wanted you dead I'd have killed you at Trasimene. Anyway, how come you're here?" He shook his head. "Here, of all the places!"

Cornelius shrugged and smiled back. "After you mauled us at the Geronium fight my legion is stood down for the winter to rest, recruit and rearm. My friend Gaius needed expert medical care so I brought him here; he's at the house of Atticus the physician."

Baldor chuckled. "Mauled you! More like we kicked your damned arses! When are you Romans going to learn that you're beaten?"

"If and when you've killed us all."

"Hah! You've still got plenty Roman arrogance!"

"No, just pride. Would you not fight for your home and your people until the last drop of your blood?"

Baldor ignored the question. "Tell me, do you … do you think the Gods are playing with us? After all this time and all these battles, we keep meeting and again now, what's the chances?"

"I don't know." Cornelius gave a slight smile and shook his head. "I do know it's good to see you without a sword in your hand and trying to kill me!"

"You're my enemy Cornelius; I'm supposed to kill you."

"And I you … but I couldn't, can't, just like you won't kill me now."

"Don't be too sure!"

"As you've just said, you would have done it before now if you wanted me dead. In a better world I would have had you as my friend … my good friend."

Baldor sighed and looked Cornelius in the eye and saw sincerity. Cornelius stared back, the pair peering as if looking into the other's soul. The moment lingered, both men perhaps remembering when they were just boys on a high wharf in Gades, their game of marbles, a tumble into the water and a life saved. Yes, friendship would have blossomed but for fate. Their reverie was interrupted by a knock at the door and Cassia stepped in with the wine. After she'd gone, Baldor filled two cups and offered one to Cornelius.

"To a friendship lost."

Cornelius raised his cup, smiled sadly and nodded. "Friendship."

"How many men have you here?" Baldor asked coldly.

"Ten."

"Ten! Why should I believe that?"

"Why should I lie?"

"Because you're Roman!" He sniggered.

"As I told you the army is disbanding for winter; most are heading back to barracks in Rome I came this way to bring my friend to Atticus; the ten men who accompanied me came as volunteers. What are you doing here and in auxiliary uniform, trying to take the town by stealth?"

"None of your business."

Andulas entered the room followed by Armaco. "Time to go Baldor; what do you want to do with him?"

"Tie him to the bed and leave him, by the time they find him we'll be gone."

Armaco, still muttering his discontent began ripping bed sheets into strips then pushed Cornelius back onto the bed tying his arms and legs to the bed legs. Gagging him, he gave him a hard smack in the side of the face, his ringed hand tearing the flesh.

"Just leave him Armaco!" Baldor snapped. "He's not going anywhere!"

"We should just kill the bastard and have done." Armaco snarled and picking up Cornelius stick went to break it over his knee. Baldor snatched it off him.

"Leave it! It's his badge of office!" He growled, then taking it and Cornelius's sword and dagger, laid them at the other corner of the room. Sighing, he moderated his tone. "I'm sorry Armaco; it's just … well it's complicated. I'll follow you down in a moment." As the men left, he turned to Cornelius. "You'll be fine until tomorrow and we'll be gone. It was good to talk and I'm sorry for the way things are, and yes I think but for the war we would have been good friends. Baal guard your footsteps, farewell Cornelius." He saluted, then locking the door headed down the stairs.

The three, along with their men quietly armed themselves, departing the inn in ones and two's and disappeared into the night.

****

Lasairiona, tray in hand complete with Livia's main evening meal paled as she entered the room and saw the woman leant to one side of her pillows. Her hand was near the water jug, it knocked over and the water dripping from the tray and table onto the floor. Vomit ran from her mouth covering her chest and the bed sheets her face deathly white, the pain still etched on her features. Quickly depositing the tray, Lasairiona rushed across to Livia feeling for her heart rhythm at her neck and found nothing; her eyes were wide open staring but the pupils very small. Sniffing at the abandoned plate of the first course she had made, she could smell nothing other than the garlic in the soup, which masked everything. Fear washed over her like a cold wave and she sat down heavily on the bed. Regardless of what she said, she would be blamed for Livia's death, more so as she had been preparing the woman's food herself. How had it happened? From collecting the raw ingredients to cooking the food she had done everything herself, her only thought was with the kitchen always busy somebody had managed to slip something into the dish. What to do? There was nowhere to run and that would only signify guilt, all she could do was ask for a physician to be called.

Her anxious shouts produced servants and slaves and then Thaddeus. Striding into the room, he looked to the bed then Lasairiona before enthusiastically calling for a physician to be summoned.

"What's afoot girl?" He snarled. "You were charged with the care of my wife and now unless my eyes deceive me I see her lying dead?" Stepping toward the bed he felt at her neck then shook his head.

"I didn't kill her, I cared for her!" Lasairiona almost shouted. "I, I saved her life in the town when …"

"So you say!"

"The town guards, they confirmed I'd helped!"

"I'm not interested in what guards or slaves say. The fact remains that since you became my wife's body slave she has become ill and now, now she's dead!"

"I didn't kill her!"

"Well, before you arrived my Livia ailed nothing."

"I cared for her, I …"

"You hate me, so I've no doubt you hated my wife …"

"You tried to rape me!"

"You're a slave, mine to do with as I please!" He said matter-of-factly. "So, to get back at me you decide to kill my wife."

"No! No! She was kind to me!"

Thaddeus ignored the reply. "Knowing you can't harm me what better way is there to hurt me than through my wife. My poor Livia! What have you done, you Harpie?" He snarled at Lasairiona while seizing her by the hair. "Guards! … Guards!"

Within a few moments, two guards stepped into the room looking expectantly at Thaddeus. "Yes sir."

"Take this bitch away and lock her up, I'll deal with her later."

"Yes sir." The pair seized Lasairiona while Thaddeus bawled renewed demands for the physician.

Later that evening the guards arrived at Thaddeus's rooms along with Lasairiona.

"Gag and bind her, then hang her from that hook by her hands." He pointed to a hook set in the ceiling. "Send Arya to me and tell her to bring her tools."

"Yes sir."

"Well Princess." He said quietly into Lasairiona's ear. "Here we are again and you guilty of murder." Lasairiona, her eyes wide in fear tried to speak but the gag was efficient. He tut-tutted as he ran his fingers over her face and the scar while speaking softly. "Once so pretty and now so ugly and all because you wouldn't amuse me. Silly, silly girl!"

The door opened. "Sir?"

"Ah Arya! Welcome my dear. You will have heard of my dear wife's demise at the hands of this bitch. She denies it of course." He gave a hapless shrug then a cruel smile. "So, you must loosen her tongue for me."

"Yes sir, her feet again sir?"

"No, no." He grinned. "Strip her and don't worry about skin damage this time, this ugly Harpie needs to admit to and pay for my dear wife's death."

A look of evil relish spread across Arya's face and she began ripping Lasairiona's dress off, stripping her naked before picking a multi-tailed whip from her bag.

"No, no, no Arya! She needs to suffer slowly; the whip is much too quick what else do you have?" Arya smiled and rummaged in her bag lifting out a quirt, a wooden paddle and a cane. "Oh! So many choices." Thaddeus couldn't restrain a malevolent chuckle, his face twisting in perverse delight. "The paddle! Yes, the paddle that's a nice slow start, pour us some wine and then you may begin."

Arya sipped her drink while running the paddle tormentingly over Lasairiona's pale skin making her shudder. She spun Lasairiona around slowly as she spoke while pointing to the parts of her body with the paddle.

"Where would you like me to begin sir, her back? ... Her thighs? Her buttocks or belly?"

"H'mm, her belly and thighs will bring much pain and prolong the process, save her back for the whip and her buttocks for the quirt. The cane will suffice for her feet later on. We have all night my dear so take your time."

Thaddeus settled back on the couch to watch, drink in hand, while Arya again ran the paddle over Lasairiona's skin, pausing as if to strike and then moving on. Lasairiona tensed waiting for the blow while twisting in her bonds. Suddenly, Arya slapped the wood across the front of her thighs making Lasairiona scream into the gag while Thaddeus watched intently. Arya worked very slowly and accurately, taking her time between strokes, sometimes hitting the same spot other times moving to fresh skin. Each strike making Lasairiona withe and cry into the gag and exciting Thaddeus. Arya was about to move the beating to Lasairiona's belly when her head fell forward onto her chest.

"She's swooned sir, shall I revive her?"

"No need to rush my dear. Come, your exertions make you look over warm so rest a while, remove your dress and loosen that beautiful raven hair then come here." He patted his thigh.

Arya smiled and seductively peeled off her dress. She was just climbing onto Thaddeus's lap when a scream followed by shouts and a clash of metal resonated in the courtyard. A dog barked, yelped and went quiet then hooves and fast footfalls sounded on the pavers below. Shoving Arya roughly aside, Thaddeus leapt up, closing his robe he ran to the window overlooking the torch lit courtyard. Opening the shutters, he saw dark shapes of mounted men streaming across it and a handful of guards running towards them, there was another brief clash of metal as the first of the guards died the rest turning tail and scattering back into cover of the buildings.

An arrow flew past Thaddeus's face, close enough for the fletching to brush his skin. He yelped and leapt back in alarm, the arrow shattering on the room wall and raising a scream from Arya.

"What's happening sir?" She cried as she snatched up her dress and ran towards him.

"We're … we're being attacked!" He gasped and made for the door.

Fear fuelled; Arya quickly shrugged into her dress. "Take me with you sir." She pulled at his robes, trying to slow him while seeking her sandals.

"Get off me you stupid bitch!" He pushed her savagely away sending her sprawling over the low table knocking it, the wine jug and cups over, her head thumped on the floor and she didn't get up. He fled the room and on down the corridor without looking back.

Chapter Nineteen

After loosing at the lighted window, Malo laid another arrow on the string, his eyes searching for movement.

"Malo! Stay here and kill any bastard on the wall or running for the gate." Andulas yelled as he forced his horse about seeking more guards who were scattering into the buildings like rabbits down a warren as the raiders chased them down.

Malo dismounted and snatched the quiver from his mount. A moment later another guard spun around clutching at an arrow in his chest, before tumbling from the wall onto the stable roof, smashing tiles and rolling off.

Leaving two warriors to close and guard the gate, Baldor and the rest of the men dismounted. Leaving their cumbersome shields with their mounts, they split into pairs and entered the buildings, chasing guards and searching for Lasairiona. Armaco, remaining mounted rode his horse up the wide-stepped entrance to the portico and the main doors of the villa. Rearing it on its hind legs, he used its strength to force the doors. The hooves struck the ornate timber twice before they flew open; dipping his head beneath the door lintel, he rode into the room. Crashes from overturning furniture, screams, shouts and the clatter of weapons followed.

On the other side of the courtyard Baldor and another warrior, Cudius forced the door of what looked like slave quarters that led into a gloomy, shadow filled corridor. The air was stale and musty and with just the yellow glow from occasional oil lamps to light the way, the pair advanced at a cautious, stealthy walk. With swords held in front of them and their other hand wrapped around dagger hilts, their ears strained for sounds that would betray an attacker. A woman appeared, saw the naked blades and screamed as she turned to run.

Baldor's heart pounded in his chest his hands clammy with sweat and tight around the spatha and pugio hilts, his nerves on the raw. Open battle was frightening enough but this dark, claustrophobic fighting was terrifying. Kicking open another door into a better-lit but crowded room brought a sour waft of overheated humanity and screams as women slaves jumped back and away from the two men.

"Any guards in here?" He growled as the women cowered away.

One woman, braver than her sisters stepped forward. "No sir! No." She said with a shaky voice while holding a hand in front of her body, her thumb intimating behind her.

Baldor pushed past her towards the back of the room, the women parting before him. Suddenly a woman was pushed at him; a guard followed and lunged at him with a short sword. Baldor, ready and lightning quick, sidestepped and drove his pugio into the man's ribs as he hurtled passed, Cudius finishing the man with a stab from his spatha.

"Anymore?" He shouted; his words lost in the women's screams.

Suddenly, another woman was pushed forward, sprawling into him sending him staggering backwards, she trying to hold onto him as she collapsed from the knife wound in her lower back. Behind her, a guard made a leap for the high window but scrabbling over the sill he was caught by Cudius who stepped forward sinking a dagger deep in his exposed back.

Recovering his balance, Baldor shouted again. "Are there anymore?" Shaking heads and a chorus of no's came back. "Lasairiona! … Lasairiona!" He shouted as he glanced around the gloomy room. "Has anyone seen a tall redhead? A Gaul! … Anyone?"

"She … she's a personal slave to the Mistress, sir."

"Where will she be? Quickly!"

"The Mistress's rooms are upstairs in the main house sir." She pointed.

Go! … Go! Out into the courtyard, you won't be harmed." He urged the women before him.

The pair followed the women out leaving them in a frightened huddle then turned the way the woman had pointed. Baldor quickly bawled identification to Malo when he saw the archer's bow swing towards him then mercifully away; darkness clearly brought risk as well as advantage. The arrow instead brought down another guard trying to jump from a side window of the main house.

Running to the main house and the doors that Armaco's mount had kicked open, Baldor and Cudius made their way through the mess of smashed furniture and pooling blood from two guards sprawled on the marble floor, one whose head lay paces from his body. The opulently furnished rooms were brightly lit with an abundance of lamps, the white plaster walls decorated with colourful patterns and pictures. Ahead, the clash of weapons, a horse's whinny and the clatter of hooves striking the marble floor sounded loud and told of Armaco somewhere deeper in the house. Baldor and Cudius hurried through the palatial sized rooms, past more bodies towards the noise and found Armaco forcing his horse sidewards to pin a guard against the wall. The man threw down his sword as he stumbled backwards, raising his hands and calling for quarter he died beneath Armaco's spatha thrust. Hearing footfalls, Armaco forced his mount about, a vicious snarl twisting his mouth but recognising Baldor, he settled the horse and shouted.

"I think that's the last of the bastards down here, some ran up there." He pointed his bloody spatha at the stairs.

Baldor nodded and ran for the stairs taking them two at a time.

Cudius, keeping pace alongside looked up and seized Baldor's mail shirt hard, halting and dragging him sidewards just as a marble bust dropped in front of him, smashing it and the stair tread to pieces where he would have been a moment later.

"Careful sir!"

Shaken by the near miss and bleeding with small cuts from the shards of flying marble, Baldor swore and grunted his thanks. Stepping cautiously and close to the wall side of the stairs, he looked upwards before advancing. Just before he reached the top landing, a guard rushed him swinging a club at his head; Baldor drove his spatha at the man's belly while raising his other arm in defence of the descending club. The guard's careless rush spitted him on Baldor's blade but the club smashed into his raised arm. The dying man's impetus knocked Baldor backwards, the pair tumbling hard down the stairs amidst cries and grunts of pain. Cudius cleared the top step stabbing another oncoming guard low in the belly then engaging another, the clash of sword blades and grunts echoing in the stairwell. Baldor, dazed, bruised and badly shaken from the fall kicked the dead guard off him then swore loudly as he tried to lever himself up using the injured arm. There was an agonising scream from the top of the stairs, followed by a guard's body crashing and somersaulting down the steps just past Baldor, then Cudius shouted down.

"Sir! Sir! Are you all right?"

"Yes! ... yes, I think so." He groaned loudly as he got to his feet. "But I think my arm is broken." Unsteady and hurting and with his forearm hanging limp he forced himself back up the stairs. Cudius stood over the wounded guard at the stair head.

"Where's the tall redheaded woman?"

The man wept and gasped while trying to stem the steady blood flow from his gut, Cudius kicked his hand away replacing it with his boot and pressed. The man screamed.

"Mercy! ..."

"Where's the redhead?" Cudius snarled and pressed harder with his foot. The man groaned horribly, the pain stealing his breath.

"The Master's rooms ... there." He pointed.

Cudius pushed his sword into the man's throat. The blood fountained as he stepped over the body. "This way sir."

The pair approached a carved cedar wood door. Standing either side of it, Cudius put his dagger between his teeth then reaching for the handle gently pushed it down. The door swung open with a small protesting squeak from the hinges. Baldor made to enter but Cudius blocked him while nodding to the body on the floor. Pushing in front and brandishing sword and dagger, he stepped cautiously into the room. Baldor, a pace behind, guarded Cudius's back, his eyes scanning all around. To the rear of the room, he saw fox-coloured hair and a naked, white body suspended from the ceiling.

"Lasairiona!" He gasped as he stepped quickly towards her. Seeing her head slumped forward on her chest and thighs discoloured with purple, black bruising he feared the worst. His stomach churned; his mind full of dread as he called Cudius from examining the other body on the floor to help. Cutting Lasairiona down while looking for more wounds they laid her gently on the settle. Clumsy with his useless arm, Baldor pushed a cushion under her head while Cudius removed the gag and looked for signs of life. Baldor searched for water, finding remnants in the overturned jug, he squatted next to her.

"Lasairiona! ... Lasairiona! It's me ... its Baldor, you're safe now!" Slowly regaining consciousness as Baldor wet her lips and wiped her brow with his dampened neckcloth, she stared fearfully at his helmeted face. "It's me, Lasairiona, Baldor!" She stared then flinched trying to move away but he held her gently. "It's all right, it's all right it's me!"

She blinked, looked confused then looked again, her lips opened but no sound came out. "Here, drink … drink!" He offered the cup.

Her eyes went wide then tear brimmed as she recognised his face squashed between the cheek guards of the Roman helmet and she eased the cup away.

"Baldor? … Baldor! You … you've come for …?" Tears spilled down her cheeks and a lump in her throat stole her words.

He leant in and kissed her gently on the forehead. "Yes, I've come for you. What … what have they done to you?" He grimaced as he moved his fingers gently across her cut and bruised face.

She threw her arm over his neck pulling him close and wept. He felt her hot tears on his skin and the sobs racking her body, she mumbled prayers of thanks into the side of his face. Cudius meanwhile was helping Arya.

Hearing more fighting outside Baldor gently urged Lasairiona up. "We need to go; can you get up?"

He pulled a throw from a nearby chair to cover her nakedness and held out his good arm for support as she eased up from the settle, she grimacing and gasping when her battered legs went to stand. Disbelief at her rescue gave way to a thankful but grim smile as she cuffed her tears away. She was about to take the throw from Baldor when she saw Cudius helping a stunned, confused Arya to her feet. Lasairiona's eyes narrowed, her face darkening like a rising storm and changing from thankful relief to fierce, blind hatred her mouth twisting into a savage snarl.

"You!" She spat. "You evil bitch!" The hate almost tangible and choking her.

"Mercy! Mercy Princess!" Arya blurted. "It wasn't my doing; I only did as I was commanded! … Please, he would have killed me!" Her fear making here step backwards and away. Lasairiona, driven by hate and ignoring her pain and nakedness stepped after her.

"You lying bitch! You enjoyed it! You revelled in it! You're his creature." She stepped closer while Baldor and Cudius looked on unsure. Suddenly, Lasairiona snatched the dagger from Cudius's belt and lunged at Arya. She, still nonsensical from the collision with the table, raised her arms in clumsy defence while stepping back until she hit the wall. The first strike pierced Arya's forearm making her scream. Lasairiona, consumed with anger seized her by the throat bringing the dagger down again, this time into Arya's shoulder. "This is for what you did to me!"

"No! Please, no!" Arya shrieked as the dagger went deep.

Lasairiona pulled the blade out then stabbed quickly again and again into the woman's chest and flailing arms, the hot blood splattering her and the wall while Arya continued to shriek then wilt under the blows.

"Bitch! … Bitch! … Bitch!" Lasairiona shouted as she stabbed repeatedly, her other hand still holding Arya by the throat as she slid down the wall. Only when Arya was a crumpled, bloody mess on the floor did Lasairiona stop, breathless and weeping again she dropped the dagger. Baldor and Cudius stared at Lasairiona, still naked, covered in blood splashes and beginning to shake. Hardened as the men were to the horrors of war they were shocked at the hate and venom they'd witnessed. Cudius recovered first.

"We need to go."

Baldor wrapped the throw around Lasairiona and helped her out of the door then glancing back at the window, he saw the yellow-orange glow of flames beginning to light the night sky.

In the courtyard, the slaves stood in guarded huddles while the raiders slaughtered the few guards who'd survived the attack and surrendered. Armaco, still mounted directed more warriors to burn everything while Andulas questioned the slaves on the whereabouts of Thaddeus.

Cudius, Lasairiona and Baldor appeared, he calling for the horses.

"Will you be able to ride?" He asked anxiously.

"Yes, yes I'll manage, just help me up."

Baldor held the horse's bridle with his good hand as Cudius helped her mount, she gasping and giving a small whimper as her thighs contacted the horse.

"All right?"

Not trusting herself to speak she just nodded.

Armaco rode up. "All good Baldor … Lasairiona?"

"Yes, all good." The relief clear in his voice.

"Sir! Sir, Look!" A warrior shouted.

Baldor looked to where the man pointed into the flame lit darkness and saw a white-robed, portly figure fleeing from the burning house into the gardens.

"Thaddeus!" Baldor growled. Looking quickly for Andulas but unable to find him he turned to Armaco. "That's the bastard! Get him!"

Armaco kicked his mount hard sending it leaping forward into the swirling smoke, the hoof beats loud and hollow in the courtyard as he lashed the reins either side of its withers seeking more speed. Forcing his horse into the darkened garden and amongst the small trees and shrubs Armaco chased the man down. Catching and seizing him by the hair, he brought his mount to an abrupt halt, Thaddeus twisting and yelling in his grip. Armaco turned his mount about and kicked it into a trot dragging the man alongside by the hair at a fast-stumbling gait. Back in the courtyard, he released him then kicked him in the back, knocking him to the ground.

Andulas, appearing out of the darkness removed his helmet and strode across to him. "Get up!"

Thaddeus, still on his hands and knees and breathless from the enforced run struggled to his feet, his fear upon him like a heavy cloak. His eyes casting nervously about the gathering warriors went suddenly wide when he recognised the big Gaul.

"Lord … Lord Andulas of the Cenomani? What … what means this?" He asked incredulously.

"Lord Andulas of the Lingone! The Lingone! You base-born dog!" Andulas snarled.

Thaddeus frowned, looking bewildered. "But … you, you …"

Andulas ignored him and seizing him roughly by his robes dragged him towards Baldor and Lasairiona. "And this is Captain Baldor Targa and his lady."

Thaddeus looked up, stared, then recognised Baldor. "Master Gestix? What? …" The confusion and fear clear in his voice then seeing Lasairiona, he paled. Her malevolent gaze and blood-spattered face frightened him as realisation dawned. "No! Please, I … I didn't know, I …"

"Liar!" Lasairiona snarled. "Liar!"

Thaddeus looked nervously at each of them. "I have money, lots of money! Take it! … Take it all!"

Andulas smiled grimly. "We will! But first …" Shouting and hammering from outside the villa gates interrupted him. Thaddeus looked hopeful but only for a moment as Andulas quickly locked huge hands around his throat. "I'm Lingone! Do you hear me you pile of pig offal? I'm Lingone! And no one makes slaves of my people or hurts my friends!"

"No! … No! N …" Thaddeus gasped, as Andulas's thumbs dug savagely into his windpipe choking off his words, he struggled and clawed at the tightening hands but to no avail. The Gaul's huge strength backed by a terrible anger closed off the airway as his thumbs slowly collapsed the trachea. Thaddeus's face coloured, growing darker as his body starved of air, he twitched, and his eyes grew wide as if they would pop from their sockets. As his body began to wilt and his bladder wet his robes with piss, Andulas snarled and gripped tighter shaking him like a dog with a rabbit before lowering the dying man to his knees. Then, grabbing Thaddeus's head, he gave a final, brutal twist. There was the sound of a snapping branch as the man's neck broke. The head lolled obscenely to one side and Andulas let him drop.

"It's good to be rid of shit!" Snarling his disgust, he spat on the body while wiping his hands quickly on his tunic as if filthy and contaminated. The sudden roar of flames as they took hold in the outbuildings lit the courtyard and belched orange sparks and burning debris high into the night sky and had him barking orders. "Mount up! Mount up we leave now! Anyone trying to stop us at the gate we ride down!"

****

Cornelius heard impatient urgings from outside the door, then the key turning in the lock.

"Sir! Sir! Are you all right?" The legionary shouted as he pushed the Landlord out of the doorway and stomped towards the bed and Cornelius. Removing the gag, he drew his dagger and slashed through the sheets tying the Centurion to the bed then went to help him up. Cornelius rubbed at his chafed skin and groaned when he struggled to flex his limbs and stand, they long since numbed from the tight bonds. "We've being searching for you everywhere sir! We thought they must have killed you."

"Never mind me! What of our men and what happened last night? I heard shouts and chaos."

"We have two injured sir the rest of us are all right."

"And?"

"An auxiliary cavalry unit robbed and burned a villa down. They slew the Master and his guards before fleeing with a woman slave and killing some town guards that tried to stop them. We killed one of them; his body is by the gate." Cornelius was about to blurt that the auxiliary unit were actually Carthaginians but stopped himself otherwise his life being spared could be questioned. "We heard they'd been seen here at the inn … you're lucky they didn't murder you sir, one more death wouldn't have made any difference to their crimes but I see they gave you a thumping anyway."

Cornelius, strangely thankful for the blow he'd received massaged his aching jaw, wetting his neckcloth he wiped the dried blood away and asked. "Centurion Laelius! What of him?"

"We presume he's all right sir, they only attacked the villa nowhere else."

"Send the men to see if we can help at all, you come with me and we'll check on Centurion Laelius."

The pair took off towards the house of Atticus, Cornelius stumbling along as his legs still refused to work properly. Silencing the legionary's questions and concerns, he tortured his mind as to why Baldor and his men were dressed as auxiliaries and ready to risk entering a Roman town for a woman slave, moreover who was the dead man?

After checking Gaius and suffering more grumbles from Atticus about soldiers bringing trouble, he checked his injured legionaries. Finding them battered from being ridden down but not critically hurt, he went to examine the dead auxiliary.

"He's a Gaul sir!" A legionary growled as he kicked and spat at the body. "Bastards can't be trusted!"

"Do you think they just got fired up on wine and ale and decided to mutiny, sir?" Another asked.

Quietly relived the body wasn't Carthaginian so to raise more questions, Cornelius just shrugged. "Maybe. As soon as Centurion Laelius can be moved without risk we're leaving for Rome."

"Yes sir!"

****

Sleet and heavy rain from the east set in on the ride back to camp making the going difficult for Baldor and the troop, a cold, miserable night camping in the hills without a fire and hot food adding to their discomfort, the loss of Cudius weighing heavy on Baldor's conscience. Huddling together for warmth, Baldor told Lasairiona of Sulis's death and what they'd found on their return to his burned tent, of the enquiries made to find her and the battles that had interrupted the search. Then finally, of the first attempt to buy her from Thaddeus, she shuddered at the mention of his name and buried her head in his neck, he using his good arm to pull her close.

The moment dawn was a grey smudge in the east they were on the move again keen to return to the warmth and safety of the main camp. The bonus to the foul weather was it kept the Carthaginian patrols small, cautious and less numerous and after some tense exchanges between themselves and a patrol until their identity was established, they were escorted into camp.

Issa barked as they approached the tent then threw herself at them as they entered her tail wagging and body shaking in excitement as she ran to each man before sniffing cautiously at Lasairiona. Andulas sent for a physician to check Lasairiona and see to Baldor's arm then bellowed for food. Glad to be out of the weather the men shrugged out of their soaked clothes into clean tunics and heavy cloaks, Lasairiona making do with a man's tunic and winter cloak. The tent was warm but the air smoky and sharp from the braziers though no one seemed to mind as they huddled around the crackling wood, cups of steaming mulled wine in hand.

The physician examined Lasairiona and bathed her thighs in cold water, cooling the area then applying Arnica ointment to reduce the swelling before removing the stitches from her face and applying cream to keep the skin supple. Both bones in Baldor's forearm were broken and required setting, the swelling from the delay in seeking treatment making it difficult to reposition them. He bit on a leather belt and growled as his skin flushed then dotted with beads of sweat from the pain as the physician manipulated the arm to position the bones correctly. Finally, the man seemed content with his work and bound the arm before fitting a shoulder sling.

Warmed through from mulled wine and an early dinner all sought their bed and finally allowed time for Baldor and Lasairiona to be alone. Issa jumped onto the bed and Baldor moved her off down to her sheepskin on the floor. She gave a disgruntled sigh as she settled and watched as Baldor helped Lasairiona under the sheets and furs. Getting up again, Issa sniffed Lasairiona's face then finally allowed a stroke and fuss before being commanded back to her bed. Man and woman snuggled as close as their injuries would allow in the small bed, their body heat a bonus to the relief and comfort each felt from the presence of the other.

Lasairiona whispered quietly into the dark, her voice shaky and heavy with emotion. "I prayed that you'd come for me ... but ..."

"But as time passed you thought I'd abandoned you."

"Yes ... no but being neither a wife nor concubine I had no right to expect you to seek me."

Baldor, glad of the darkness to hide his embarrassment cleared his throat. "Wife? Concubine? They're just names; I'd like to think you're my woman? ... A woman that chooses to be with me?"

"Am I not that?"

"Yes you were, you are. However, remember you're also a free woman that chooses whether she goes or stays. You're too beautiful, too proud to be caged as property of another."

There was silence for a while then her lips found his in the dark and she kissed him tenderly. "I love you Baldor, wholly and freely and not because you rescued me but for the way you've treated me since I was given to you. Many would have treated a daughter of their enemy differently."

"You cared for me when I was wounded."

She managed a small laugh. "You thought I would have killed you then."

It was Baldor's turn to laugh. "Yes, yes I thought you would."

"I don't expect you to love me, not yet." She said, her tone serious and stopped his impending interruption with a kiss. "I know you still mourn your wife and I understand."

"I ... I."

She kissed him again. "You came for me Baldor." She whispered. "You risked your life, your friends and your men all risked their lives for me ... just for me, so you care." She sounded close to tears. "That's ... that's more than enough for me right now." She snuggled as close as she could and mumbling her prayers fell asleep. Baldor, as weary as he felt and warmed by Lasairiona's words was kept awake with the guilt over Cudius's death at the villa gate. For Cudius had come willingly on the venture, fought bravely and saved his life on the stairs so tomorrow he decided, when he reported to Hannibal, he would pray with him as he'd promised and pray especially for the warrior Cudius.

****

"Good morning, sir." Baldor greeted Hannibal as he entered the tent.

Hannibal smiled warmly. "Hail Baldor!" Leaving the scribes he was working with, he gestured Baldor away to the rear of the tent. "Come, come sit. I trust that's not serious?" He gestured to Baldor's slung arm.

"No sir, it's broken but reset, I'll recover fully."

"Good, good! Now, by your demeanour I take it your venture was successful. You have your woman?"

"Yes sir, thank you." His smile faded a little.

"Ah! I sense a but."

"Yes sir, I lost a good man."

"Fights are not won without casualties Baldor, you know that." He said not unkindly. "I imagine it was bloody so losing one is kinder than many." He placed a hand on his heart. "Baal bless and keep the fallen."

"Yes sir." Baldor bowed his head.

"Who fell, my friend?" He asked guardedly.

"Cudius, a warrior from Lord Andulas's retinue. He saved my life in the fight but was speared at the gate as we fled the town."

Hannibal bowed his head. "Baal bless and keep Cudius."

"On behalf of Cudius, thank you sir." Baldor bowed his head.

"So, you rescued your woman and returned with all your men bar one?"

"Yes sir."

"Then thank the Gods Baldor, for to enter an enemy town, attack it and come home with your prize for the loss of one man is a victory indeed."

"Yes sir." He answered quietly.

"But Cudius's death weighs heavily on your conscience?"

"Yes sir … However, I wish to thank you for permission to go and the use of the men."

"A promise is a promise Baldor." He smiled warmly.

"Yes sir it is and thus I would fulfil my promise to you … I would offer my prayers to the Lord Baal Almighty for my success and for Cudius."

Hannibal beamed. "Come! Come through where we won't be disturbed." He led the way into his private quarter and a small altar with miniature golden effigies of Baal and Tannith on it. A sweet, spicy smell of cinnamon emanated from a tiny oil burner that steamed gently on the altar top. Dropping to his knees, he gestured Baldor alongside. There was silence between them for a moment as they bowed their heads, closed their eyes, placed a hand on their heart and settled themselves. Hannibal was about to speak when Baldor fidgeted, looking up and around suddenly anxious. Hannibal placed a comforting hand on his shoulder and smiled; Baldor managed a hesitant, nervous smile and settled again. Hannibal began.

"Baal Almighty, Lord and father … Tannith mother of us all, we offer our thanks for the success and safe homecoming of your son, Baldor Targa and his return to your grace and favour." He paused for a moment. "Lord, mother, I thank you both for this man, Baldor Targa, a brave warrior, a good man and a true friend to me, your son."

Silence followed, the time stretching, eventually Hannibal tapped Baldor's leg lightly. Baldor cleared his throat.

"Baal Hammon, Father and lord of us all, Tannith mother … I thank you for the safe deliverance of my men, my woman and myself and ask … beg, that you forgive your errant son his transgressions and his absence from your grace." He swallowed hard and took a moment breathing deeply; Hannibal remained still, his head bowed. Baldor began again. "I also ask … crave, your care and love for Cudius, a brave man who gave his life and saved mine while helping gain what I desired … and also for another, Hattam who gave his life seeking the truth."

There was a long silence and sensing Baldor was finished, Hannibal closed the prayers.

"Lord Baal, Tannith mother of us all, again I thank you for my friend here and your care of him and me, please bless and keep us both."

As the pair rose to their feet, Hannibal placed a hand on Baldor's shoulder and smiled warmly, Baldor gave a timid smile in return.

"I'll pray to Epona for Cudius as well, sir. He deserves no less."

Hannibal, quietly delighted at Baldor's return to piety nodded and gestured him through to the main tent.

"Wine and breakfast, Baldor?"

"Yes, thank you sir."

"Who is Hattam and what news of your stolen possessions."

Baldor looked suddenly morose. "Hattam was Armaco's man, his enquirer and searcher for the men who burned my tent and stole my belongings. The last Armaco heard from him, he had a lead to a Greek and was asking further. His body was found outside the camp while we were gone, he was obviously coming close to someone and they murdered him."

Part 3

A fight for grain brought not food but a harvest of death.

Anon

Chapter Twenty

The plain of Cannae in the Apulian District, 29th of July (Quintilis) 216 BC

Winter had come and gone and the year turned, spring had long since passed and summer itself was now at its zenith, the fight at Casilinum a distant memory. Apart from small skirmishes and the usual patrols, the men had enjoyed a mostly peaceful existence; both they and the horses were now in peak condition from living well. The army had left Geronium just a month or so ago when food supplies finally became exhausted; plundering their way further south, they had captured the Roman grain store here at Cannae and set up camp. The Romans had followed and boldly made camp on this south side of the river less than twelve stades from the Carthaginian one. The embankment and palisade of it seemed to shiver and shake in the August heat making it impossible to see men or horses clearly.

With the Roman arrival skirmishing between the two sides had commenced and continued for some days with no advantage for either side and which, by midday ceased altogether when the hot Volturnus wind from the southwestern hills blew in, raising huge clouds of dust.

Baldor gazed from the escarpment at the crop and grass rich plain of Cannae just below him. A breadbasket for Rome, it spread flat and wide like a tabletop with the river Aufidius meandering lazily through it toward the distant sea. The early morning sun was already heating the parched land and blurring the horizon as the hot air wriggled and squirmed above it, the distant ground shimmering as if pools of quicksilver laid upon it. Enjoying the heat warming his skin, he breathed deeply relishing the scent of dry grass from the plain mixing with the aroma of fresh baking bread from the camp. His attention was caught by large patrols of Numidian cavalry splashing over the river heading north on their sand-coloured ponies to harass any foragers from the newly erected and huge, second Roman camp.

Sipping honeyed-water, he flexed and rotated his left arm and wrist as his thoughts wandered. Fabius's term as Dictator had ended with the dying of the previous year stirring the Romans from their apathy, and all through spring and summer they'd prepared once more for war. Appointing two new Consuls and raising additional legions to support those remaining of Fabius and the prior Consul, Geminus, they were now here in the large camp across the river. Reports spoke of a staggering eight Roman legions supported by a similar number of auxiliaries making for sixteen legions overall and giving a scarcely believable total of eighty thousand men, battle was coming.

Issa's tail banging against his legs brought a smile and he reached down to ruffle her ears. At a year old she was now well above his knee height, her body thickened with muscle and filling out what was once spare skin. She pushed her head against his hand a low rumble in her throat. Lasairiona came behind him, her arms slipping gently about his waist and snatching him from his thoughts. The sweet smell of her perfume filled his nose as she hugged him close and planted a gentle kiss on his cheek.

"Good morning my love, breakfast?" Her voice soft and seductive.

Baldor smiled and turned. "Yes, I'm hungry."

She smiled coyly. "Well, you were awake late! Come, it's ready." Following her into the tent he smiled to himself, she'd recovered well from her ordeals at the hands of Thaddeus; her body had healed quickly, the scar on her face now no more than a pale, pink line; her mind though had taken longer to throw off memories of her suffering. However, with the passing of time and relative peace along with his care, her demeanour had brightened. He'd also realised that what had begun as his lustful desire for her had slowly changed, first to caring and then to love. He wasn't sure when or how it happened but setting her striking beauty aside, this woman with her quiet and caring ways had eased beneath his skin then into his heart. She was slowly filling the void left by Aiticia and his broken heart was beginning to mend. The pair were enjoying their repast when the dull thud of hooves on the grass produced Armaco who dismounted and shuffled into the tent doorway.

"Armaco! Good morning."

"Captain, Lasairiona!" He gave a grim but strangely satisfied smile, hinting at the news he bore.

Lasairiona rose and pulled another chair to the table. "Come Armaco, we have plenty to share."

"Thank you lady but no, I breakfasted at dawn with Andulas, when you're early to bed, you're early to rise!" When Lasairiona looked bashful, he smirked then chuckled.

Ignoring his friend's teasing, Baldor asked. "What's to do, Armaco?"

"We've found that bastard Greek! … Pardon my language lady." He added quickly. When Baldor looked confused, he continued. "Haemon, the one who killed my man Hattam, and he was carrying this." He laid Baldor's silver hilted dagger on the table, his gift from Hannibal. "Unfortunately, your helmet and all your other stolen gear has been sold."

Baldor jumped up his voice a low growl. "Where is he?"

"Back at Andulas's tent but sit down and finish your meal."

"No, I'm …"

"Relax, he's already told us all we need to know."

"Which is what?"

"That he was put up to the job by another Greek …"

"Another Greek!" Baldor asked incredulously. "I don't know any Greeks, why …"

"You might not but Sakarbaal does, another Greek called Hephaestus …"

"Sakarbaal!" Baldor snarled and strode towards his weapons.

"Calm yourself Baldor; it's not what you think." Armaco guided him back to his chair. "Listen carefully, Sakarbaal called at Andulas's tent late last night looking for you."

"Why would …?"

He raised hands to silence Baldor's interruption. "Sakarbaal was in a wine tent last night and overheard this Haemon, who was drunk, mouthing off to another man, Lycidias about this Hephaestus and wanting more money for the risks they'd taken; especially now enquiries were being made. Sakarbaal put two and two together for he knows this Hephaestus just happens to be a creature of Bodeshmun."

"I knew it!" Baldor snarled. "I bloody knew that bastard was behind all this!"

Armaco had to calm him again. "Listen! … Listen!" He said forcefully while putting a restraining arm on Baldor. "Sakarbaal is not involved in any way. Apparently, he and Bodeshmun parted ways after the Trasimene fight when Bodeshmun threw him and his men out of his retinue."

"Do you believe him?"

"Yes. He talked at length to Andulas and me last night about what Bodeshmun had said about taking revenge on you. He'd had a few drinks and there was plenty of time to trip himself up if he was lying."

"Do you think that's why he apologised to me and sought peace?"

"Yes, we think he's distancing himself as much as possible from Bodeshmun, I'd say he hates the man."

Baldor chewed his lip as he thought. If Armaco was convinced by Sakarbaal's words, the man must be telling the truth. "So, the thieves what about …"

"Andulas sent some of our lads to grab them while they were on the way back to their tent last night."

"Did anyone see?"

"No!" Armaco snapped indignantly and shook his head. "Shush man and I'll explain! We knew there was three men that robbed your tent, kidnapped Lasairiona and slew Sulis, now we have their names, this Haemon and his two accomplices, Lycidias and Bannus. Lycidias is dead and Bannus was knifed by the lady that night at the tent." He smiled at Lasairiona.

"So, we need to put this Hephaestus to the question?"

"Why bother? We have our proof from this Haemon we just need to kill Bodeshmun and this Greek lackey."

"Baldor, take this to the General." Lasairiona interrupted urgently.

"It's a little late for that Lasairiona." Armaco said and smirked. "This Lycidias didn't want to come with our lads last night and struggled too much so they killed him. Criminal or not the General wouldn't like it as it happened in camp."

"It's too late anyway." Baldor snarled as his voice dropped low the words spat like hot venom. "I'm going to kill Bodeshmun and these Greeks and anyone else that's involved."

"Aye! But like Andulas said we do it quietly and cleverly."

"Please Baldor! Take it to the General." Lasairiona implored as she placed a hand on his arm. "Please!"

Baldor slipped his arm around her pulling her close but speaking firmly. "I'm sorry but no, these men are responsible for your suffering, Sulis's death, Cudius's death, my injuries and stealing from me."

"The General will see justice done; he promised you! Please Baldor, you don't need any more trouble the war is bad enough!"

Seeing the ghost of her ordeal on Lasairiona's face and her angst, he lowered his voice and calmed his ire. "I'm sorry my love, I have to do this. The wrong done to the three of us demands it, my pride as a warrior and a man demands it."

She surprised him when she threw his arm off, slammed her cup down and got up from the table her face twisting into fierce anger. "Men and their damned pride! Go ahead then fight some more! Is the war not enough?"

"Don't worry lady; I'll be there to watch his back!" Armaco grinned smugly. The grin disappeared quickly when Lasairiona rounded on him, her tone sharp and bitter as bile.

"You had better Armaco Salamar! For I'll hold you to it, mark me on it!" Before he could answer, she was gone.

Arriving at Andulas's tent, they found Haemon naked, gagged and tied to one of the large roof poles and the dead body of Lycidias dumped in the corner. The air was hot and stale with the stink of sweat and piss, two huge Gauls, torso's bared and lathered in sweat stood to one side of Haemon, one massaging bloodied knuckles while the other reached for a cup of water and a plate of salt. Haemon's face was a mass of dark blood and bruises his eyes almost closed from swelling, his broken jaw hanging slack, his bare chest criss-crossed with long shallow cuts and white from a frosting of salt.

"Has he told all he knows?" Baldor asked flatly.

"Aye, salt in the wounds brings out the truth." Andulas replied grimly.

"Lemon juice would have been cheaper and hurt just as much, which would have been good enough for that bastard!" Armaco snarled. "I still say cutting his balls off would have loosened his tongue quicker and saved a lot of hard work."

Baldor took the water and hurled it in Haemon's face, the liquid bringing the man back to his senses. Baldor pulled the man's head up by his hair as his lips twisted into a hate-filled snarl, his words spilling out quietly but chillingly cold.

"You're responsible for many deaths and much suffering, Haemon the Greek. You can greet Charon for me and tell him there will be more scum like you to fill his Hades bound boat before I'm done!"

Haemon twisted in his bonds, peering through swollen eyes he shook his head and shouted into the gag. Baldor grunted in effort as he punched him hard in the solar plexus and then in the pit of his stomach before kneeing him in the groin. As Haemon groaned and sagged forward, Baldor snapped his head back with a vicious uppercut then head butted him.

"That's a blow from each of us, one for Sulis whom you murdered, one for my woman who you sold to slavery and one from me for hurting what I love! The last are for Cudius and Hattam whose deaths you caused." He spat in Haemon's face. "Now your miserable life is forfeit for those crimes."

Haemon groaned and fought for breath while Baldor picked the man's belt up from the floor and stepped behind him. Flinging the belt around Haemon's throat and wrapping the ends around his fists, he pulled it tight forcing the man's head back hard against the post. Pulling savagely on both ends of the belt, he began strangling him. Haemon didn't die quickly as the belt was broad and he continued to writhe and twist as it sunk slowly into his flesh, gradually cutting off his air supply. His face slowly darkened to the colour of over-ripe plums then as his bladder gave way his body began to wilt. Growling from the effort and pent-up hate and seeking further purchase so to finish the grim work, Baldor placed his foot on the pole pulling harder while growling like a dog over a bone.

Eventually, Andulas had to place a hand on Baldor's shoulder to have him stop, Haemon very much dead. Baldor dropped the belt and stood back breathless from the effort, his face slowly losing the rage that had twisted it. Andulas wrapped an arm around him while steering him to a chair and placing a cup of wine in his hand settling him. Baldor gulped the wine and muttered.

"You're right Andulas; it's good to be rid of shit!"

Andulas signalled to his men. "Remove this pig turd, smuggle it and the other out of camp and dump them in the river well away from here."

"Yes Lord."

He turned back to Baldor while gesturing for Armaco to pull up a chair.

"So, at least two more men need to die, we can't take the matter to the General now, so we need a plan."

****

"Sir! … Sir!" The Optio called into Cornelius's tent. "Consul Lucius Aemilius Paullus requests your presence at his quarters in the main camp."

"Yes Optio, tell him I'll be there directly." Cornelius jumped up from his breakfast reaching for his weapons belt and helmet.

With thoughts racing through his head as to the reason for his summons, from his estrangement to Paullus's daughter Aemilia, the war to possible news of his father or home, he crossed the river to the main camp and presented himself at Paullus's tent, his heart very much in his mouth.

"Ah, Centurion! Come away in." The big man beckoned and smiled warmly.

"Greetings sir and congratulations on your appointment."

"Thank you." He gestured to the wine.

"Yes, please sir. You're well? Aemilia and the family …"

"All well, Centurion." He said matter-of-factly then cleared his throat. "Aemilia sends her regards and had me bring you this." His tone sombre as he offered a folded, sealed parchment.

"Thank you." Cornelius dipped his head and pushed the missive into his tunic but caught the heady scent of Aemilia's perfume on it. Was this the official break of their betrothal? However, a perfumed letter hardly intimated such; Lucius offering him a cup snatched him from his thoughts.

"You're well lad?"

"Yes sir, thank you."

"Good! …"

"Sir, can I ask news of my family?" His tone anxious. "My mother and brother, and my father and uncle in Spain, do they all fare well?"

Lucius noted the concern in Cornelius's voice and smiled. "Yes lad, all are well. Your mother sends her love and this." He smiled warmly as he passed another sealed parchment over. "I can tell you that your brother is dispatched to Spain where your father and uncle are doing well. They're encouraging the Spanish tribes held under Carthaginian rule to our banner, thus keeping Hasdrubal Barca's hands full in south Iberia trying to subjugate the rebellions." He chuckled. "He'll not be venturing to his brother's aid here this year."

Cornelius felt a warm glow in his heart at the news and sighed in relief as he tucked the second parchment alongside the first.

"Thank you sir, you and the Gods are most kind … Can I ask? This … this here, we'll win and finish it now, you think?"

"If we're careful yes. I say careful because though the plain is empty with no places for trickery or ambush the Carthaginian cavalry remain a concern. As you know, they're numerous, battle hardened and bloody dangerous! And the plain is ideal cavalry country."

"Yes sir but also good for us, for the legions."

Paullus nodded and sipped his wine. "Agreed but we still need to be wary of the plain. Yes, we have the numbers and the ground this time but many of our men are new. Granted, they've trained hard over winter and on through these summer months and are confident and spoiling for a fight but most are as yet untried in combat. However, we do have a core of veterans and former Consul, Geminus is also here in support of myself and my co-Consul Varro, so we're ready."

Cornelius cleared his throat. "May I ask sir, what of your co-Consul Varro? Is he like yourself, experienced?"

Lucius smiled. "Ah! You've heard! Consul Caius Terentius Varro, the novus homo, a new man. He's an interesting fellow, brave, keen and the men like him, I like him and he's not untried for like myself he served in the second Illyrian war so has some military experience. We've agreed to maintain the usual alternate daily command but have brought both Consular armies together as one rather than the usual separate entities." Cornelius seemed to relax a cautious relief brightening his features. Lucius smiled again, he liked his prospective good-son, he was courteous, brave and of good family. "Cornelius."

Surprised, Cornelius looked up quickly for Lucius usually referred to him by his rank. "Yes sir."

"I've another matter to inform you of and again it's a pleasing one." He walked to his desk and opened a box containing a wad of parchments while Cornelius looked on bemused. Lucius filtered through them before pulling one out and walking back to Cornelius and handing it to him.

"Cornelius Publius Scipio." He said formally. "Under the circumstance we find ourselves, that of war, I'm empowered by the senate to promote you to Tribune for your service, bravery and tenacity shown against the enemy. The senate will formally acknowledge this honour when we return to Rome. Congratulations Tribune!"

Cornelius just gawped dumbstruck while Lucius pushed the parchment into his hand and shook the other.

"Why … why me sir?"

"Because you're a good man Cornelius and for all the other reasons I've just given you."

"But … but my men, my friend and commanding officer Gaius, what of them?"

"They'll be fine; it's time to step up Tribune!" He patted him on the shoulder. "Be back here tonight at stand-down and I'll introduce you into the mess and formally announce your promotion to your new colleagues." He picked up his helmet from the table. "You must excuse me Tribune; I have a meeting to attend … later?"

"Yes sir, yes of course."

Cornelius made his way back to his tent his mind in a whirl and full of questions and more than a little daunted by his new position. What to say to Gaius and his men while wondering what was in the letters?

Sitting on his bed he pulled the parchments from his tunic and again caught the sweet scent of Aemilia, he gazed at it for a while strangely nervous as to what it said. Having given her a wide berth when he was last in Rome, he hadn't heard from or spoken to her since their falling out over a year ago. Finally, he forced his fingers under the seal opening the letter. The writing was small and neat and in Aemilia's hand, her words clearly private and not entrusted to a scribe to write.

Dearest Cornelius,
I pray this letter finds you safe and well.
With my father's appointment to Consul, I entrusted this letter to him, as I knew he would place it personally in your hand and my words would be safe.

You and I did not part on good terms and a year has passed since last I saw you. I have heard nothing from or of you since that day, except that you were once again briefly in Rome after the battle at Geronium, thus I called on your mother seeking news of you. You'll be relieved to know she and your family are all well, she sends her love and prayers and is full of pride at your promotion as am I.

I did hope that you'd have called on me to perhaps reconcile our differences before taking the field again. However, I imagine your pride would not allow it. As you can see, I have chosen to put my foolish pride aside and my hope into this letter for I love you deeply. I can only hope and pray that you still feel the same about me? I don't wish for us to be estranged, after all we are, were, betrothed?

In truth, you've never left my heart or been far from my thoughts and prayers and I deeply regret both my temper and harsh words that day and for not waiting to hear you out. I pray we can start over, unless my cruel words and curt dismissal of you was too much to bear and you have found solace and love with another with a kinder tongue.

Now that my father has taken the field, I better understand your desire to fight for our people and city and despite my fears for your safety; I would support you rather than berate you for it. Forgive a foolish woman who selfishly put her needs and desires before those of our people and city. My only defence is that I love you more than life itself and wish you home and safe to me.

I pray daily that Mars spares you and that Vesta keeps you safe that I may see you again. All my love, your Aemilia.

25th day of Quintilis, feast of Furrinalia.

Cornelius finished reading, his heart very much warmed and a lump in his throat while feeling a fair amount of guilt for he'd neither thought of nor prayed for Aemilia for some time. He re-read the letter then locked it in the small box with his personal affects. A moment later, he took it out again and re-read it once more, smiling, he inhaled the fragrance from it then tucked it safely inside his tunic close to his heart. Pouring himself a wine, he broke the seal on the other letter and as it opened a gold neck chain fell out. Picking it up, he recognised a finely wrought effigy of the Goddess Salus suspended from it wrought in blue-black haematite. Holding it in his hand, he sipped his wine as he began to read.

Greetings my son,
I trust my words and prayers find you safe and well. It is quite wonderful to send a letter knowing you will receive it owing to the kind undertaking of Consul Paullus.
Congratulations on your promotion, my pride knows no bounds as I'm sure your father, brother and uncle's will when they hear of it. You will be pleased to hear that your brother is dispatched to Spain where your father and Uncle Gnaeus are being successful against Hannibal's brother and his Carthaginian savages.
I must act the concerned citizen now instead of the weak, fearful mother of a son at war and say we are all praying that the coming battle is the last and brings a victory that see's the barbarians broken and driven from our country. Play your part well my son be what you have always been, brave, honourable and lead your men well, I know you will bring honour on our house.
Now, speaking as a mother with all the fears and concerns for her son, I say do your duty and do it well but without recklessness or bravado. Live to come home son

so we can celebrate as a family and give thanks to the Gods for deliverance. I have enclosed a necklace of the Goddess Salus, a gift from a loving mother to her first-born son. Wear it always and she will keep you safe and bring you home to me.

My prayers and love are with you always.

Written on this 17th day of Quintilis in honour of Victoria and as an omen to you for victory.

Your loving mother, Pomponia.

Placing the letter among his affects, Cornelius stood and poured more wine then settled back in his chair, his feet resting on the small table as he let out a long-satisfied sigh. Fastening the necklace about his neck he felt content inside, his heart warm and mind settled from the support, concern and love from both his mother and Aemilia instead of the berating and anger he'd suffered previously. Thoughts of his promotion both scared and thrilled him at the same time. However, as young as he was for the post, he could at least face his new colleagues with considerable military experience behind him many of whom could not. Now, all that was needed was a victory here on this plain of Cannae and his satisfaction would be complete. Was it too much to ask of the Gods? Finishing the wine, he dropped to his knees to pray.

Meeting with Lucius as commanded, the pair made their way to the mess. Entering a grand tent, his name and rank were announced right after that of Lucius and brought handshakes and words of congratulations from those close by. He was served wine and ushered through to the main room where men collected in groups around a long table, it fast being laden with platters of food and jugs of wine by a small army of slaves. With dusk falling the canvas room was warmly illuminated by oil lamps set around on tall stands else nestled amongst the dishes on the table, the smell of roast chicken, beef and fresh bread tantalising his taste buds. He was dazzled by the platters, jugs and cups which were all of chased silver and in stark contrast to his simple horn cup and bronze bowl that he carried in his pack.

At only nineteen years old, he knew he was very young to hold the rank of Tribune. However, when Lucius spoke, officially confirming his position, heads turned towards him and in many cases dipped in salute and he saw only respect. Yes, his family name gave automatic esteem, but his own military record and experience reinforced it, saying this man had come up the hard way and earned his Tribune's purple stripe.

Some of the older men spoke to him of his father and uncle offering their regards, the younger men, many of whom were fresh to their post asked of his thoughts on the campaign and news of the Carthaginian warriors, was it true they were cannibals and was Hannibal more monster than man?

The sound of a gong saw the men move to their couches for dinner while Paullus and Varro stood together to address the assembly. The two men were vastly different in stature, Paullus being a raven-haired bull of a man while Varro was balding, of medium height and slender; both were aged similarly in their mid-forties. Cornelius took stock of both and was heartened by what he saw in the way of good camaraderie as they smiled and chatted together waiting for the men to be seated and settled, perhaps this time things would be different. He took a moment to glance around the table and noted the upbeat atmosphere and self-assurance emanating from the men. He allowed himself a cautious smile for the command group was in good spirits, confident but seemingly without bravado or contempt towards the enemy. He also drew comfort from the huge number of men the Consuls had brought with them, this being the largest force ever assembled by the city. Though many were new and untried in combat they had been well trained over the last months, that fact plus the flat, open ground of the plain could surely only bode well for the sons of the 'She Wolf'.

Varro rattled his cup on the table and the men quietened and settled to listen, he took a moment to look around the room nodding to those he knew and smiling at all. The men before him varied widely in both age and experience from young, fresh-faced youths through to grandfathers, their time and experience with the legions as wide as their age difference. However, it seemed all had come determined to do their part to rid their country of the Carthaginian invaders.

"Gentlemen, a moment please before we dine and a few words on behalf of my colleague Consul, Lucius Aemilius Paullus and myself, Consul Caius Terentius Varro. We have gathered here in great resolve to see the invader driven from our land. We've chosen our time to fight and are ably prepared with our men well trained, ready and well positioned for the coming battle. Our main camp here on the north bank of the Aufidius dominates the fords across it and the plain beyond, while our smaller camp on the southern bank protects our water supplies and flies in the face of Carthaginian aggression." The men cheered at this and Varro gave them a moment before carrying on. "This time there's no ground for Hannibal to use in trickery or ambush and we'll dictate when and where we fight not the Carthaginians. As is custom, I pass command to my colleague tomorrow with alternating days of command to follow. However, this time … this time, we together as one army and with the help of the Gods will bring the Carthaginians to battle and destroy them."

Men cheered and rattled their cups else slapped the table in support of their Consuls. Cornelius was greatly relieved by what he saw and heard, yes he thought; if they were careful and with the help of the Gods, they may finally see an end to the invader.

Chapter Twenty-one

The plain of Cannae in the Apulian District, 30th & 31st of Quintilis (July) 216 BC

The sun was just rising above the distant ocean the dark orange sphere unobscured by cloud but not yet high enough to dazzle, the western sky still in grey shadow from the departing night. With the day barely new, the cornu wailed over the Roman camp sounding a 'Stand-to'. Sentries dashed to Paullus's tent while sleepy legionaries emptied from their tents seeking the reason for the alarm. Like a disturbed anthill, the camp seethed into life, men quickly arming themselves while Centurions bellowed at them to form up and cavalrymen ran for their mounts.

"Consul! Consul Sir!" A sentry called urgently into Paullus's tent.

The big man appeared, wiping sleep from his eyes and calling for his armour while summoning the sentry into the tent.

"What's afoot man? Are we to be attacked?" He kept his voice as calm and level as he could though his heart was pounding in his chest.

"The Carthaginians sir, they're crossing the river."

"Are they in battle array?"

"No sir, no! They're screening the crossing with cavalry but it seems they're only moving camp to this side of the river."

"Moving camp?"

"Yes sir, their whole army is on the move."

"And what of our camp on their side of the river?"

"Signals from them say they're on alert but remain watching and waiting for orders sir?"

"These cavalry screens, how large are they?"

"Huge sir! Regiments of light Numidian and heavy Libyan-Phoenician cavalry."

"So their column's well protected then?"

"Yes sir."

While the two men conversed, a servant encircled Paullus's waist with the belt of leather pteruges tying it off at the small of his back.

"Keep me informed of the enemy's movement's soldier and make sure Consul Varro is acquainted of the situation." He said while lifting his arms as more servants offered up his bronze breastplate, locking it together with the back plate. Others brought his helmet, baldric and weapons while another crouched to slip greaves into place over his shins. Slipping his helmet on, he strode out to the parade ground where order was fast coming out of chaos as maniples quickly became cohorts and then legions.

"Is he seeking battle Lucius?" Varro asked tensely as the two men came together.

"Not from what I'm told Caius, it seems they're moving camp to our side of the river."

"To what purpose do you think?"

"Jupiter knows but it flies in our face that we cannot stop it and weren't prepared for it either." He growled.

"What's the damned Carthaginian at?"

Lucius flicked his head to the front of the camp and the two men set off. Standing by the gate, they watched the Carthaginian army crossing the river upstream from the Roman camp and saw the multitudes of cavalry the sentry had mentioned. The cavalry faced the Romans, their huge numbers defying any interruption while their infantry comrades and baggage train passed safely behind them.

"If we could only drive their cavalry off we could hit them on the march." Caius spoke aloud as he watched the slow column of men and carts making their way parallel to the river and westwards towards a ridge.

Lucius growled in his throat. "Aye but we can't match his numbers in horse and this Hannibal knows his trade, he's covered himself well and by the time we mobilise most of his army will be across." He shook his head and snarled. "Look! He knows we're awake, he's strengthening his cavalry with divisions of skirmishers just in case we do move."

Caius looked to where Lucius pointed and saw thousands of lightly armed skirmishers interspersing the cavalry divisions. "Why move camp though?" He asked again.

Lucius didn't answer immediately.

"I can only think he's trying to negate our greater numbers, there's not enough room here to deploy our full strength so he's seeking battle this side of the river rather than the plain. Also, he's demonstrating that he can move with impunity."

Caius snarled his tone bitter. "We'll teach you this time boy! You'll dance to our tune, I promise you!"

The day passed without great event while the two sides watched each other and the Carthaginians set up camp on the ridge. The water details and foragers from both sides went almost unmolested though some Numidian cavalry did harass one detail from the smaller Roman camp, the act being another demonstration of dominance and lack of fear of the Roman numbers rather than any military objective.

With evening coming and the camp established, Hannibal called his officers to a meeting. Most arrived filthy from the march and covered in dust whipped up in the afternoon by the hot Volturnus wind to invade men's armour, eyes, ears and mouths. Cups of welcoming wine were downed quickly with refills eagerly sought.

"Gentlemen! Gentlemen, thank you for your attendance, I'll not keep you over long." Men quickly took their seats and looked to their General. "It's been a good day, we've rubbed the Roman noses in the dirt once more, they've stood by impotent while we marched and set up camp in front of them." The men cheered, Hannibal smiling and giving them a moment before quietening them. "We're in a good, dare I say safe position here on this ridge, the lack of space between our camp and theirs helps negate their huge numbers so I don't think they will seek battle here. Tomorrow however, we'll prepare anyway while antagonising and harassing their water parties and foragers anew with our patrols."

"Speaking of their numbers sir, word is circulating that they outnumber us by more than two to one." Maharbal said.

"It's true!" Hannibal shrugged while smiling and casually refilling his wine cup then standing to pace the tent. "But are we not the better men? Have we not proved it? Our victories at Ticinus, Trebbia and Trasimene say so and remember they outnumbered us on almost every occasion and we still won. Our army has been together and fought together for over three years. We know and trust one another, and our men trust us else they wouldn't be here for as you know, unlike the Romans our men are not one people but a mercenary army that relies on success to keep it together. Therefore, I say that after three years we are successful!" There were shouts of 'Aye!' and the sound of hands slapping the table. "Outnumbered or not we have the battle experience and many of you are the same officers who've commanded and led since we left Spain. How many commanders have the Romans had?" There was some smiles and laughter now and Hannibal smiled back mischievously. "As you keep beating and killing them there have been many; Publius Scipio injured and defeated at Ticinus, Longus beaten and disgraced at the Trebbia, Flaminius who lost his head and his men at Trasimene! Geminus's whole cavalry arm slaughtered or captured to a man." The tent filled with laughter. "Old Fabius who wisely wouldn't fight us was the brightest amongst them despite his servant Minucius who would fight but then lost, thus they send two more against us!" He gave a hapless shrug as the tent filled with an uproar of cheers and laughter as the men raised wine cups to themselves and their General.

"What do we know of these next two lambs, General?" Maharbal asked.

Hannibal had to wait until the hoots of laughter died down, his tone becoming more serious. "I'm told both have some military experience. Paullus is the more cautious of the two, Varro, like Flaminius before him is popular with his men and the Roman people so to maintain this admiration he may be the one that'll bite at us first. However, neither man is a fool nor glory seeker and they're being careful around us just like old Fabius. It seems they may be learning for they've not split their army like the previous Consuls, hence their numbers. However, they'll still have alternate days of command, so we'll test each man's character and watch their reactions. I think that unlike Fabius they won't need too much goading to fight for the army they've brought is not here for show." As the men quietened, he casually refilled his cup then resting his fists on the table leaned on them, his tone quiet and serious though he smiled readily. "Don't let their numbers daunt you, as you know we are usually outnumbered but I tell you this I would take quality, our quality over their quantity every time." The men rattled their cups again while voicing agreement. "And remember! Alexander of Macedon was outnumbered in every battle he fought against the Persians and was like us many stades from home, yet he carved an empire." He paused to drink and watched his men from over the rim of his cup, putting it down he looked up and down the table a warm smile on his face. "I do wonder what Alexander could have accomplished if he'd had men like you to support him."

The men cheered, clashed their cups and shouted for their General. Hannibal smiled as he saluted them their morale was high, their camaraderie good and their trust in each other and himself clear, all he needed do now was pick his day and position and he already had a plan.

****

The next morning, the last day of Quintilis, Hannibal walked the camp speaking to soldiers and officers alike as they sharpened weapons, repaired mail and armour and readied themselves for battle the following day. He didn't go dressed in his finest war panoply but as an ordinary soldier, thereby putting men at ease when he stopped to converse and encourage them. As word spread of their General being amongst them men gathered about him as he went, he answering their questions and sharing their jokes and banter. Tomorrow he said, they would test the Roman resolve and see if they would stand against the 'Lion's Brood'.

By the time he returned to his own tent it was late afternoon and stifling hot with the gusting Volturnus beginning to blow the dust in swirls across the plain. Having taken his midday meal in the open air with one group of men and talked, laughed and encouraged all, he was exhausted but quietly content at what he'd seen and heard of the feeling in camp. With reconnaissance of his men's demeanour complete he judged their temperament mildly apprehensive as he'd expect before battle, however their outlook and mood remained positive but not overconfident. That, he decided was a good thing, overconfidence brought underestimation and consequently mistakes; thus, a little trepidation was a good thing. His men were all well prepared, being well fed, rested and were it seemed spoiling for a fight. Relaxing into his chair with a cup of wine, he pondered the question put to him a score of times that day.

'If we win this fight General, will the Romans sue for peace?' He'd answered honestly that he expected it to be so, for no nation could sustain the crippling defeats they had subjected the Romans to, one more battle and just one more victory and he felt sure this aggressive, belligerent nation would finally succumb. Tomorrow was Paullus's day for command so they would probe and test the man's mettle and this huge army.

****

"What! … You're telling me the very thing I warned you against has happened?" Bomilcar Bodeshmun growled at Hephaestus as he jumped up from the table his dark eyes narrowing and brow furrowing to a savage scowl.

"Lord, I was firm in my instruction to this Haemon that the gear and the woman were to be sold well away from the camp."

Bomilcar stepped close to his Greek adjutant, his face coloured in anger, spittle flying as he snarled into the man's face.

"Yet here you are telling me this base fool Haemon has done exactly the opposite! And now that questions are being asked because of his failings, he has the audacity to demand more money for the work as he deems the possessions stolen from Targa's tent were not enough."

"Yes Lord, he …"

"You'd better find this Haemon quickly and shut him up for good!" He growled while stabbing a finger into Hephaestus's chest.

"Lord, he's … he's disappeared."

Bomilcar slapped Hephaestus hard on the side of the head surprising him and sending him stumbling. "Disappeared! … Disappeared where, deserted, killed, died of the pox?"

Regaining his stance, Hephaestus shook his head. "I don't know Lord. He demanded more money and said he'd meet me again last night in the wine tent where he and his cronies drink but he never appeared."

"Baal Almighty! I'm surrounded by fools!" He bawled and turned to swipe the wine jug and cups from the table splashing wine across the tent wall like dark blood from a severed artery before clattering in a heap on the floor. "I gave you a simple task! … A simple bloody task!" His voice rose to a shout, which he then managed to lower when he realised. His words instead coming out in a low gravelly tone but with no less amount of anger and malice. "Gods above man! All you had to do was whisper in this thug's ear of what was required and pay him some money. Baal in heaven! How hard can it be?"

"Lord, I …"

Bomilcar silenced him with a wave of his hand. "Who's asking questions?"

"I don't know Lord. All he said was questions were being asked about the robbery."

"Tannith in heaven! Do you know anything? ... And what of Targa's whore?"

"There was no mention of the woman, Lord."

Bomilcar paced the tent a hand cupping his chin as he thought, Hephaestus watching him warily from the corner of his eye.

"So, our thug has disappeared, we don't know where but must consider the worst. Someone is asking questions or knows something and that someone can only be Targa or his men, who else would care about a dead slave, a missing whore and a burned tent?"

"Yes Lord."

"It appears we need to finish the job ourselves and remove Targa. I was going to kill the damn boy anyway; this mess just necessitates the need to do it sooner rather than later."

Hephaestus paled. "But Lord ..."

"But nothing man!" He snapped. "You're to blame for this mess so you'll help me sort it out!"

"Lord, murder has already been done over this."

"So, a slave was killed! What of it?" He shrugged.

"But Targa is a Captain and a friend to Hannibal ..."

"So?"

"Lord, I want no further part in it. I serve you faithfully, I always have but ..."

"And you will continue to serve me how I say, else your family back in Carthage will be thrown off my estate with just the garments on their backs and you!" He prodded him hard in the chest again. "You! Can find another Lord to serve."

"Lord, if we're caught ..."

"Well, we'll make sure we aren't caught. Like you, I've no wish to be nailed to a cross and I'm sure your wife and children have no desire to be homeless."

Hephaestus looked at the ground as he chewed his lip, his face showing small grimaces and a nervous tick that pulled at the corner of his mouth.

Bomilcar casually rested a hand on his dagger hilt and asked. "Well! What is it to be? Are you with me or against me?" Hephaestus hesitated. "I'm waiting!" Hephaestus saw Bomilcar's fingers wrap around his dagger hilt, it was obvious he wouldn't be leaving the tent alive if he declined. Lords such as Bodeshmun could pass off the death of a retainer with a myriad of reasons and no one would question much. Then, depending on the reason or charge laid upon the retainer's demise, could also see their family's lives or liberty forfeited.

"I'm your man Lord, as always. What's the plan?" He said quietly.

"Aha! So it seems you do have some sense in that thick Greek skull after all! The plan is simple and involves just you and me, the less folk involved means less chance of repercussions, unlike this last debacle."

"Yes Lord."

"Battle is coming and one more dead Captain on the casualty list, regardless of whom he's friends with will hardly draw attention. Anyway, to ease your newfound tender conscience, all I need you to do is watch him and let me know when he's on his own. Do you think you can manage that?"

"Yes Lord."

"Good! Now, fetch me some more wine then ensure the men are ready for tomorrow."

"Yes Lord."

It was early evening when Baldor headed to his tent with Issa at his heel and panting from the heat. Having spent the day encouraging and preparing his men for battle the following morning, he was tired, hungry and despite his positive talk to his men, worried. It was more than just the usual nerves before battle; for the question of the huge Roman numbers had come up again and again throughout the day and was unsettling him. He'd countered his men's concerns with Hannibal's words and examples, now he had to believe them for himself. It was much easier to be brave and resolute when in the company of his men or at Hannibal's table with his peers than to be alone with his own thoughts.

The camp was strangely quiet with just the low buzz of conversation carrying on the air interspersed with the rasp of whetstones on metal and the ting-ting of Smith's hammers ringing on anvils as they worked late into the day. The usual loud and lively chatter, shouts and laughter that spoke of men drinking, gambling or even arguing were missing. Thankfully, the atmosphere was not that of dread or fear but more a quiet apprehensive caution, ostensibly it was not unlike any other night before a battle only amplified to a greater degree. Approaching his tent his nose caught the scent of dinner and took his mind to his body needs. The small table within was already set along with a basket of fresh bread, bowls of butter and olive oil with plates of cheese, olives, capers and jugs of wine and water, while the main course gently simmered in a pot suspended over a small fire by the side of the tent.

Lasairiona smiled as he entered. "Come, dinner is ready, eat and then you can rest." She ruffled Issa's ears as the dog pushed at her legs, tail wagging excitedly.

"Thank you." He smiled warmly as he kissed her. "I'm hungry all right."

She poured the wine and added water to it. "Clear head tomorrow?"

"Yes, I'll …"

"Tell me of tomorrow!" She interrupted, her words coming out in a rush the dread in her voice clear. "Please tell me true, don't sweeten it or give me false hope for I can see you're worried."

Baldor chewed his lip while stroking her cheek tenderly and giving her a warm but sad smile. "All right … we think battle's coming tomorrow and the odds are heavily stacked against us."

"How many are they?" Her voice dropped almost to a whisper.

He cleared his throat. "We have reports of eighty thousand men." He heard her sharp intake of breath.

"And you have how many?"

"About half that in infantry plus ten thousand cavalry."

"This is it then Baldor, the final throw of the dice the battle to end it all?"

"We hope so."

Lasairiona shook her head slightly and her eyes filled, their icy blueness augmented brightly by the moisture, her sorrow seeming to make her only more beautiful. She didn't cry though the tears spilled down her cheek. Seeing her angst pulled at his heart.

"Hey … hey, come on." He said quietly as he gently brushed the tears away. "Numbers don't guarantee victory; they've always outnumbered us but never beaten us yet. Many of these Romans are new to war while we have been fighting together for over three years. Experience and quality are what counts not numbers."

"But so many!"

"Which is one reason why we moved camp they now lack the space to field them all, another reason being we show them we don't fear them."

"I fear for you regardless of their numbers … for once in my life I have someone who cares for me, who loves me …"

Issa, sensing the tension and unhappiness came and laid her head on Lasairiona's lap while giving a small whine, her tail wagging slowly. Lasairiona patted her head gently. "It's all right girl, it's all right." She whispered.

"Don't fear my love, please!" Baldor smiled and leaned over the table to kiss her tenderly on the brow. "I have an able General and good men around me; you know that." He said kindly.

"I know, I know." She brushed at her tears. "I'm sorry; I should be strong for you but I love you so much, I couldn't bear it if, if … I just want the war over and you safe and for us to live our lives in peace."

"When the war's over I promise you we will."

Lasairiona managed a sad smile though her eyes sparkled and her body seemed to grow from an inner strength, her voice firming. "Eat, I've laboured your ears enough." She pushed the bread and olives towards him. "The lamb stew will be nearly ready."

"Once we've eaten I'll clean my armour and sharpen my swords and then we can have some time."

"It's already done."

"What?" He looked at the weapon tree in the corner of the tent that held his mail shirt, helmet, greaves and swords. The bronze helmet was burnished bright with the horsehair plume brushed, the mail shirt cleaned and glinting from a scrubbing with river sand, his two falcatas out of their scabbards and lightly oiled. "What … who? Did you do this?"

She managed a full smile at last. "I'm the daughter of a Gallic Warlord remember, I've seen and helped with war panoply before, the difference now is I love the man I've done it for. You'll find the blades nick free and sharp."

Baldor rose from the table and picked one up, sighted it and thumbed the edge approvingly.

"Thank you, thank you so much! This has saved me a lot of time and work tonight." He kissed her again as he sat back down.

Mischief replaced her prior sadness. "Which means you'll have more time for me and don't expect to sleep too early my love; I want payment in full for all my work … but eat first, you can't love or fight on an empty stomach."

Smiles and light laughter finally filled the tent as the pair kissed across the table before feeding one another of the bite size food. Seeing he was hungry, she tore some bread, buttered it and passed it to him, he wolfing it down along with some olives then finally remembering his manners he offered her the bowl. She smiled and nibbled at an olive teasing at the outer flesh with her teeth while watching him with eyes that now shone like ice on fire. Her eyes never left him as she reached for another; he picked his cup up and swilled the wine then grabbed her hand urging her up from the table.

"Bed, now!" He laughed and pulled at her hand.

She slipped from his grip. "No … no, you need to eat …"

"I'll survive!"

She pushed him back to his seat while wriggling from his grasping hands.

"Good things come to he who waits." She said, the pout of her lips and provocative, sultry tone doing nothing to calm his urgent desire.

"Very well, we'll wait for the rest of dinner." He countered while laughing and reaching for her again.

"No! The lamb is ready now." She giggled.

"So am I!"

"Oh, my love!" She said with mock sympathy. "I'm sorry, I shouldn't tease." The husky allure of her voice belying her words. "Please My Lord, enjoy your dinner and then … then you can do what you like to me!"

"You'd better bring that lamb now then!"

"You don't wish more olives first?" She teased again.

"The lamb now! Then you girl!"

"Girl, is it?" When he gave a mock growl and made to get up, she jumped back from his reach and gave a bow. "Dinner will be served, My Lord." Then ducked outside, returning with the stew pot and served him.

With dinner finally done, she mixed more wine in his cup then sipped from it, her eyes peering seductively at him over the rim before offering it to him. As he took it to his lips, she rose from the table and stood back while slowly unfastening the shoulder straps of her dress, holding them in place she turned away letting the garment fall to the floor. Naked and barefoot, she stepped out of it and walked towards the back of the tent and a curtain that screened what passed for a bedroom, she paused briefly to look back over her shoulder.

Baldor watched her go, his heart already hammering in his chest, his wine going down in gulps as he looked at her body. Her fox-coloured hair reached midway down her back, her skin pale and flawless like the purest marble, her waist narrow, her buttocks firm atop shapely thighs and long calves. Then all too soon, like a brief apparition of a beautiful Goddess she was gone. Abandoning the wine, he unlaced his long cavalry boots while cursing his fingers for not working fast enough, removing his dagger and belt and shrugging out of his tunic; he threw it to one side as he followed after her.

It had been fully dark for some time before the pair sought sleep, exhausted but relaxed from their lovemaking Baldor held Lasairiona in his arms, her head resting on his chest her arm laid over his waist. Running his fingers through her hair, he breathed deeply inhaling the sweet fragrance of her perfume emanating from her heated skin, it mixing with his own musky, male smell and the scent of sex that came from the bed when they kicked the sheets back so to cool off. Outside, the camp was now totally quiet with only the occasional call from the night birds to disturb and both soon fell asleep.

Chapter Twenty-two

The plain of Cannae in the Apulian District, the 1st of Sextilis (August) 216 BC

The dewfall chill woke Baldor just before dawn broke. Easing the sheets over Lasairiona, he motioned Issa back on her sheepskin then slipped quietly from the bed and found his tunic. Picking her dress from the ground, he sniffed at the perfume on it a warm smile creasing his face. Placing it on the chair, he went to a small wooden stand that held tiny gold effigies of Baal and Tannith, the two being gifts from Hannibal. Alongside and also in miniature but wrought simply in bronze, the Gallic deities, Epona and Sirona stared back at him. Lighting an oil lamp, he placed a small dish filled with scented oil on top of it to heat then dropped to his knees and bowed his head, his prayers coming out in stilted whispers.

"Baal Hammon, Lord of us all … Tannith Goddess, please hear your son's prayers. Help … help me lead well and be brave against my enemy. Should I fall today …" He took a deep breath. "Should I fall, please see my woman safe and spare my friends and men if you will." He fidgeted and cleared his throat. "Again Lord, mother, I apologise for my past transgressions and lack of respect and ask that you accept your wayward son into your grace and … and that you'll welcome me when I approach your door." The last words came out hoarse and thick with emotion as the thought of his demise stole his resolve. Picking up the effigies of Baal and Tannith one at a time he gently kissed each.

Hearing then seeing the oil beginning to bubble in the dish, he wafted the sweet-smelling steam over his head. "Father, mother, if I fall today and the Lord Baal accepts me I will have joy that I see you once again.

Until then, father I'll try to be brave and bring honour to our house. Mother ..." His eyes filled and a lump rose in his throat. "Mother, I'm sorry that against all your wishes I've taken the warrior's path, please forgive your wayward son." He waited a moment to settle his breathing and let his heart slow. "Gestix, brother, I miss you every day, I miss your wisdom and your love." He managed a sad smile. "I'm trying to be a better man, Epona bless and keep you brother." He then picked up the image of Sirona, Lasairiona's Goddess and chosen protector and stared at the strange little image of a woman with a dog on her lap, a snake twisted about her arm and her other hand holding three eggs. "Goddess, I've never prayed to you but I do so now for my woman, my love. She reveres you above all others and I ask your protection for her. Please protect her if I'm killed and cannot." He kissed the greening bronze, placed it back on the stand and stood to go and arm himself. He paused and fished the silver cameo from his tunic then kissed it. "I won't' forget you, I promise. Tannith keep you always."

The trumpet sounded the 'Stand-to' just as Baldor finished fastening the straps holding the falcatas on his back. He heard the soft thud of hooves outside the tent and muffled voices, Andulas, Armaco and his men were here.

"Captain!" Armaco's loud voice carried into the tent.

Baldor stepped out into the pale light. "I'm here! Good morning brothers."

Andulas and Armaco dipped their heads and returned the greeting while Armaco pulled on the reins of Baldor's mount moving it forward ready for him to mount. Baldor looked surprised to see a riding blanket already fastened in place. Armaco sniggered.

"I thought you may need a bit of help this morning!" He laughed as Baldor grimaced, Andulas doing his best to hide his mirth behind his hand.

"Thank you but I can manage." Baldor replied as he reached for the reins and looked to mount.

"You may need your helmet then? I didn't bring you a spare one." Armaco quipped then smiled and shrugged. Andulas couldn't suppress his laughter, while Baldor shook his head and turned back to the tent. "She must be quite a lady, Captain!" Armaco called after him then jumped as Andulas punched his arm.

"She! Is quite a lady." Lasairiona said as she stepped from the tent door with Baldor's helmet and padded cap in her hand, a blanket held over her shoulders covering the thin shift she'd pulled on, Issa padding alongside her.

Armaco had the decency to blush and stuttered an apology. "I beg your pardon Lasairiona."

She raised a fist at him but smiled. Her countenance became serious as she passed Baldor his helmet, her eyes moist as she threw her arms around his neck, the blanket falling to the floor her tone sharp in his ear. "You should have woken me!"

"I'll be back later, don't worry!" He said as confidently as he could.

"Sirona keep and protect you my love." She pushed the tiny effigy into his hand and kissed him then turned to Armaco. Forgetting the fallen blanket, she took hold of his mount's bridle and looked up at him. "Remember Armaco, you promised to keep him safe!" She snapped. "I'm holding you to it!"

Armaco tried to focus on her face as he went to answer but couldn't help notice her bare shoulders and the low cut, thin shift that barely hid her breasts. Despite his usual rough, brash ways, he was caught off-guard and strangely flummoxed by the vehement beauty before him, making him stumble for words.

"I will." Was the best he could manage. Then, when she smiled warmly, kissed her fingers and placed them on his hand, he answered firmly. "I will … I promise."

Suddenly remembering the blanket, she looked momentarily embarrassed and picked it up wrapping her shoulders again, she took Issa by the collar as she approached Andulas.

"Sirona keep you safe, My Lord." She smiled and dipped her head, he smiling and bowing his head in return.

With Baldor mounted the column moved out, Lasairiona and several other women watching them go while Issa whined mournfully. Andulas turned to Armaco shaking his head and chuckling.

"I never thought I'd live to see the day!"

"What?"

"You! Lost for words?"

Armaco, having recovered from his vocal disarming by Lasairiona pushed his mount between Baldor and Andulas.

"Well, the lady is beautiful and with all due respect Baldor, how on earth do you leave a woman like that?"

"What choice do I have when you're outside my tent bellowing,

'Captain' Loud enough to wake the whole camp."

"You'd better make sure he gets back safely Armaco." Andulas said with a smirk.

"I'll make sure all of us get back safely." He threw both arms in the air triumphantly. "There's nothing to fear, Armaco is here!"

The men close by all laughed while Andulas turned to Baldor.

"I feel much better now the old, cock-sure Armaco is back."

"Aye, if all else fails he can talk them to death."

"What's the punishment for thumping your Captain, Andulas?"

"In your case you may not live long enough to find out, for if the lady hears you've hurt him … Well?"

"You know, I might just take the risk!"

The chuckles and talk ceased as the troop exited the camp and a messenger arrived at the gallop with orders for them to assemble on the left wing. Men sobered as they saw the preparations for battle for looking at the massing numbers, Hannibal was fielding his entire army. They were directed between the huge screen of javelin men and slingers already forming a defensive skirmishing line and the front ranks of their massing light and heavy infantry divisions. Trotting through the sand-coloured dust clouds raised by thousands of feet, Baldor led his men to the left wing where General Hasdrubal was assembling the heavy cavalry. Meanwhile, infantry officers bellowed commands while pointing to where they wanted men positioned, the troops marching to their allotted place and setting their banners.

Trumpets blared in the nearby Roman camp and velites spilled out of the gate. Moving at double pace they spread quickly across the camp frontage in a wide, dense block screening the legions exiting behind them, before advancing a few paces at a time as the legionary ranks thickened in their rear and sought more space. Columns of more legionaries and trotting cavalry turmaes appeared from the other three gateways from the camp, the Roman cavalry, like their Carthaginian counterparts riding out to the wings.

It was mid-morning before both armies were deployed and the dust finally settled, each side watching the other for the first sign of attack. The Roman lines however were backed right up to their camp rampart, more like a force defending a city wall than an army seeking open battle. An eerie silence settled over the ground as men waited.

Hannibal and his senior Generals appeared. Beneath the standard of Carthage, they rode slowly across the front of the army, the men cheering and raising spears as they passed by, Hannibal raising his hand in acknowledgement of their adulation. The Roman ranks however remained quiet and unmoving.

Midday became early afternoon and the relentless heat of the August sun cooked the warriors in their mail and armour, men sipped their water sparingly, mindful that battle might still come. Just as the Volturnus began to blow and strengthen at the Carthaginian's backs, a huge warrior stepped out from their ranks carrying a war spear and walked towards the Roman lines. Pausing out of javelin range, he raised the spear to throw and then with a short run and deep grunt that carried over the plain, he hurled it. The throw was huge, the spear thudding into and then sticking up from the ground but falling well short of the Roman ranks. The man shouted to the Romans then waited, with no response he turned his back and waited again. Shrugging massive shoulders and raising his hands in a hapless gesture, he walked back to his lines as the Carthaginians erupted into cheers, their spear shafts and swords beating their shields.

Caius looked to Lucius and growled. "We'll have to fight now; the cunning young savage is forcing the issue." Lucius squinted into the sun and chewed at his lip but said nothing. "Lucius … Lucius!" Caius badgered. "We need to go now; the die is cast for us."

Lucius looked at the narrow space between the armies and his men packed tightly together, his features drawn in consternation. "There's no space Caius!" He growled.

"Jupiter in heaven man, we've no choice! Give the order; let us have at them and now, before we're too late!" He beseeched but when Lucius didn't reply, he vented. "Gods above man, are you blind? Unless we attack, he's claiming the land and the battle by the spear! We have to fight! Our honour demands it!"

"He's not Alexander claiming Asia, Caius!"

"No, he isn't but the men know what it means, we have no choice other than to fight!"

"The winds behind them, it's whipping up the dust and we are looking into the sun." Lucius countered, his tone bitter. "It's already too late in the day and we can't fully deploy here in this space either, our numbers are wasted."

Caius looked at the faces of the men arrayed behind him and saw grim anticipation, a fervent need to get on and fight, to get it over with, anything was better than more waiting.

"Damn you, Lucius! Damn you to Hades!" He spat. "You are wary of the open plain and now this space is too tight?"

"Tomorrow is another day."

"Aye! My day! I'll finish what you won't!"

Caius pulled his mount about with a savage twist on the reins while the trumpets signaled retiral and the Roman army began to fall back to camp.

Cornelius heard the orders being relayed and then another huge roar from the Carthaginian ranks drowned out everything. Looking across he saw weapons raised aloft in jubilation as men cheered, some jumping up and down, others pointing and laughing, the thump of weapons on shields starting again. Once again, Hannibal had humbled his enemy and this time without a blow being struck.

Chapter Twenty-Three

The plain of Cannae in the Apulian District, 2nd of Sextilis (August) 216 BC

The first ghost light of dawn on the tent wall woke Baldor, gently untangling himself from Lasairiona's embrace he eased from the bed. Issa jumped up, stretched and gave herself a shake then bounded across the tent towards him; he bent down to stroke and fuss her while seeking his tunic and boots. Would today be the day the Romans finally fought? He managed a grim smile and wondered at that, for yesterday had seen the Romans humbled, how could an army's morale come back from that? Despite the huge enemy numbers, the Roman decline of battle had left his own men jubilant and confident, seeing the refusal as fear of them.

Lasairiona came behind him, embracing him and dropping her head on his shoulder, her naked body warm against his, her scent sweet and heady.

"Will it be today?" She asked quietly.

"I don't know." He rubbed his cheek gently against hers. "I hope so, and then it's done."

"Yes, it's the waiting that's the worst." She hugged him close and he felt hot tears on his skin.

"Hey! It'll be all right … I'll be all right, I promise." He said softly with more confidence than he really believed then kissed her cheek.

She sniffed hard and cuffed at the tears. "I know you will." She said firmly. "I've prayed to Sirona to keep you safe and she's always cared for me, so I won't fear for you." She lied convincingly.

A single trumpet blast announced dawn to wake the camp and go to breakfast.

"If you win can …"

"We will win." He affirmed and smiled. "We will! And yes, then we can live in peace." He pre-empted.

"In Carthage?"

"No … no, Andulas has offered us a home …"

"But I'm Cenomani!" She interrupted sharply. "How will that work; how can we live there? My tribe and Andulas's hated each other!"

"I asked that and Andulas assures me that despite feuds and war, tribes and people mix. People are just people at the end of the day intermarriage and acceptance happens no matter what's gone before, you must have seen it?" When Lasairiona still looked unsure, he continued while doing his best to hide a wry grin. "Anyway, Andulas is Lord of the Lingone and what he says goes in his lands and by then I hope you will be my wife, so there'll …"

"What … what did you say?"

"Andulas is Lord of the Lingone and what he says goes." He smirked and chuckled, then grunted when Lasairiona punched him in the back.

"What did you say?" She repeated quickly, excitement lightening her tone.

"Andulas is …" She bit his ear lobe making him yelp. Grinning at his teasing he turned to face her, his hand caressing her cheek, his tone finally serious the words gentle. "I said … will you be my wife?"

"Oh!" She dropped her head a little, her tone hesitant her reply stalled.

"Oh?" He repeated, suddenly sounding very awkward and unsure. "Do you need time to consider?"

"Well, no … not really."

"What then?" He cleared his throat, clearly uncomfortable with the way the conversation was going and his embarrassment mounting. "I don't understand."

"There's a problem." She gave him a sad but seductive look.

"A problem! Surely, it's just yes or no?" His words tetchy as his pride rankled.

"The problem is, I'm a Chief's daughter and Armaco says you're just a Carthaginian peasant."

"What?"

"Armaco says you're a …"

Unable to keep a straight face or hold her laughter any longer she threw her arms over his shoulders. "Of course, I'll be your wife!" She said quickly while showering his face with kisses. Then, holding his face in both her hands, she looked at him intensely and smiled, he saw her eyes filling with tears again. "I love you; Baldor Targa and I accept your casual offer."

Relieved and managing to laugh at her teasing he kissed her full in the mouth. "I could have put it better I suppose but I love you … I love you dearly Lasairiona of the Cenomani, my heart is yours."

"And mine yours, Captain Baldor Targa and that's all that matters."

He wiped gently at her tears and kissed her again.

"We won't reside in the village for Andulas is giving us our own steading, we'll have peace Lasairiona away from here, away from most folk, I promise."

"As long as I have you, I don't care." She smiled then tittered. "Baldor the farmer, I like it!" She hugged him tightly then picking up her dress began rummaging through their food stocks. "You need breakfast."

"You'd better put that dress on else forget breakfast."

She turned towards him unabashed at her nakedness her eyes suddenly afire, her lips slightly open in a seductive pout, holding the dress up she let it fall. Baldor was half out of his seat when the trumpets sounded and repeated.

"Damn it!" He growled.

The moment was broken, Lasairiona grabbed the dress from the ground and slipped it over her head then began putting food on the table while Baldor shrugged into his leather shirt and pulled on his boots.

"Eat my love, I'll bring your war gear and help you ready."

The trumpets sounded twice more as he wolfed bread and cheese while Lasairiona helped him into his war panoply. He was just ready when hooves outside the tent announced his men along with a shout from Armaco.

"Captain! … Captain Sir! We need to go now!" This time there was urgency in his voice. Lasairiona opened the tent flaps and Baldor stepped out, Issa following. "Good morning sir, lady." Armaco dipped his head and before Baldor could ask, he expounded. "The Romans are crossing the river to the plain and drawing up for battle; it looks like they've found their balls at last!"

"They're up early and moving fast then!"

"Aye! Trying to look keen after yesterday's loss of face I guess."

"All of them?"

"Aye, thousands of the bastards are already across and their camp here is spewing thousands more."

"And us?"

"Full mobilisation Captain. Today's the day it seems, we're to cross the river and form up under General Hasdrubal on the left wing."

"I've had no message from Hannibal?"

"The idiot messenger came to Andulas's tent looking for you, he gave me the message but I sent him here to let you know." Baldor just shrugged. "I guess he didn't find you?"

"No matter! Brief me as we go."

"I brought your mount anyway." Armaco lifted the reins.

"Where's Andulas?"

"Gone ahead to let General Hasdrubal know we're on our way. Bastard Romans! They've set us by our ears this morning." He hawked and spat. "Beg your pardon lady."

Taking his helmet from Lasairiona, Baldor kissed her, she managing to control her emotions and remain strong while pushing the effigy of Sirona into his hand again.

"Later." She said and smiled. "Issa, come." She turned away leaving him to his men, her angst and tears hidden from all. Inside the tent, she fell to her knees to pray.

Finishing her prayers, she looked for Issa. "Issa! … Issa?" Running to the door, she caught a glimpse of Issa as she and the men disappeared down the camp road.

Raising clouds of water spray that coloured momentarily like a rainbow in the bright sunlight Baldor's men forded the Aufidius, a few stades downstream the Romans were also crossing. On the plain huge clouds of yellow dust rose obscuring much of the view as both sides positioned themselves. Trotting along the riverbank they were met by a Marshal.

"Hail Captain! Keep to this bank and head downstream, you'll find General Hasdrubal with the heavy Spanish and Gallic cavalry on our left flank. Baal keep you sir."

"And you." Baldor waved his men on following the river.

Armaco came alongside. "We've got company." He pointed.

"Issa!" Baldor growled. "Issa, go home! … Home!" His voice lost in the rumble of hooves; Issa just kept pace with the horses.

Coming up on the rear of Hasdrubal's cavalry Andulas met them and led them to their position.

"The General wants us here Captain, hard against the river."

"Excellent! No worries about our left flank then."

"Baal almighty! We have a good position for once." Armaco still sounded like he was grumbling but the three men smiled.

"You brought the dog?" Andulas asked in dismay.

"No, the dog brought herself." Baldor dismounted and scolded Issa, then seeing her drop her head and look sad, he reneged and ruffled her ears. "Baal keep you too Issa!" He squashed his face against hers, she, licking his and whimpering.

Time passed as the armies assembled. Officers bellowed, runners dashed about the lines with messages and units shuffled or moved until commanders were content with their position. Horses whickered and shied, some rearing and tossing their heads as they sensed the tension building in the men. The hubbub gradually eased as the shouts and activity died away and with the two sides finally in position the dust began to settle. The sand coloured plain was now a blaze of colour from brightly painted shield faces, helmet crests, bright coloured tunics and gently fluttering banners and standards. Sporadic bright flashes came from helmets and spear tips as the sunlight reflected brightly from the burnished metal. The tension increased as men sweated and waited. A messenger cantered up.

"Captain Targa … sir, you're to accompany General Hasdrubal to General Hannibal, this way please."

Nodding to his comrades, Baldor cut out from the line and followed the messenger.

"Ah good morning Captain, come! We're to review our position and the enemies with General Hannibal." Hasdrubal said as he led on.

The men trotted along the front ranks of the army towards a mounted group positioned forward of the front line's centre and complete with banners and the disc and crescent standard of Carthage. For the first time in battle that Baldor had seen, Hannibal was dressed opulently. His helmet sported a magnificent purple horsehair crest that tumbled down his back over a splendid purple cloak with a leopard skin stole draping his shoulders. His bronze breastplate polished to a gleaming luster, his black-faced shield bearing the crescent and disc of Carthage picked out in bright bronze.

"Gentlemen well met! I believe today is the day." Hannibal pushed his mount forward to shake Hasdrubal and Baldor's hands and beamed a smile. "Come; let's review our men and our enemy." Then turning to the Roman lines he began the briefing, pointing as he spoke. "Varro is in overall command. He's anchored his cavalry under Paullus on their right wing against the river facing you, General Hasdrubal."

"No matter sir." The older man growled. "If we can't ride around them we'll ride through the bastards!" This raising some light laughter from the group. Hannibal grinned.

"Once the skirmishers are done General, drive Paullus and his cavalry off, you know what to do from there."

"Aye sir."

"As usual the Roman centre holds their legions and auxiliary infantry; they're under their former Consul, Geminus. Varro himself is on their left with his auxiliary cavalry anchored against the hills facing you General Maharbal and your Numidian horse on our right. He's trying to ensure you can't get past him or flank him either, the man's thinking … well, maybe?" He smiled.

"His position looks sound sir?" Maharbal commented grimly.

"It does. He's trying to ensure we can't manoeuvre; however, this lack of space could be his undoing. Also, he hasn't taken into account the elements, by early afternoon the Romans will face more of the sun than us and we'll have the southern wind at our backs." He smiled. "That'll add nicely to the trouble we're about to give him!"

As Hannibal finished explaining the Roman troop dispositions the men stared at the depth of the assembled ranks facing them, the sight was truly daunting. General Gisgo broke the pregnant silence.

"Baal Almighty sir! Their frontage must be ten stades at least … and their depth! They're thicker than mites on a mangy dog. I've never seen so many men."

"True General Gisgo, very true! However, I wager not one man over there has the name Gisgo and therewith lies their problem!" The quip made the group laugh and broke the tension. The ranks drawn up behind them, hearing the laughter began to cheer, the good spirit spreading quickly through the army and growing in volume. Hannibal smiled and pulled the group together to shout above the noise. "General Mago!"

"Yes sir."

"You take the centre with our Spanish and Gallic heavy infantry; they'll form our front line but I want them arrayed convexly."

"Convexly?"

"Yes, it makes a bulwark against the legions' advance helping break their line. I'll command our heavy African infantry behind you but place them to either side, leaving a gap for your Spaniards and Gauls to fall back into if the push from the legions becomes too great."

"Yes sir."

"Just hold them as long as you can and hopefully they'll keep committing more and more men."

"Yes sir."

"If you see your line breaking under the pressure, drop back before it collapses."

"Yes sir."

"Now, in case Varro's just parading to raise morale we'll strike first. Gentlemen to your positions and may Baal keep and bless you all. Skirmishes to the front!"

Cornelius listened as Varro rapped out his orders to the command group then finished with a speech.

"This ends here today. We have the men; we have the ground and we have the blessing of the Gods! We outnumber them and there's no chance for Punic treachery or any way for them to outflank us, so finally they must fight us as men."

"Consul Varro." Paullus said officially. "You've deepened our infantry formations considerably, that's not the best use of our firepower."

"True but it allows deployment of our greater numbers and will help with our impetus going forward." He raised his hand to stifle Paullus's reply. "Our cavalry are well secured on both flanks and with you and me in command we'll ensure they hold while we use that infantry depth and weight to crush their centre."

Lucius however was not to be silenced. "There's not a lot of space for the legionaries to operate."

Varro smiled. "We can't have it all ways Lucius; surely you must be content with …"

"And gone noon they'll have the Volturnus at their backs and ..."

Varro, tiring of Lucius's comments snapped. "By then sir they'll be almost finished for we'll not be overlong about our business. Now! Let us have at them! Gentlemen to your positions! Velites forward!"

As trumpets sounded all along the lines, the group cheered and the waiting ranks hearing it joined in. Soon the deafening cadence of weapons beating shields began. For once, Cornelius managed a smile then kissed the effigy of Salus hanging at his neck – today was the day the sons of the 'She Wolf' took revenge on the 'Lion's Brood', he closed his eyes to pray.

Baldor mopped sweat from his face with his neckcloth and watched as brightly trousered, bare-chested Gallic skirmishers and Balearic slingers exchanged javelins and slingshot with the velites, the bravest closing for swordplay, bodies already littering the ground. Owing to the convex Carthaginian centre, he could clearly see the waiting heavy troops. Gauls, this time in mail shirts and bronze helmets with long broad swords and oval shields, the Spaniards in fish scale corselets and crested helmets. Could they hold the push from the massed legions when it came?

As the tension mounted and he quietly fretted with the waiting, he sought to talk then remembered his prayers. He gave a grateful sigh; at last, he could seek comfort and ask a blessing while also praying for his comrades' lives. Bowing his head, he muttered his reverences to Baal and Tannith asking their protection. Then, pulling the tiny statuette of Sirona from his purse he prayed for Lasairiona. A trumpet blast close by made his mount bridle and snatched him from his devotions as General Hasdrubal called for the advance and Baldor waved his men on. Kissing the image of Sirona, he slipped it back into his purse then pulling the cameo from his shirt kissed it. The trumpet sounded again and the horses went to the trot. Relieved to be moving, he mumbled a final prayer to his parents and Gestix.

The skirmishers, having fought to a stalemate and seeing the cavalry move broke off the fight, the velites dropping back through the legionary's ranks, the Carthaginian skirmishers nearest to their advancing horsemen now running alongside. Determined to hold their position the Roman cavalry remained stationary and were hit at the gallop by Hasdrubal's men; the Roman horses naturally shying and turning away in panic from the incoming charge. This was no fluid, swirling cavalry action but a bloody, head-on battering of horseflesh and men. Horses collided, heads tossing as they whickered and screamed in fear, others skittered and reared trying to evade the incoming charge else went down crushing their rider. Men on both sides spilled from their mounts as the impetus of the fierce clash took its toll while heavy war spears ruptured mail and leather armour alike. Some closest to the river were knocked hurtling down the bank the riders jumping clear else falling to be crushed under the tumbling, screaming mounts.

Paullus, magnificently armoured and dressed in a scarlet tunic and cloak raised his gladius, shouting for his men to hold he was hit on the helmet by a slingshot. Badly shaken and concussed he reeled drunkenly on his horse, his bodyguards coming alongside and steering him away. As they turned to the rear, his men seeing his departure and already succumbing to the brutal Carthaginian attack began to flee.

As the fight opened up to chase, Hasdrubal reined alongside Baldor, pointing and shouting above the din. "Captain! Take your troop, follow Captain Harbro, and see these Roman bastards off! Once there's no sign of them rallying come back here immediately and help me attack their left wing under Varro."

"Yes Sir!"

Baldor waved his troop on in pursuit while Hasdrubal marshalled his men ready to ride across the rear of the battle to attack Varro's auxiliary cavalry.

Back in the infantry centre, the whoosh of the departing Roman pila was followed quickly by a trumpet blast and the legionaries roared, drew gladius s' and attacked at double step. The Gallic carnyx wailed their baleful, brassy note in response while the men roared defiance and raised shields against the incoming metal shower. Pila fell, piercing or rattling and banging on shields like heavy hail else slipping through gaps and skewering men. The last few paces between the enemies closed quickly, men on both sides shuffling tighter together against the incoming impact. A moment later, the Romans smashed into the bulge of the convex Carthaginian line. As their shields hit those of the Gauls and Spaniards, the throaty roar became a groan as flesh and blood absorbed the bone jarring impact. Men shouted their hate, shields battered while blades flashed and stabbed, hot blood misted the air mixing with the rising dust. The weight of the Roman attack was amplified by the densely packed ranks behind, driving their comrades on they pushed the Spaniards and Gauls slowly back. Mago and his officers shouted themselves hoarse to hold the line while calling more ranks forward in support. Managing to slow then stop the Roman push the fighting rose to another level of intensity as the enemies came closer than lovers. The iron stink of blood mixed with that of stale sweat and emptying bowels, the combatants so close that the dead and dying couldn't fall and were held up by the crush of their comrades. Then, with the Roman ranks still pressing from behind the push began again, driving the Spaniards and Gauls slowly back, men going down as they tried to step back while fighting to the front.

Still chasing the fleeing Romans, Baldor grunted as he drove his spear into the back of an equite. The man threw up his arms, dropping his sword and shield, his back arching as the heavy spear burst through the mail shirt into his lungs, his body along with Baldor's spear tumbling from his mount. Seeing the Romans scattering in all directions Baldor had his signaler sound the recall. Taking a moment while his men rallied, he saw Issa alongside panting from the run and the heat and her tongue lolling. Turning his mount, he detected a limp and dismounted to check his horse's legs, Armaco reined in.

"All right?"

"I think so." He answered while running his hands around the horse's fetlocks. "I think it's something in the front hoof."

"Take that Roman mount."

Baldor shook his head. "They're still not using bridles! This won't take long to sort. Take the troop and follow General Hasdrubal."

"I'll wait for you."

"Go! ... Go! I'm all right!" He shouted as he prized a sharp pebble from the hoof with his dagger. "The General needs us as soon as possible, go!"

Armaco grunted and kicked his mount on, Issa racing after him. Harbro arrived moments later with his men and Baldor waved him past intimating he was fine.

Slipping his shield over his back, he mounted again. He'd just turned his horse to follow his men when he was hit from behind with tremendous force. A fighting spear broke on his shield tipping him from his mount. His horse whickered and sprung away. Landing heavily, he groaned as the wind was knocked out of him and his face smacked the ground hard. A horse stamped in front of him and a man dropped lightly from its back.

Breathless, Baldor scrambled to his feet, dust and blood in his mouth. "You!" He gasped wetly from bloodied, burst lips while unslinging and dropping his shield and snatching for both falcatas.

"Yes me, boy! The last person you'll ever see!" Bomilcar threw the broken spear down then drew his spatha and dagger to run at Baldor.

Though shaken and bruised from the fall, Baldor surprised Bomilcar as he also ran and met the attack. Fueled by intense hatred and desire to kill, the pair growled in effort as their blades clanged and scraped with fast, hard strokes their feet raising dust as they stepped quickly. Seemingly matched in skill and speed and realising the end was not going to be quick they separated, seeking breath and eyeing one another.

"I'm your nemesis boy! Your doom!" Bomilcar taunted. "It was me who had your tent robbed and your bitch sold to be slaved and whored!"

Baldor snarled, baring bloodied teeth as he felt the anger flowing through him like hot venom, twisting his gut and misting his vision in a red haze.

Bomilcar sought to feed the anger. "Come boy, come!" He beckoned with his spatha. "When you're food for crows I'll hump your bitch then give her to my men." Giving a hollow laugh he spat then moved seeking a new line of attack.

Baldor's hot retort dried in his throat as his memory recalled Gestix's teaching. *He wants you angry, angry men make mistakes! Keep your temper Baldor! He'll die just as quick and be just as dead once you're done! Keep your mind on what you're doing.'* Feeling a strange calmness come over him, he spat gobbets of thick blood and gave a cold smile. Extending his left arm, the falcata outstretched to fend off a rush he raised the other blade above his shoulder as he crouched slightly. The pair attacked again. A blur of metal ensued as each man fought with both weapons, the lightning speed interspersed with gasps, grunts and the almost constant ting of blade on blade. Pushing apart for breath once more the dust from their feet drifted on the rising breeze.

Baldor, younger and perhaps fitter from three years of war was the first to attack again. Composed and methodical he drove Bomilcar backwards in a flurry of sword strokes so fast the man struggled to counter and his retreat ended in a stumble. Seeing an open defence Baldor seized the moment. Raising his leg, he stamped the flat of his boot into Bomilcar's midriff knocking him backwards, his spatha slipping from his grasp. Landing heavily, and breathless and shocked at the skill, Bomilcar snatched for his dropped weapon while pointing the dagger at Baldor as he scrambled back and away. Baldor stopped, the words coming at last.

"Get up you piece of shit! Get up! … I'll kill you on your feet!" Then memory of another lesson came to him. *'Give no quarter Baldor for you'll receive none.'* Raising a falcata high he roared and stepped in to kill.

Suddenly the thump of hooves came behind him. Turning, he had to duck quickly as the horseman swung low with his sword as he passed, the blade cutting only Baldor's helmet plumes. The horse came to a sliding, whickering halt, the rider jumping down and unslinging the shield from his back.

"Hephaestus! Kill the bastard!" Bomilcar shouted as he scrambled up from the ground.

Baldor looked quickly from one man to the other. Deciding Bomilcar was closest he attacked again hoping to finish him before the other closed on him. Bomilcar sneered and quickly backed away and Baldor realised he'd have to fight both. Setting his stance, he pointed a falcata at each man, his head flicking cockerel-like watching as the pair stalked him. Taking the initiative, he went for Bomilcar again driving him back before turning quickly as Hephaestus rushed him. Hit hard by the man's shield he staggered backwards but managed to deflect the stabbing sword with one falcata. He swung low with the other at Hephaestus's legs cutting him above the knee and making him jump back. Bomilcar, seizing his chance attacked and cut at Baldor's ribs with his spatha. The mail shirt turned the blade's edge, though Baldor grunted and gasped in pain from the force of the blow. Stepping back for space, the two men followed him and though Hephaestus limped, his body remained well hidden behind his shield.

"It's your last day Targa!" Bomilcar sneered as he flexed both spatha and dagger.

Baldor's breath came fast his chest heaving, his ribs hurting and his head pounding from the fall. A brief prayer slipped across his smashed lips, his mind racing as he eyed the men stalking him, he was going to die here. Hephaestus stepped closer then rushed the last few paces to attack. Baldor responded with a flurry of high speed falcata strokes battering the man's shield and sword blade driving him back again before turning quickly to face Bomilcar coming at his side. The next moment a grey blur hit Hephaestus's shield as Issa threw herself at him, the dog's weight sprawling him onto his back. Before he could recover, she was standing on his chest growling and tearing at his sword arm as the man screamed.

Baldor immediately turned on Bomilcar. Flinching from the pain in his ribs he brandished his falcatas, the man raised his spatha though his face now showed fear. A scream from Hephaestus that became a wet gargle was drowned by Issa's growls as she savaged then tore his throat out. Bomilcar stared at the dog as it lifted a dripping, bloodied maw from the twitching corpse and stepped cautiously towards him growling low. Taking advantage of the distraction Baldor knocked the spatha from Bomilcar's grasp with a vicious sideswipe. The man whipped about with his dagger, pointing it first at Baldor and then Issa as both advanced on him. Baldor stepped in quickly, one falcata engaging the dagger, the other swung low at Bomilcar's legs slicing deeply down the thigh muscle and glancing off his greave. Bomilcar's leg folded and he collapsed onto one knee as Baldor stepped away while Issa crouched to spring at the man and the still outstretched dagger blade.

"Issa away!"

Issa stopped; her eyes narrowed; a feral snarl lifted her lips baring large, bloodied teeth. Bomilcar brandished the knife while looking from dog to man then Baldor attacked again. A feint from one blade was followed by a vicious slash from the other that sent the dagger spinning away. A moment later the other forced, point first into Bomilcar's chest. The man groaned deeply as the blade pierced leather cuirass, flesh and ribcage to burst a lung. His face twisted in agony; his scream stolen by the air leaving his chest.

Baldor gave a roar of triumph as the second blade chopped into Bomilcar's neck jarring hard against his spine and spraying Baldor in hot blood. Bomilcar's head lolled obscenely and as the man wilted, Baldor stomped a boot hard in his chest, he was dead before he hit the ground. Baldor spat forcefully on the corpse. "Bastard! ... Bastard!"

Breathless and shaking with emotion he stared then fell to his knees and dropped his falcatas.

"Issa here!"

Issa ran to him, barreling into him hard, her body pushing into his embrace her tail thrashing like a whip while she whimpered, her tongue licking his bloodied face. He pushed his head against hers while ruffling her ears, his chest heaving in grateful sobs as he muttered into her smooth coat "Bless you Issa! Bless you! ... Bless you Gestix!"

Chapter Twenty-Four

Positioned deep within the hastati ranks behind the princepes and not yet engaged, Cornelius had seen the Carthaginian cavalry attack rout Paullus's cavalry then disappear from sight. Though disappointed, he was not too perturbed for cavalry actions usually played out in a chase away from the battlefield. However, when they reappeared, marshalled to good order and galloped across the Roman rear to attack Varro's cavalry on the Roman left, he felt his stomach tighten. Before he could contemplate further, a loud roar like that from a giant's lungs rose above the clash of weapons and the screams of men as the Roman leviathan surged forward, the Carthaginian front line was broken!

Trumpets blared the advance and legionaries stepped quickly after their frontage. Cheers and smiles rose around Cornelius as men realised they were winning and despite him calling for order, he was forced along in the press. Owing to the space between the ranks being halved, the ordered lines quickly squashed and mingled together becoming a solid mass and men jostled for space. Following their comrades in front, they stepped over and on the bodies of the dead and dying both friend and foe alike as they pushed on.

Mago's Gauls and Spaniards were forced back, the Romans engaging the full Carthaginian frontage while pushing the convex line deeply inwards. Behind Mago's men, Hannibal and his Libyan troops waited on the flanks, leaving empty space for the Gauls and Spaniards to fall back into.

Out on the Roman left wing, Hasdrubal's cavalry rode at the gallop deep into the flank and rear of Varro's allied cavalry who were already engaged at their front by General Maharbal and his Numidians. Again, the stationary Roman mounts succumbed to the incoming charge and bloody carnage followed. Shocked by this surprise attack the Roman auxiliaries panicked. Despite Varro's cries to rally, those that could turned their mounts and fled eastwards off the plain, leaving their comrades to fight and die and the legions to fight it out unsupported, though still winning against the Carthaginian centre. General Maharbal and his Numidians took up the chase to ensure they didn't rally. The pursuit saw the lightly armed Numidians at their raiding best, herding and killing the fleeing auxiliaries like lions picking off sheep.

With the slaughter of the remaining Roman auxiliaries almost complete, Hasdrubal had the recall sounded and reined in while calling for his Captains. "Gentlemen!" He waved his commanders close just as Baldor and Issa caught up. "We rest briefly then reform again, this time to attack the rear of the Roman infantry centre … Captain Targa, are you all right?" He asked when he saw Baldor's blood splattered chest and mouth.

"Yes General, apologies for my lateness."

Hasdrubal nodded. "Gentlemen, to your troops and on my signal form line." The men nodded acknowledgement then sawed on their reins pulling their mounts quickly about. Calling for their standard-bearers they spread out, the banners focal points for each troop to gather at and reform ready for the next attack.

Armaco, seeing Baldor's blood-streaked face and Issa's red spattered coat reined in next to him.

"What in Baal's name happened to …?"

"I'm fine!"

"You were when I left you! Baal Almighty, man! Your lady will have my balls for earrings."

"I'm all right Armaco, thanks to Issa." He managed a bloody smile.

"Issa?"

He nodded and spat more blood then wiped his mouth. "Aye, Issa! Moreover, Bodeshmun is dead along with his Greek lackey."

"When? … Where?"

"Later."

As the last few of Varro's cavalrymen who hadn't fled died, the Carthaginian cavalry formed around their troop standards to make a wide frontage across the plain. Baldor, back in command stood forward of his troop, Issa alongside. Resting their mounts, the men caught their breath as they looked to the huge infantry battle raging in the centre of the plain. It was clear the Romans were having the best of it as they continued forcing their huge, armoured mass deep into the Carthaginian centre driving the Spaniards and Gauls back before them.

"We're ready General!" One of the Captains called.

Hasdrubal just raised his hand in a halting motion while watching the battle intently. Time slipped by while the men, though grateful of the rest fretted as they watched their infantry comrades pushed ever backwards by the legions. Back they went, their dogged resistance becoming hurried as the push from the now densely coalesced Roman legions increased. Driving the Gauls and Spaniards hard the Romans, so intent on destroying the Carthaginian centre passed the Libyan columns arrayed on the flanks. Suddenly, a war horn wailed twice above the din and the Libyan columns turned ninety degrees to form line and face the legionaries passing in front of them. Another horn blast saw shields locked together and spears lowered.

"Now!" Hasdrubal called to his signaler. "We go now! Sound the advance!"

The trumpet blew loud and long and the horses sprang forward. Holding a canter, they ate up the ground as they headed for the rear of the Roman centre. As the Libyans roared and attacked the Roman infantry flanks, Hasdrubal's trumpeter blew again taking the cavalry to the gallop.

Such was the crush amongst the legionaries that Cornelius could no longer see more than the men in close proximity to him and nothing of the Carthaginian cavalry charging their rear. With the space between the ranks now non-existent and the Carthaginians attacking on all sides the Romans were jammed tighter together than shoaling sardines. He'd lost control of his men and only the outer ranks of what was now just a huge, armoured mob could fight back, maniples could not move to offer support and those men that had pila had no space to raise and throw. As the Roman push slowed and finally stopped, panic set in amongst them as the Carthaginian vice began to squeeze.

Vicious fighting continued into late afternoon then the Volturnus wind picked up and strengthened. Blowing and gusting across the plain it drove dust into the Roman faces while the August sun beat down, cooking men in their bronze helmets and mail shirts and adding to the stifling heat from the packed bodies. The stench of death rose along with the temperature and wind while blood, entrails, ruptured bowels and piss slicked the ground as men screamed, died and went down. Men on both sides wearied while weapons blunted and short intervals of rest became necessary though the Romans remained almost completely contained.

Battle raged on into early evening with the Romans continually attacked on all four sides, their numbers diminishing like a sandbar washing away with a high tide. Desperation saw parties of legionaries break from the main body to make sorties into the enveloping enemy, most were savagely repulsed though some managed to slip through to flee. The bulk of the Roman mob however stood its ground still offering fierce, dogged resistance.

Weariness from both sides and frantic, horrified desperation from the Romans saw more men manage to break out from the Carthaginian vice and scatter. Cornelius and his men, positioned so deeply within the ranks had barely fought and as the Libyans stood back to reform and a small gap opened, they took their chance to break out and run. Fighting as they went, they managed to put a small distance between themselves and some Libyans who turned to follow. Running hard, Cornelius passed Paullus sitting awkwardly as if he'd collapsed then tried to rise, his back leaning against a rock his head tilted back and helmet gone. Battered and exhausted, his pallor grey-white, he'd clearly been left for dead. His face and neck were streaked in dried blood from the slingshot strike earlier in the day, his hand holding his thigh where blood trickled quickly through his fingers adding to the pool at his feet. Glancing behind, Cornelius gauged the distance of the chasing Libyans then turned back to Paullus shaking and badgering him.

"Sir! … Sir! Come …"

Paullus opened his eyes. "Go lad, I'm finished! … Go!"

Cornelius hesitated and held out his hand. "Here sir! I'll help, please!" He urged.

"Go Cornelius! … As your Consul, I command you to go."

Cornelius stared, his heart pounding, fear and horror filling his mind, his legs suddenly weak. Hearing bloodcurdling cries, he looked up and saw the pursuing Libyans closing the distance. Two legionaries grabbed him by the arms dragging him stumbling and running after his fleeing men. Managing to shake the pair loose, he stopped and drew his gladius and turned back then groaned inwardly as he saw Paullus, who had risen to his feet gladius in hand; go down amidst frenzied spear and sword thrusts from the pursuing Libyans. Leaving the dying Roman the

Libyans raced towards Cornelius. Realising he couldn't fight them all he turned to run.

The onset of dusk or perhaps exhaustion were the only things that slowed the bloodlust and stopped the slaughter, the Romans battered and weary threw down their weapons and asked for quarter. The Carthaginians, as drunk on bloodlust and victory as they were, were also exhausted and the fighting gradually ceased.

Baldor reined in his troop and gazed over the field, as far as he could see the ground was thickly strewn and piled deeply with bodies most of which were Roman. No one spoke as they stared at the grim spectacle before them. Tens of thousands of bodies lay stiffening in death, the hot air humming loudly with clouds of black flies that swarmed over the offal that had once been men. Crows and ravens charked, squabbling and flapping as they moved from body to body picking and tearing at eyes and lips or seizing at entrails. High above, circling lazily on the hot thermals the sky was dotted with red kites as they awaited their turn at the dead. Other than the birds, nothing moved amongst the piles of bodies for most of the wounded had been dispatched as the Carthaginians advanced against the shrinking Roman lines. Many men had been crushed from warriors trampling over them else suffocated from the dead bodies piling on top of them.

Baldor's hands were red and sticky, his mail shirt splattered with congealing blood, his lips and cheek swollen and lumpy from his fall his ribs aching but other than that, he was miraculously whole. His horse hung its head and gave an exhausted whicker, its face, chest and flanks spattered red. As he stared blankly at the carnage, his newfound piety had him quietly mouthing prayers for his salvation and unexpected victory over Bomilcar. Armaco bled through a rent in his mail above his waist but declared it was nothing. Andulas was a grim spectacle with dust clinging to the blood that streaked his face and chest though it wasn't his own, he as ever, seemed untouched by wounds. Baldor looked to both and gave a small-relieved smile, his words from a parched throat just a harsh whisper.

"The Gods are good brothers, bless you both. A dry sob shook his chest and he swallowed hard to hide his emotion.

A ragged cheer rose from some infantrymen as victory and the size of it began to dawn, others took up the shout and it spread across the field growing in volume. Baldor's troops began to cheer making their weary and still nervous horses bridle and stomp. Baldor, Armaco and Andulas raised their swords to the sky, grim smiles brightening their faces for the 'Lion's Brood' had not just won a great victory but torn the 'She Wolf's' cubs asunder.

Later that night beneath torchlight, Hannibal's Generals and Captains filled his tent, all were dust caked, bloodied and still in their war panoply. The men, weary but jubilant slaked their thirst with wine while heaping plates with the quickly prepared food, most not having eaten since dawn. Laughter and high spirits filled the tent. Hannibal, as weary and grimed as his men circulated and joined in the banter, letting the men have their moment. As time grew late, he called for order and men quietened to listen.

"Gentlemen, I salute and thank you all for your brave actions today." He held his hand over his heart and bowed his head, then quietened them quickly as voices rose in response. "It's late and we are all weary, so I'll not keep you over long. We've destroyed the might of Rome here on this plain today; their dead are still being counted though we already know they greatly surpass those we killed at Trasimene or the Trebbia." The men cheered loudly, he let them while smiling and nodding then gaining quiet again, he continued. "This battle has to conclude the war; Rome has no field army now and no choice other than to sue for peace on our terms." The men cheered again. "Let the men rest, then ..."

"General." Maharbal raised his cup in salute. "My congratulations on a victory well won but I say don't delay. Send me ahead now with my cavalry while the Romans are in disarray and in five days you could be feasting as victor on Capitol Hill."

Some men shouted hearty 'Aye's' while others shook their heads saying the army needed to rest. Hannibal, smiling warmly quietened them again.

"General I thank you for your bravery and outstanding command today and your gallant offer but as you rightly imply Rome is still many days away. Your cavalry would be unsupported as we are in no shape to follow on so quickly."

"Let me at least try General." He asked eagerly.

"No General." He replied kindly. "Even if Rome were closer we have no siege train to ..."

"Regardless sir, you know Alexander would have been banging on their gates within a day." Maharbal pushed.

Hannibal firmed his response. "No General Maharbal, no we wait and we rest."

Chastened, Maharbal bowed his head respectfully though he mumbled into his cup. "Truly, the Gods do not give everything to one man. You know how to win a victory Hannibal, but you don't know how to use one." Hiding his disappointment in his cup, he swilled the wine and sought more food.

Hannibal continued. "Tomorrow we'll burn and pray for our dead, Baal bless and keep them all." He dipped his head and mumbled a prayer, the men doing likewise. Leaving a few moments for silence, he raised his head and smiled. "Then … then we'll divide the spoils amongst all while sending ten representatives from amongst the prisoners to Rome, they to arrange ransom for the thousands we have here as captives. We'll also send an envoy with our terms to the Roman senate."

Men cheered loudly and turned back to eat while Hannibal circulated once more, not as a triumphant General but just a man amongst friends. It was late when he found Baldor. Taking Baldor's offered hand, he embraced him warmly.

"I rejoice to see you my friend."

"Likewise sir, Baal is merciful and good."

Hannibal smiled amiably at Baldor's piety. "Thank you for your bravery and efforts today."

Baldor smiled and saluted. "I have Issa to thank, sir."

"Issa?" Hannibal asked, then quickly recollecting the name looked at the dog stood quietly alongside Baldor.

"Yes sir, she saved my life."

"May I?" Hannibal asked as he reached for a joint of meat from the table, then presuming consent gave it to Issa. She, wagging her tail as she took it and immediately settled to eat. "Baal bless and keep you Issa for saving my friend's life." He gave a wry smile while watching Issa pull and tear at the meat. "You are truly blessed Baldor Targa. You have friends you can trust, a faithful dog and a woman whom I surmise must be as beautiful and bewitching as Helen of Troy for you were prepared to risk all and fight for her."

Baldor blushed and tried to hide his discomfort with a smile. "Yes sir, I believe the Gods love me."

Hannibal smiled and laughed lightly then purposefully averting Baldor's eyes, looked up at the tent roof.

"Yes, I believe they do Baldor. Let's hope." He cleared his throat. "Let's hope, Lord Bodeshmun is also loved by the Gods for I don't see him present at this gathering." Still looking away but placing a hand firmly on Baldor's shoulder as if giving pause, he spoke quickly over the words forming in Baldor's mouth. "We should offer a prayer for his departed soul when we pray next." His fingers gripping Baldor's shoulder then released.

"Er, yes sir ... yes we should."

"But now." Hannibal looked back at him. "Now, I thank Baal Almighty for your life and that of your friends whom I surmise are also still with us?"

"Yes sir, thank you sir. Lord Andulas and Hypolokhagos Armaco are both hale."

Hannibal nodded and smiled warmly. "Good! For tomorrow, we'll all be rich men."

"You think this will be the end of it, sir? The end of the war?"

"I hope so and Baal as my witness I pray so, a little peace would be most welcome."

"And home sir?"

"Yes! ... Yes, I've dreamed of such." He looked away again.

Baldor cleared his throat and took a breath. "Sir, when peace is established may I have your leave to go home?"

Hannibal turned back and smiled. "You're seeking wife, hearth and home Baldor?"

"Yes sir. A chance at another life, a quiet one."

Hannibal smiled warmly and placed his arm over Baldor's shoulder. "I would miss you; miss our talks ... and even the trouble you bring me!" He laughed. "Yes, Captain Targa once peace is established you have my blessing and leave to go, though I reserve the right to visit you wherever you may settle."

"Thank you sir, thank you! You would be most welcome at my house and table."

"We'll talk more on this later Baldor as it draws late and we are all seeking rest. However, my word is my promise, when this business is done and we have peace you can leave for home."

Issa, picking up Lasairiona's scent took off towards her before Baldor saw her waiting outside the tent in the torchlight. She, wrapped in a shawl against the night's chill fussed the dog while staring anxiously into the darkness. Baldor raised a hand and kicked the horse on. Lasairiona, recognising his helmet and horse as they passed through a pool of orange light, took off towards him at the run the shawl falling from her shoulders, Issa keeping pace alongside. Baldor jumped from his horse just as Lasairiona threw herself at him, her arms wrapping about him, her fast, tumbling words lost as she buried her face in his neck her tears hot against his night-cooled skin. Hugging her close, he felt her body shake as she cried with relief while Issa whimpered and brushed against both. Baldor ran his hands through her hair and kissed her, her perfume sweet like ripened fruit the heady, musky tones filling his nose.

"It's all right." He said softly as he breathed her scent in. "It's all right and I'm all right, Andulas and Armaco are all right. Sh'sh." He kissed her again then gently eased her face from his neck. Her eyes, wet with tears seemed to sparkle and he kissed her brow and lips. Shaking her head, she traced fingers lightly across his swollen lips then holding his face in both hands, showered it with kisses. Not trusting herself to speak she snuggled back into his neck again her body still shaking, stifled sobs racking her frame. Neither spoke; with darkness affording privacy, they just held one another. As the shaking and sobbing subsided Lasairiona gathered herself, stepping back she cuffed the tears away and smiled.

"Come my love, you must be weary and hungry."

"Hungry for the sight of you." He said and pulled her close again then stepped towards the tent his arm holding her close his other holding the reins of his mount.

Lighting more lamps in the tent, she settled Issa on her bed then helped him out of his mail before producing a small bowl of steaming rosewater so he could wash. Too late to heat buckets of water so to bathe he washed the dust and blood from his face then slipping his tunic off began sponging dried sweat from his chest. Words seemed un-necessary between the pair, embraces and kisses seemingly more than enough to convey their feelings. Lasairiona took the sponge from him and continued gently washing him while pausing to examine the purple-yellow bruises on his ribs. She pressed tentatively on each rib and though he grimaced slightly she was content that no bones were broken. Washing his back then stripping his loincloth she carried on.

It wasn't long before he took the sponge from her and dropped it in the bowl then kissed her full in the mouth.

"I think I'm clean enough."

She smiled. "Supper?"

"I've eaten what about you?"

"Yes, I …"

"Good!" He interrupted and pulled her close.

"Bed then? You must be exhausted?"

"Bed!" His fingers began unhooking the straps of her dress, his lips tracing tender kisses over her shoulders to the base of her neck.

Though surprised by his ardour she responded quickly and stepping away, she let the dress fall and made her way to the bed pulling him by the hand.

With their passion spent and sleep coming, they laid in each other's arms and she asked quietly.

"Is it over?"

"It is for me my love, I'm exhausted." He sniggered.

"She punched him playfully and he groaned. She gasped when she realised she'd hit his bruised ribs then climbed on him hugging and kissing and apologising."

"I asked for that." He chuckled as he kissed her. "I take it you mean the war? Yes, I believe it's over, more importantly the General seems to think so, for no nation can recover from a defeat like that." He paused, as he thought of the carnage on the field, that grim spectacle he didn't doubt would haunt him for years. Clearing his throat, he moved on. "Envoys go to Rome tomorrow seeking their surrender and once a peace is concluded I have permission to go."

"Go? … You mean away from the army, away from the war … away from here?" The excitement clear in her voice as she badgered.

"Yes."

"To make a home?"

"Yes, it'll be time for … what did you call me?"

"Baldor the farmer."

"Yes, that's me, Baldor the farmer, the peasant that married a Chief's daughter."

Lasairiona laughed and snuggled closer. "The Gods have blessed us my love, I have you and we'll have peace and hopefully the rest of our lives. I will ask no more." The pair were quiet for a while; Baldor's breathing deepening as he drifted to sleep when Lasairiona shook him gently. "Baldor … Baldor!"

"Yes." He mumbled sleepily.

"We haven't prayed or given thanks properly for our good fortune." She went to get out of bed but he threw his arm over her holding her back.

"Tomorrow." His voice slow, drowsy and heavy with sleep. "I promise we'll pray tomorrow."

"We shouldn't presume our luck or dreams without giving thanks for it." She persisted.

He kissed her back and pulled her closer. "I'm sure the Gods will forgive us this once ... sleep."

She snuggled back down in his arms, he already sound asleep. She however, wide-awake and uncomfortably mumbling her prayers, asking forgiveness for the tardiness in giving thanks and promising to make a sacrifice tomorrow ... hoping the Gods would listen and forgive.

Cornelius wasn't sure how far he and the few survivors with him had ran. Breathless and exhausted they finally stopped as darkness halted their pursuers and hindered their own progress to a cautious blundering in the gloom. Resting his back against a tree, he sipped from his water flask and tried to calm his nerves. His tunic was wet with sweat and plastered against his body, his heart still racing from the run and heavy from the slaughter he'd seen. How in Jupiter's name had it come to this? The mightiest army Rome had ever fielded, fighting on near perfect ground for their legions slaughtered like sheep at a sacrifice.

The horror of it all weighed him down, seemed to smother him, his thoughts as black as the surrounding darkness. He shook slightly, the tears of frustration and dismay adding to his sweat-wet face. This was the fourth battle and the fourth time he'd been forced to run, why was he still alive when so many were dead?

Jammed in so tightly he'd only been able to fight as his century was finally exposed to the Carthaginian onslaught that came on mercilessly, scything men down like ripened wheat. Even then, he and his men had found no space to move or fight properly; pushed from behind, stumbling over the dead and dying, most of his men had perished quickly on Libyan spears. Hanging his head he felt ashamed for being alive, a failure, for he hadn't been able to lead properly or well and the wounded were left where they lay. An Optio shaking his arm interrupted his despondency and hopelessness.

"Sir! ... Sir! We need to go."

"What?"

"We need to keep moving sir; away from here, the Republic is finished, over! The Carthaginians are unbeatable."

Cornelius shambled alongside the Optio as the group moved off.

"Which way?" One man asked.

"Does it matter? As long as we don't go back there." Came from another."

"If we reach the coast we take ship and leave, if we find ourselves heading north we skirt Rome and keep going." Said another.

The sentiment was quietly echoed by others in the group as they shuffled along in the dark. Cornelius listened for a while and realised that amongst the legionaries there were others of rank, none however looked to counter the despondency or decision to abandon Rome and the people. As Cornelius's nerves settled and rationality returned, he thought of the men he'd lost, the death of Lucius and where in Hades was Gaius? Had he also fallen? Moreover, what of the people waiting back in Rome, the mothers, sisters, daughters and wives of the dead men … what of his mother and Aemilia, were they just to be left to the mercy of the invader?

"Stop! … Stop!" He hissed as he grabbed for those closest to him while calling the rest of the small party to halt. "Listen, listen to me! What kind of men are we that will leave our people to the mercy of the invader? You saw the essence of their mercy today, how can we as Romans, as men, live and breathe while leaving our people to be murdered and enslaved?"

"We can't beat them!" A man growled. "Jupiter knows we've tried!"

"Then we try again!"

Grumbles and sharp discontent came back at him. "You stay and fight then." Came harshly out of the dark.

Cornelius sighed and tried a different tack. "Very well then, I'll stay. As bleak as things seem, I'll stay and fight again for my people, for my family, for Rome and our way of life. You can go; you can run away; I can't stop you and I won't blame you. You may live for a while longer; either overseas or in hiding here but when your time comes as it comes to us all, ask yourself this. Even if we fail again and we die, would it not have been better to fight? To enter Elysium as a man who'd tried to save his people, who'd fought as best he could for his way of life, for his freedom and for those he loves. Would you not wish to have taken that choice instead of a few short years of miserable life, skulking, hiding and hanging your head in shame?"

This time the silence seemed deafening, the only sounds that of men's breathing and the shuffle of harness. The silence stretched. Then, way off in the distance a wolf howled and a pheasant squawked in alarm and one of the men spoke quietly.

"Lead on sir, back to Rome."

The group shuffled quietly off into the darkness.

Historical Note

The idea for the Carthaginian escape from the valley in the Ager Falernus district using the cattle drive over the saddle as a diversion is true. It was very successful and credited to Hannibal's Quartermaster General, Hasdrubal. I chose to make it Baldor's idea so to place him back in favour with Hannibal.

Hannibal obviously knew and understood the character of his enemy Fabius, very well and counted on him remaining undecided and impotent while the action took place. A marvelous piece of trickery and bluff by Hannibal against a man who fully expected to be tricked by the ever-wily Carthaginian. However, in fairness to Fabius he would have been a brave or perhaps rash General to lead his rudely awoken men into the darkness, without knowledge of where and how many the enemy were.

Fabius was recalled to Rome by the senate more than once to explain his delay and procrastination in confronting the invaders. Especially so when his own property was purposely circumvented and left untouched by the marauding Carthaginians.

Fabius's Master of Horse, Minucius, was very different in character to his superior and held with the traditional Roman values of fortitude and aggression. During one of Fabius's sojourns to Rome whereby Minucius was left in command, his men did attack and cut up a large Carthaginian raiding party and chased them back to their camp at Geronium. Despite neither side being ready for full battle, the fight and numbers involved escalated with the Romans gaining the upper hand from both surprise and the arrival of substantial reinforcements. This fight being the only time to date that Hannibal was caught off guard and thus the Carthaginians suffered the worst of it until the arrival of General Hasdrubal with cavalry and infantry support. The Romans withdrew but left the Carthaginians badly mauled and with a greater number of casualties.

The Roman senate, unable to take power from Fabius but seeing a slight change in fortune by a different General changed the law and appointed Minucius alongside Fabius and with equal powers. Hannibal, upon seeing the Romans split their army in two once again and noting the ready aggression of Minucius, immediately moved to the offensive and set a trap outside the Roman camp to draw him on. Minucius took the bait and his army was very badly mauled and only saved from annihilation by Fabius marching in support. It suited both sides to retire though Hannibal could claim victory by the number of casualties the Romans suffered.

Fabius's term as dictator finished with the end of the year 217 BC and winter saw an end to the campaign season. Although he had avoided bringing Hannibal to battle and was despised for his delaying tactics, his actions had allowed time for Rome to recover from the disaster at Trasimene and recruit and train new legions ready for the coming year. Some historians now think that Fabius's tactics went a long way in preserving the Roman state and positively affecting the eventual outcome of the war in Italy.

The following year 216 BC, saw no major conflicts throughout spring and most of the summer though the Carthaginians continued their depredations, slaughter, and living off the land. The senate appointed two new Consuls, Lucius Aemilius Paullus (Cornelius Scipio's potential father-in-law) and Caius Terentius Varro. Along with the largest army Rome had ever placed in the field, the Consuls brought Hannibal to battle on the plain of Cannae.

Paullus did refuse battle outside the large Roman camp on the first of August, though the casting of the spear by the Carthaginians to claim the day is my own idea and taken from Alexander's supposed action when invading the Persian Empire over a century earlier. With Varro in command the following day, second of August, the Romans crossed the Aufidius and deployed for battle. For all the plain suited the Roman legions it also suited Hannibal's cavalry, thus Varro attempted to negate their flexibility and any chance of being outflanked by anchoring his own cavalry on the riverbank to his right and again against the hills on his left. The idea seemingly to hold the Carthaginian cavalry in place while the Roman heavy infantry destroyed the Carthaginian centre.

Owing to the size of the Roman army, estimated at around eighty thousand men the distance between the ranks was halved in a bid to array them all, consequently, it critically hampered their ability to fight or manoeuvre. The Romans did break the Carthaginian infantry lines and in true fashion made straight for their centre expecting to break it apart and carry the day. Hannibal however, had allowed for this expected hammer blow and as his Gauls and Spaniards fell back before it, he turned his heavy Libyan spearmen in from the flanks to envelop the

Romans on either side. When General Hasdrubal's cavalry attacked the legions in the rear, they were effectively boxed in.

With the lack of space between the Roman ranks being squeezed further by Hasdrubal's cavalry, the Libyans and the reforming Gauls and Spaniards, the Romans were forced into a huge, disorganised mob with no space to fight effectively, slaughter being the outcome.

General Maharbal did suggest that they follow up the victory at Cannae quickly by advancing on Rome. Hannibal declined, electing to rest his men and citing a lack of siege equipment to take Rome if it did not surrender. Both points of view are valid. If the Carthaginians had approached Rome straight after Cannae the city may well have capitulated as their field army was destroyed. However, if the Romans refused to surrender and barred their gates, Hannibal would have had no choice other than to lay siege, his lengthy experience at Saguntum three years earlier perhaps giving him pause.

Owing to this third catastrophic defeat of the legions, both Hannibal and Baldor surmise Rome is finished and must sue for peace. Cornelius however, despite his experience of the slaughter and in true character of his people refuses to accept or contemplate surrender … the war will go on for both men.

Estimates of the casualties at Cannae vary but most historians settle on a figure of six to eight thousand for the Carthaginians and their allies.

The Roman casualties however, numbered some fifty to sixty thousand men killed, with four to five thousand taken prisoner. The dead included many men of high rank; Consul Paullus and the previous elected Consul, Gnaeus Servilius Geminus. Marcus Minucius Rufus perished along with two Quaestors, twenty-nine Tribunes and around eighty senators or high-ranking magistrates. Consul Caius Terentius Varro survived Cannae and returned to Rome.

This death toll would not be equaled in battle for over two thousand years until the advent of the machine gun and the first day of the battle of the Somme in July 1916, when British casualties numbered similarly.

Ever since the battle of Cannae, Generals have sought to imitate it. This masterful tactic of double envelopment or pincer movement being seen as the ultimate tactic to decisively defeat an enemy in the field.

Also, by Garrett Pearson

The Lions and the Wolf series

The Orphan Cub (I)
In Hannibal's Shadow (II)
The Brood at Trasimene (III)

Other Books

Stamford and The Unknown Warrior

Printed in Great Britain
by Amazon

34309151R00169